For Peg & Dale —
my old Wayne County
HFH friends!
Kris

One Man Short

By

KRISTEN AMMERMAN

Infinity Publishing

ISBN 0-7414-2192-5

Cover illustration by Mark Ammerman

Published by:

INFIꞶITY
PUBLISHING.COM

1094 New De Haven Street, Suite 100
West Conshohocken, PA 19428-2713
Info@buybooksontheweb.com
www.buybooksontheweb.com
Toll-free (877) BUY BOOK
Local Phone (610) 941-9999
Fax (610) 941-9959

Printed in the United States of America

Printed on Recycled Paper

Published November 2004

Chapter 1
Turning Up Missing

Kasi Short's husband picked a real tidy time to turn up missing. That's one of the marvelous wonders of the English language – that someone can both turn up and still be missing at the same time. And that's just what Joe Short did.

There I was, salivating from the savory smell of the freshly popped white fluff over which Kasi was dribbling hot butter in the kitchen just behind me. I could hardly wait to cram the first food I'd had in ten hours into my mouth, even if it was just popcorn. I sat on the edge of my client's polyester paisley sectional, in front of a soundless, flickering, 24-inch Sony, and waited edgily, doing that little knee jiggle Micky claims I've done since kindergarten – the one that originally meant I'd been reading ahead and couldn't wait for everyone to just turn the page.

And suddenly, Joe Short turned up missing. Right there in the living room.

Kasi, approaching from behind the couch, started to lean over my shoulder to pass me the bowl of Orville Reddenbacher. My hand left the arm of the sofa to receive it, and suddenly the woman let out a sharp, little dog-being-stepped-on whelp and her forearm jerked up like the handle on a released one-armed bandit. I flailed at the lurching bowl, but my swipe only served to swat the green plastic container like a basketball blocked just as it was about to kiss the rim. Glorious, deliciously puffy, white kernels flew in all directions, cascading across the couch and onto the thick-piled carpet. "Joe! It's Joe!" screeched Kasi, gaping at the TV and bouncing up and down in place, a veritable human pogo stick. "Oh my God, it's Joe!" she squealed. "Is he dead? Oh, my Lord, did they find him dead? Oh my god! Ohmygod, ohmygod, ohmygod!" she wailed, grabbing my wrist and pumping it as if it would gush forth answers to her plea.

"Hold on, Kasi! Hold it!" I grabbed the butter-spattered remote from the couch with the hand that wasn't being jerked, and frantically pushed the volume button. "—Next on Pennsylvania's own 'Unsolved Mysteries,'" concluded the announcer as a worn black and white photograph of a man was followed by a commercial.

"Unsolved Mys—"

"—See, it's not the news, it's that William Shatner thing," I soothed, simultaneously attempting to shake her loose.

"No, that's 'America's Most Wanted,'" her voice crept upwards, approaching a contralto keen. Her grip tightened, viselike.

"No, no," I disagreed. "'Most Wanted' is with the guy whose son was abducted. Shatner must be the 911 thing."

"'Unsolved Mysteries' is flying saucers and spontaneous combustion and bumble bee communication," Kasi moaned, eyes now blankly fixated on a model selling perfume in her underwear. She still had a tight grip on my arm.

"And missing persons," I added, peeling her fingers back one by one, as gently yet forcefully as I could.

"But — but — " and she let go her grasp and commenced pacing, obliviously grinding the spilled popcorn into the rose-colored carpet, her strong little fists clenching and unclenching, her joggers' lungs pushing nervous puffs of pre-hyperventilated carbon dioxide past barred teeth. "But what's he doing on 'Unsolved Mysteries?'" she gasped at the TV. "*I* didn't put him there! Until a week ago, the cops hardly considered him missing!" And her blue eyes sizzled hotter than the wood heaters Home Depot was now hawking on NBC.

Things went rapidly downhill from there.

The thing is, between August 5, when Joe Short disappeared from his now-distraught wife's home, and only hours prior to his re-emergence September 24th on Pennsylvania's premiere mystery re-enactment show (the selfsame day I met Ms. Short), I was blissfully ignorant of this man's existence.

Earlier in the day on the 24th — the day of the popcorn shower — Mickey Daniels and I had been working a cheating wife case. We had followed Mrs. Hernandez straight from her 10 a.m. hair appointment to Mr. Garcia's brother's unoccupied apartment. In the time it takes to screw on a telephoto lens and aim it at an opportune gap caused by a broken Venetian blind in a rear first-floor bedroom, we were able to catch Mr. G. and Mrs. H. *in flagrante*. In a big way. ("Very big!" Mick had said admiringly, zooming in and clicking away.) It was embarrassingly easy.

But by mid morning, my man Mick's normal good humor had waned, and he had taken on a decidedly peaked look, begun to sniffle and sneeze, and then suddenly expressed the urgent need for a bathroom — now! Seeing as how (and we could, actually) Mr. Garcia's brother's powder room was at that moment occupied by post-coital cleansing, and we were only four blocks from Mick's place anyway, I thought it best we exit forthwith and repair to my partner's abode. We had, by then, sufficient photos to win Mr. Hernandez an uncontested divorce. Besides, I had a hidden agenda.

While Mickey was occupied in the bathroom down the hall, I hauled my ungainly 5'10" frame onto a wobbly dining room chair, and with my head in M.D.'s oregano-scented kitchen cabinet, I sur-reptitiously glued a bogus Buns Bisque Cannibals Soup label over a real can of Healthy Choice Chicken Supreme. I'd been carrying those labels around in my shoulder bag for weeks, just waiting for the right chance to use them. And now that Mick, the human germ magnet, seemed to be coming down with another of his bugs, I might just get to use my – er – gag.

When he finally emerged, I was seated nonchalantly at the kitchen table, pretending an interest in my field notebook. "Hey, you got any soup? Soup's good for a cold," I suggested innocently.

He was bleary-eyed. He seemed drained of his naturally insouci-ant ease – deflated, like a wilted flower. But as I knew he would, he obediently sauntered to the cabinet, opened it, and, after a few sec-onds, extracted my strategically-placed can. "E-li-i-i-za!" he groused, supplying an entirely unsatisfactory "there she goes again" look. His normally bright blue eyes were dull with incipient fever. This wasn't nearly as much fun as I'd anticipated.

"Read the ingredients! They're a hoot!" I cajoled, trying to prod him into good humor.

"No!"

"Aw, come on!"

"Big buns, little buns, cute buns, not-so-cute buns, downright ugly buns, a lot of bisque, bisque helper, Life Savers, antacid, and occasional turmeric," he read flatly from the bogus nutrition label, one thick, dark brow arched incuriously.

I jumped up, bumping a knobby knee on the underside of the pine table. "Ouch!" But no mere bruise could detain me. "Look at this!" I enthused, grabbing the can out of his hand and pointing my digit at the nutritional information. "Contains less than 100% of anything, including all that preceded that which was a total part of each whole item!"

"What's that supposed to mean?"

"Nothing, silly. Absolutely nothing. Isn't it great?"

"Wonderful," he conceded stuffily to shut me up. Too miserable to feign interest or display even fake disdain, he sank into an overstuffed chair that let out a tired, low creak in mimic of his defeated moan. "But where's the chicken noodle?"

We did eventually sit down to some toast and oatmeal, as Mick had suddenly lost all interest in canned foods. But before he had taken more than two bites of Wonder Bread and one of Quaker Oats, he began to bring up ingredients much nastier than those on my ersatz label, and by late afternoon, I felt it incumbent upon myself to personally escort the Mick to Mrs. Daniels's Motel for some R & R.

There, Mrs. D. fed Mick some homemade chicken gumbo deluxe, which he thankfully kept to himself. And I, perpetual bearer of bad news, was unceremoniously hustled out of the house with the suggestion of urgent errands beckoning elsewhere. "Really, dear," Mrs. D. tsked at the door. "You're not terribly nurturant."

The reference to my apparent lack of nurturing tendencies was Mrs. D.'s latest stab at that subject closest to her heart – the fact that I have recently "lost" my husband. (May he long remain among the missing!) Obviously, from Mrs. D.'s viewpoint, the reason for my sorry status is my apparent failure to look after my ex sufficiently. I wonder what excuse she's manufactured for herself to explain Mickey D. not having a woman to nurture *him*...

But mothers are like that. At least ours is.

Oh yeah, Mick is my twin brother. Or so Mother, alias Mrs. D., claims. I continue to explore alternative theories and options to our apparent relateness. (Not so much to Mickey as to Mother.)

At any rate, I returned later that evening to Mick's apartment to feed his cowfish, Churchill (the fish looks just like Winston, I swear), and to make sure we hadn't left the stove on. At about 8 p.m., just as I was fixing to leave, the business phone, which rings at Mickey's and my apartments as well as the office, jingled. Mickey D.'s recorded voice announced the offices of Samuels and Daniels, Private Investigators, and directed the caller to leave a message after the tone. I had no intention of picking up. On the contrary, I was looking forward to heading straight home for a TV dinner followed by a few chapters of the latest Margaret Maron mystery. But when the machine beeped, a throaty voice seemed to start right in the middle of a thought, as if the

4

woman had been talking to herself and simply decided to pick up the phone mid-soliloquy.

"—I was on my way to the market to buy him lobster, for Pete's sake. Lobster! I *hate* lobster! If he wanted to leave, why not just say so? No warning, no inkling, no nothing. The cops making little suggestions, little hints, that I either chased him off or killed him off, though they don't seem to care one way or the other. Maybe the Mafia did him in. Maybe he got amnesia and he's wandering around The Greater Philadelphia Area not knowing who he is and where he lives. Am I the only one who cares?"

There was a pause and I was momentarily caught in-between, mentally intrigued by the woman's quandary, my curiosity piqued, but my body nevertheless resembling park statuary. Then there came a long exhalation of breath with a squeaky catch on the end. And the voice quietly, almost defeatedly, recited her name and phone number. I found myself picking up on the last number. "Mrs. Short?"

"Oh, you're there?" The dull, matter-of-fact tone in her voice said she'd suspected all along that someone was monitoring the call, but had been resigned to the likelihood that no one would respond to her plea for help.

"This is Eliza Samuels," I said. "I can come over right now if you'd like."

She gave me directions to her house and added that she was making popcorn, as though it were an extra incentive for me to come over. Pathetically enough, it actually was.

It had all started (or so Kasi Short informed me as I sat on her sofa, sipping Diet Coke and glancing from time to time at the light on my pocket recorder) when she left work early on the afternoon of August 5 to prepare for her husband's 45th birthday celebration.

Pacing back and forth across the oak-paneled living room, stopping once to turn off the TV, once to turn up the volume control on the intercom from the children's room, she related to me the events of that day. Her voice had a throaty, sometimes crackling sound to it, too deep for the small but sturdy body. The energy level was high. The blue eyes sparked, then seemed to fade, only to flare again, in sync with her emotions. Shoulder-length blondish hair bobbed as she moved. It seemed she should be a smoker, do something with her hands. They were sensitive, small, darting — like she was.

She had left work early on August 5, punching her personal security code into the monitor box at the electronic exit gate at Vortex Institute, as modern technology released her and her Volvo through the barred entrance onto the wide access roads of Research Office Park. She maneuvered into the frenetic late afternoon traffic on the Schuylkill Expressway, caught the Blue Route, and breathed a sigh of relief as she eased onto the off-ramp at Lochmore. From there she drove directly to the automatic teller machine at Lochmore Savings & Loan to withdraw cash to buy fresh lobster for Joe's favorite meal. Today was his birthday and she had planned a little party. It would just be the four of them. Joe wasn't generally much on socializing, and lately he'd seemed a little depressed over hitting the big four-five. But Kasi wanted to make it a special evening.

She inserted her card, punched in her access number, the amount of $100 from checking, and waited. In a few seconds, the machine spit her card back out and informed her she had insufficient funds. She was disgusted. These damn things were always acting up. Maybe, she thought fuzzily, the machine thought she was using the wrong number. So she did it again. "Insufficient funds," it repeated. Well, this is ridiculous! The third time she asked for the same amount from savings. The machine swallowed the thing whole, blinked, and all but licked its lips and burped. Kasi whipped into a parking space, stomped into the lobby, and blasted the nearest teller. "The damn thing ate my card!" she accused the woman.

"Let me check your account, ma'am," the teller ogled her myopically from behind dense glasses. "What is your account number?"

"Why, I've banked here for years. I don't know my account–"

"On your checks, ma'am? On your savings book? Don't you have them with you?" said Glasses.

"Well, yes," she allowed. And she fumbled in her pocketbook and came up with the checkbook. "See, I have $1,283.79 in there," Kasi pointed to her balance. "And look, $3,420.13 as of July 30th in the savings. See?"

"Yes, ma'am. Let me check the numbers." And the teller took her savings and checkbooks across an aisle to a computer fifteen feet away, keyed in some numbers, scrawled some more figures on a pad, and returned a moment later. "You have a balance of $3.79 in your checking account and $100.00 in your savings, Mrs. Short. Would you like me to enter your balance in your savings book?" She stood poised with a red pen over the savings book, the left brow raised ever so slightly in disinterested doubt above a quarter-inch thick lens.

Kasi stared at the teller. Her eyes dropped to the woman's name-tag. "Miss Strunk," she said, and paused.

"Yes, ma'am?" the right brow rose to match the left.

"You must be mistaken," she said softly, using the voice she'd heard Ms. Wenkosky, the owner of her daughter's day care center, use with the preschoolers when she wished to stress a safety point. "I seem to be missing upwards of forty-six hundred dollars. Now where do you suppose it went?" She was practically whispering.

"I don't know, ma'am," Miss Strunk replied, almost as softly. "I could check again."

"Please do," she said in her very best Thumbelina voice.

Miss Strunk returned to her computer, punched in some more numbers, and called to another teller. She whispered something to the second woman and the latter scuttled busily toward a rear office, glancing back over her shoulder at Kasi. Miss Strunk keyed in more numbers and scrolled through more pages on her screen. She nodded her head as though she had solved a problem. Just then the second teller returned with a young man in a three-piece suit and they both huddled by the computer. The two tossed accusatory glances between one another and the impatient customer like children playing Hot Potato. Finally Miss Strunk gathered up her figures and the bank employees approached the counter together. "How are you today, Mrs. Short?" the young man asked, false jocularity twisting the corners of his thin lips.

"Shitty." She exploded, instantly regretting it.

He chuckled as if she were the most sadly misguided person he'd dealt with in weeks. His hand grasped the lapel of his jacket proudly, as though it had a five-star general's bars sewn on it. "Well, Miss Strunk informs me you believe your balance to be higher than our records indicate. She has rechecked the numbers, and they seem to be correct. It appears that your husband withdrew funds from the account this morning, lowering your balance to the level Miss Strunk reported to you."

"Huh?" It was all that came to mind.

"This *is* a joint account," he stressed.

"Well, yes, but he wouldn't take that much out without—" and she clicked her tongue at the ridiculousness of the situation. "It ate my card!" It was the only legitimate complaint left to her.

"Get Mrs. Short's card for her, please, Miss Strunk," said Three-Piece. "I'm sure you can straighten it out with Mr. Short when you get home. But if you'd like to give him a call—" his hand motioned toward the phone in his office.

"No. No, that's all right. Thank you." And she grasped at the card that Miss Strunk was now proffering, as though it were a key to a bank vault. But it was a vault that held only $103.79. Why $103? Why in the world had he taken all that money out of their account? Though inside her head, screams three octaves above high C were squeezing toward her larynx, the sounds that exited her mouth were remarkably civilized. "Thank you," she said simply and primly as she made her retreat.

Kasi climbed quietly into the car, drove home, pulled the Volvo up the steep drive to the back of the house, and turned off the ignition. Joe's car was gone. "Shit! Shit! Shit! Shit! Shit!" she spat louder and louder, slamming the palm of her hand over and over again on the steering wheel. "What the hell's going on?" she wailed. A creeping, unfocused fear bordering on pain gnawed at her chest. Suddenly it surfaced — the children! She'd forgotten to pick up Eva at day care. A bolt of panic stabbed her heart. Brando! What about Brando? He'd been home with Joe today. Joe was supposed to take care of him. The Popeye's Playroom Day Care didn't take children until they were one year old. Joe, a musician, usually worked nights and had been home alone days with the baby since she'd gone back to work four months ago when Brando was two months old. She jumped out of the car and ran through the house, calling "Joe! Joe!" Then "Brando! Brando!" as if the infant could actually answer, "Right here, Mom!"

She stopped and listened to the house. It was empty. Still. Sepulchral. Its emptiness tickled the back of her neck. Kasi shivered and reached for the phone.

"—Mrs. Short! We were beginning to worry that your sister might be seriously injured. Eva's been—"

"Is she all right?" Kasi cut off Ms. Wenkosky.

The day care owner paused. "Who?"

"My daughter!"

"Eva? Well, yes, she's fine. But we were concerned about your sister. I'm sure Mr. Short wouldn't have left Brando here if—"

"Brando's there?" Relief flooded in, then backwashed over other doubts, other questions.

"Then your sister—?" The voice on the other end of the line was obviously confused.

"My sister?" Kasi parroted. I don't have a sister! What the hell is going on here? "What did my husband tell you? He — um, he and I haven't made contact all day. I didn't realize he'd left Brando with you, and I got involved — forgot to pick up Eva."

"Oh, that's okay. We're open until six, you know. Brando's been a good little boy. Mr. Short didn't leave any diapers, though, and the ones we have are awfully big for such a little tyke. I guess he was terribly rushed, though, worried about — about your sister..." She left the opening, but Kasi didn't bite, and she continued. "He asked when he brought Eva this morning if we would take Brando, too, for a few hours, seeing as how it was an emergency. He said your sister was in an accident and he wanted to be with you at the hospital, that one of you would get back to us as soon as possible."

"Oh, I see," Kasi's mind raced but she tried to remain calm. "Well, I guess we just missed each other at the hospital. It was a false alarm. She wasn't hurt after all. We got all bent out of shape for nothing!" and she laughed choppily.

"Oh, that's good." Ms. Wenkosky sounded uncertain.

"Well, I'll be right down to get the kids. Thanks for keeping Brando in a pinch. I really appreciate that!"

"Well, as long as it's an emergency, we like to help," the daycare operator said. "But only in an emergency," she repeated, more forcefully.

"Yes, well I'll be right down. Goodbye." And she hung up.

Later that evening, over takeout pizza at the kitchen table, Kasi gingerly questioned Eva. "So what did Daddy say when he left you at Popeye's Playroom this morning?" she prompted, nonchalantly shoveling a spoon of creamed spinach into Brando's mouth.

"Said he loved me." The four-year-old hadn't questioned her father's absence from the dinner table. It was not uncommon. He often had evening rehearsals or left early for a distant gig.

"Did he tell you what he was going to do today?"

Kasi took a bite of pizza. "No, what?"

"Oh, I don't know. Nothing special, I guess. I just wondered if he told you anything unusual."

"Said, 'Remember I love you.'" Eva reached for another slice of pepperoni. Kasi choked on hers. Eva didn't even look up. She was swinging her legs against the chair leg, picking at the cheese that was dribbling off the side of her pizza. "'No matter what,' he said." She was chewing, talking through the pizza. "He had something in his eye and he had to leave quick," she garbled over a mouthful of crust.

Kasi rose hastily, bumping Brando's highchair. "I've got to go to the bathroom," she swallowed through a burning lump in her throat.

"You finish your pizza and watch your brother." And she went into the bathroom, shut the door behind her, clicked the lock into place, and screamed a soundless scream at her reflection in the mirror.

That last part I sort of imagine, because Kasi didn't actually tell me that she ran into the bathroom and screamed. It's just that I have a vivid imagination sometimes and tend to fill in the blanks. By the time Kasi got to that part of the story, though, she was crying. And I didn't know what to do. If Mickey D. had been there, he'd have held her or comforted her or something, but as Mrs. D. has pointed out, I'm not too good at the "nurturant" stuff. I'm more the look, listen, and absorb type. Sort of like a paper towel with rudimentary sensory orifices.

That night of the pizza-that-should-have-been-lobster, Kasi sat up waiting. For what, she wasn't quite sure. For some reason, she didn't really expect Joe to come home. Not that night, anyway. But she expected an answer, some kind of explanation. Where had he gone? Why had he taken their money? Was he okay? Was he in danger? Why hadn't he told her? Why? Why? Every possible avenue she let her mind wander down was a dead end. None of it made any sense. They were relatively happy, for God's sake. He'd never been real demonstrative (in fact, he could be downright stiff most of the time) but she felt that he loved her. He was good with the kids. They both had jobs in fields they enjoyed and were good at, a nice house, nice friends. Why would he take the money and not tell her? Call her? Leave a note? And at that thought, she ran through the house, looking everywhere for a trace of a note, a clue, an answer. Nothing had been touched. Nothing. Nothing! Even his precious saxophone sat mutely in its case in the corner of his study.

Then she became afraid for him. Little things started to jump into her mind, to tickle her fear. Just the night before, they'd been settled on the couch watching a late night gangster flick after the children were asleep. Watching movies was one of the few things they still did together, what with their conflicting schedules and the kids and all. But this night, Joe seemed fidgety. He couldn't seem to get interested. He kept knocking the movie, suggesting they watch something different. But Kasi was really into it. *The Inquirer* had given it a real good review when it came out a year ago, but they'd missed it at the theater.

Halfway through the flick, during a commercial, Kasi went to the kitchen to grab a couple cans of Coke and a box of crackers, and when she returned she saw he had switched to a news magazine program on CNN. A bunch of politicians, foreign policy experts, and military people were sitting around talking about the precarious political situation in the former U.S.S.R. "We're missing the movie," she said. He'd switched then to Jessica Hahn trying to make a post-Baaker Love Connection, and finally reluctantly relinquished the control and rose as if to leave the room.

"Come on, Joe, the don's enforcer was about to teach that little guy a lesson for selling drugs in his territory and not giving him his cut of the take," she tempted.

"Nah," he said, shrugging indifference. "Marbles has to go again." He stepped into his loafers and took the mutt's leash from the hook inside the coat closet door, threw a trench coat on over an old pair of sweats, and the two of them shuffled out just as the little swarthy guy took a burst to the kneecaps from an Uzi. It was so unlike Joe to leave in the middle of the action. It was his original love of these heart-stopping adventure films that had engendered in her a similar interest. Why suddenly the apparent turnoff, she wondered now in retrospect.

She'd fallen asleep almost as soon as the movie was over. He must have come in and found her on the couch, and not wishing to disturb her, gone into his study and worked late into the night on his latest musical score. Because when he finally woke her and led her, groggy and disoriented, to bed, she saw the clock on the night stand said 3:15.

"Want to know how the movie ended?" she mumbled.

"I already know. Somebody double-crossed somebody. They made him pay. It was messy."

He helped her undress in the dark, his wet sweatshirt brushing against her. She vaguely remembered him telling her he had "almost lost his Marbles," and relating a wild chase the dog had taken him on into the bushes after a cat or a rabbit, but she fell back to sleep while he was gently tucking her in.

He was already up when she rose the next morning, and at the breakfast table he seemed preoccupied with the morning paper. "Happy birthday, honey," she said, bending to kiss him goodbye. "What's that?" He had a deep bruise under his right eye.

"Ran into a tree branch when Marbles went after that damn cat!" he groused.

And that's the last she'd seen of her husband.

Maybe Joe had gotten himself into trouble? Maybe he needed the money to bail himself out? What kind of trouble? Could there be some gangsters after him — maybe a bad debt from a loan shark? But no, that was out of character. Maybe he had meant today to take care of whatever it was, and then get home in time to tell her and straighten it all out. But something had happened. Something terrible had happened and he hadn't been able to get back to her. Oh my god! Oh my god! What am I going to do? She bit her lip, paced up and down the hallway. Suddenly she started at the sound of the phone ringing. Joe! But it was Glory Ribbono calling from He Just Left, the bar where Joe's band was playing that evening.

"Kasi? It's Glory. The guys are warming up to go on, hon. They're all set up and Joe still hasn't shown."

And at that, Kasi lost it. It took Glory five minutes to calm her down sufficiently to determine that Joe was indeed missing, had been missing all day, and that he had taken most of the couple's liquid assets with him. "Hold on, Kasi. Stay put. I'll be there as soon as I can," she stressed slowly and deliberately.

It normally takes forty minutes to drive from Ardmore to Lochmore, but Glory, wife of Rocky, the bass fiddle player, made it in twenty-five. Over the course of the previous several years, the two women had sat together, passing the time in many a nightclub and bar while listening to their husbands play. The realtor and the software expert had more in common than their partners' music. They had become good friends, socializing outside of the bar as well as in.

Glory had never heard Kasi sound this way before. It was kind of scary. She pushed her wavy black hair away from her face and glanced at her dark reflection in the rearview mirror. Got to be strong for Kasi. Can't look freaked, she told herself, biting her fleshy lower lip as she pulled into the Short's driveway.

As soon as she determined that Kasi was still in one piece, Glory went in search of the kids. She was disturbed to find Brando sleeping in a dirty diaper in the playpen, and Eva still up, sitting in the bathroom on the closed toilet seat, playing Game Boy. After she tucked them into their respective beds, "Aunt Glory" returned downstairs to find Kasi pacing the kitchen, smoking a Kent. "What is *that*? You don't smoke!"

"They were here. He left them here."

She was smoking Joe's cigarettes! Glory pulled out a kitchen chair and herded the distraught woman into it. "Tell me what you know," she said, as she started a pot of coffee and cleared away the remains of the barely touched pizza.

Kasi told her everything — about Joe leaving Brando at the day-care center with a bogus excuse, the cryptic and apparently emotional leave-taking with Eva, the missing money, and the silence. And then she told Glory her fears surrounding his reaction to Thursday's movie. "Maybe he gambled with someone. Maybe he owed some-body something. Maybe they had something on him. He's been nervous lately, more non-communicative than ever. A loan shark? The Mafia? Glory, they play in those Mob-connected joints all the time!"

"Oh, come on, Kasi, just because he didn't want to watch a gang-ster flick?" And she reached up maternally to brush her friend's hair from her eyes. It was damp from salty tears and sweat.

"Well, what else, then?" Kasi wailed, pulling away in exaspera-tion. "What else? He didn't withdraw four-thousand, six-hundred dollars and thirteen cents from our account to have a burrito at Taco Bell!" she shrieked. "And he left $100 in the savings account! If we go below $100, the bank charges us a $5.00 service charge. See? See? He was still thinking of me!" And at that, she broke into full-blown, hysterical, hiccupping gasps. Glory took her in her arms and hugged her tightly, rocking and rocking.

"Now, now. There, there," was all she could think to say.

Glory spent the night, falling into an exhausted sleep on the living room couch some time after 4 a.m. When she awoke around 7:30, Kasi was seated in the same rocking chair she'd been in all night, but now she was gently holding her slumbering son. "You didn't sleep," Glory surmised.

Kasi shook her head in acknowledgment. "Do you want to stay here with the kids while I go to the police station, or should I get Eva up and we'll all go?" She seemed calmer, determined.

Glory sat on a bench in the waiting room of the Lochmore Police Station, tending Brando in his stroller and trying to keep Eva occupied, as Kasi answered questions for a missing persons report on the far side of the room.

"Well, young lady, your husband has to be missing 24 hours before we can make out a report," said the desk clerk, whose nametag read "Cpl. Bankowitz." "We can't be spending a lot of man-hours searching for someone who may have just stepped out for some air," he said, smiling and putting a warm, moist hand solicitously on the back of hers. "You understand."

She pulled her hand away, and shot him a warning look. "He *has* been gone 24 hours!" she insisted. "That's not a breath of air. He could have personally inflated the Hindenberg with the amount of air he's had!" From anger to fear to hurt and back again she went. But that was *her* prerogative. This condescending fool had no right to pass judgment. Kasi brushed a hank of hair away from her blazing eyes and drew herself up as tall as her five-foot-four frame would allow.

Cpl. Bankowitz's eyes appraised the shapely woman before him. Older than he first had thought. Thirty-five or so, but still a looker. "But you say you didn't miss him until you got home from work last night at 5:15," he remarked, pointing to the form she'd just filled out.

"But he'd been gone since 8 a.m. *That's* when he dropped the kids off at the day care." Her mouth was pulled into a firm, straight line and her eyes were sparking.

"Now, now, little lady," Cpl. Bankowitz said, reaching again for her hand.

"I'm not your little lady!" she suddenly shrieked. "I am reporting the disappearance of my husband!" Her voice became strident, rising with each tightly clipped sentence. "My husband of nine years. A forty-four — no, forty-five-year-old man — from off the face of the earth. Whoosh!" And with that she flung her arms toward the ceiling, as though demonstrating the takeoff of a UFO into the sky. Other officers, riveted now by the distraught woman's vocal outburst, rolled their eyes to the ceiling in response to her gesture. The lieutenant, coming out of his office to investigate the ruckus, paused behind the restraining gateway of the inner sanctum to watch. "He took $4,600.13 out of our account and just vanished! Whoosh!" Kasi whooped, making the skyward motion again.

On the other side of the room, Glory quickly arranged Eva on the bench by Brando's stroller, admonishing her to stay put, and hurried across the floor. A circle of male officers stood around Kasi, staring, most with their mouths open wide enough to catch a fly ball. You'd think Kasi was exposing herself or something. Of course she was, in a way. But they were certainly not helping matters, thought Glory with disgust. She took Kasi gently but firmly by the elbow. "Come on," she said softly. "We're going to straighten this out." And to Officer Bankowitz, she said sternly, "Those little ones need looking after," and nodded briskly in the direction of the children. "Lieutenant, may we have a word with you?" she stated crisply to the man with the most stripes on his shirt, who had attempted to retreat into his office, albeit a bit too slowly.

He glanced over her head at Bankowitz, who shrugged, clueless. Resigned, the man in the lieutenant's uniform with the name "Lt. Franken" over his heart, posted an insincere, conciliatory smile on his lips. "Why, certainly, ladies, you come right in." And he opened up the gate and ushered them into his office.

They had barely taken their seats when Cpl. Bankowitz appeared apologetically at the lieutenant's door. "I'm really not good with—" and he awkwardly ushered Eva into the room before him, wheeling Brando after. The women gave him cold looks.

"Now what seems to be the problem, Mrs. ..?" Franken asked.

"Kasi Short. And this is my friend Glory Ribbono." And the four adults started to parry theories, accusations, and conjectures. As the men volleyed and the women spiked, Eva wandered around the room touching things lightly — the picture frame on the lieutenant's desk, the department sports trophies on a table, the officer's dress coat slung over a chair. Touching lightly, here and there, never landing, always flitting, her wide eyes jumping from face to face, object to object.

Was there something wrong with Joe and Kasi's marriage, the policemen wanted to know? No other woman? No other man? Didn't he have to take care of the kids an awful lot? Did he perhaps resent that? Maybe the guy just wanted a break... Perhaps he was out on a bender? How did she know he didn't drink on the side? Take drugs? Gamble? He spent a lot of time in bars with his work, didn't he? He disappeared on his birthday? Maybe the guy had a midlife crisis or something. Had he acted strangely lately? The man didn't want to watch a gangster movie? That's a little farfetched, ma'am, don't you think? Why would someone be after your husband? Why would he need all that money? Come on, think! Just how well did she know this guy, anyway?

And then the women would serve and the men spiked. Why, indeed, would he take the money without telling her? What would make him do such a thing? He'd always been steady, reliable, dependable, predictable. Why this all of a sudden? It made no sense.

When they got up to leave they had more questions than when they had come in. "We'll look into it," Lt. Franken promised, holding Kasi's complaint between both hands with the ceremonial respect a priest pays the Host at communion.

"I bet he files it as soon as we walk out of here," hissed Kasi as she pushed Brando's stroller through the front door.

Yep, thought Glory silently, glancing back at the men, still standing, heads together, by the inner sanctum gate.

"They think Daddy went for a walk?" asked Eva, obviously incredulous, as she took her mother's hand.

And a smile came to Kasi's lips in spite of herself. "Nothing gets by you, does it, honey?" And she stooped and planted a kiss on her daughter's nose. "Don't worry, honey. Don't worry."

The women returned to Kasi's house. Kasi resumed pacing the floor. Glory did the dishes, helped Eva color by numbers, chased Marbles away from digging in the zucchini patch. Eventually she told Kasi she'd better go home. "I'll check on you later. Try to get some sleep," she advised her friend gently.

When she questioned him at home, Glory's husband seemed clueless. "The guy's been a little distracted lately," was all Rocky could offer. "I don't know — just not always there, like, you know? He's missed some cues lately. A couple of weeks ago he forgot the vocals on songs we've done for years. Nothing major. Nothing you could really put a finger on. He said everything was fine." The big man shrugged.

What about other women? Naw, he'd never seen Joe with anyone but Kasi, Rocky insisted. How about friends Kasi might not know about? No, Joe wasn't much for bosom buddies — nobody he hung with outside of work. Inside the bars, in between sets and before and after gigs, he was always buying some guy he hardly knew a beer. Remember when she and Kasi drove out to Atlantic City to watch them play at The Trump Castle, and Kasi got pissed when Joe spent all his break time huddled in a corner, helping some stranger get drunk? Well, that was Joe's way. On breaks he'd be up at the bar or sitting in a booth, laughing and joking with some local yokel, hunkered down, drawing the fellow out, asking him about himself. He was always wanting to know where a guy was coming from, where he was going, what he did for a living. Always taking an interest in some loser like he was offering the fellow a special treat or something by keeping him company. Joe was a real sociologist, seemed to have a special affinity for the lonelies you find in the places they played. Liked to make them feel good, I guess. But he'd never known Joe to extend a friendship outside the place. "He liked to study people, but not really get involved with them, you know? He was his own one-man Lonely Heart's Club Band, I guess," Rocky mused.

"You talk like he's dead," Glory accused.

"Well, I guess I'd miss him if he was," Rocky allowed. "We couldn't very well play for long without him."

"Jeez, don't get all broken up or anything," she spat disgustedly. "For Christ sake, you've spent hundreds and hundreds of hours over a period of eight years with this guy. The man just drops off the face of the earth and you guess you might miss him?" She threw a dirty sock he'd left on the bathroom floor at his face, and stomped out of the room. "Would you maybe miss me too if the ground opened up and swallowed me?" she tossed back over her shoulder.

"Jeez, what did I say?" Rocky mumbled, going back to his shaving. Eleven a.m. on a Saturday morning and she's asking me deep questions. How can a guy be sensitive to these things at eleven a.m. on a Saturday morning when you been up 'til three-thirty, four o'clock, for Christ's sake?

The next day, Kasi remembered the car. Joe had been driving the Toyota lately, and he'd had it when he disappeared. It was in her name, because she'd bought it before they met. Maybe she should report it stolen and the police would have to take some action to track it down, wouldn't they? They track cars, but not people, she thought, disgusted and discouraged. Miss a ten-year-old Toyota, and they'll put out a report on a nationwide computer. Miss a 45-year-old man, well hell, he's just gone on a bloody walkabout.

So she called up Cpl. Bankowitz. He gave her a hard time over it. After all, it was her husband, why didn't she give him a chance? She was so angry she hung up on him, but when Glory called her later, Kasi told her about the car and Glory called the station to make sure they had, indeed, put it on the national computer network of stolen vehicles. They did have a missing person report out on him now, too. At least they'd done that much, she reported back to Kasi.

Kasi got off the phone with Glory and bent to scoop up Brando, who was lying on his stomach, rolling a can of green beans across the kitchen floor. "Golly, you're getting big, boy!" She rubbed noses; he smiled and squealed happily. Making noises was one of the little guy's favorite things. "Can you believe your father is missing all of this? That silly man! What's wrong with him? Huh? What's wrong with him?" The happy, teasing lilt of her voice did not vary, but the look in her eyes clouded. Brando hesitated in his noise making, but continued to smile. She walked with him into the living room and sat down on the couch, holding him on her lap.

"Was that Daddy on the phone?" Kasi's heart sighed at her daughter's words as Eva sashayed into the room.

She looked up to see that the little girl was wearing almost an entire tube of her mother's brightest lipstick on the lower half of her face, and an expectant look in her chestnut eyes. Kasi immediately softened. "Oh, Eva! Why didn't you ask me first? I would have helped you. You've gotten it all over you!"

The four-year-old, ever stubborn and independent, declared, "I wanted to do it myself. Don't I look pretty?"

"Well, you look — red." Brando laughed out loud.

"Mommy!" Eva wailed, and then remembered why she'd come out before she'd gotten to the eye shadow. "Was that Daddy?"

"No, honey. It was Aunt Glory. Now go get me a wet washcloth and let me take off the excess lipstick before you get it all over your clothes." Of course, it was already all over the little girl's hands, but strict discipline didn't seem appropriate right now. They were all too strung out for the extra strain.

But Eva continued to stand there, red hands on hips. "When is Daddy coming home?" she asked, her voice suggesting Kasi was hiding him from her on purpose. God, she worshipped that man!

"I don't know, Eva. We've talked about this."

Eva stamped her foot. "I want Daddy!"

"I know, honey. We all want Daddy. But we don't know when he's coming home. Come sit with Brando and me. I'll make dinner in a few minutes." And she patted the couch beside her. Eva hesitated, pouted, pulled one foot along the carpet. She wandered first to the right, then to the left, but she couldn't hold out much longer, and so she finally came, indirectly, and therefore, she thought, on her own terms, to sit beside her mother. Kasi put her arm protectively around her red-smeared daughter and hugged her close, but not too tightly. Eva started to hum, and then sing a little song her father often sang to her. Kasi's eyes clouded over and her mind leapt back, replaying the last few weeks, looking for clues, signs, answers to why her world had suddenly come crashing down without the slightest notice.

That night she sat up late again, staring off into space. Her brain was in a place people's minds go when they have experienced extreme sleep deprivation or unbearable torture, or a combination of the two. It was a nowhere land, at the top of a precipice. One sudden move in any direction might have sent her spiraling into breakdown. It seemed the walls themselves were humming.

She heard a loud knock.

Kasi started, lurched, sat down again on the couch. My imagination, she told herself. It's midnight, after all. Then it came again. Persistent. Hard. Kasi jumped off the couch. Someone's knocking on the door. It's midnight and Joe is gone and I'm here alone with the kids, and someone's knocking on the door. "Who's there?" she squeaked.

"Al," said a deep voice very clearly. "Where's Joe?"

"Joe?" It was like her mind couldn't register why some guy was outside her door calling himself Joe. Her mind said, I don't know an Al, but he knows Joe. That's not Joe. Who's Al? And it got all mixed up in her mind.

But all she said was, "Joe?"

But no one answered.

For the longest time she stood five feet from the door, peering at it. "Who's there?" she asked tremulously. Again no answer. "Who's there?" more loudly. No answer. "Who's there, god damn it!" And she reached out, grabbed the knob, and flung the door open, steeled for battle. There was no one there at all. And there wasn't a sound but the tremendous thu-thump, thu-thump, thu-thump of the pulse in her temples and the gentle whistle of a light breeze through the trees.

The wind knocked on the door and called itself Al, she said to herself in almost bemused self-mocking. He's gone with the wind and the wind doesn't even know it!

She locked the door, dragged herself slowly back to the couch, and collapsed into a nightmarish sleep.

19

Of course, in retrospect, she allowed as it might not even have happened. Yet part of her believed someone had come looking for Joe — some ghost, some apparition of the night.

In relating her vision-come-visitor story to Glory, she was convinced the man was a thug who had arrived to exact revenge. What if Joe had been gambling all this time — borrowing money from someone to cover his losses, and somebody was after him to get the money back? She was constantly nagging him about the amount he blew every week on Pick Four and the Super Seven. And he was always betting on the Sixers and the Phillies. If he had lost control and gone on a gambling spree, he'd certainly be back soon, begging her forgiveness. Should I let him back? Should I make him leave for good? Don't I still love him and need him?

But wait, if he'd taken their money and used it to repay the loan sharks, why were they here looking for him? Maybe they were casing the joint to rob it. Maybe they hadn't gotten enough out of him, and had killed him and now they were looking for post-mortem perks. Her mind went wild.

The next morning she called the police again and told them about the caller, admitted she was afraid. Was the man threatening, they asked? Well, no, not overtly, but—. Bankowitz handed her over to another officer. Officer Shirley Schwenk was appreciably more sympathetic. She suggested Kasi write down everything that had happened in the past week. Maybe there was a clue there, she suggested. So she did that. She sat down at her Mac and wrote it all out. When she came to the part about the money withdrawal, she stopped.

Kasi called First Federal and began asking questions. They passed her from one person to the next, until finally they put on a woman who admitted her initials were on the withdrawal slip Joe had filled out when he withdrew the money from their account (through the drive-up window). Yes, she remembered Mr. Short. It was Friday morning and the man with Mr. Short had leaned across and asked for twenties. She'd had to go get another wrapper. That's why she remembered.

Another man in the car! Kasi immediately called the police back. They sent a detective down to question the teller. For a while they thought he might have been coerced into the withdrawal. But under questioning, the woman said, "Well, the other guy had a long beard, not much different than Mr. Short's," and they discovered she'd been confusing Mr. Short all along with another customer, Mr. Lyon, who had a beard to match his name. So they were back to square one, and the police seemed to lose interest again.

A few nights later there was a phone call. No one on the other end. And then, the following night, another. She told the caller to stay out of her life. She told the person out there to go ruin someone else's hopes and dreams. For all she knew, she was telling it to a perfect stranger, or someone's malfunctioning computerized telemarketing machine. Or even Joe himself. But there were no more calls like that.

The police had come to the house and interviewed her again. Taken her statement. Talked to the guys in the band. Nothing. Joe had simply disappeared from the face of the earth. Kasi couldn't shake the feeling that someone else besides the police was looking for him, though. And that he himself was still around, somewhere out there. She had no concrete evidence to support her feelings, however. And recently she had developed the distinct impression that the police suspected *her* of something foul or deceptive. "Do you have insurance on your husband, Mrs. Short?" Lt. Franken asked the last time she called the station.

"Yes, I do. As a matter of fact we added to it just before Brando was born," she replied. "Do you have insurance on Mrs. Franken?" she countered.

"Yes, Mrs. Short, but Mrs. Franken is not missing."

"Well, at least you're finally admitting my husband is missing!"

Kasi and I'd been talking for a couple of hours. Actually, Kasi was doing 95 percent of the talking. The recorder and I were merely absorbing. Marbles, a large, longhaired spaniel mix with freckles on his snout, lay at my feet, twitching in his sleep.

"Are you hungry?" Kasi asked unexpectedly, a wan smile on her face. When she smiled I saw she was really quite pretty, although her eyes were somewhat sunken above tight cheeks void of make-up, and furrowed lines were etched from her eyes past her hairline. They were troubled eyes, but they had a light Mickey D. would probably call "sparkly" under different circumstances.

"Now that you mention it—" I had gotten so involved trying un-successfully to be nurturant for Brother Daniels that I hadn't eaten myself, I realized with a sudden pang. I'd forgotten until then about her incongruous comment over the phone about popcorn. When I'd arrived, we'd immediately started talking and the promised snack had completely left my mind. But now that she'd brought up food, I realized I could actually go more for a medium-rare T-bone and a baked potato smothered in butter with a crunchy salad on the side…

"How about popcorn?" Kasi asked.

Hey, what the hey. Beggars can't be choosey. "Sounds great," I smiled, with a tad of false enthusiasm. But she was understandably preoccupied and didn't notice, disappearing into the kitchen.

This, of course, was when I took the opportunity to ransack the living/dining room — visually, of course.

On the wall over the dining room table was a family portrait, pre-Brando. There was a serious-faced but pretty little girl with wavy blond hair pulled back in a ponytail, her head cocked slightly away from the camera, toward her father, but with her deep brown eyes looking into the lens beneath long, dark lashes. The effect was almost coy, coquettish. Standing behind, with a gentle hand on her daughter's shoulder, was Kasi. It had to be Kasi, and yet she almost looked like a younger sister of herself. It couldn't have been much more than a year prior — in fact, the swell in her loosely flowing shift and the fullness of her breasts revealed the photo was not all together pre-Brando. But the face was younger, vibrant, almost triumphant. It said, "This is my family and I'm proud of us." Next to her, but separated by at least two feet, stood Joe Short. In contrast to his wife, he looked much older than his apparent forty-four. More like late forties, even fifty. Wavy, unruly dark hair flecked with gray framed a ruddy, high-cheeked visage. But the eyes were hidden behind thick, dark, almost sixties-style glasses. The thin lips pointed to his right as though he were talking out of the side of his mouth to his wife when the photographer snapped the picture. It gave him a sort of sneering, William Buckley sort of look that said, "I told you I'd go along with the photo thing, okay? I don't have to pretend I like it." His left hand was at his side; his right arm stiffly disappeared behind his wife's back. (The photographer coaxing, "Come on, Mr. Short, let's put our arm around Mrs. Short. That's it. Let's smile, now. Have you any last words before I shoot?") Joe did not appear to be a happy camper. Kasi's somewhat idealistic presentation of supposed marital bliss was chipping. And they'd picked this as the best picture — one to hang over the dining room table? Hmm.

There were a few other framed photos — one of Eva dressed in little-girl frills and sitting on the living room couch, holding the newborn Brando in her lap, a posed, exaggerated smile crinkling her face.

And there was one of a man playing a saxophone on stage. By squinting and standing just six inches away I could see it must be Joe, though his hair was longer and his thick glasses gone, and the stage spotlight shining almost on his head put his face half in glare, half in shadow. He was leaning back from the waist up, torso twisted, pelvis thrust forward. The horn was to his lips, the instrument tipped back, giving the body and instrument the shape of a tilted quarter note. His eyes were closed. This was a different Joe Short altogether.

A fourth photo showed Kasi, gown-bedecked and shaking the hand of a scholarly-looking gentleman in a tuxedo. In her left hand she held a gleaming plaque. The sign behind the dais read, "Computer Innovators of America. 1998 Awards."

"Do you like it with butter?" Kasi called from the kitchen.

"Oh yes, please. Lots, if you don't mind." And I moved back to the living room and switched on the TV to make it appear as though I was innocently occupying myself, but set it on mute so I could hear Kasi when she came. "Not much on the tube on Wednesday nights. Guess a lot of people whoop it up on Hump Day, huh?" There was a sort of concurring grunt from the kitchen. I slid over to the bookshelves that sat next to the stereo on the east wall of the room. *Artificial Neural Networking*, *Fractal Turbo Pascal*, *Digital Bus Handbook*, *Switching Theory*, volumes I through V, *Applied Linkage Synthesis*. Obviously Kasi's. The next row was *How to Toilet Train Your Child*, *Surviving the Terrible Twos*, and the standard Dr. Spock titles. Then a row of thriller and science fiction novels — Asimov, Le Carré, Ludlum. I opened the cover on *The Matarese Circle*. "Happy birthday to Kasi from Sandi. Enjoy!" The shelf next to the bottom appeared to be mostly true crime. Joe McGinniss's *Fatal Vision*, Steven Levy's *The Unicorn's Secret*, Frank Abagnale Jr.'s autobiography, *Catch Me If You Can*. "The Amazing True Story of the Most Extraordinary Liar in the History of Fun and Profit!" read the last jacket. There was something inside the book, causing a bulge about mid-point. When I opened it, a thin, light piece of wood fell out.

"Do you want more Coke?" Kasi called out.

"Yes, please, and ice this time." I hate ice in my Coke. Waters it down and I never feel like I'm getting my money's worth. But it gave me time to pick up the reed, stuff it in my pocket, return the book to the case, sit back down on the couch, and focus in on the soundless TV before Kasi walked into the room, holding my soda in one hand and balancing a huge bowl of popcorn in the other. She put the soda down on the end table.

And that's when she dumped on me. She glances up to see a picture of a guy she thinks is her missing husband, lets fly with the popcorn, and starts hopping around like a ping pong ball.

"Are you sure that was him?" The teaser promo had just briefly flashed a photo on the screen. The guy didn't look to me like either the reluctant family man or the rapt saxophonist enshrined in celluloid on the dining room wall behind us.

"Of *course* it's him," she snapped. "Don't I know my own husband?" Well, actually, that's exactly what I had begun to doubt, but this was obviously neither the time nor the place.

"Well, Kasi, let's go to the videotape!" I said, grabbing the nearest VHS cassette and popping it into the VCR. At least that way we can have it to review once reality sets in, I thought. We didn't have to wait long. The story of the man Kasi claimed was the missing Joe was the first to be shown on what turned out to be "Pennsylvania's Unsolved Mysteries," a statewide version of the popular nationwide show hosted by Robert Stack.

"It's him!" she interposed every twenty seconds. "See?" "Why, that bastard!"

I cheered silently. At last, she's actually expressing anger at the guy. After all, the story we were watching was a tale of abandonment — not abduction, not Mafia-style hit men out to settle a score, but simple disappearance. The guy — (and mind you, at this point, I'm still not convinced it's the same guy we're looking for) — is simply a putz. He starts a family, glides along through life as though everything's hunky-dory, and then he just up and leaves them without a trace.

The tale was a simple one. A young woman named Ayn Curtis (underneath her name, superimposed on the screen, was the identifier "Missing Man's Daughter") was looking for her father, who disappeared with no explanation and no warning nine years ago, when Ayn was eleven. Her mother had recently died and now she wanted to find her father — and if not her father, then answers as to why he disappeared.

A little bit about his background was given. He was a musician ("See? See?" Kasi practically gloated, pointing a trembling finger at the screen.) Jack Curtis had been married to Sally Swingle Curtis, an executive administrative assistant in Kimbles, Pennsylvania. He was 5'10", needed corrective lenses, and had a port birthmark on his upper left arm ("Yes! It's shaped like Florida!" Kasi crowed). He and his band had sometimes traveled on gigs throughout the Poconos, into New York and New Jersey, and even played occasionally at resorts in Atlantic City. ("That's where we met — Atlantic City! We met in Atlantic City!" she wailed. "The bastard told me he was divorced! He

24

told me his wife couldn't have children, and that she ran away with another guy in the band!")

"Shh! Shh! You'll wake the children." I said it as much to calm her growing hysteria as from a fear of Eva awakening and coming into the living room to view her alleged father on TV. The woman was practically bouncing off the furniture. To tell the truth, I can't remember ever missing Mick's soothing presence more. All I could think to do was pick the popcorn up off the floor. ("A dirty house reveals a cluttered mind," my mother always says. She also claims that dirt is older than time and that the rules of ethics change every ten years. The woman is the only creature alive who, by the simple force of repeated misrepresentation, can change a platitude into a nonsensical neologism. But if you say something often enough, people accept it.) And that's why I kept saying to Eva, "It'll be all right. It'll be okay. We'll find the mother — I mean, your husband. Don't worry." Be happy. Let your smile be your umbrella and everything will be right as rain.

We watched the tape three times. By the time we'd taken down the host's 800 number for the third time ("I want to make sure it's right," Kasi explained nervously), I had concluded the following:

- ☐ Sally Curtis and her daughter had been sadly duped.
- ☐ If "Pennsylvania's Unsolved Mysteries" were to run a story on Kasi's case, the casual viewer could easily mistake if for a re-run of the Curtis's story.
- ☐ If Jack Curtis had managed to leave his loving family and disappear without a clue for nine long years, we might as well kiss goodbye to the hope of Joe Short walking back in that door under his own volition any time soon.

Kasi called the 800 number and told them briefly what she knew about the man they called Jack Curtis. An appointment was arranged for three days later with the program director, a Mr. Tadford Ames, at the Embassy Suites in Plymouth Meeting.

"It's on Saturday. Is that all right?" she asked when she got off the phone.

"Are you sure you still want us to investigate this?"

"He's still missing, isn't he? In fact, he's more missing now than he was three hours ago," she declared. Somehow that made perfect, illogical sense, so I didn't press her. "They said they would give my number to that girl, Ayn Curtis." Her voice faded and she looked away as she said the girl's name. "Explains why he called Eva 'Eva Ann,' even though her middle name's Leigh, after my mother. He always claimed they just sounded right together." She said it sadly, almost nostalgically, as she folded the paper with the 800 number on it into smaller and smaller pieces.

Then she swiveled her head slowly about the room with the detached look of a stranger in an unfamiliar place. Her eyes lit upon the photographs on the wall. She walked to them, ran her fingertip lightly over the glass, tapping each one gently, like a doctor tapping the chest of a congestant patient. Suddenly she snatched the family portrait from the wall, smashed it on the back of the bookcase, and plucked the photograph from beneath the shattered glass. She ripped Joe raggedly from the picture, searing off part of her own shoulder and grazing Eva's left ear in the process. "He's gone! He's gone for good and I hate him!" she screamed. "He fucking lied to me from Day One! He took my trust. He shit on my trust! I hope the bastard rots in hell! Heaven help him when I catch up with him! When one of his ex-wives or sons or daughters catches up with him and rips him limb from limb!" she cried, symbolically shredding him into smaller and smaller pieces as she sobbed great, racking sobs of grief, anger, and betrayal.

I put my arm around her and held her tight and pretended to be Mickey D. and Mrs. D. and Mother Teresa all in one. Damn it, Mickey, you *know* I need you to do this kind of thing. Damn that damn disease you have that makes you sick at the drop of a hat! Damn all men whose sex drive is stronger than their immune systems and their brainstem put together. Damn all the good people who don't realize how anxiously death and pain sit on your shoulder and all the bad people who don't care. And damn the bastards who reach into your soul with warm fingers that turn to ice just when you let down your guard.

I held Kasi for a long, long time, then watched her stand in the dark over her children's blessedly slumbering forms, and finally told her I had to leave.

"I'm sorry," I said, as she saw me to the door and handed me the videotape.

"It's not your fault."

"No, not that," I said, looking down at the cassette. "I taped over 'It's a Wonderful Life.'" And she smiled wanly, tears glistening in her eyes.

Chapter 2
To Beat the Band

"You *are* getting out of bed and going with me tomorrow," I informed Mickey on Thursday afternoon. Ayn Curtis and Kasi Short were to meet at Ayn's apartment the following morning, and Kasi wanted us to be there. It turned out that Ayn was now living in Philadelphia, and was anxious to hear whatever she could about her missing father. Mickey's old excitement was evident as we discussed the case in his childhood bedroom in our mother's house.

"He'll do nothing of the sort!" the matron herself pronounced, sashaying into the room with a glass of fruit juice and a handful of pills. "And you get off that bed. You'll catch it, too!" she scolded, fluttering at me as though I were a pesky fly that wouldn't go away.

I didn't get off the bed but I shifted my weight some so she could pull M.D.'s eiderdown quilt up to his neck, even though it was only September. "You can't get *it* from sitting on a bed, Madre. Trust me on that one."

"Eliza!" Mick warned with an uneasy smirk.

"Germs are everywhere," she tsked, ignoring reality as usual, fluffing Mickey's pillows as though they were life itself needing no more than a simple whack! into place from her to make them right again.

"His germs are not germane in this instance," I smart-alecked. "They are only exploitative parasites playing piggy-back, as it were. Not real germs of their own, actually, so they don't exactly count as primary germs but as—"

"Eliza!" Mickey warned sharply this time.

"—sycophantic germs," I concluded quickly and clapped my jaw shut as The Mick swiped at me with the water bottle, which I adroitly avoided by scooting down to the end of the bed. All right, so I can't help myself sometimes. I can't stand her obtuse blindness. And his ultra-sensitivity to it. And my own maddening uselessness. So I babble.

He coughed a chest-deep rasp. "This is just a cold," he said when he caught his breath. "I'll be up tomorrow."

"You're not—"

"—I am," he cut her off.

"The last cold you had—"

"—I'm going to work tomorrow."

YESSSS! I mouthed over the old lady's sculpted hairdo. That's it, Mickey. Fight the damn bastard. Fight, fight against the dy—

"—Well, don't come running to me when your goose gets out of the barn!" Mother said sharply, staring straight at me and poking a long, manicured nail in my direction. "You're playing with fire and the wind's going to go out of your sails!" And with that she flounced righteously out of the room, holding Mick's lunch tray before her like a torch to light her way.

The Mick and I looked at each other in wary astonishment. "When your goose...?" I asked dubiously. "Should we be worried about her, or what? She's moronically mixing metaphors!"

"Germs are the devil's playground," Mick mocked, and we both snickered guiltily. Something nasty — something real — was obviously getting through to the old broad, and her reaction to it wasn't a pretty sight. Suddenly the sights and smells of the room felt heavy to me — the brown bottles of Mickey's everyday drugs grouped on the nightstand, the minty smell of cough syrup, the pasty odor of antiseptic Mother practically coated the room with.

"I gotta go," I said. "See you later. Get better fast." And I was out of there.

-------The rest of Thursday afternoon, while Mick was ingesting vitamin mega doses and watching the "Mysteries" videotape, and Kasi Short was mentally preparing for her meeting with Ayn Curtis, I did a little background checking.

First I got ahold of Sara Barklee, an ex-Vortex Institute buddy of mine (in the catch-as-you-can, get-'em-while-they're-hot industry of computer engineering, employee turnover is high). Yes, she knew of Kasi Short. Vortex had 1,500 employees on its 400-acre "campus" complex. But Kasi Short was a standout — a rising star. With the company for twelve years, she was considered a programming whiz woman — one of those rare hackers who could see the Bigger Picture, beyond the mathematical maze of code to the solution.

Her bio in the latest Vortex employee directory showed a masters in computer science from Bryn Mawr and various company and industry awards. Hobbies: jogging, skeet shooting, playing with her children, listening to her husband's band. Must ask her what the hell one did with a skeet after one killed it.

I got the names of a few of Kasi's co-workers from Sara, but I didn't follow up on them right away. Checking up on your own client is a delicate matter.

Checking up on Joe Short was another story. I interviewed Rocky and Glory Ribbono as the former changed the oil on his '69 Mustang in the driveway of their small Victorian in Media in a neighborhood with a feel of tarnished silver — classic but in need of a polish. The Ribbonos had apparently seen better days, too. The Mustang wasn't so much a classic as a hanger-onto. "Rocky's the original owner," Glory offered.

"My Dad was so proud that I graduated from high school, he bought it for me," Rocky added. "I was the first Ribbono this side of the Atlantic to make it through high school."

"Last thing you did right, far's he's concerned," Glory noted.

"Yeah, well, maybe that'll change soon," Rocky mumbled, un-screwing the plastic cap on another quart of oil.

"Rocky!" Glory was obviously caught by surprise. "You prom-ised! You said you'd find legitimate part-time work until you can find a replacement for Joe!"

"Yeah, well I tried!" and he threw the oily dipstick rag on the ground. "You *know* that! I got no skills. I'm not a shirt and tie kind of guy, honey, I'm a musician. Joe was good. We can't make it without a good horn. And Joe was our lead vocalist. The rest of us are back-up, back-seat. We tried Chip Werner but he just didn't click. Sam Angel's a *putz*, and Mike Zimmerman wanted too much of the cut. Our contracts have been voided, our extra gigs have dried up, and I got blisters from putting on Sunday shoes and scraping and bowing all over Phily for a dumb-ass job. I ain't no salesman, no stock clerk and no waiter. And you haven't sold a house in two months!" He looked away from his wife, suddenly finding an interest in his size eleven Reboks. "Besides, Pop says all I have to do is collect the money." He mumbled the last statement.

"No, Rocky, no! You said you'd never do that!" Glory was prac-tically crying. I felt like a witness to marital rape.

"Glory, honey!" he caught a flailing wrist as it ineffectually swiped at his meaty upper arm. "We're gonna lose the house if I don't." He looked over her shoulder at me as she struggled to slip his grasp. It was a "What's-a-guy-to-do?" look; a "Talk to her, will ya?" plea. Glory pulled away and ran into the house.

I bent over, picked up the oily rag and placed it on the fender. "Your father — he's not trafficking in drugs, is he?" Are you planning to sell your firstborn? When did you stop beating your wife? (One thing that amazed me when I first got into this business was that often when you ask people these kinds of personal, potentially incriminating questions, they actually answer.)

"No, no. Video machines. Mostly poker." He lowered the hood, picked up the rag, and began mechanically polishing the hood with an unsoiled corner of the rag. The base player's voice was low, understated background, like his fiddle.

"Poker? You mean the ones that pay back money, as opposed to 'for entertainment purposes only?'"

"Well, you can set 'em either way."

"Isn't that illegal in Pennsylvania? And Mob controlled?" I put it right out there. I'd read the official Crime Report on La Cosa Nostra.

"It's a family business. Not a Family business with a capital 'F,'" he stressed, meeting my eyes to make sure I understood the distinction. "We're Italian but not "Connected," with a capital "C." My grandfather started with pinballs back in the '40s. Then it grew into video machines — Pac Man, Donkey Kong, that sort of thing. But it's the poker machines that make the money. Sure, the payoffs are technically illegal. But everybody does it. Hell, they used to rig the old pinballs to pay off! You tell the old man it's illegal and he'll tell you where to go. It's more like a game to him, I guess. My father always expected I would take over. Actually wanted to send me to college so's I could learn bookkeeping!" he snorted. "Not to study music, though. Oh no, couldn't see no future in that." He walked around to the side of the car and kicked the tires a little too hard. "Maybe he was right."

He spit on the car and wiped; spit and wiped. "Then there's the little scratch games and the pull-tab games they sell to bars and clubs, even service organizations. The old man's made a bundle off of them. Quarters add up. Pays a hell of a lot better than tweaking strings."

"Or blowing a horn?"

"Yeah, sure," his dark eyes scanned my face for a quarter-beat, and then he resumed the rhythm of spit and shine.

"What if your old man gets caught?"

"Already has. Paid some fines. Got put on probation. They confiscated the machines and smashed 'em up, just like they was whiskey stills. Hell, within a month he had just as many joints stocked with new ones."

"So Glory's afraid the same'll happen to you."

"She don't have to worry. I'll just be a gopher; empty the machines, divvy up the take." Spit and shine. Spit and shine. "Better hours, steady work, good pay."

"But?"

"Glory don't want me to."

"And you?"

"Hell, ain't no harm," he said defensively, then kept on shining. We didn't talk for a while. Finally he said, more softly, "I've watched people stand at those things for hours at a time. They go up there with five dollars in quarters and then when it's gone they go to the change machine and get five more, and five more. And then they go across the street to the ATM and take out another $20, and when that's gone they hit their friends up for a loan until payday. And they start stopping by on the way home from work to play a few games. And they forget to go home for supper..." He was looking at his shoes again. He seemed to have played out his interior tug-of-war. I shuffled my feet, feeling a bit uncomfortable.

"But I need a job," he said, and started shining again. I just watched, mesmerized by the motion, intrigued with Rocky's moral dilemma. "You know," he said, finally glancing at me suddenly as if making sure I was paying attention, "my old man offered Joe a job more than once. He did that to all the guys in the band. Thought if he lured them in, I might see a good thing and come, too." He reached down and adjusted the mirror. "Before this "Unsolved Mysteries" thing came up, I wouldn't have told you this, 'cause I think a lot of Kasi and I wouldn't want to hurt her," he allowed. "But Joe took Pop up." He was still playing with the mirror, swiveling it back and forth. The sun of a late fall day glinted off it, reflecting light on the sober, rugged face. Rocky shrugged his shoulders. "But it didn't last. He did some servicing and bagging, made a few bucks and then quit. Joe told me it just wasn't his style. I think he done it for the cash. Kasi always made four times what he did. Kind of hurts a guy's ego." His voice went way down on the last statement.

"Did Joe play the machines?"

"Oh, yeah. It's hard not to. I remember a few times he got a little mad at himself 'cause he blew whatever he'd made. But it didn't last long. He couldn't go too far, because he don't have a whole lot to begin with. He wouldn't ask Kasi for money. That's why his emptying out that joint account was such a mind blower."

"Did he play the lottery?"

"Yeah, he bought tickets now and then."

"How about the bigger stuff, when you went to Atlantic City?"

31

"No."

He seemed so sure. "No roulette, no blackjack?"

"Uh-unh. At the casinos he played the guys." Rocky watched my eyebrows rise in surprise, then looked away quickly, his face turning a dark fuchsia. He made himself busy again, polishing that mirror. But after a brief moment, he continued. "I ain't sure, mind you, and I never really clued in onto this 'til just recently," he said, then paused and took a deep breath. "...But I think Joe was a switch-hitter." He glanced up to see my reaction. When I gave none, he continued. "That would explain why he kept leaving these women — starting a family and then moving off again. Maybe he was trying to stay straight, but it went against the grain, ya know?" He had hit his stride now, more confident in his analysis. "He was always working up some guy at the bars and the nightclubs we played. Get him alone in a corner, buy him a beer or two or three, laugh and joke with him. Sometimes after the gig was over the guy'd still be sitting there in the corner, at 2:30, 3:00 in the morning, waiting for Joe. And when we left, Joe'd be there with 'em." Now he was polishing the roof.

"Half the time, Glory don't know when I get home," he commented matter-of-factly. "Can't stay up and wait all night on a week night. She's got to be to work at 9:00. Same with Kasi. There's plenty of opportunity in this line of work for a little extra-curricular action if you're so inclined. Yet I never, in all the years we played together, seen him with another woman. I told Glory that; Kasi, too." And he spit once more, this time on the ground. "But what I didn't tell 'em is I seen him with a *lot* of men."

We paused silently in the late September sunshine for a few minutes. I could see Glory standing at the kitchen window, hand on chin, elbow on sill. "No women, then?" I poked one more time. It had seemed the most plausible reason to disappear. After all, he left one woman and then found another and left her. It sounded as though he'd met Kasi when he was still living with Sally Curtis, and while supposedly playing a gig in Atlantic City. But if a guy could leave one woman for another without a trace, why not leave a woman for another man, also without a trace? Maybe the man at Kasi's door the night after Joe disappeared....

"No women," Rocky confirmed.

"And no serious gambling?"

"Nothing anyone would come after you for. He didn't go in the hole. Never spent more than he had," Rocky insisted, seriously wounding Kasi's favorite theory.

"Anything to blackmail him on?"

"Other than the guys?...."

Hmm. We absorbed that one a little longer.

Finally I asked, "What do *you* think?"

"I think Kasi better forget about him. He fucked her good." He was mama's boy enough to blush at his own words.

"Yeah. Well, thanks for your time and your honesty. And good luck with your — your job search." I ventured a smile and a wave at Glory's form in the window.

"He played a mean horn," Rocky allowed wistfully as I turned to go. It was the closest he could come, under the circumstances, to acknowledging he'd miss the guy.

But as I got into my car and drove away, I wondered just whose horn Joe/Jack was playing with now. After all, he left *his* at home. As "Saturday Night Live's" Roseanna Roseannadana, the character who was always misquoting people, once panned, "Sax and violence don't mix." Or something like that.

Next on my list was Billy Randolph, the band's piano player. Randolph was at his day job (apparently the only job he had now that Joe Short was among the missing). He was a kindergarten teacher in Conshohocken. By the time I had maneuvered my way past the administrative office and located Randolph's room from a map posted by the employee mailboxes, the kids had gone home for the day and Randolph was sitting at his desk, correcting papers.

"Do they have tests nowadays in kindergarten?"

He raised his head, eyebrows arching inquisitively, and started to rise.

"No, don't get up." I extended my hand.

It was enveloped by a large, smooth hand the rich brown color of apple wood. The pressing of the flesh was more on the order of a brief handholding than a shake. His eyes were expressive, welcoming. "You must be Jodi's mom. I hear she'll be transferring to our class later this week. I'm sor—-"

"No, no, I'm not Jodi's mother." It was a shame to cut him off; I could listen to that reassuring resonance all day. Must give great harmony. His hand dropped. I proffered my card. "I'm sorry I couldn't call ahead. I'm here about Joe Short."

"Joe."

I thought at first that he had said, "No." He just stood behind the desk, looking down at it as though Joe were there somewhere among the papers. Finally he raised his head and an apologetic, sad smile came to his sensuous lips. "I'm sorry. I guess I just feel guilty about all this."

GUILTY? Now wait just a minute. Male kindergarten teacher. Missing musician with possible bisexual tendencies. My mind was doing sexual gymnastics to beat the band. Had these two done a little *pas de* do-re-mi? Practiced a bit of chamber music, perhaps? Tickled each other's ebonies and ivories? I envisioned a lover's quarrel, an off-stage spat, leading to — to what?

"Excuse my manners, Ms. Samuels," he said, glancing at my business card. "I'd offer you a chair, but—" and he pointed toward the miniature desks.

Now come on, Eliza! Just because a man — a big, brown, hunk of a man at that — is a kindergarten teacher with a sensitive way doesn't make him a homosexual, right? If being attached at the hip to Mickey D. for that long didn't teach you anything, it should have taught you not to type people based on preconceived stereotypical notions. Never mind that this guy's got beefcake eyes and boiler room buns (oh, yeah, I checked *that* out when he stood up) and a smile to launch a GQ cover. And yet, it was too good to be true. That old saw about all the good-looking, sensitive ones being gay was certainly gnawing on me now. Goodoleboy Rocky musta been looking in the wrong direction when he was gay gazing, I concluded.

"Oh, that's okay, I'll just lean up against one of these if that's all right." Randolph gestured acquiescence as I perched on the edge of the desk in front of his. He sat back down, heavily, as if weighted.

"You feel guilty?" I prompted.

"Yes," he said. He was quiet for a minute, fingering a No. 2 pencil, his eyes staring at a point four inches to the left of my face. "I saw him last night."

"My God! Where is he? Everybody's looking for him. His wife—-"

"On TV, Ms. Samuels. I saw him on the TV."

"Oh." Come on, get a grip, Eliza. Stop jumping to conclusions. Start being a detective again. Damn it, Mickey. I need you here to protect me from my own cupidity.

"I was just kind of flipping through the channels, and there was Joe's picture. I recognized him immediately. No doubt about it," and he put down the pencil. "I blame myself."

Okay, we're back to square one. "Why is that, Mr. Randolph?"

"Billy."

"Okay, Billy, why do you blame yourself?"

34

"Well, you see, I know Joe probably better than anyone." Here it goes. And at that, he got up and moved around to the front of the desk, leaning his cute toosh against the lacquered wood veneer and folding muscular arms across a well-defined chest. "I'm the one who brought Joe into the band."

"Oh, really?" This was hard to concentrate on.

"Yes." And he proceeded to tell me How Joe Short Joined the Band. "We were playing in Cheltenham. We were about to lose our lead, a helluva sax player. We had an ad in the trades for a month or more, and Delbert had agreed to stay with us until we got a replacement. We had a biweekly gig — Thursdays and Saturdays — at a small club called The Blue Chip. I saw this guy sitting at the corner of the bar both days for two weeks running. He'd nurse a Seven and 7 most of the evening. Sometimes he chatted up a few of the regulars, but mostly he watched the band. When you're up there playing for a while, you get to looking at the patrons, deciding what they do, why they're there." He crossed one leg over the other at the ankles, and recrossed his arms in the opposite direction over his green chambray shirt and white silk tie.

"The second week, I sat next to him at the bar during break and we made small talk. He told me he liked our sound. I told him we were losing Delbert and looking for a replacement. Do you know he never let on that he played?" He shook his head in remembered puzzlement. "He just said, 'Hope you find someone.' I sat by him again the next week. He mentioned he was going up to Atlantic City that weekend to party. At the time I remember thinking he didn't seem like the partying type, you know?" He shook his head, looked off into space as if there were an answer there.

"So how did you find out he was a musician?"

"Kasi."

"I thought he didn't meet—"

"That's the weekend he and Kasi met in Atlantic City."

"But—" My mind, doing mental gymnastics, slipped right off the balance beam. "But wasn't he playing for a band when they met? A band from the Poconos?"

"Yeah, apparently, from what the TV says, although at the time I believe he told us it was Cleveland he was from. I don't know what he was doing here. I never figured that out. I just know that a month later, he's back and she's with him and they're sitting at the bar. He's lost his beard by now, but it's him, no doubt in my mind. And when the gig's over, and we're packing up, I go up to the bar to get a beer, and she leans over and introduces herself before Joe and I can even nod our acquaintance. She says, 'I hear you're looking for a lead. My fiancée here plays saxophone and he's wonderful.' And the rest is history."

And with that, Billy Randolph got up, stretched, and loped around to the back of his desk again. "I should have known then he'd go out the same way he came in, without a trace." It almost sounded logical the way he put it. Blows into town and blows back out again, like an anchorless tumbleweed.

"So why do you feel guilty?" I wondered how Randolph's logic played it out.

"Damn it, I should have warned Kasi!" He balled up a piece of paper and threw it in the wastebasket. "I never had the heart to tell her I met Joe before she did, that he'd been here before. There was something strange about it all. I couldn't figure out which came first — the chicken or the egg — moving here because of her or the band; finding the location, then the band, then the girl, or did it all just fall together simultaneously?" Charcoal eyes peered at me as though I could decipher his puzzle. "I could never figure Joe out. And I could never figure what Kasi saw in him, either. She's so warm and intelligent. A real trusting woman. I didn't want to break that trust, I guess." He looked at me, a slight curl of his lips signaling regret.

Hmm. No love lost there. Bitterness, not passion. Regret, but not over Joe. Billy Randolph was playing with his pencil again. I shifted my weight. The edge of the desk was making my butt sore. "So do you think he found — someone else— and left Kasi for her or him?" There, I threw it out. Let's see if he chomps on *this* one.

He allowed me a thin, almost bemused glance from under thick eyebrows. "Joe Short didn't leave Kasi for a woman *or* a man," he said softly but firmly. "Joe was brilliant in his music, his art. He could blow the roof off if he was in the right mood. But in human relationships he was a phony, a stand-in, a cardboard cutout, like those life-size pictures of the presidents that people pay big money to have their picture taken with. Short came here because something he wanted was here. The people were peripheral, secondary. If he's left, it's the place, the circumstances he's leaving, not the people. As for sex, Joe Short didn't have any. Hormonally, biologically, he was a male; psychologically, he was a wasteland. He was asexual, almost anti-sexual. I swear, those kids were produced by immaculate conception. How that poor woman put up with him is beyond me."

And that's about all the wisdom Billy Randolph cared to offer on the subject of Joe Short. Except for one passing comment as he saw me to the classroom door. "It's cute, though, how Joe left little clues, almost as though he were teasing someone — daring them to find him out," he smiled with appreciative irony lifting his eyebrows.

"What do you mean?"

"His aliases, for instance."

I gave him a blank stare.

He smiled gently as if to excuse me for my ignorance. "The name 'Curtis' in Latin means 'Short,'" he explained as he shook my hand and wished me well.

So J/J had changed his family and his location, but kept his name and his avocation. And something passing for a semblance of humor in his taunting cockiness. That might be a weakness to explore – a possible key to his eventual discovery. But as of now, we were still coming up one man short.

I left Wildwood Elementary and eased my Cabriolet into the thickening traffic on the Sure to Kill (otherwise known as the Schuylkill Expressway, or Route 76), thinking all the while how this felt like a colossal waste. How can I take this poor woman's money to try to figure out the workings and whereabouts of a very elusive man whom apparently nobody really knew to begin with? The people he spent the most time with couldn't even agree on his sexual preferences or whether he actually had any. He gambled but he didn't really. He was peripherally involved in illicit activity, but probably not on an indictable level. He liked to talk to strange men in bars, but he'd never follow up on anything. He left one woman for another just to switch bands? My natural inclination was to tell the woman to forget the slob. Find yourself a real man, if there are any left out there. If not, stick with the dog. He's at least loyal.

But there was one more band member to go — George Diego, the guitar/fiddle player. I caught up with Diego as he emerged from giving a private lesson at the State School for the Blind, between Lancaster and Haverford Avenues, inside the city limits. I stopped a woman guiding two boys with canes and she pointed Diego out, just 100 yards away, carrying his guitar case clutched to his chest as though it possessed no handle. When I approached and offered my card, explaining my mission, he totally bypassed my outstretched hand, instead sucking me to him like an enthusiastic octopus, his dark eyes gleaming. "She sent you to me!" he effused. "I knew she would." And the little guy embraced me with a surprisingly powerful grip.

Uh-oh! I thought, attempting to diplomatically pull away from his hold. I'm not the touchy-feely kind. My people's people's people's people and all of their people were British. On both sides, forever. We WASPs don't feel very good about tactile familiarity. Studies show you can watch two friends chatting in a restaurant:

- ☐ If they're British, they will *not* touch;
- ☐ If they're Americans in, say, Florida, they *might* touch one another twice an hour;
- ☐ If they're in Paris and they're French, two times per minute;
- ☐ And if they're Puerto Rican, they can't keep their hands off one another — would you believe every 20 seconds!

So Jorge and I are having a cultural clash right at ground zero here, before we've even been properly introduced. In fact, he's so effusive and smothering and I'm so taken aback that I almost miss the underlying message here: George and Kasi; Kasi and George. Suddenly that song, "Looking for Love in All the Wrong Places," wells up, taking on a new meaning. It's not Joe's love life that's been elusively staring me in the face; it's Kasi's.

"She won't talk to me," George wailed. "She won't answer my phone calls. Since Joe left, I am nothing to her! But now you've come. She's changed her mind? It's a sign. She needs me. She wants me, yes?"

Backing up out of reach to the proper "safe" WASP distance of three feet, I forced George to stop touching me and resort to touching himself. He had put down his musical instrument and figuratively taken up his corporeal organ. Forced to find a socially acceptable replacement, he stood there wringing his sensual/sensitive hands and bouncing anxiously on the balls of his feet.

"She said she loved me!" The vibrato in his voice was like a beckoning wave tickling at the shoreline as he crept closer. I sidled back.

"Now that Short's gone we can finally be open! We can finally be free!" Fortissimo!

"But she won't talk to me! I will die! I will mortally die!" Crescendo! Profundo! Excitidado! (?) I thought an emotional string was going to break and go flying, straight at me, in the form of one very high-strung Latin hombre.

"Look, Mr. Diego—"

"George. Call me George." And we did opposing two-steps.

"Look, George, maybe we should go somewhere and you can tell me your story?"

"Certainly! My apartment is just a few blocks from here—"

"No, thank you very much, I don't want to put you out. Isn't there a coffee shop near here?" A WASP coffee shop. Booths with four-foot wide tables. I was visually measuring his limbs. His musician's fingers looked longer than his arms. Seems safer inside a commercial establishment than out here with no manmade barriers between us.

He reluctantly relented. There was a Denny's on the next block. I staked out a booth and for the next half-hour, learned all about George's version of his affair with Kasi. He spoke passionately and openly. But once he started to get it out of his system he calmed down a bit, and picking up on my body signals, backed off physically as well. There was a great deal of fidgeting going on below table level on his side of the booth, however.

It turned out George had been with the band for only a year and a half. He had approached Kasi almost immediately, she had readily responded, and they had been having an affair almost from the start — through her pregnancy with Brando, his birth, and up until the time of Joe's disappearance. I found myself both titillated and repulsed by the thought of the two of them having an affair while she was carrying her husband's baby. Or was she?

So I just blurted it out: "Is Brando your son?"

"No."

It was the shortest visible ejaculation of our entire exchange. What could I say after that? Are you *sure*? Did you have blood tests? Who came up with his wacky name, anyway?

I *did* ask him how much Joe knew.

"Short, he didn't know and he didn't care," George brushed off the question like a crumb from the tabletop. "Joe couldn't have cared less. He paid next to no attention to her. She was little more than a symbol to him; a prop: The Mother, The Wife. They didn't *love* one another."

A vibrato encore. He was digit wringing again.

"*I* was the only thing that was keeping Kasi together through this — the only loving, caring part of her life. I thought she would just stay with him through the pregnancy; that it was too unsettling a time to leave him, and as soon as things calmed down a bit, she would come to me." George sighed deeply. "I don't know why, but she felt a responsibility of some sort towards him. Women, they mother men, you know." And he looked at me with soulful eyes.

39

Not me, buddy. Just ask my mother!

"But now he's gone, there's no reason to turn me away. I call on the phone and she hangs up. I go to the house and she shuts the door in my face."

The midnight visitor? Had Kasi been hallucinating? Transferring feelings of guilt about George onto the shadowy "Al" of an over-wrought imagination?

"Okay. Let's leave that for a moment," I rapidly switched tracks. "What do *you* think happened to Joe Short?" I did my best to look into those dreamy brown eyes without blushing or cringing.

"I don't know, lady." Suddenly the passion was out of his voice and he fidgeted as though he needed to use the little men's room. "Hey, I gotta go. Ask Kasi to call me, hey?" He pulled a wallet out of a tight back pocket and slapped a few dollars on the table, made a slight nod of the head and disappeared, his cased instrument hanging loosely from a strap around his neck, like a giant sling.

By the time I'd done the band, I was physically, emotionally, and mentally exhausted and felt as though I needed a shower or two. Mrs. D. had invited me for dinner, but I just couldn't face the quiet polite-ness, the pointed evasiveness, especially given the highly unlikely event that she would allow Mickey out of bed to join us. So I pulled into a self-serve gas station and used the outdoor pay phone. When she answered, I begged off, complaining of fatigue. As I expected, she didn't cajole or ask me to reconsider, yet I felt almost instantly regretful, put upon by her refusal to whimper just a little. If she'd made the slightest hint, I would have willingly crumbled. I knew she wouldn't, but I was foolishly disappointed. It's a little game the two of us play sometimes. I know it's childish, but I can't seem to control myself. Miffed, I said, "Let me talk to Mickey, Ma." She hates 'Ma.' She can take Mother or Mom or even when I teasingly call her Madre; anything but 'Ma.' Ma is 'K-K-K-Katie over the cow shed.' Ma is Minnie Pearl. Ma is Kentucky moonshine and dandelion wine. Everything Mrs. Daniels's highbrow upbringing taught her to disdain. And I – ungrateful offspring that I am – love sometimes to rub her nose in it.

And of course, when I uttered that word, she handed me over to Mickarooni with nary a squeak. If I'd called her anything else, she would have said he had to rest. Curious, hey? Works every time.

WASPS have strange, exotic cultural rituals of manipulation. (And other Americans refuse to admit we're ethnic, too!)

Finally Mickey D. came on, sounding like a dog trying to cough up something he found on the front lawn and should have peed on, not eaten. "You sound much better!" I lied.

"Thanks. I feel much better."

Yeah, right. "Well, the show must go on." I filled him in on what little I had, garbled and contradictory as it was.

It turned out Mick hadn't taken the afternoon lying down, either (figuratively, at least). He'd called one of the few still-loyal friends he had from his days in the FBI — one who hadn't turned his back and slunk away when Mick was drummed out of the original good old boy club itself for ironically being inclined toward the same sexual persuasion as Sir Edgar Hoover himself. Mick's old friend Jake Janus had run a check on both Joe Short and Jack Curtis for us, and drawn a complete double blank. Couldn't even find a Social Security number. "Nada," Mick declared. With his head blocked up, it sounded like baby babble.

"How could he not have a Social Security number?" I asked. There was a scowling teenage face peering at me from outside of the phone booth. He had an orange shock of hair coming out of the top of his head and two rings in his right nostril. I turned my back to him.

"Jake said there's a lot more undocumented people out there than you'd imagine. Don't get a number and you don't get Social Security in your old age. But you can evade paying taxes, too — income as well as Social Security. And if you're self employed all your life...." He blew his nose. "Then again, maybe he doesn't expect to live to see old age."

The kid was pounding on the door of the booth, gesturing at his watch. "Hold on a minute. This is an important call!" I hollered. The little bugger just tapped his foot impatiently on the pavement. His IQ appeared to be about the same as his shoe size. I turned my back. "So maybe he's evading taxes. That's not a felony offense."

"Well, actually, it is," Mick pointed out.

"Not the type you run away for. The IRS wasn't after him, as far as we know. Of course, Kasi hasn't exactly been up-front with me. Who knows—"

"Lady! I gotta make a phone call!" The big foot was *on* the door.

I turned ever so slightly and opened up my blazer so the butt of my revolver showed where I tuck it into the waistline of my corduroys. The kid's eyes got big and he turned and walked away hastily. "Tee-hee," I snickered to myself.

41

"You all right, Eliza?" That brotherly concern in his raspy voice.

"Just a rug rat. Showed him the caliber of woman he was messing with."

"You're not exactly nurturant, you know," he jibed.

"Tomorrow, Mick. Nine a.m. We're going to meet Ayn Curtis and Kasi Short, The Ladies Who Were Left Behind."

"Yeah, yeah. If *She* takes the bars off the door."

"You be ready. I'm coming to take you away."

"Ha-ha, he-he," we sang in unison like two pre-adolescents, and signed off.

Now that I'd turned down La Mere's pot roast surprise, I was hungry. I was also feeling that I should go back to see Kasi and confront her about all I'd learned — especially her liaison with Georgie Porgie. But hey, this was a missing person case, not a murder investigation. And I was at her house until late last night, up early this morning, and honestly wiped out from interviewing people all day and psychologically sparring with my mother.

So I did what any well-deserving, single, all-American WASP does after a full day's work. I visited the Lochmore library, went home, took a nice hot shower, and ate a TV dinner in front of the tube. Budget Gourmet. Something chickeny. Watched a re-run of Cheers and part of the news. There's a chance of showers on Sunday. The SVRR, which used to be the KGB, says the Ames spy case was no big deal and how come everybody got so uptight about it? A terrorist bomb blew apart the queen's Rhododendron garden at Balmoral. A Mafia boss got sentenced to "life plus 120 years" (translated: 15-20) after one of his hit men turned state's evidence. And a six-year old in Durham, North Carolina shot his father dead as he was raping the kid's 12-year-old sister.

Then I turned off the TV and scanned the book I'd borrowed from the library, Frank Abagnale Jr.'s *Catch Me If You Can*, the one I found Joe Short's reed tucked into at Kasi's house. The cover sort of sums up the gist of the biography. It calls Abagnale an "outrageously daring impostor who practiced law without a license, performed surgery with no medical training, flew a Pan Am jet, taught at college, passed himself off as an FBI agent, and became a millionaire before he was twenty-one."

The guy got caught now and then, but he got away — every time but the last one. Did Joe Short aspire to be an Abagnale? Was he a con artist without the necessary flamboyance? Pick up with one woman, get bored, and just move on to the next? But he wasn't making money. Both of his wives had had better jobs than he, but they didn't make the kind of money to marry for. He was a legitimate musician. The other guys had said he'd had the talent to go much further, way beyond their little band. But the group he'd left in the Poconos was apparently neither better nor worse than the one he'd joined down here. He didn't seem to have the ambition to go for more — a recording contract or a band that had a big name. Other talents? A little amateur photography and apparently skeet shooting with the wife on a Sunday afternoon. Nothing to write home about.

Not exactly the adventurer Abagnale was. Maybe it was just a distraction for Short; a fantasy. He broke away from one all-too-ordinary existence looking for adventure, only to put himself in an almost identical situation. Perhaps it was simply time to move on and try it out again. As guilty as I was feeling by now about taking Kasi's money, I couldn't wait to meet this Ayn Curtis and find out if someone from Short's previous life could fill in some of the gaps.

I turned off the light and snuggled under my electric blanket. The nights were getting colder. Nice to be warm and dry and fed.

Ought-oh! I turned on the bedside light. The Cow Fish! I forgot to feed The Cow Fish. Damn that Mick and his maddening illnesses. Hell, she isn't going to starve. Plenty of larvae to suck on if she gets desperate. Or she could milk herself. I turned the light off. This is why I don't have pets. They would die. I could never be a mother. I would starve and neglect my young. Not that I wouldn't *mean* to be a good mother. It's just that it's better not to get involved. If you don't love something, when it dies or leaves or disappoints you, it doesn't hurt so awfully bad.

Chapter 3
Ayn's Story

When I arrived Friday morning, Mickey was ready, standing out on the porch, looking like an overgrown first grader watching for the school bus, the lunch Mom had packed for him dangling in a paper bag at the end of a long, sinewy arm. Unlike me, when Mickey's well, he keeps in shape, swimming, playing tennis, lifting weights. He's still—

"—Come on, move over. I'm not going if you drive."

"Aw, Mick, I'm an excellent driver!"

"And I'm Mario Andretti. Move over."

When it comes to driving, you gotta let The Mick have his way. It's a male thing. He says it's 'cause I'm a menace to the driving public. But in reality, it's got something to do with testosterone.

At any rate, with my excellent map-reading skills (these are definitely required; no street in Philadelphia starts out and ends up with the same name its full natural length) and Mickey D's amazing patience with people who think that they have the right-of-way merging *into* traffic, we managed to arrive safely half an hour later at 910 Buckhouse Lane, a narrow street in a middle-class neighborhood several blocks from Temple University.

There was laundry hanging on the front porch of the rambling, slightly worn, two-story Victorian, which had, from its tired, borrowed look, presumably been a long-time rental unit for Temple students. The brisk, late September morning air sent a line of T-shirts strung on a rope the length of the porch flapping against one another. "Outside of a dog, a book is a man's best friend," I read out loud the front of a shirt facing us as we climbed the stairs to the porch.

Mickey paused as we reached the top of the stairs and tugged lightly on the shirt, turning it so that the back was in view. He read, "Inside of a dog, it's too dark to read. ...Groucho Marx." A chuckle of appreciation quickly developed into a chortle of glee, and Mick and I were standing there, still snickering over the shirt a minute later when Kasi parked her Volvo across the way and started hesitantly across the street. "Eliza!" Mickey poked me, his laugh turned to a ticklish cough. "Stifle! Our client's coming."

I introduced Mick and Kasi, now straight-faced. "We were waiting for you," I said. She was bouncing on the soles of her feet, the sky-blue eyes darting. "I didn't bring the kids. I thought—"

"That's fine. There's plenty of time for that," I assured her.

"Ms. Short, she'll be just as anxious as you," Mickey said, laying a hand gently on her shoulder.

"Yes, you're right. Absolutely." Her darting eyes landed thankfully on Mick's calm face. "Call me Kasi, please." Amazing. He charms women like a Svengali. It was M.D. who obviously got all the nurturant genes. When you share a womb, there's only so much of one thing to go around, I figure.

Mick took the initiative and knocked. A small, dark, oval face peered out at us, then went away. "Ayn! They're here!" a high, uninflected voice beckoned. Footsteps. Whispering. Silence. Footsteps coming and going. Then another face. This one rounder, high-cheeked, black-eyed. The girl from PA's "Unsolved Mysteries." She opened the door slowly and stood still. She glanced from me to Kasi. Kasi gasped and swiped her hand before her eyes like a windshield wiper as the girl's eyes settled on her calmly. "I'm Ayn." The girl said. "You must be my father's latest wife."

Kasi reached forward tentatively, whether to shake Ayn's hand or give herself support against the doorframe, I'm not quite sure. She ultimately managed the latter as Ayn stepped back into the house. "Does that make you my step-mother?" the girl shot over her shoulder. "Or just the concubine at the Summer Palace?" The comment came like a whiplash, angry, sharp, and stinging.

"Why...why!" Kasi gasped, grasping ineffectually for the retreating shadow as I did the same.

But Mickey was faster than both of us. "Ayn!" he said with authority, moving quickly to her side and turning her gently with his lithe hands, like she was no more than a cotton T-shirt he was flipping in the morning breeze. He put his face close to hers and peered into her eyes. Surprised, she made no attempt to pull away. "Outside of a father, a diamond is a girl's best friend," he said softly. "Inside a father, it's too dark to tell the difference between the family jewels and cubic zirconium."

Ayn stared at him, expressive mouth falling open, dark eyes squinting. She looked from Kasi, still flailing half-heartedly by the doorway, to me, to the philosopher poet himself.

45

I understood her completely — or so I thought. She had been busy asserting her right to be angry with her father. He had abandoned her and was still missing. In his place a target had appeared, a symbol of his life without her — a choice he'd made which excluded her and her mother and included a stranger and a new family. But I sensed this flippant hostility didn't fit her comfortably. Slowly the corners of her mouth turned up and she released a quick little smile. "Very good," she allowed with a bit of a smirk, "but T-shirt psychology doesn't exactly explain life, does it?" Then she scowled slightly. "Who are you, anyway?" she squinted at him.

"Michael Daniels, private investigator hired by Ms. Short," he said, offering a hand. She shook it slowly with a slight, almost dismissive smile that said, "Surely you understand we can not afford to be amused right now."

"And this is Eliza Samuels, my partner." We shook hands. Her fingers were long and narrow, her nails bitten to the quick, much like my own.

I took it from there. "Ayn Curtis, I'd like you to meet Kasi Short, who has been married to a man known to her as Jack Short for nine years now." And Mick and I virtually pushed the two women at one another.

They shook hands slowly. "Excuse me," Ayn said in a Presbyterian church whisper. "It's just that I'm—"

"—Angry," said Kasi graciously.

Ayn raised her eyes and met Kasi's gaze. "Yes," she said, almost surprised. A flicker of respect or even understanding seemed to spark between the two.

We moved through a couple of garage sale-furnished rooms with close ceilings and came to a little screened-in porch touched by the morning sun.

Kasi sat on a bench against the west corner, and I took a seat beside her. Ayn perched on a stool against the opposite screen, her back to the sun. Chakra, the Indio-American woman who had first come to the door and who turned out to be Ayn's housemate, silently served us sweetened iced tea in tall jelly glasses, then hovered by the doorway to the house. Mickey stood in the middle of the room, in a sort of monitor's stance. "Why don't you tell us about your childhood," he prompted. "I'm sure Kasi would like to know as much as she can about her husband's past, and then she can tell you what she can about his present — up until his second – or most recent disappearance."

"Well, okay," the young woman allowed. She propped her feet up on the rungs of the stool and pushed a strand of wavy dark brown hair behind her ear.

"My mother met Jack Curtis at a honeymoon resort in Laketown, Pennsylvania, in the Pocono Mountains," she began. "Her maiden name was Sarah Swingle, but everyone called her Sally. Her best friend from high school, Greta, was a waitress at Paradise Regained. Mom would pick Greta up from work now and then. It was Greta who introduced her to Da— to Jack Curtis." She'd started out slowly, glancing, when she looked at anyone, at Mickey, who nodded occasional reassurance. Otherwise she looked at her lap, at the brick laid patio, at the large palm frond on the floor beside her stool. But little by little she seemed to gain momentum, like a snowball rolling downhill. It was as if she'd been hoarding this story all her life.

"When she met him, he was playing in a band that entertained the guests at Paradise Regained and three other nearby resorts owned by the same company. He was also the resort photographer, taking pictures of the newlyweds in heart-shaped bathtubs and giant-sized champagne glasses filled with bubble bath, then selling them the photos in overpriced little 'Honeymoon Commemorative Albums.'

"Mom was a secretary. She worked at the AT&T satellite station in Kimbles, near Hawley. She was about 25 when they met, shy and inexperienced. He was about the same age, said his folks came from Ontario, but had been dead since he graduated high school. They started going out." She swung one shapely bare leg against the rung of the high stool, the other foot tucked beneath her khaki shorts. Kasi hung on her every word, crossing and recrossing her legs and making occasional startling little painful sounds from the back of her throat. The Mick coughed quietly into his handkerchief and looked out at the climbing sun behind Ayn's gold-flecked hair. I observed.

"He proposed marriage almost immediately. She resisted. She was very shy with men, you see. Competent in many things but lacking in self-confidence. You know — she was very good but very small inside." At that she suddenly looked directly at Kasi, who moaned softly. Mickey and I exchanged "Well, isn't-she-deep-for-a-20-year-old?" glances, and Ayn resumed.

"Then she got pregnant. She admitted to me once that she thought about abortion. She didn't think she was ready to be a mother. But he would have none of it and that settled that. They got married and bought a little house near Hawley. For a while, my father worked as a

47

photographer for the Army Depot at nearby Tobyhanna. He wasn't a bad photographer, you know." It was almost a challenge.

"Yes," Kasi responded for the first time. "He used to keep a darkroom in the basement," she said quietly, fading off as Ayn jumped down from her stool and disappeared into the house. We looked at one another. Chakra asked if we wanted more tea. I couldn't place her accent. It wasn't exactly Main Line, but it wasn't off-the-plane East Indian, either. Mickey was the only one who wanted a refill.

A moment later, Ayn returned with a 5x7 wooden frame hugged to her chest. "He took this of me," she said, thrusting it at Kasi.

"My God, it looks like Eva!" Kasi gasped, leaping from her seat.

"Eva? Eva? What do you mean, *I'm* Eva!" Ayn wailed, grabbing at the photo as if to take back her name. "That's what he called me. How did *you* know?" She was trembling with emotion.

"Our daughter's name is Eva. *He* named her that," Kasi whispered gently, patting the hand that grasped the picture frame tightly. "He called her Eva Ann."

Ayn pulled away, raised the frame above her head, and smashed it with all her might against the red brick floor. "There can't be another Eva! My mother named me Ayn, but *he* called me Eva!" she wailed.

"After his grandmama," Kasi finished for her, trying to gather the recently orphaned woman child into her arms. Ayn did a little dance on the brick, her feet pumping up and down as if to run, but her body was enveloped by the warming arms of the woman with whom her father had committed bigamy. "He named his favorite girls for his beloved Grandmama," Kasi said, soothingly patting the distraught girl's head and back. "You have a sister now, you know," she said, wiping the tears that flowed unbidden down Ayn's face. "And a brother." And she withdrew pictures of Joe and the children from her pocketbook and showed them to her husband's daughter. "And they have a big sister."

Ayn took the snapshots, holding them with ravaged fingertips, her eyes at first wary, then peering hungrily. Kasi bent over and picked Ayn's photo from among the shards of glass Chakra was quietly sweeping into a dustpan. The roommate was like a ghost servant, inconspicuous, solicitous, and silent. Kasi and Ayn peered separately at the images of children left behind. "How could he do it?" Ayn breathed.

"*Why* did he do it?" Kasi stressed. It was clear Kasi's hurt was turning again to anger. Ayn's hurt was much more primal, undeveloped — an abandoned child's confusion turned inward.

"What happened between your parents?" I asked. I couldn't take much more of this. They were acting like relics — remaining fragments, surviving parts of a man nobody seemed to know. It was making me angry. When someone's dead — or gone of his or her own volition, you should let go. If you don't you will become a shadow of them, an echo, a fossil. Mickey must have sensed my impatience and frustration, because he, too, urged Ayn to resume.

Ayn continued to hold the pictures of her father and the children, but she resumed her narrative. "I was eleven when he left. I don't know any more how much of what I know is from my own memory or how much came from my mother. She was obsessed with him, you know."

And with that she began to relate what she knew of Curtis's disappearance. He had apparently failed to return from one of his regular gigs in Atlantic City, New Jersey. The band he was playing in at the time had maintained connections from the days at the honeymoon resort, which was partially owned by an outfit that also owned casinos in Vegas and Atlantic City, and they played occasionally as a back-up or stage band at one of the Jersey establishments. She'd never known which one.

For six or more months before he disappeared, Jack had gone on increasingly long trips with the band. Sally Curtis had become vaguely ill several months before Curtis began to "stray," and she eventually took a leave of absence, followed months later by her being laid-off at work, where she never returned. She had always been their main and only steady money-earner and finances became extremely tight. It was at this time that Ayn would hear her parents arguing late into the night. Jack would become sullen and storm out, disappearing for a day or more at a time.

So when he failed to return from the gig, it was a while before they were really sure he wasn't just dragging his feet. "He'll be home soon, honey," Sally, tilting another beer, would tell her daughter.

But he didn't come home. Finally Ayn called the drummer in the band. "Let me talk to your mother, sweetheart," he told her. When Sal got on the line he said, "We haven't been to Atlantic City in three months, Sal. The band was dissolved a month ago."

Sally Curtis keened and keened. Finally the local constable arrived, hat in hand, to investigate what had been called in by the neighbors as an "animal complaint." He found Sally clutching one of Jack's old sweaters, soaked with her tears, rocking and wailing and

49

pausing only long enough to pop the top on another Schlitz. Ayn sat on the front stoop and held her hands over her ears. The incident was to go down in local gossip legend as "The Time That Poor Thing's Good-For-Nothing Left Her and She Took to Howling at the Moon."

Children and Youth Services took Ayn away for a few weeks and put her in the county group home. When they let her go home again, it was to a mother who had retreated behind a wall of self-recriminations and denial. She never blamed Jack, only herself. In Sally's private family lore, Jack became some kind of saint she had driven away through her drinking and nagging. She apologized daily to Ayn for leaving her fatherless.

Sally continued to drink and never returned to a professional position of relative authority or responsibility. Instead, she worked in the county's small library, shelving books, updating the card cata-logue, and reading constantly.

"What did she read?" It was Mickey with an irrelevant question, just as things were flowing. I gave him a dirty look. He coughed, sneezed, and blew his nose.

"Romance, mostly," Ayn responded. "History. Some mysteries."

"What do you read?"

"I'm studying criminology at Temple. With that and temping, I don't have time to read much."

"What happened to your mother?" Kasi asked gently, getting us back on the subject. "And what brought you here?"

Sally Curtis had breathed her last labored breath looking over her daughter's shoulder, past the dialysis machine, through the Reverend Matthew Saunders, at a vision past the third story window of the critical ward at Pocono General Hospital. "Jack?" she panted in a final, tremulous withdrawal. They said the alcohol had finally killed her, but it was Jack Curtis who'd figuratively uncorked the bottle and tipped it to her lips. It took nine years, but he'd done her in, leaving Sally's last question mark echoing through the halls of the terminal ward.

Ayn had only been in Philadelphia for three months now, moving south on a whim after her mother's death. "It was just that a college pamphlet arrived in the mail about then," she mused. "In fact, it was a little late, considering I graduated high school two years ago. There was an 800 number to call about financial assistance. And when I did, they said that there was not only assistance, there was actually a scholarship left by an alumnus from my area, earmarked for students from Wayne or Pike counties, and since nobody else had applied to

Temple from Wayne or Pike, it could be mine if my grades were good enough."

"Serendipitous," breathed Chakra. I almost jumped. I hadn't even noticed she was still there, she was so almost invisible. It was the first thing she'd said since the iced tea. I glanced at Mickey and caught him shuddering and I suddenly felt guilty for bringing him out in the cool fall air. What if he got pneumonia again?

But Ayn interrupted my guilt feelings. She explained that she had meant to make a clean break of it — to find herself, put her past behind her, and start on the way to a career — maybe study pre-law. She'd sold the cottage on Lake Wallenpaupack to a couple from New Jersey who thought they could commute to their high paying jobs in Syosset and live in the seemingly bucolic charm of the Poconos for a quarter the price of their split-level in Hopatcong. She let the house go for a prayer because that was all she could hear as she went from room to room — her mother's broken, drunken prayers to her father to come home. They whispered from the wallpaper: "When your Dad gets back," they hissed. "When Jack comes home."

But everything had just kind of fallen together here. She'd found this apartment, made friends with Chakra, who originally had the apartment next to hers, but who had moved in with her to share expenses after a small fire in her own apartment. Classes at Temple were going well.

"What made you go to 'Pennsylvania's Unsolved Mysteries?'" Kasi prompted.

"Well, after a month or so, I signed up with Corporate Temporaries for part-time secretarial work. The first place they sent me was Lane Industries, and that's where I met Grace Johnston, who was also a temp. We fell into a discussion about family, and she said she was adopted and wanted to find her birth parents. At first I told her both my parents were dead," Ayn sighed, looking out the window at the changing leaves. Silence fell again, but this time no one interrupted. Eventually she resumed her story.

"She approached me later in the break room and asked if I would go to a support meeting with her, to keep her company. What could I say?" The dark, almost Oriental-looking eyes sparked. "So I went with her to Ozbip."

"Oz—?"

"Adult Adoptees Seeking Their Biological Parents," Chakra chimed in crisply, again startling me.

"But after the AASBP meeting, we went out for coffee and she got real emotional about finding her Mom," Ayn recalled. "Suddenly

I found myself spilling my guts to her about Jack. 'I *knew* you were a soul mate!' she cried, grabbing my hand. 'Something told me I had to invite you to that meeting! They won't take my story, but maybe they'll take yours!' Grace was sort of into New Age," Ayn explained, a bemused half-smile on her lips. "She claimed she'd had a dream about meeting me, and that she felt compelled by her spirit guide, who came to her in dreams, to turn me on to getting in touch with my roots. Back home, I suppose she would have become a BAC."

"A BAC?" Mickey D. and I harmonized.

"Born Again Christian," Chakra explained tentatively, peering from behind round black eyes to see if we were BACward, and therefore potentially offended. I had the feeling she was ready to take any perceived offense upon herself to protect her precious roommate. There was something very unusual, almost spooky, about this girl and her relationship to Ayn.

"I'm not," I said helpfully.

"What? Not what?" Mickey D. was lost, like a computer searching the wrong drive for information and caught in a loop.

"It's okay, he's neither offended nor Born-Again, he's sort of lapsed Episcopalian, aren't you, Mr. Daniels?" I jibed. The attention had been thrown to Mickey and he was obviously floundering, having lost the gist of the conversation.

"Oh yeah," he backpedaled weakly, in response to my affirmative coaching nod. This is why it's sometimes fun to play practical jokes on The Mick. But once again, I digress.

Well, to make a long story short, Grace had insisted Ayn should get her father's story on "Pennsylvania's Unsolved Mysteries," the local network's answer to the nationwide TV program that explores everything from life after death to conspiracy assassination theories to the Bermuda Triangle and long lost relatives.

"I don't believe in that stuff," Ayn told Grace.

"That doesn't matter, I'll do the believing," Grace assured her.

"Why would anyone care about a man who's been missing for nine years?" Ayn resisted.

"Well, you care, don't you?"

"I don't know." The only reason I would do it, Ayn told herself, was for Mom. Then, in a wave of grief, regret, and anger, she remembered Sally was dead. "What's the sense?" she rose abruptly from the table, knocking over her cappuccino.

"You owe it to yourself," Grace said, grabbing her by the arm.

"Why don't *you* go on 'America's Most Wanted,' or whatever it is?" Ayn asked as she threw down a few dollars and marched out onto Front Street, dogged by Grace.

"'Unsolved Mysteries,'" Grace corrected. "He's missing, not wanted, right?"

"Good question. Can you give me a few years to figure that one out?" They were marching down the sidewalk, Grace still grabbing at Ayn's arm, Ayn's gauchos and nostrils flaring. Then she turned and pointed at Grace with a long, slender finger. "Well, why don't you?"

"I did," Grace said, deflated. "They wouldn't do it. Said they had a thousand adoptees looking for their parents." There were green tears coming out of the corner of her eyes, dripping through her mascara. Ayn crumbled, let Grace take her arm as they walked more slowly down the street. "Here," Grace finally said, digging with a tissue-fisted hand into her pocketbook. "Here's the number. Call this guy. Tell him about your father. If you could find your father, I'd feel so much better," she said, and thrust a name and number into Ayn's hand. "Maybe then Dharma will let me sleep at night."

"Dharma?" Mickey D. queried.

"Her spirit guide," Chakra and I unisoned. It was really scary. Mickey D. gave me a weird look but the others didn't even seem to notice.

Well, Ayn didn't use the number. In fact, the next day Grace called in sick, and then Ayn was sent on a temp job at a different company, and she lost Grace's number. She virtually forgot about America's Most Mysterious until she got the call from Tadford Ames.

She was coming out of the shower the following Saturday morning, dripping all over the floor, when the phone rang. "Ms. Curtis?" the voice said. "I'm Tadford Ames, program coordinator with 'Pennsylvania's Unsolved Mysteries.' I understand you have an interesting mystery you wish to explore. Is there some time when we could meet and review the case to see if P.U.M. is interested?"

"But I — but how?" Of course, she realized Grace had contacted the program herself, sure that Ayn wouldn't on her own. She felt irritated and apologetic all at once. "That woman shouldn't have called you," she said. "You don't understand. It was a long time ago."

"Well, what little of the story Miss Johnston told me was quite intriguing," Mr. Ames explained. "Perhaps its worth exploring. I'll be in your neighborhood on other business today. What do you say I meet you for lunch at Tweeky's at noon?"

Tweeky's! She'd always wanted to go there. "That's a little expen—"

"It's on me, of course," he broke in. "I just want to hear your story."

"But it's been nine years—"

"I have another appointment at eleven, so I really must be getting back to work now. See you at noon, then. I shall call ahead and reserve a table. Ask for Mr. Ames. Bye, now." And he hung up.

Even Mickey D. raised an eyebrow on that one.

"So I went," Ayn sighed. "What else do you do?"

Mickey D. shrugged. I shrugged. Kasi shrugged. I refused to sneak a look at Chakra to see what she was doing.

"So tell us about Mr. Ames," I said after finishing my fourth Fig Newton. Chakra had apparently decided we were honest-to-goodness, not-gonna-leave-soon guests, and brought out cookies to soak up our tea. By now the ladies' room was calling to me, but I was afraid to leave for fear I might miss something.

Slap! A fly came to a messy end, squashed between flyswatter and screen. Chakra flicked its remains onto the floor with the end of the instrument of death. Well, scratch off the Hindu hypothesis.

"Mr. Ames," I again prompted Ayn.

"Tadford is a fascinating man," she finally said. Her eyes had lit up and her body posturing changed completely. It was like watching a butterfly come out of its cocoon.

"You only went to him with your story a month ago?" Kasi asked.

"He came to me," Ayn reminded her.

"And your story went on the air that quickly?" Mickey remarked. "Awfully fast turnaround for TV, isn't it?"

"The Wacko Waco story was being filmed while David Koresh was still holed-up inside the compound," I noted. "They're so quick these days that if the World Trade Center had been 100 stories higher, they could have used the first of the escapees from 9/11 as mini-series extras before the whole thing collapsed. There was practically a book out on the Nicole Simpson murder while the whole world was still watching on TV as O.J. and Cowlings tooled around California in that Bronco."

54

"But this is just one missing man," Mickey D. said doubtfully.

"Tadford said I'd waited long enough," Ayn said almost defensively. "He wanted to ease my suffering."

Whoa! Tadford. Suffering. This might explain the Monarch-like metamorphosis. I sensed more than a professional interest in Mr. Ames. "So Mr. Ames is ready to film another update to the story?" I prompted.

"Oh yes, he's very excited. He wants to do it as quickly as possible. He says other calls have come in," she noted, her color rising.

"What sorts of calls?" Kasi asked eagerly.

"He wasn't real specific. I called him this morning. He said some people saw Dad — er, Jack, or Joe — whatever his name is, years ago, but others maybe since he left you. Tadford didn't give me any details. He's taking care of everything, though. I guess we'll learn tomorrow."

"Tomorrow," Kasi echoed. And on that cue we all sort of rose and stretched. We made plans to meet together for coffee an hour before our scheduled 3 p.m. meeting at Tadford Ames's hotel suite. Then Kasi crossed the room and hugged Ayn gently. Mickey D. and I sort of sidled out of the room and left them to themselves.

"So," I said to the narrow back which escorted us to the front door, "are you a student, too, Chakra?"

"I am a computer support analyst," she said as she opened the door.

"Oh, really? Ms. Short is in computers, too."

"Oh?"

"Yes, she works at Vortex."

"Yes? So do I."

"And you haven't met? I'm surprised—"

"There are over 1,500 employees at Vortex," Chakra said softly. "And I just started there recently."

"Oh. Of course. Well, it was nice to meet you. Goodbye."

"Goodbye."

We passed the "Too Dark to Read" T-shirt on the way out, and as we got in the Cabriolet, Mickey mumbled, "That must have been Chakra's." We waved goodbye to Kasi as she emerged from the house and headed for her car.

Mickey D. drove himself home. "I can't take any more of Mom's mothering. She'll kill me with kindness," he admitted.

"I told you."

"*You* took me there."

"I *had* to. You know I don't do nurture."

"I don't want nurture and I don't need nurture. I want to be left alone." He was sulking now. Ninety-nine point four percent of men sulk. I think it's another of their hormonal things. Our father sulked himself to death. But that's a different story.

"Come in and have some soup with me," Mickey D. relented as I started to scoot over into the driver's seat.

"You sure you want me?" I was acting hurt now. I swear I come by this behavior genetically.

"I'll let you have Buns Bisque," he tempted me with my own label trick, the old spark back in the eyes.

"Spleen With Bean or nothing," I countered, and things were back to normal.

We were eating our soup surprise (the gag labels were so sticky that when we peeled them off they took the original labels with them, and we couldn't tell what we had until we opened and sampled it) and Mrs. D's packaged chicken salad sandwiches when Mickey's office phone rang.

I answered, "Samuels and Daniels, Investigators," and before I could finish, a voice squealed, "Marbles in the back yard with a bone!"

My first thought was, are we playing that old board game, Clue now? Mr. Mustard in the parlor with the candlestick? The butler in the dining room with the flowerpot? But this was no game. Kasi was hysterical. I couldn't make sense of her panicked babbling. "Calm down, Kasi, calm down!" I begged ineffectually.

Mickey took the receiver out of my hand and pushed "speaker" on the phone. "Kasi!" he said, both sternly and gently. It was a voice that said, "I am in control. Listen to me."

"Now stop and catch your breath. Count to ten," he directed. And he started to count slowly, "One. Two. Take a breath," he ordered. "In. Out. Three. Four. Slowly. Deeply. Five."

At first she just seemed to hiccup. Then she was panting. Then just breathing heavily. Finally we could hear her whispering the numbers in unison with Mick. It was as though he was tele-hypnotizing her.

"Now tell us real slow and easy what's going on," he directed.

56

"Marbles brought me a bone," Kasi said.

I pantomimed a panting dog for Mickey's edification. He shook his head in understanding. "Marbles brought you a bone?" he repeated.

"It's a hand."

There was silence. It felt as though we were waiting for the punch line or something.

"I'm afraid it's Joe's," she said so very softly.

"Oh, shit!" Mick and I said in stereo.

"Stay right there, Kasi. Don't move. Don't touch it. Don't do anything," I said, grabbing my car keys off the table. "We'll be there in five minutes."

"Shouldn't I call the po—"

"—Wait. We'll take care of that. We're leaving now, Kasi. Don't move!" And we were out of there.

-------   .

"Jesus, don't you hate it when that happens?" I stripped the gears as we were trucking down Old Chester Road, and Mickey D. cringed.

"Don't swear," he said.

"Who's swearing? Kasi's over there holding hands with a dearly departed skeleton. Not only is the case over for us, things look mighty unfortunate for our client. To say nothing of our missing person."

"You're so mercenary," Mickey practically spat at me. "The guy's dead, for Christ sakes! Gone. Over. Nada. Don't you have any feelings?"

Whoa, I struck a nerve. He's getting sensitive on me! The old Mickey would have just groused, even joked, but not bitten, lashed out like that. Still, I couldn't let him think I noticed. Can't acknowledge it because then the fear of loss becomes too close, too real, too scary. "Now look who's swearing!" I countered, squealing the brakes on purpose as I whipped onto Kasi's street. I glanced sideways at the Mick and almost ran over Eva on her Hot Wheels, racing down the middle of the street, her golden hair flying.

"Jesus!" we both screeched simultaneously as I slammed on the brakes.

She whizzed right by us, pedaling like a demon. "That's Eva," I hollered at Mickey as I threw the car in park and we both jumped out and raced after the little lightning rod.

"Hold up, honey. Slow down, Eva!" I yelled after her. She kept on pumping. And here came another vehicle straight at us — a black

Cadillac, going hell for leather. We were screaming and running, gaining on the little bugger, but the car was gaining faster. Finally, the driver lay on the horn. Just then I grabbed the back of the Hot Wheels and pulled her up short. The driver slammed on his brakes, jumped out of the car and the next thing I knew he was flying by me, straight for Mickey. "What the frig's wrong with you people letting her ride down the middle of the road like that?" the man screamed as he streaked by. "I coulda hit her!"

I was busy keeping a handle on Eva's getaway vehicle. She had finally stopped pedaling, realizing it wasn't getting her anywhere. But then she jumped out of the tricycle and headed off under her own locomotion.

"Whoa, Eva! Hold on, there!" I grabbed her by her pullover and brought her up short. But her legs kept pumping.

I glanced back to see Mickey bent double and the driver sort of jumping around him like a sparring boxer. "Hey!" I yelled, grabbing up Eva, unceremoniously slinging her under my arm and hurrying toward the men. "What's going on here?" I hollered, scurrying up behind the guy.

Mickey was panting and holding his side. He swallowed, gasped, tried to catch his breath. One hand waved me off. "Nothing," he gasped. "Nothing. I'm fine."

"What did you hit him for, you moron?" I said, twirling the guy around with one hand and grasping the still-flailing Eva under my left arm. Hell, I'll take him on with one hand!

"I didn't hit him, lady, he was like that," the little driver turned abruptly toward me, a worked-up, accusatory look still smeared across his face. "What you let your kid ride in the street for? I coulda— Ms. Samuels?"

"George!" I almost dropped Eva.

"Eva!" George exclaimed.

"George? Who are you?" We all looked at Mickey D. He was still red in the face, but the breathing was more controlled. Best thing at these times is to simply ignore Mickey's failing health, just like Mrs. D does.

"This is George Diego," I explained to Mick. "He played guitar and fiddle in Joe Short's band. Remember, I told you about our interview..." I hinted, making "hot" wrist-waving signals at my face with my free hand when George turned his back to me. "George, this is Michael Daniels, my partner." They shook hands.

Eva had finally stopped wiggling and was lying almost limp and silent, like a sack of coffee beans under my arm.

"So what brings you here today, George?" Mickey D. managed, almost smoothly. Still quick on the rebound. Can't get up and down the floor at times, but if you post him under the basket....

"I came to see Kasi," Diego said, and his eyes suddenly lit up like a fire.

"I thought she didn't want to see you," I reminded him.

"I know, I know!" he said excitedly. "But she wants me now. She wants me. She called me and told me to come. She needs me! She needs me!" And he raced back to his car.

Mickey D. and I exchanged looks. "The plot sickens," I grumbled.

"Here," Micker said, smiling gently at Eva. "Give her to me. Come here, sweetie." And she opened her arms willingly to be engulfed by his. I walked back to my car and Mick, holding Eva, followed Diego's Caddy as it pulled into Kasi's driveway. I brought up the rear.

I wasn't quite sure what to expect inside. Did she call him after she found the bones or before? Did she call him first or us first? Did she suddenly want to make up with him, now that it was apparent her husband was dead, or did she want to confront him with the evidence and go from there? One thing was obvious: whether the bones were really Joe's or not, and whether or not George had anything to do with it, he still had a real boner for the lady.

I didn't have to wait long for the answers to my questions. I parked the car in the street, got out, and as I was approaching the driveway, saw George back hurriedly out of the front door, numerous objects pursuing him. He ducked a book. An orange thunked him in the solar plexus and a Barbie doll thudded into an upraised arm. "But Kasi honey, I love you!" he wailed as he retreated, wincing at every hit. Just as he reached the car a hard white object slapped him in the face and he yelped, jumped about a foot in the air, and upon landing, scurried in one sleek motion into the front seat, slammed the door, and narrowly missed me as he reversed onto the street and gassed away in a screech of spinning tires.

I cautiously sidled up the driveway and stooping, examined the last item that had caught poor George. "I gotta hand it to you, Kasi, if you're trying to destroy evidence, you're doing a good job of it," I mumbled, unloosing the scarf that was draped around my neck and tenderly scooping up one slightly chewed, slightly cracked bundle of bones. Definitely a human hand.

Inside we had a distraught, highly emotional woman pacing and crying; a man standing there, wheezing lightly and cradling a small, clinging bundle of life; a disheveled, shaggy dog panting and peering almost guiltily from the corner of the room; and the shrill cry of a baby wailing like a saxophone with a attitude problem coming from somewhere down the hall.

As they say, I'm not nurturant, so I did the logical thing. I put down the other guy's hand, took my own, and dialed the police.

Chapter 4
Who?

We were treated to the entire cast of characters from Lochmore's Police Department — Lt. Franken, Cpl. Bankowitz, even Patrolperson Schwenk.

Finally, County Coroner Jack O'Neil showed up. "This is a bit premature, men, don't you think? I need a body. I can't pronounce a hand dead. People survive without hands," he growled, shuffled back to his car, and drove away.

Men in uniform with shovels and pickaxes moved into the back yard. They dug around among the dead cornhusks and zucchini in what was left of Kasi's garden. All they unearthed was some rotten potatoes, a few arrowheads, and a rusty old flashlight. There was talk of bringing in a backhoe. There was mention of a dog trainer. ("Or maybe one of those pet psychologists. What do you think?" Lt. Franken, looking reflectively at poor Marbles, asked Sheriff Ronald Twizzard.) I like Lt. Franken. He only checked under my nails once. Twizzard wanted us to all take our shoes off. Even Eva.

Kasi balked at Eva. She started getting feisty about then. Twizzard threatened to arrest her. "For what?" she challenged. "Picking bones?" Twiz backed off. He doesn't have honest-to-goodness policing rights in Pennsylvania, anyway. A sheriff's no more than a glorified jailer in the Commonwealth of Pennsylvania, though there are always a few exceptions statewide who've been known to push the boundaries of their mandate.

Suddenly Kasi pivoted on her heel and went eyeball-to-eyeball with Franken. "Where's my husband?" she spat. "If that's part of him, I want to know and I want to know now! You've sat on this case for seven weeks, telling me he ran off. If he'd run off, don't you think he would have taken his bloody hand with him?" She was screaming now, and it was all The Mick and I could do to keep her from hauling off and bopping the guy one. I wouldn't have blamed her, either. These fellas hadn't exactly been beating the bushes for old J/J.

Eventually it got dark and the search was put on hold. "The dog gets loose now and then, hey, Mrs. Short?" Lt. Franken suggested almost gently to the now-subdued woman. "We'll widen the search into the surrounding neighborhood tomorrow," he said, patting her on the shoulder. "You get some sleep now, you hear?"

"Thank you, sir," Mick said, shaking the lieutenant's hand. It pays to keep good relations with the police when you're in our shoes. They get kind of gummy sometimes. Mick put out his hand to shake Bankowitz's hand, but the man pretended not to see him. I tried to catch Mickey's attention, give him the who-needs-that-bastard look, but he avoided my eyes. There's history there. Communication between law enforcement agencies. Rumors. Gossip. Macho posturing. That's what I put it all down to. Homophobia's nothing new to Mickey. But then again, neither is sexism new to me. Not even Franken offered to shake *my* hand.

We waited until Glory Ribbono arrived to stay with Kasi and the kids, and then we got the heck out of there. Mickey was so tired he didn't even complain about my driving. "I'm taking you home with me," I said. And again, he didn't argue. I hate it when he doesn't argue.

We both dragged ourselves up the back steps of the house on Oxford Street. I fixed us some hot chocolate and Mickey lay on the couch in my sunroom as I settled into the old Amish rocker across from him. The streetlight outside the quadruple row of windows along Oxford was our only illumination. We listened to the night — the owl that likes to sit in the Dutch pine outside my window and coo softly; a tomcat down the block; my landlords, the Doctors Doyle, both PhDs in literature at Lochmore College, yelling in Old English at one another downstairs; a distant ambulance siren.

"What do you think?" I said.

"Definitely not a natural death," M.D. responded.

"George?" I offered.

"I seriously doubt he's got it in him."

"Yeah," I agreed. A siren wailed then faded. We both took another sip.

"Kasi?" I pitched.

"Doesn't make any sense."

"Yeah, no insurance."

"*Her* dog."

"Fatherless kids."

"She was getting away with the affair, anyway, and obviously didn't want to marry the guy."

"She thinks George did it."

"Naw, not really. She's just looking for a scapegoat. She quit talking to George when Joe disappeared, but she didn't turn him in tonight."

"That's true. Didn't even mention him."

"Neither did we."

"No."

Another sip. That damn cat sounded like he was wailing for his "Mama." I got up and shut the only open window. It was getting chilly. "Here, put this over you," I said, taking Mother D's afghan off the back of the couch and sort of tossing it at Mick. He put his empty cup on the rattan coffee table and tucked the blanket around his thin body.

"Passion?" Mick finally suggested.

"Passion?" I asked.

"Yeah, anger. Spur-of-the-moment. She finds out Joe's going to leave her or he's had an affair with another woman or a man, whatever. Or he's been doing something illegal, and she hits him in anger and kills him. Maybe even by mistake. Then she panics. Chops up the bones and buries them somewhere. And Marbles digs them up. She freaks and figures if her dog dug them up, maybe some other dog did, too, and now they're all over the neighborhood so she better be the first to bring it to the attention of the police."

"What about the cash withdrawal?"

"She could have gotten George to do it. Could have even done it herself, dressed as a man."

There was a thud on the floor beneath my rocker. One Dr. Doyle throwing something at the other Dr. Doyle downstairs. Luckily they both have terrible aim.

"Naw," I concluded. "I watched her when she saw him on TV. She was afraid he was dead. If she already knew he was dead, she wouldn't have dropped the popcorn on me."

"Popcorn?"

"Not hungry now. Too late. Some other time."

Mick didn't even bite. "What about Ayn?" he suggested.

"What about her?"

"Maybe the TV thing was a red herring. Maybe she came down here a few months back and ran into him. Maybe she came explicitly to look for him — had some reason to believe he was here. Perhaps somewhere along the line he contacted her. At any rate, she found him, and out of hurt over his abandonment and its effect on her and her mother, she killed him."

"Then she arranged to be on nationwide TV in search of him?" I poohed. "It doesn't wash. And if she could arrange that, she could have disposed of his body a little more efficiently."

"I guess."

"What about Mr. Ribbono?" I suggested.

"Rocky?"

"No, the old man. Rocky Sr. or whatever. He's the Mafia guy, right? Video games is big business. Maybe there's more to that than we know. Doesn't cutting off a hand mean something to the Mafia, like you've dishonored them or something?"

"The Arabs cut off your hand if you steal something," Mickey D. said.

"Maybe he stole from Mr. Ribbono."

"Then why'd he need $4,600.13 from Kasi's and his account?"

"To pay off Mr. Ribbono?"

We both looked off into the night. I rocked and The Mick hacked softly.

"Who?"

"Who what?" I responded.

"Who?"

"What the—?" Suddenly I realized I was talking to a bird brain. Mickey was asleep. The owl outside the window repeated his eternal question. I brought another blanket from the cedar chest and covered the slumbering form. Then I sat back down in the rocker and watched my brother sleep. In that light you'd never guess he was HIV-positive.

Chapter 5
Regret

The phone jarred me awake and I listened to my own disembodied voice inviting the caller to leave a message when a male voice said, "Hello, Samuels & Daniels Investigators." Mickey had beat me to the punch. He was standing there, a towel wrapped around his waist, his bare feet leaving a small puddle on the tile floor of the sunroom. Late morning sun from the skylight hit his head and made it look as if gold stripes interwove with his dark brown hair.

"No, Kasi, it's not what you think. She's my sister," he grinned into the phone and gave me a side snicker. "Yes, I suppose we do look a little alike, come to think of it." And with that he arched his brows sardonically. "No, she's divorced now, but still Samuels. That's right. Yes. That's quite all right. I know you've had other things on your mind. How *are* things going? Um-hm. Uh-huh. Oh, really? Well, don't worry. Do you have an attorney? You should probably consult him. Yes. No, I don't think—"

I limped into the kitchen, sore from my night in the rocker, and put the water on for coffee. Then I headed for the shower.

After I dressed and returned to the kitchen, I found Mickey D. mixing some unborn chicken embryos with cow's secretions and preparing to pour the whole mess into a buttered pan. "Where did you find those? I'm not eating them!" I curled my lip at him.

"Come on, eggs are good for you!"

"Like hell they are! Eggs are enough to gag a maggot. Eggs are good for one thing — throwing at nasty neighbors' houses on Halloween. You know I don't eat that stuff. I'm white and over 21. I can eat what I want." (This is a very WASPish, very childish, and very typical argument we're having, in case you hadn't noticed.)

"Bush wouldn't eat broccoli, and look what happened to him!"

It went on like that for a bit. Micker ate all the scrambled eggs and I had my usual breakfast — grape juice, a Little Debbie oatmeal marshmallow cookie, and coffee.

"So what did Kasi say?" I asked after scanning the *Philadelphia Inquirer*. There was not a word about body parts. "Wait — did you take your medicine?"

The Mick had the nerve to give me a dirty look. I gave him a patented "Mom" look in return. "Yes," he relented, sourly.

65

"Good. Now what did she say?"

"They were there first thing this morning. They've fanned out into the surrounding area. Her neighbors are starting to call."

"So much for keeping it out of the newspaper," I groused.

"She wants us to come over. Do some looking around ourselves. I think she hopes we'll find something first."

"Then she obviously doesn't know where to look!" I said excitedly.

"Such faith!" M.D. tsked, flicking a tiny remnant of yellow off his plate with his finger. It hit me in the cheek.

Had there been any food left on the table, and had I not been sufficiently mature to take into account the fact that this is an ill man, we would have had Animal House XV, Food Fight scene revisited, right there at the kitchen table. But I have risen above that. Instead, I stepped on his big foot with my size 12s as I walked by with my coffee cup on the way to the sink. "Oh, excuse me," I dripped.

"Oh, Mom called while you were in the shower," Mickey noted as he dumped his plate in the sink and turned the water on.

He'd pushed the button, he got the response. "She mad 'cause her little boy didn't come home to her?" I snarled.

"Why do you have to be so hard on her? She's just concerned."

"Yeah, right. Concerned you haven't found the Lord yet. That we'll both rot in hell when we die. That our sins will somehow bring her down, too. That her friends might notice we're not the traditional little married children with children of our own and a house in the suburbs with a dog and a cat. That's what she's concerned about. That's why she won't face reality. Reality's too damn impure."

"Stop it, Eliza! She's in pain. Why must you put the knife in and twist it, too?" I turned to see his face was beet red now. He was breathing heavily again.

Still, I kept on. I couldn't seem to stop. "She drove him to it!" I hissed. "She dogged Dad and dogged him and dogged him. 'Why can't you be more of a man, Roderick? Why can't you make as much money as my father, Roderick? Why didn't you get that promotion, Roderick? How come your daughter's a tomboy, Roderick? How come your son's a sissy, Roderick? Why are they suspending you, Roderick?' He pulled the trigger, but she sure as hell put the gun to his head!" I cried, and immediately regretted it.

But he didn't slap me like he should have, like you slap an hysterical woman who's gone too far. He just turned his back on me and walked out of the kitchen, leaving me trembling and fighting back tears of pain and remorse.

"Jesus, Eliza, sometimes you're just like her," he said softly as he walked away.

And I thought I would die. I leaned my thick head up against the kitchen wall and bled a little bit internally. Just two minutes and you can go from lovingly ribbing one another to this. Just two minutes. Why do I do this? Why?

The ride to Kasi's was in virtual silence.

Chapter 6
Body of Evidence

We spent the better part of three hours getting in the way of the police. Kasi's attorney, Robert Preston, was following them around, too (Mickey kept whistling "76 Trombones" under his breath whenever the guy made an entrance or an exit. It made me feel much better. Mick works real hard at not holding a grudge. I wish I could be like him...sometimes.) Atty. Preston was apparently an old friend of Kasi's from high school. It seemed to me he was overly pleased about Kasi's husband's disappearance. Another fly in the ointment?

Preston had counseled Kasi to come clean about her dalliance with George Diego. With the kids safely tucked away at Auntie Glory's, she was unburdening herself to Patrolperson Schwenk, having refused to have anything to do with "that Sexist Sergeant Bankowitz," who still hovered vicariously on the periphery. I heard her firmly insist Brando was her husband's son.

The cops had pretty much decimated the Short's back yard. It looked like a dozen groundhogs had been playing connect-the-dots. But the only additional things they'd turned up were a child's boot, a 1974 Delaware state license tag, and a few lost marbles. Honest.

They had a forensic specialist taking prints and dirt samples of the poor dog's paws. He looked very unhappy and decidedly guilty.

Then they moved down the block to dig in an empty lot.

At about 1:30, Mickey D. remembered our date with Ayn. "We've got to go talk to her," he nudged Kasi gently.

"Oh, Lord, you're right," she sighed. "I wouldn't want her to hear about it from the police."

"Or the press," I noted, thinking out loud. "It won't be long before they come sniffing around, looking for a first-hand account."

"Eliza!" Mickey cautioned.

"What?" I said innocently. Afterall, sometimes I *am* innocent.

At any rate, we finally agreed we would depart *en masse* to meet her at the coffee house in Tadford Ames's hotel, as pre-arranged. Then we would all go and explain to Ames that the follow-up to his story on Short/Curtis was a little different than expected. By the time we made our excuses to the cops, explained the situation to Atty. Preston, and left him there to guard Kasi's rights in her absence, it was only ten minutes before we were due to meet Ayn. It took twenty minutes for Mickey to drive the Blue Line to where it meets the Northeast Extension of the Pennsylvania Turnpike at Plymouth Meeting and the Embassy Suites hotel at which Ames was staying. So we were ten minutes late when we walked into the lobby and located the coffee house.

"We're to meet a young woman here," I told the hostess. "Has she taken a seat?"

"No one told me they were expecting anyone. Let me check a moment," she said. She returned almost immediately. "There are no single women patrons in the restaurant," she stated.

"Oh? Is there another restaurant in the hotel?" Mickey D. asked.

"The main dining room doesn't open until 5:00," the woman said. "The lounge is open. You could check in there," she added.

"Go ahead and take a table," I suggested to Kasi and Mick. "I'll check and if she's there, I'll bring her in." I knew Micker was dying for a bite of something. We hadn't eaten since that disastrous break- fast. But the lounge was empty except for two men talking loudly at the bar. I rejoined my companions in the coffee house.

"Maybe she went ahead to meet Mr. Ames," Mickey D. sug- gested.

"She did seem a bit enamored with him," Kasi allowed. "She's at that age when a little bit of attention from a man crowds out every- thing else." It sounded as though she were speaking from bitter ex- perience. "I expect he's a little old for her, though, being a program director and all, don't you think?" she asked rhetorically.

"Well, let's get a sandwich or something and if she doesn't come by 3:00, we'll call up to the room," I said. "You have the number, don't you?"

"Yes, room 303," Kasi said, and following Mickey's suit, ordered a BLT.

"And what would you like, ma'am?" the waitress asked.

"Just coffee," I said.

"I thought you were hungry," Mickey D. prompted.

"I thought so, too," I said, almost as surprised as he. I'm not known for missing an opportunity to eat. "But I'm just not right now," I said. "Maybe some Saltines?" I asked the waitress.

"Saltines?" She raised an eyebrow.

"With butter." I added.

"Butter?"

"Butter," I said firmly. And she finally went away.

Kasi looked at me curiously, but said nothing. Micker wasn't about to say anything.

"Why don't we try calling her at home?" Kasi asked after she and Mick had finished their BLTs and I'd nibbled on a few Saltines.

"You have her number?"

"Yes. I'll go call," she said, and I got up and let her scoot out of the booth. She came back a few minutes later. "There was no answer," she said, a worried look on her face.

"Does she have an answering machine?" Mickey asked.

"If she does, it's not on. What if she heard something about the — the hand? Oh dear."

Nobody said anything for a while. We sat there and had another cup of coffee. "Give me her number," I finally said to Kasi. "I'll try her again."

It rang four times. On the fifth ring, a breathless voice answered, "Yes?"

"Ayn?"

"This is Chakra," she panted. It sounded like she'd just run the mile.

"Hello, Chakra, this is Eliza Samuels. Is Ayn there?"

"No, Ayn is not here," she said. It was hard to tell if the tight tone in her voice came from exhaustion or exasperation.

"We were to meet her at 2:00. Do you know where she is?"

"No, I do not know. I'm sorry, I must go now. I have something on the stove." And she hung up. I had visions of her boiling bones. Finger joints. Leg bones. Elbows. Skulls. I shook it off.

I returned to the table and repeated the conversation, including the panting but omitting my gory visions. "It's almost 3:00," I noted. "Maybe we should call up to Mr. Ames's room and see if she's there. Are you sure we said we'd have coffee before the meeting, and not after?"

They concurred. Mickey shrugged. "Here," he said, laying a twenty on the table. "Pay and by the time you're done, I'll have reached Mr. Ames." And he went out to call.

Kasi insisted on paying (which is as it should be; she's the client, M.D. was just being chivalrous), so I put Mick's Thomas J. in my pocket and left three George Ws on the table for the waitress. Mick was still standing by the public phone in the lobby when we left the register. He was looking in the phone book. "No answer," he said, thumbing through the white pages. "I talked to the front desk and they said Ames's key is gone. He must be out."

"Well, it's just 3:00," Kasi allowed.

"There," Mick said, his index finger on a number. "PaCo Studios. 919-4000. Maybe we were supposed to meet him at the studio."

I'm surprised M.D. hadn't memorized the number years before. After all, in his younger, wilder, pre-Jason days, he hung out there enough. Jason, the guy who's been replaced by a cowfish — the guy who announced he was dying and Mick might be, too, and then vanished back to California from whence he had come — *that* Jason used to be an assistant producer for PaCo, the same studio that does Pennsylvania's version of Undissolved Miseries, along with numerous other stellar productions.

So after Mick asked to speak to Tadford Ames and was told the program director was not there, he asked for Darnell Pigeon, a set director with "The Rich and Powerful" (PaCo Studios hasn't had an original show in twenty years. They simply make their own versions of successful national shows.)

Suddenly I could see The Mick's face blanch pale. "He's not with 'The Rich and Powerful' anymore," he told us in an aside, then he started to cough.

Oh shit, Darnell's probably got *it* too, he was thinking. I *know* Mickey was thinking that. Then he suddenly stopped coughing. "Excuse me?" he said into the phone. "Oh. Okay. Thank you. Thank you very much." And he flashed us a relieved smile. "He's with 'Mysteries!'" he said. "They're connecting me." Then he gave me a look that said, "Please, get her out of here for a minute, would you?"

And I took Kasi's elbow. "Did you see the fountain over there?" I prodded. "Let's go throw a penny in for good luck. We'll leave Mickey to find out what he can." Thankfully, she went along without protest.

"I sure could use some luck," she allowed. Mick flashed me a look of gratitude as we moved away, toward the opposite end of the lobby.

Mick was on the phone for quite a while. Later I learned Darnell had been initially noncommittal about Ames's whereabouts. He had heard, mistakenly, through the gossip grapevine, that it had been Mickey who'd dumped Jason, instead of the actual hit-and-run which had been perpetrated on my brother by his partner. Mick didn't tell Darnell much – just enough to egg on his natural tendencies – but in no time Darnell was eating out of his hand. "That Ames fellow is a real schizoid," he told Mickey conspiratorially. "What say we meet at the Bistro and I'll fill you in on everything that's happened around here since you 'dropped out,'" he suggested. The Mick said he'd love to — later. But now he just needed to find out where Ames had gone so he could talk to him. It was important.

Well, Darnell allowed, Ames *did* get a call first thing this morning. Pigeon had been there early working on a set for an upcoming shoot when Ames showed up and went into his office to play back his phone messages. Darnell and a stage hand were just outside his door, carrying a false wall to set in place, when Ames rushed out of his office and practically ran into the wall.

"Holy Mother!" Darnell swore. "Hold onto your boxers, Buster. Where are you going so fast?"

"Got a tip!" he hollered back over his shoulder. "Might have found that Curtis fellow!" And he was gone.

"Can you find out where Curtis was supposed to have been?" Mickey begged, now at his most alluring.

"You mean listen to his phone messages?"

"Well, maybe he wrote something down in the office," Mick suggested.

"You want me to listen to his phone messages," Darnell repeated. "You sneak, you," he teased. "I could get in big trouble," he whined.

"Aw, come on, Darn," Mick cajoled. "For old time's sake."

Pigeon giggled. "Well, I guess I could try. Give me your number. I'll call back." And that's just what he did. Eons later, after Kasi and I had tossed every penny, nickel, dime and quarter we could find into that damn fountain, Mickey came nonchalantly strolling toward us, a smug look plastered on his all-American face.

"Tadford Ames got a phone call this morning," he stressed. Then he paused for effect and waved a piece of paper before us like it was a winning lottery ticket. "939 Raritan Circle, Apartment 1-B," he said, practically licking his lips. "That is where your husband, dear lady, was seen just yesterday. Ames has apparently gone there to check it out."

"Yesterday?" I said in disbelief.

"Yesterday?" Kasi echoed, her knees buckling a little. "Then the hand—"

We were still staring stupidly at Mickey when the look of triumph on his face changed to one matching Kasi's and mine. "Ayn?" he puzzled. "Ayn!" he repeated, more loudly. I turned around to see Ayn Curtis crossing the lobby. She had turned at the sound of her name and started coming toward us. Her step seemed hesitant, as though, having first been headed in one line towards the restaurant, her feet now had trouble switching direction. "Oh, I'm sorry I'm late!" she said, her face flushed. It was apparent she had been hurrying. "Would you believe I ran out of gas? I can't believe I did that. I've *never* done that before. I hope you haven't been waiting all this time out here for me?"

"Ayn, he's not dead, Ayn!" Kasi effused. She was simply boiling over. "He's been sighted. He's not dead!" and she grabbed the girl and tried to do a little dance of excitement.

But Ayn held back, a puzzled look on her face. "Not dead?" she said, her hand to her throat as though having it there would help her swallow this new development. "What — what do you mean?"

"We thought he was, but now he's not and we're going to go find him," Kasi babbled. Her facial expressions kept changing, like she was trying to figure out whether to be happy or angry, relieved or disgusted. Excitement was the overwhelming effect. She was like a hounddog who's picked up the scent after a long dry spell, panting and all but drooling.

Ayn, on the other hand, appeared to be in a state of shock. Her eyes were red and bloodshot, as if she hadn't slept. She turned to Mick, her face a cloud of confusion.

"I'm afraid you've skipped some chapters," he said gently, and started to explain the events of the previous 24 hours as Kasi hustled us impatiently to the car.

This time I drove, and it's a good thing, too, because Micker can't drive and talk at the same time, and somebody had to fill in poor Ayn. Kasi was supposed to be the navigator, since nobody knew where Raritan Circle was. But the woman was so excited about being hot on the trail of the husband she thought just yesterday someone had at least partially chopped up and buried, that she couldn't think straight. She was holding the street map upside down for about three miles, and we ended up going right when we should have gone left, north when we should have gone south.

We stopped at three gas stations and two convenience stores, and asked for directions from three vagrants and a woman wheeling a baby carriage with a dog in it, but it was finally just chance that we stumbled onto one end of the circle when we thought we were near the opposite loop. By now we were in Southeast Phily. Very poor, very ugly, and very uncomfortable for your average WASP. Rather obvious we weren't in our own neighborhood. "Lock the doors," Mickey cautioned.

Ayn, in the back seat with Mick, had been virtually silent throughout Mickey's narrative, whereas Kasi, sitting up front with me, had been running her mouth like maple tree sap on a warm night in March. "There's no numbers. Where are the numbers?" Kasi asked, frenetically. "Oh, there — 840. We're close. Another block!" She reached across as though she might turn the wheel to make the car move faster.

"Hold on, Kasi, I think we passed it." I did a U-turn and sure enough, there it was on the right — a turn-of-the-century, four-story brownstone that had obviously seen better days. Kasi was already out of the car and halfway up the sidewalk before I turned the engine off.

"Wait a minute, Kasi!" I said, jumping out and quickly following. Mickey got out of the back seat and bent over, his head inside the car.

"Come on, Mick!" I hollered, worried that Kasi was going to get away from us.

"Ayn says she doesn't want to go," he responded.

I glanced between Kasi and Mick, and then across the street at three homeboys hanging in the 'hood. "Hi!" I said tentatively, sort of testing the water.

"Yo!" responded a tall, twenty-something man swigging from a paper bag. The other two guys just kind of glanced at us and looked away like they couldn't be bothered.

"Come on!" Kasi squirmed at my elbow.

"Just a minute; hold on," I told her. On the one hand, I didn't want to go into that apartment without The Mick. On the other hand, I didn't think it was a good idea to leave Ayn out here by herself. I was getting ticked that Ayn wouldn't cooperate. I walked the few steps back to the car and bent over next to Micker. "You okay?" I asked Ayn. She was looking about as white as you can look in East Phily without being mistaken for a surrender flag. She was scrunched up inside herself. She resembled a turtle trying to get down into that turtleneck for protection.

Ayn shook her head slowly in the affirmative.

"Look," Mickey straightened up and said softly in my ear, "I think she's afraid of confronting him here, like this. I'm not so sure it's a good idea, either. We should have come by ourselves."

"Kasi's not going to wait now!" We both glanced at her, fidgeting by the apartment building door. She was practically wetting her pants.

"I guess not. But what happens if J/J's in there? How's he going to react? What's he going to do?"

"How the hell do I know?"

We went back and forth like that for a few more minutes. It was, I'm afraid to admit, decidedly unprofessional. Finally, Mick bent down and said to Ayn, "Will you be okay by yourself for a few minutes?" She nodded yes. "Okay. Lock the door there. If anything happens, blow the horn real loud and long, okay?"

"Okay."

"You're sure, now?"

She shook her head yes again.

Then he closed and locked his door and sauntered over to the men standing by the hydrant. "Hey, you got an extra cigarette, man?" he asked. The short guy handed him a Winston and the dude with the "Malcolm X" cap on backwards lit it for him. Mickey took a drag on it, said, "Thanks, man," and blew a puff toward the car. "Could you keep an eye on my sister for me?" he said. "She's carsick. We'll be out in just a minute."

"Sure, man," said the guy with the sack of booze. "They all your sisters?" he asked.

"Yeah."

"Whew!" said Malcolm Jr.

Whew? What's that mean? And since when did The Mick smoke cigarettes? Just being around people that smoke usually makes him cough. What a piece of work!

"Come on!" Kasi hissed at us.

Giving Ayn a little smile of encouragement, I patted my side as I walked with Mick up the sidewalk behind Kasi. Yep, my little .32 Browning revolver's right where I want her. Who knows what the creep will do if we zero in on him unexpectedly? Of course, by now, Tadford Ames might have found him, or he could have been tipped off and left already. Then again, he might have been watching our little charade on the street in front of his apartment and skipped out the back door ages ago.

Chipped concrete steps and a bent wrought-iron railing led to a dented metal fire door that looked like someone had driven a semi into it. Kasi tentatively pulled it open, revealing a dirty hallway and a staircase. I glanced at mailboxes inside the door, as though I expected to see "Jack Curtis" or "Joe Short" scrawled there on a piece of yellowed masking tape. There were broken parts of bicycles and baby strollers and corrugated boxes strewn about the floor by the stairway. The place smelled of cheap wine and old vomit.

"Where's 1-B?" I whispered, but the sound was swallowed up. "Where's B?" I asked again more loudly. A baby cried and from the apartment just inside the door, a large dog began to bark loudly. An upright "1" and an upside down "A" hung from a nail on the door.

"Shut-up, damn it!" a woman screamed. The dog barked more loudly. "Shut-up!"

There was a TV blaring in the opposite apartment. Kasi stepped up to it, and squinting, said, "It's 1-D. 1-B must be down there." Before I knew it, she was hurrying down the hall and Mick was loping to get ahead of her. I brought up the rear, unsnapping my holster. Mickey D. doesn't wear a gun, and hasn't since the FBI. He prefers to use finesse, he says. When that doesn't work, there's always his black belt in karate. Still, this whole scene had me very nervous.

The Mick caught up to Kasi and grabbed her by the shoulder. "Behind me," he said sternly but softly. "If he's in there, you'll get your chance to see him soon enough," he whispered. She bit her lip, nodded, and complied. I positioned myself at the left side of the doorframe, my right hand on my gun. Micker was at the right, one hand holding Kasi's arm as she reluctantly hugged the wall. Mick and I looked at one another, and I nodded. He reached out and knocked loudly. We listened. The dog down the hallway was still barking, the baby was still crying, and the TV across the hall was blaring reruns of Bonanza, but there was no sound from inside Number B. Mickey knocked again, louder. Still no answer. And again. From inside the apartment, only silence. I reached out and turned the knob. It opened with an awful squeak.

"Stay here!" I commanded Kasi in a hiss. She shook her head no, but stayed against the wall as Mick and I did the cop show entrance — cover, scan, lurch; cover, scan, lurch. No one in the kitchen. No one in the bathroom. No one in the bedroom. Nobody moving in the living room.

On the contrary, he would never move again. He was sitting straight up, his back against the dirty plasterboard of the east wall, a bullet hole in the middle of his forehead.

"Oh no! Oh no! Oh no! Oh no!" her voice got louder and louder as it came from behind me, then suddenly got softer and softer. Mickey D. took Kasi's arm and held her back. "No, it's okay, it's okay," she said softly, holding one hand over her mouth. "It's not him."

"Well, who do you suppose it is?" I asked rhetorically.

"Al. I think it's Al," she said inexplicably.

———

I sent Kasi to the car to get the camera and check on Ayn. Mickey D. scouted the other rooms more carefully to be sure no one else was with us. If you didn't count "Al" propped up there in the window, the place was practically unfurnished. A worn-out, single mattress was thrown on the floor of the bedroom; in the living room, there was a lawn chair with a third of its mesh runners missing, seated next to an upside-down milk crate with yesterday's paper on it; and in the kitchen was a sorry-looking '60s era Frigidaire with a half-empty carton of milk and a hunk of Braunsweiger on the top shelf. On the filthy counter lay a bag of Frito Lays, a plastic plate, a paper cup, and some McDonald's eating utensils.

The gun was nine inches to the right side of the body. It was a 9 mm Browning. Mick pulled out a handkerchief and raised "Al's" left hand.

Just then, Kasi came in with the camera. "What are you doing? Shouldn't we call the cops? What if someone sees us?"

"It's okay. We're not disturbing anything," I said over my shoulder. "Why don't you ask a neighbor if you can call?" I suggested. "Here, let me have that," and reached for the camera case. "Where's Ayn?"

"She wouldn't come in. I told her about Al and she said she really felt sick. She looks it. I don't like leaving her out there..." It was obvious Kasi was uncomfortable being there too. I didn't blame her. My stomach was doing little cartwheels when I paid attention to it, and I was glad now I'd only ordered Saltines for lunch. But we sure as sugar weren't going to leave that apartment without finding out all we could first.

"Why don't you knock on a door and have them call 911?" I prompted again. She nodded and disappeared.

"Here, look!" The Mick said, holding the limp hand up with his handkerchief. There was something scrawled in ink on the guy's palm. Something I couldn't make out.

"Hold it, I'll get a picture." And I snapped a bunch while Mickey held him for me.

"Look here," he noted, turning the hand over. There was a bloody scratch mark down the back of the hand. Closer inspection showed the dead guy's fingernails were bitten to the quick.

"This wasn't suicide," we said in simulspeak.

"Do you really think this is Al?" I asked.

"She never saw Al. She's not even sure he wasn't a figment of her imagination!"

"We better hurry up," Mickey D added. "The cops will be here soon, and I'd just as soon not be caught holding hands with a dead man, taking portraits, and giving manicures."

I went into the bathroom with the intention of washing my hands, and thought better of it. Then out into the hall to see if Kasi needed any help. It was then that I saw the blood — a dozen minuscule specks in the left panel of the recessed molding on the front of the door, starting about three inches above the doorknob and moving toward the right. In the relative darkness of the dimly-lit hall, and in the midst of our anxious entry, we had easily overlooked them among the flecked and peeling once-white paint, but now that the door was open to the light inside the apartment, the little spots were clearly visible.

"I found the murderer's blood!" I hollered to Mickey.

And with that, the first contingent of men and women in blue stormed through the front door and corralled us like stray cattle.

Naturally, we were the bad guys for being there in the first place. And unfortunately we got a crew that Mickey D. and I know from way back. Sgt. Stanley Staszewski was a thorn in the side of our dad, even before The Scandal at the Phily Police Department precipitated Dad's early "retirement" from that august body, and the bastard's been leaning on Mickey ever since he left the Fibs. It seems everywhere we go, we run into this idiot. And apparently he keeps tabs on us. Staszewski backed Mickey up next to the refrigerator, his beer belly practically rubbing buttons with Mick's belt buckle. "Yesterday ya dug up a hand, today a whole body. Maybe tomorrow you'll find a crypt full of archeological remains for us, ya think?" Staszewski snorted. Zewski's brains must have been a graft from a baboon's butt.

"Be careful, there's blood on the door there," I said as a detective hustled us into the hallway. "The murderer's blood."

"Murderer, hey?" Staszewski pushed me aside to follow Mickey out the door. "You carry a gun, Daniels?" He was in Mickey's face.

Mickey was ignoring him.

"I asked you something, boy. Do you pack a gun?"

"No," I said, pushing myself between them, "I do." And I pulled out my permit and shoved it at him. While he was studying it, Mickey D. walked away.

Staszewski looked up from the paper and grinned. "I forgot, your gun's not loaded, is it, Daniels?" he snorted and slapped another officer's back as he walked by. "Hear that?" he chuckled. "I said Daniels over there has a gun, but it's not loaded. He needs his sister for protection."

"Sergeant!" Captain James Stanford called from inside the apartment. "Get forensics down here, STAT! We've got a homicide."

We were almost to the front door of the building when Captain Stanford called out, "Hey! Don't go anywhere. We need to ask you some questions."

I nodded acknowledgment, we stepped out onto the stoop, and Mickey immediately started hacking.

With the arrival of the police, the neighborhood had come to life. The street was filled with people. Ayn's trio of "watchers" was at the front of the gathering crowd of onlookers as we headed out to check on her. "Hey, you shouldn't have brought your sister, Mac," said Marlboro Man. "This is a bad scene. Dangerous for her."

"I appreciate that, man," Mickey D. caught his breath. "Hey, you know anything about this dead dude?"

"Shit," he said, and sidled up right next to Mickey. "I wouldn't tell them pigs shit!" and he crunched knuckles with The Mick and, in an exaggerated saunter, followed by Sad Sack and Malcolm X Jr., he disappeared into the growing crowd.

"Wait!" I hollered ineffectually after them as the sound of arriving patrol cars and the loud crowd drowned out my voice and the police began to push back the neighbors, cordon off the scene, and separate us from the onlookers. Ayn remained holed-up in the back of the Cabriolet, which was now surrounded by neighbors gathering to discuss the murder.

They kept us there for two and a half hours as forensics and crime scene investigators, the coroner, the photographers, and the press came and went, questioning neighbors and collecting evidence. Nobody heard nothing. You know, what with the dog barking and the TV blaring, and the kid crying and the homeboys playing their rap real loud, what's to hear? Gunshots ain't real rare around here, see?

They grilled us over and over. I was getting sick of it. "Do you want to know what I had for breakfast?" I offered.

"Very funny, Miss Samuels," Staszewski smirked.

79

"Ms."

"What?"

"It's Ms. Samuels."

"Oh, I thought Daniels was the one with the married name," he quipped. Mickey'd had enough. He lunged at him. But Captain Stanford stepped in between them.

"Staszewski," he said. "There's apparently another witness outside in the car. Would you bring her in, please."

"Aw, come on, the kid's sick," I whined. "We're not material witnesses. We didn't see anything you didn't see." I'd been hoping Ayn wouldn't be noticed. She wouldn't have any input of use to the cops, and she seemed so screwed up just now about her father.

"I just want to see what she has to offer," Stanford said, not unkindly.

The body was still in the room, but they had moved it. He was now laid out with a sheet draped over him, and the attendants from the morgue had just arrived and were preparing to lift the body into a large white bag.

Just then a female officer came in, holding Ayn lightly by the elbow. Her coloring hadn't improved a whole lot since the last time I saw her. Mickey D. went to her and patted her gently on the back. She almost cringed, appearing frightened, her eyes darting around the room, trying to avoid the body.

"It's okay, Miss Curtis," Captain Stanford said. "I've been told you're somehow a part of this ever-expanding adventure of The Missing Man. Mrs. Short here has explained it all to me," he said, motioning to Kasi, who was seated, subdued, on the milk case just outside the entrance to the kitchen. "Sort of," he added, and smiled ironically. "At any rate," he continued, "It appears that you're all here because some guy named Tadford Ames was supposedly coming here to find your husband — or, I mean, father — Mrs. Short's husband. Is that right?"

Ayn nodded.

"Is that a yes?" Lt. Stanford prodded.

"Yes," she said softly, her hand at her throat, absent-mindedly playing with the high neck on her sweater. All of yesterday's hurt, biting sarcasm was gone out of her.

"Okay. Now, Mrs. Short says the man we have found here is not her husband. I just want you to take a look for us and confirm that this is not the man you knew as your father — I mean, the man who was your father." He shuffled his feet a little. "Well, you know what I mean." I couldn't help but smile.

While the lieutenant was talking to Ayn, the EMTs had placed the body in the bag, zipped it up, and were ready to move out, so Stanford directed the attendants to unzip the bag and Mickey D. led Ayn slowly across the living room.

"Do you know this man?" Captain Stanford asked as the three of them stood there, looking down.

Ayn swallowed hard and nodded. "Yes," she whispered. "It's Tadford Ames." And she burst into tears.

Chapter 7
Dead Ames

First question: Who the hell is — or was — Tadford Ames? Was he just a misguided, over-zealous television programmer, or did he have a hidden agenda that would make him so interested in finding J/J that he went by himself to the location of the man's last sighting and got himself murdered in the process? The answer to these questions might just lead us to our missing man. Before we could go down that particular alley, however, the police "invited" us down to the station for more questioning regarding Ames. Basically, the session went on a fast train to nowhere. Ayn was the only one who knew the program director, and she claimed to have met him only in regards to the show and — oh yes, for dinner. Twice.

So there *had* been hope of a romance there. Poor kid! What she was looking for was both a father and a father figure. She got neither. Instead we'd found molding processed pork liver and a would-be beau with a bullet through his brain. But the more they grilled Ayn, the more the feisty side of her that we had met just yesterday seemed to re-emerge. Now here was a survivor! Go, Ayn! I cheered silently, as she gave Staszewski tit-for-tat. The kid had sarcasm down to an art — a woman after my own heart.

Finally, Glory Ribbono came to pick up Kasi, and we were allowed to escort Ayn back to her Geo Prism. She explained that while she was on her way to meet us that afternoon, she'd run out of gas. She was standing beside her stranded vehicle when a Good Samaritan stopped and poured enough gas from a spare can into her tank to get her to the hotel, albeit over an hour late.

"You better get some more gas now before you run out again," Mickey D. cautioned.

"Yeah, I know, you're right."

"We need some, too," I noted.

"Why don't we go to a station, get some gas, and then we'll follow you home," M.D. suggested. "I'd like to make sure Chakra's there. I don't want to leave you alone. It's been a tough day." That's Mickey D.'s patented brand of chivalry. What's a girl to say when faced with that?

She said the expected: "You don't have to, I'll be all right. Really." But Mickey held firm. So we followed her to an Exxon half a mile away, and while Ayn and I pumped, Mickey D. did the windows on both cars. I filled up Cabri, but Ayn put just $3 in her tank. You know how students are — always short of cash.

Then we followed Ayn home and relinquished responsibility to the solicitous ministrations of attendant Chakra.

"Feel better now?" I asked Micker as we drove away.

"I'm not sure," he mused.

"Why's that?"

"Later. Right now we've got to get a handle on the slippery Tadpole." I could see his cogs grinding.

We drove to our little office, twenty minutes away in Lochmore. Lochmore used to be where the gentry lived. They'd hop the train from their high-rise jobs in downtown Philadelphia to their grand estates out in the "country." It's been a long time since Lochmore was country, but it's still composed of some of the richest real estate in Pennsylvania.

Lochmore College, a very well-endowed liberal arts institution of high repute, situates the town at the peak of yuppiness, but saves it from outright stuffiness. Neither Mickey nor I are either yuppies or, I assure you, stuffies. We do, however, *come from* a long line of stuffies. Our mother's father, Grandfather Longacre, was one of the founding fathers who rode the train daily into the city and was picked up at the station precisely at 6:00 p.m. by his gardener, Gilbert III, in the Studebaker. His father, Great-grandfather Longacre, did the same, and was picked up precisely at 6:00 p.m. by his manservant Gilbert II, in the carriage. Great-great Grandfather...well, you get the point.

The "town" part of Lochmore is tiny, and its very existence seems to have been physically designed around what has sustained the village — the train and the college. If you are driving south into Lochmore on her main street — Route 320 or Old Chester Road — you pass beautiful stone structures of the college, playing fields, and well camouflaged parking lots on either side of the two-lane road. As soon as you approach the village, the road seems to be sublimated, passing underneath the station and the track. As your car rises again to the normal level of the terrain, you are already out of beautiful downtown Lochmore. In order to see it, you must make a quick left as soon as you emerge from the underpass, and find the pie wedge-shaped business district hugging the one-way, one-lane street that circles the upper level of the overpass, alongside the railroad track and the train station. The pointed, inside angle of the pie wedge points directly at the track and the college across the way. Another pie wedge facing the opposite direction carries two more blocks of businesses.

You will find the usual necessities — hardware store, drugstore, bank, post office, tailor, weekly newspaper office. Also a few trendy gift shops and a couple of nice book shops. A co-op grocery, a family restaurant and, of course, The Nook, the established "in" place to eat. And then there's our offices.

Samuels & Daniels, Private Investigators, is situated on the nipple of the teat that feeds Lochmore — the angle of the pie wedge that points the way to the station and the college. We share the second floor over the drug store with a dentist, a chiropractor, and Miss Marsh, who is 89 and has given piano lessons in the same two rooms since 1932. If it happened in Lochmore and Miss Marsh doesn't know about it, it's not worth knowing.

When we're busy, we don't use the offices a whole lot. They're mainly a reason to have a presence and a place for clients to call. There are two desks with swivel chairs, two naugahyde chairs for guests, a couple of filing cabinets, a copy machine, a phone, an I-Mac computer, a coffee machine, and a bathroom. The big office picture window looks down on — what else? — the train station.

As soon as we got in the door, Mickey was on the horn to his friend Jake with the FBI. While he was talking to Jake, I went into the bathroom, which doubles as a darkroom, and started developing the film, after which I blew up some prints and hung them to dry.

"What's it look like?" Mickey asked when I emerged.

"Hard to say. Let 'em dry a little. What's Jake got?"

"He's plugging old Tadford into the computer, but it'll take time. Heck, it's 9 p.m. He's gonna check and call us in the morning." He stretched back in his chair, his long arms behind his head, his eyes closed, letting his lean body go slack.

"Tired?"

"Yeah."

"Wanna go home?"

"I guess."

"Where?"

He opened one eye. "I don't know."

"Want to come stay with me for a while?"

"I'm not sure." He curled his lip up, like he was thinking on it.

"I won't preach or rant and rave any more."

"Promise?"

"Promise."

"Okay," he said, letting the back of the chair go vertical. "But first we have to stop and feed Churchill."

"No problem."

"And then we have to call Mother."

"Aw, come on, it's late."

"You promised."

"I only—"

"—You promised."

"Okay, already." No use getting into that again.

Kasi called again the next morning as I was sitting down with the newspaper and my usual breakfast repast. Mickey D. was still snoring out on the sunroom couch.

"I can't believe those morons can't find the rest of my husband!" she huffed.

"Good morning, Kasi," I said, swallowing a bite of cookie. "Cops haven't — umm, dug up any more evidence?"

"If they have, they're not telling me."

"Do you still think the hand was Joe's?"

"Lord, I don't know. They say it's the right size. What else can I believe?" she wailed. "First I just wanted him back. I thought if he could forgive me for George..." she sighed and paused, "...then I could forgive him for whatever. Things were tough sometimes between us, but I didn't have anything else solid, you know?"

"Hmm."

"Then I got worried. You know — possible gambling debts, secrets from his past catching up with him, 'Al' — what have you. And then I realized I knew next to nothing about him and his background. *That* made me angry. I stayed angry at him for ages. Then I got mad at everyone else for not giving a damn — for not helping clear up the whole thing so I could get on with my life. Then when Marbles showed up with that hand...well, I figured the fat lady had sung. I didn't know whether to be the grieving widow, the injured wife, or the angry avenger, but I thought it was over." She paused, muzzled the receiver and hollered something to Eva in the next room. I slurped on my Welch's.

"You know George didn't have anything to do with it, don't you?" she said into the receiver.

"Mmm."

"I just had to lash out at someone and George was easy. The whole thing with him was easy — easy to start and easy to end, you know?"

"Mmm."

"Then I started feeling sorry for myself — started to grieve, sort of. And just as I was getting into it — just as I was working up to a semi-respectable dose of angst, I realized something. You know what?"

"No, what?" I stretched the phone chord over to the refrigerator and topped up my grape juice. She really would have been getting a lot more out of this if Mickey D. had answered the phone, I thought to myself.

"I can't grieve."

Silence. Maybe I should say something here. "Oh?"

"No. I can't grieve. You know why?"

"No, Kasi, why?"

"I didn't love him, that's why. Hell, I didn't even *know* him, how could I love him, right?"

"I guess."

"With Ayn it's different. She was in love with the idea of being loved *by* him after all these years, and now even the chance of hating him, up close and personal, has been taken from her. You know?"

"Yeah, I guess."

"You were married once, right?"

"Uh, yeah." Now we're getting personal. This is supposed to be about you, Kasi, remember?

"What happened?"

"We suffered a mismarriage early in the relationship."

"Oh, I'm sorry, a miscarriage is—"

"No, marriage, with an 'm,' as in mistake."

"Oh!" And she chortled dryly. "Maybe that's what this is — only it's like having a child with autism. He looks normal. Sometimes he almost acts normal. But you can't reach him, you can't make contact. That's it — we had an autistic marriage and I never knew it."

"Well..."

"Can you believe that? I never even knew it."

"Kasi, it's not your fault, you know." Thinking back on it, I believe that was one of the nicest things I've ever said to someone.

"Really? You think so?" she almost whispered.

"Yes, I do." And we both basked in that for a while.

Finally I got tired of basking. "Kasi, can I ask you something?"

"Sure."

"Do you think Joe killed Tadford Ames?"

"I don't know. I just don't know," she sighed.

"Why did you say it was 'Al' when you first saw the body? I mean, isn't that a little freaky? You said 'Al' was just a voice — a noise outside the door that vanished when you opened it up."

"I know. I know. It just felt like that's what Al would look like — or feel like. Until Ayn fingered him as Ames, he felt like some sort of resolution to my 'Al' question. But as I can't see how it jibes that they're the same, I just don't know. It's just one more confusing factor in this never-ending nightmare."

"It's okay. Don't worry about it. We'll get to the bottom of this," I assured her, though I wasn't all that sure myself. "You still want us to look into it?"

"Oh, yes! Definitely! Whatever it takes! I need to know. That's the only thing I'm sure of. I need to know why."

"Okay. We'll keep on it. I'll talk to you later. Stay in touch."

"Bye."

"Goodbye."

The *Philadelphia Inquirer* had a few paragraphs on Page 13 on Ames's demise, quoting the police as saying it was a "suspicious death," and listing the victim tentatively as Tadford R. Ames, 39, a program director with PaCo Productions and a resident of Embassy Suites Hotels.

They'd apparently contacted someone at PaCo, because the article said he'd been with the company for "a short time," having come there from a movie company in Wilmington, North Carolina.

The cops were being close-mouthed, which usually meant they didn't have a clue. Unfortunately, we didn't have many, either.

I scanned the paper for something about the hand, but there was nothing. Zilch.

Finally I got out the prints I'd made the night before and laid them on the kitchen table. I took my handy dandy magnifying glass out of the first aid drawer (I mainly use it to remove slivers), and pulled the accordion light fixture over the kitchen table to within six inches of the photos.

"Hmm," I declared as Mickey D. shuffled stiffly into the room.

"It's raining," he said accusingly.

"Good morning, Sir Grump."

"I mean *pouring*. It wasn't supposed to rain. What are you doing?"

I looked up. He was absent-mindedly running his long fingers through that lovely thick hair that should rightfully have gone to me, as a member of the sex to whom beauty is supposed to be all-consumingly important. "I'm checking out the handwriting."

"Whose handwriting?"

"The writing on the hand, silly."

"Well, why didn't you say so?"

"I did."

"You said handwriting."

"Well, it's certainly not a footnote."

"Humph!" And he took milk out of the refrigerator and drank from the carton.

"Hey! Don't do that. You've got germs!"

"Don't sweat it. There's only an inch. I'll buy you more."

"If you're going to stay here, buy *you* more."

"Okay." He came over, and resting a knee on a chair and his elbows on the table, peered over my shoulder. "What's it look like?"

"Dog."

"What?"

"All I can make out is d-o-g — 'dog.' There's something before it, right there by the, — er, lifeline — which, by the way is longer than you might expect, given that he's dead and the paper says he was only 39." I glanced down at my palm for comparison's sake. "Let me see your hand," I commanded.

Mick started to comply, then pulled it back. "Forget that," he sniffed. "Let me see the prints." And he picked one up, then another, stooping to study them under the magnifying glass. "Looks like an "H" before the "dog," and something curly before that. Hdog."

"Hotdog," I offered.

"Yeah, right, the guy's being murdered and he writes 'hotdog' on his hand, then sits back and dies."

"In this case, nothing would surprise me," I declared.

The phone rang two sharp rings, then a short one — the office phone. "I'll get it," said Mick.

It was Jake. Mickey hit 'Speaker.' "What have you got for us, man?"

"Another nowhere man."

"You're kidding!"

"Nope. This one's got a Social Security number, but we traced it back and it seems the original Tadford Ames died in Ontario at the age of three. He and his whole family were wiped out in a car accident in 1957."

"Maybe he's *not* 39, then," I mused. "That would explain the lifeline." I've gotten rather obsessed with stuff like that lately.

"What's that?" asked Jake.

"Nothing," Mickey said abruptly, shooting me a dirty look. "It's just my sister. Remember Eliza?"

"Oh, sure. Hi, Eliza."

"Hi, Jake. Thanks for all your help."

"The least I can do. Say, there *is* some good news in this," he added.

"How so?" It didn't sound like much good to me.

"It gives an in for the FBI to investigate," Jake said.

"It does?" I asked.

"Federal crime," Mick explained.

"That's right," Jake agreed. "Appropriating someone else's Social Security number and identity gets the Feds' attention real fast. But you'll have to bring it to their attention through 'proper channels,' Mickey," he reminded him.

"Yeah, well, they're not exactly taking my advice lately," Mick groused.

"If there's anything I can do, just holler," Jake offered.

"Thanks, Jake."

"Yeah, thanks, Jake," I chimed in.

"Bye."

After breakfast, Mickey D. did some deep breathing exercises, working his way up to a conversation with Darnell Pigeon. I couldn't help but snicker. "Hey — *you* wanna do it?" Mick challenged. He was definitely in a crabby mood today.

"Somehow I don't think he'd respond quite as well to me," I snorted.

"Well then, lay off. The guy's a cretin — one of the gossiping, back-biting, snippity troublemaker types."

"Well, in this case that should serve us just fine. He found Ames for us, didn't he?"

Micker closed his eyes, took a deep breath, and dialed PaCo. Pigeon was on the line in ten seconds flat. I had to hit 'Speaker' this time, with M.D. giving me a disgusted look. Heck, I wasn't gonna miss this!

"Hey, I'm glad you called. I've been looking for Daniels in the phone book." Darnell sounded breathless, as if he'd run to the phone.

"It's Samuels & Daniels."

"Oh. I *told* you he was into something heavy, didn't I? A bullet through the brain! I think it's drugs," he whispered hoarsely. "Pankratz has been in one big zombie haze since he hired this Tadford fellow."

"Who's Pankratz?" Mickey D. asked.

"David Pankratz, studio manager. He's the one who brought Ames on. Hold on a minute." Muffled voices in the background. A few seconds later, Darnell came back on. "Look, I can't talk here. Meet me in half an hour," he hissed.

Mickey D. raised his eyes to the ceiling and shook his head in dismay. "Should I just call later?" he asked wistfully.

I bit my lip to suppress a laugh.

"No, that's no good. The walls have ears around here. Meet me at The Bistro at 10:30. I'll be the one in the gabardine suit." And he giggled and hung up.

"Oh, Jesus!" M.D. moaned.

"You shouldn't swear," I said prissily, grinning widely.

"Yeah, well what are you going to do while I give my quart of blood?"

"Tag along?" I ventured hopefully.

"Not on your life!"

I stuck my tongue out at him. "Well, maybe I'll visit Ayn," I announced. "Did you get the feeling she's been less than totally truthful about this whole thing?" I mused.

"Bingo!" M.D. proclaimed. "If you get a chance, find out where she *really* was yesterday," he said. "She sure as hell didn't run out of gas," he added.

"Why do you say that?"

"There was one of those free car wash tickets on her dashboard when I washed the windows last night. The kind you get when you buy ten gallons of gas at some stations. It was dated early yesterday morning. If she ran out of gas, then she used up more than nine gallons in under six hours."

"Oh? And when were you going to clue me in on this, partner?"

"I just did, didn't I?" And he turned toward the bathroom. "I've got to shower and get dressed. Where did we put the clothes I brought last night?"

"Hall closet." And I put my head down and fidgeted with the buttons on my sweater. Okay, I admit I've been a little snippy lately.

A bit too caustic, perhaps. A tad touchy, maybe. But that's just because I don't know what to do about certain things regarding Mick and his health and all. And M.D. knows that. But to hold back evidence to spite me? We're partners, damn it!

Suddenly Mickey D. stepped back into the room and grabbed me gently by the chin. "Hey," he said gruffly, blinking into my face with those baby blues. "I want you to know I'm still here, functioning and viable. I'm still sharp. I'm still active. I'm still earning my keep."

"*I* never said—"

"—I said it. You've been doing more and more. I've been doing less and less. I guess when I saw the ticket, I thought I could figure it all out and come up, single-handedly, with the answer, like a one-man FBI, a Sherlock Holmes. I wanted to prove that I still had it."

I pulled away from him. "You *do* still have—"

"—I don't have what I want, Eliza. I want TIME." He practically spat it out. He was standing there in his shorts, balling a towel between his hands. And for once I was speechless. Finally, he broke the awful silence. "Just allow *me* to be bitchy every now and then. You get to do it all the time. People expect it of you. But me, I've always been the accommodator, the mollifier, the steady-as-he-goes type. Well damn it, *I* want to bitch now and then."

"Okay, so go ahead and bitch. Who's stopping you?"

And the saddest smile spread over his face. He let the towel drop loosely at his side, and turned and walked away.

"Jesus, all I said was 'clue me in,' already," I mumbled as he disappeared into the bathroom. There was a terrible lump in my throat. Maybe I'm getting Mickey's cold.

Well, I changed my mind about going to see Ayn. I didn't quite know what I needed to ask her yet, and to tell the truth, the thought of being around that Chakra woman had me a little spooked. That and the fact that Mickey D. mentioned it might be a good idea if we went to see her together. After that teamwork speech, I decided not to press things.

So instead, after M.D. shuffled off for his reluctant assignation with Darnell, umbrella in hand, I called my old friend Trisha Petersen. Trisha and I go back a long way. We were roommates in college. She was Pre-medicine and I was Pretending. To know what I wanted to do, that is. For the longest time, I'd had it all figured. I'd get a B.S. in criminal justice and then attend the police academy to follow my old man into the ranks of the men and women in blue. But then came the scandal at the station, and the wild scenes at home with Mom, and finally, the .38 through the brain in the basement. Accidental. Cleaning his service revolver. That's how the police report read. That's how the insurance company paid it. Nobody else was fooled, least of all his kids. We were high school sophomores at the time.

The likes of people such as Sgt. Staszewski and his ken looked on my father with much the same scorn as they now heaped on Mickey D. for simply being himself. Someday we'd find out what really happened to make Dad do what he did. Mick and I would investigate the hell out of that department and get to the bottom of things. I think that's why Mickey turned to criminology and the FBI after Dad died, with the intention of getting in there and blowing the cover off that scam. He and I had never believed Dad had done what they claimed. We didn't want to believe.

But we'd both lost our steam — I through an overall pessimistic haze that settled in after my marriage to Bozo, and Mickey when his natural idealism got quashed by the Morals Police at the FBI. That and one hit-and-run lover that left him with internal injuries he will almost certainly never recover from.

Well, all I meant to say was that Trisha Petersen fulfilled her career goal. She had become a serologist with the Pennsylvania State Police. Her job was to analyze blood. Trisha was the one they turned to when they needed expert scientific analysis for paternity suits, rapes, and murders. Trisha was the one I turned to after Mickey tested HIV positive. I'd made her do every test in the book on him, hoping they were wrong, that someone had screwed up somewhere. But the only one who'd screwed up was Mickey D. And he'd finally called a stop to the tests.

"Hey, Drac, it's me, Eliza. How's it going?"

"Type A! Where you been hiding?"

It was good to hear her voice. All those wild college memories came flooding back. I realized I'd been out of the loop for a while. "How's Tom and the kids?"

"Fine. Well, Ben broke his arm falling out of a tree last week," she sighed. "But Tom's up for a promotion at IBM."

"Bad time to be at IBM," I opined.

"Well, yes and no. He's in outsourcing. Tom thinks it's a good time if you can hang in there. How's Mickey doing?"

"Pretty good. Catching a lot of little bugs. Nothing major." Trisha was the only one of my friends who knew about The Mick. Only one besides Mom D., in fact, and Mom refused to acknowledge it. So I wasn't used to talking about it. I changed the subject. "Hey, Trisha, you ought to be getting a case soon that we're working on."

"Oh yeah? Which one's that?"

"Tadford Ames. Murdered in South Phily yesterday. We've been doing a missing person on the prime suspect."

"Hold on a second, Eliza, they delivered a few samples this morning, but I haven't had a chance to look at them yet. I've been tied up with a bloody rape/murder from Easton, and a probable murder/suicide from Equinunk. Just a second, I'll go check the paperwork and see what they brought me."

A minute later she was back on the line. "This one isn't it. Looks like a child support paternity suit," she mumbled, and I could hear paper rustling. "Here! Here it is. Ames, Tadford. Blood and tissue samples from the autopsy. And a few slides of 'possible related.'"

"What's that mean?"

"It means they think it might be Ames's blood, too, but they're not sure."

"Those morons! It's not Ames's, it's the killer's! That's what you've got to determine. Whoever dripped his or her blood on that door killed Ames! You don't shoot yourself in the head in one room and fling little blood spatters against the door on the way out after killing yourself!" I blew air, exasperated.

"You haven't changed, Type A. You'll blow a gasket before you hit 40."

"Nope, I'm doomed to grow old and mean, like my mother."

"Your mom's not old."

"Well, mean, then."

"I don't think she's mean, either. Let's do lunch soon."

"Yeah, I'd like that. Could we sort of combine it with a little info on Ames and his executioner?" I begged.

"It's quite a process — usually three weeks, but I'll rush it for you."

"Can we meet for lunch, then?"

"Sure, I'd love to. How about The Easel?"

"Great! See you then. And thanks, Trisha."

Another call from Kasi. The cops were talking drug dealing. Had she ever seen her husband take drugs? Had she ever taken drugs with him? Could they see her arms? Weren't the trips to Atlantic City really drug runs? How did they finance their house? Could they see her financial records? How dare they!

And they'd been grilling the guys in the band, too. Billy Randolph had even called her and very pointedly asked if she had "sicced that amorphous xenophobic cretin Staszewski" on him. "And I always thought we were friends," Kasi wailed. "Even Glory is getting short with me. They're coming down on Rocky through his old man, nosing around and talking about laundering money and stuff," she practically spat. "I just want closure on this thing. I want closure!"

"I know, Kasi, I know. We're working on it." I told her that Mickey D. was interviewing people at PaCo as we spoke, and that I had a blood specialist checking out the murder scene samples. "Say, have you had your dog for long?"

"My what?"

"Your dog."

"Who, Marbles?"

"Yeah. Where'd you get him?"

"From a friend. Why?"

"Well, he wasn't ever trained to sniff drugs or anything, was he?"

"What? What's all this about drugs?" The exasperation was dripping from her. "We got him as a pup when Eva was a baby," she declared.

"I'm sorry, Kasi, it was a long shot. Just something we found at the scene." And I told her about the writing on Ames's palm.

"Hey, I'm a computer programmer, not a palm reader," she sighed. And we signed off.

I went for a walk in the rain. Walking sometimes helps me sort things out. This time it just made me wet.

Okay, let's say Ames is Al. If that's true, he knew J/J was missing before he ever contacted Ayn about doing the TV show. If that's the case, he set her up to do the show to flesh out J/J, which meant he either 1) already knew she was J/J's daughter; or 2) she isn't J/J's daughter afterall, she's Ames's accomplice.

Accomplice in what?

We apparently need to look into Ayn's background just a tad.

Mickey came home ten minutes after my walk was over, looking shell-shocked. "He pegged me right off the bat," he sighed. "It'll be all over Society Hill by tonight. How could he know? Do I look like I have—?"

"—Hell no, you just have a pathological aversion to dishonesty. It's a real character flaw in you, Daniels."

"Don't call me Daniels."

"Besides, who cares about Society Hill? Who do we know in Society Hill? I think the last case we had over there was a missing Persian, about two years back. And I don't mean the Iranian variety of homo sapiens, I mean the feline."

"I know a lot of sapiens in Society Hill — homo and otherwise," he said, playfully tugging on my hair.

"Oh, go on, who cares what he thinks he knows about you? What's he know about Tadford Ames?"

"Mostly gossip, but interesting gossip. Seems our 'program director' stormed the place six weeks ago, swept all other pre-scheduled programming aside, and rushed his own projects onto film, the Jack Curtis segment at the forefront. He was able to throw his weight around because he apparently came equipped with an unlimited supply of exotic drugs for Mr. David Pankratz, who manages the entire circus from a distant cloud of drugged haze, provided, gratis, by his latest supplier, now his *late* supplier. Apparently, a great number of the cast and crew were also floating free, courtesy of Mr. Ames. I detected a distinct and persistent sniffle coming from Darnell's nose and I wasn't in the least concerned about catching another cold." Micker plopped down tiredly on the couch.

"So it *is* drugs."

"Well, it gets more interesting," he said, kicking off his loafers and tucking his feet in between two sofa cushions.

"Yes?" I took to pacing between the couch and the window.

"Darnell and some others have been suspicious from the start, or so he claims. Jealous of his unearned influence is more like it," M.D. scoffed. At any rate, just last week Darnell had made contact with a friend who works with the movie studio in Wilmington, North Carolina that Ames supposedly came from. They had never heard of the guy or anyone matching his description. "By the way," Mick interrupted himself, "Did Ayn ever mention Ames had a thick accent?"

"Not that I recall. What kind?"

"Darnell called it 'east of the Iron Curtain and west of Nome.' At any rate, Darnell claims he and his cohorts were just waiting for the right time to expose Ames, but they were leery of Pankratz's reaction, and apparently also enjoying the fruits of his deception as long as possible."

"TV and big screen people don't often mix," I mused, "so Ames probably thought his cover would last long enough for him to make contact with J/J, for whatever reason."

"Well, he made contact with *someone* all right," Mickey grunted.

"All this is no more than some sort of drug war?" I raised a brow.

"Much too complicated," M.D. agreed. "Drug dealers usually just find the guy who did them wrong and mow him down."

"Mob-connected?" I ventured.

"The set-up's too sophisticated and the execution — sorry — is too sloppy," Mickey D. opined.

"They pulled off JFK's assassination," I asserted. Being related to an ex-Fibber, I had absorbed this particular conspiracy theory long before the recent spate of TV movies.

"Yeah, but the Mob had the active assistance of the CIA in that one," Micker argued. "They wanted him gone as much as the Mafia did. And this is one they haven't exactly pulled off. Not yet. Besides, it was too polished, trying to make it look like a suicide, yet too sloppy, leaving the blood on the door and the writing on the hand. Not professional but not gangsterish," he shook his head. "And just where does J/J fit into all this?"

"If he didn't off Ames, who did?" I posed.

There was no reply.

"And if he did," I added, "who was our mutt Marbles playing patty-cake with?"

"It only takes one hand to pull a trigger," M.D. noted quietly.

"Well, whether J/J's operating with a full set of digits or not, I have no idea," I said. "All I know is it feels like we're trying to drive the Indy on a tricycle. We've got to get more horsepower."

Mickey D. started preparations for a spaghetti dinner while I prepared a salad and went through my memory bank of contacts. Suddenly I whacked the cutting knife down on the chopping block, sending a sliver of onion flying. "Jeez, why didn't I think of him before? Ira Fahnstock!"

"Who?" M.D. was rummaging in my shelves for sauce seasonings.

"Other side, other side," I said, pointing to the left cabinet. "Don't you remember Ira? Hornrims, squeaky little voice, the only kid who had a receding hairline in the ninth grade?"

"Ira the Bean?" He was dumping God Knows What into a pan of simmering stuff. It was starting to smell awfully good.

"Yeah! Gosh, why did we call the poor kid that?" I mused.

"He wore a beanie, silly — a yarmulke. We were kids. Cruel WASP kids."

"Maybe that's why he was going bald so early. The top of his head never saw the light of day."

"You're still cruel."

"I know," I smiled. "Anyway, remember how he went every summer to that Orthodox Jewish camp?

"Camp Tonawanadonadega, or something? How could that be Orthodox?"

"I don't know, but it was in the Poconos!" I declared triumphantly.

Mickey D. just kept stirring the brew. "Is there a point to this?" he asked finally.

"Yes."

"Oh, good," and he poured half a bottle of wine into the spaghetti sauce.

"Mickey!"

"The point?" he tried to divert my attention.

"Ira's uncle owned that camp!" I declared. "Ira ended up being the manager and caretaker. We could call him up and ask him to check on Ayn's story. It's on the same lake as the town she grew up in."

"Is that the best we've got?"

"What more do you want? There's nothing else in the Poconos besides camps, honeymoon resorts, lakes, black bears and people who used to live in Jersey. How hard can it be?"

"And what's going to make Ira Fahnstock do this sleuthing for us?" The Mick asked as he drained the spaghetti and poured it into a large bowl.

"Because Ira Fahnstock has always carried a torch for Yours Truly!"

"Pah!" M. D. sputtered, slopping sauce into a gravy boat. "How so?"

"Because Ira Fahnstock got his first kiss *and* his first hickey behind the scoreboard of Stourbridge Jr. High — in the sixth inning of the playoff game with Damascus — from me! Tongue and all. I was extremely generous, too!" And I gave my brother my most self-satisfied Cheshire grin.

"You hussy!" he snorted as we sat down to a very luscious repast.

"Now *this* is why I asked you to stay," I smiled, smacking my lips and reaching for the sauce.

After dinner, it took me several calls to find the right Fahnstock in the White Pages, and then a bit of convincing to get Ira's number from his father.

"Eliza Daniels? Daniels, Daniels...Are you Elliott Daniels's daughter? Joel Daniels? No? Were you bat mitzvahed with my daughter Sarah? You were never bat mitzvahed? You're not Jewish? Are you sure? 'Daniels' is a good Jewish name. It means 'God Will Judge.' Your maiden name is Samuels? Well, that's Hebrew, too. It means 'Asked of God.' Are you ashamed of your heritage, young lady?"

I hadn't expected a Hebrew lesson, but I was rather intrigued at Mr. Fahnstock's revelations. Wouldn't it be a hoot if Mother found out she'd married a closet Jew? As steeped in WASPism as she was, it would be quite a come-uppance. But Christians, now that I thought about it, were notorious for stealing Jewish names and not owning up to it.

Finally, Mr. Fahnstock ran out of patronymic etymological comments. There was a pause, as though he were doing a rewind of the recorder in his brain. I could almost hear the soft hum and click as he returned to the beginning of our conversation. "...You knew my son in grade school?...You know, Ira is happily married."

When I finally convinced Mr. Fahnstock that giving me his son's phone number would neither be a breach of privacy nor a threat to his marriage, I scribbled it down, thanked him, and triumphantly dialed Ira's number.

It took another several minutes to get through Mrs. Ira Fahnstock to Ira. She seems so curious about my intentions in speaking with Ira that I wondered if he had confessed to his wife about his first kiss with Eliza, the *shiksa* from Lochmore. Finally, I was passed through to Ira.

"Eliza Daniels?"

I almost expected, "Ben's daughter?" to follow, but he remembered me, apparently warmly. (Okay, I admit I was not always this sassy. I've become increasingly flippant as the years go by. So it's not a total stretch to imagine me as a sweet, desirable, young thing, is it?)

Following the usual niceties, I brought up the purpose of my call. No, he didn't know any Curtis family. "Curtis, Curtis—" and I could visualize him scratching his bald pate — or the yarmulke which crowned it. It took me a long time to explain the situation and what I was looking for. I was beginning to think a personal trip to the Poconos might not be a bad idea, but then Ira said he'd be happy to see what he could dig up for me.

"Really? You sure you don't mind? I mean, I could fly up and check it out myself, but..."

"Oh, no, I'm sure that would be an inconvenience for you. The nearest airport is Scranton, which is 50 minutes by car. It would take about as long to drive as it would to fly and then pick you up. Of course, we'd love to have you. We could put you up in one of the bunkhouses... But no, I don't mind at all. It ought to be interesting, actually. Things are kind of dull around here when camp's not in session. There's only maintenance and a few adult weekend retreats throughout the fall. Say — how's your mother?"

"Fine. Bet it's pretty up there now."

"Well, yes."

"How long do you think it will take?"

"Oh, a day or two. Give me your number."

"Call collect."

"Oh no, I couldn't."

"You're doing me a great favor, Ira."

"For you, Eliza, I'd be happy."

"Thanks, Ira. Talk to you soon."

"Bye."

"Bye." And I hung up.

"For you, Eliza, I'd do anything!" Mickey mocked, making fat, kissy-slurpy noises. "Ira and Eliza sitting in a tree, k-i-s-s-i-n-g," he taunted.

I threw the sofa pillow at him. Drat that speaker button! Stupidest thing they ever did to a telephone.

"Oh, by the way, I forgot to tell you, Darnell shot a hole in the theory that the murderer left a message on Ames's hand," Mickey noted.

"What's Darnell know about Ames's hand?"

"Well, the cops asked him about it. Asked him why his phone number was on there."

"Say what?"

"Yeah. Seems they chopped it off and sent it to the FBI lab to be analyzed."

"Was it hand-delivered?"

"I doubt it was parcel post," Mick snorted. "Anyway, down there they put the thing under ultraviolet and they came up with a whole lot of writing. Seems Tadford was in the habit of writing notes to himself on his hand. One of them was Darnell's phone number."

"How'd he explain that?"

"He claims that when Tadford first started working at PaCo, he didn't have a key or a car, and Darnell told him if he wanted to get in after hours, just call him and he'd pick him up and let him in."

"I bet!"

"Darnell says Ames was always writing things on his hands. That's what he told the cops. So they've pretty much given up on your 'hotdog.' writing."

"Doggone it."

I got a smirk for that one.

That evening I broke down and did the monthly paperwork — book balancing for both the business and myself. Check writing, invoicing, and more check writing. All because Mickey asked me if I wanted to go to see Mother D. with him, and I needed an excuse not to. Maybe having him stay here isn't such a good idea. At any rate, he called around 9:30 to say La Mere had talked him into staying at her place since she had his bed made up and all.

"What an extraordinary idea!" I said.

"Oh, come off it, Eliza. Grow up!"

"I'm throwing your toothbrush away."

He hung up!

I went to the sunroom, turned out the lights, and sat on the rocker. I find it's the best place and way to think when I don't want to scare myself. This is also the spot where I allow myself to talk out loud about what's happening and listen to my own analysis. It helps me to work through things.

"Now let's explore this, Eliza. It appears that your natural manner of communicating is not working. Afterall, you were only kidding with Mickey and he just didn't get it. *You* knew what you meant, why didn't he? This is not a good sign. Mickey, of all people, is supposed to know exactly what you mean."

"Yes, but perhaps things are wearing on him. Maybe he's just tired of all the effort. You know, the effort to keep on keeping on. Dealing with you and your love/hate relationship with Mother D. is a bit much for a guy to have to put up with, on top of everything else. Even for an angel like Mickey D."

"But that's his role, to put up with things. That's what M.D. *does.*"

"Doesn't mean he likes doing it all the time. What do you want him here for, anyway? He just crimps your style. He's messy. He listens in on your phone conversations. You can't walk around with your clothes half off like you normally do."

"Because I just do. It's like having a slumber party. When we were little, the Micker and I would flash messages at night between our bedrooms with a flashlight. Then when Mom and Dad went to bed, we'd meet in between and sleep together on our blankets on the floor, like we were having a slumber party."

"But you're not kids anymore. He can't stay here forever. What's the point?"

"I miss him. I miss him already. I don't want to miss him, so if we do things the same now that we did then, it won't change. It will stay the same forever."

"You're afraid. Afraid of his dying."

"No! He's not dying!"

"He will, though."

A siren wailed nearby. The Doyles' German shepherd started to bark. I got up and crossed to the window. The streetlights shone on the still-wet street below.

"You know what?" I said to myself.

"Hmm?"

"Maybe you *are* a lot like your mother."

Chapter 8
Stacking Shoe Boxes

I went walking in the morning. It was gorgeous: Indian summer warm with a fresh fall flavor. The leaves were turning all kinds of beautiful, with a warm breeze blowing the early curlers off the trees. Winter can't be far behind, I thought, then quashed the idea. Today I'm going to think positively.

What I was really trying to do was think about the case without really thinking about it, you know what I mean? Like letting your mind go blank in order to let truth shine through the cracks; turn off all the lights in the house at night and you can see what's goin' on outside in the dark better. A Zen Buddha kind of thing, I guess.

But it just wasn't working. My mind was blank and still nothing was coming through. Perhaps there's nothing out there.

When blanking out the light doesn't work, and Mickey's not around to bounce ideas off of, I have a third method to examine the facts at hand: computer games. A rousing game or two or three or four of Tetris is a sure bet for loosening up the old creative juices. So I wandered back to the apartment, flicked on my Power Mac, sat down, and proceeded to maneuver tetragons.

Now, Tetris was a game invented by someone who had a small amount of imagination which was channeled into a very prescribed, focused, narrow boundary. The game itself tells you some 30-year-old researcher at a computer center in Moscow came up with it, and they gave the guy the Crest of Lenin or some such thing for bringing all that foreign currency to the U.S.S.R. But I imagine its original inception to have been something like this:

I figure the genesis of the idea came from some poor working slob in a warehouse, say deep in Siberia. It's a shoe warehouse. The workers stand around all day and wait for the shoes to arrive, so they can stack them in the warehouse. And the warehouse is full of shoe boxes, because their distribution system is so screwed up that nothing ever gets where it's supposed to. (This program was written pre-democracy, mind you. Nowadays they've solved all that bureaucratic inefficiency because they all turned into capitalists the minute Yeltsin faced down the tanks in Red Square. Now all it takes is the proper bribe to the Russian Mob to get something done).

But back in '85 or whenever this program was developed, there were few forklifts or modern machinery to stack all those size 12 black boots, you see. So the workers had this pulley system rigged up that grabbed the boxes, hoisted 'em up and then dropped 'em into place, four at a time. (Tetra = four — get it?)

Sometimes the boxes don't land where they're supposed to, and they leave gaps and it's really a mess and everything falls down and you have to clear it out and start all over again. And every once in a while, they actually come and take a load of shoes away so that people can stand in line in the street for their size twelve black boots, whether they need them or want them or not, 'cause that's what's available today and you take what they got or you don't have anything, understand?

Anyway, the warehouse hack stacks these boxes of shoes, four at a time, all day, five days a week, fifty weeks a year, and when he goes home at night, his mind replays shoe box stacking maneuvers in his head, even into his sleep.

So to make a long story shorter, he describes his nightmare to his wife's brother's Red Army pal who recently got sent to computer school in Kiev, and the guy makes a video game out of it, wins the Breast of Brezinsky Award, and sends the poor box stacker a dozen of the software games, none of which can he so much as insert in a floppy drive 'cause he's only seen computers at the library and you have to have a special permit to use 'em.

This game that I imagine was stolen from the shoe stacker's head is the game I play when I need to let the light in. It empties the mind of all thought. I just sit there and maneuver little boxes — four at a time — into stacks on the warehouse floor. If I stack them correctly, they don't pile up real fast. If I get sloppy, they fall on top of each other and I have to start all over again. That's all there is to it. It's wonderful. Serves absolutely no useful purpose. You should try it some time. I'm sure any number of mindless computer games could serve the same purpose.

So anyway, I sit down to Tetris and start playing. Not doing very well. Gaps where I failed to stack the boxes correctly are gathering everywhere, and the boxes are getting closer and closer to the ceiling. But just as the train on the periphery of my imaginary "warehouse" is about to come into the Komsomolskay Metro to haul away some boxes, it comes to me like a veritable avalanche of shoe boxes — *Mr. Marlboro and his homeboys down on Raritan Circle!*

The boxes start to fall faster and I'm losing my pace. *Marlboro Man said something strange. What was that he said?* Another hole;

another. I need four level ones so I can stick them over there in that corner and lower the wall. *He said, "Hey, you shouldn't have brought your sister, Mac...Bad scene. Dangerous for her." Strange he called him Mac, so close to 'Mick,' but I didn't remember Mickey telling him his name. Maybe he calls all white guys "Mac."* I lay in a few lines of boxes real solid, and the threshold lowers. I'm breathing easier. I'm past 10,000 points. *And when Mick asked him if he knew anything about Tadford, the guy said, "Shit, I wouldn't tell them pigs shit!" Not that he didn't know shit, but that he wouldn't tell shit.* And I slam four in a row straight-up instead of sideways in the slot, and in five seconds flat, the shoe warehouse fills up to the brim and entombs me.

I sat back and looked at the screen but only saw the Marlboro Man looking back at me. It was like he was saying, I know what you're up to and I'm on your side. Your secret's safe with me, but take your sister home, would you?

Shit, we gotta go find that dude!

I immediately reached for the phone to call Mickey, dialed his number, then remembered he'd stayed over at La Mere's. I redialed and after the third ring, Mother D. answered. "Hi, Mom. Beautiful day, huh?"

"What's wrong? Are you all right?"

"Nothing's wrong. I just said beautiful day. Micker there?"

"He's sleeping. He really needs to rest, Eliza. This could develop into pneumonia."

"Mickey's a big boy, Mother. He knows when to rest and when he needs to work. We've got an important case. I gotta talk to him."

"He's sick."

"Aw, he's got a simple cold. This one won't kill him, Mother. Not this one."

There was a pause. "You're so — so bloody crass!"

"Ew-ew!" I really hadn't meant to start this. Honest. So I took a deep breath. The morning was clouding over. "Look, Mother, I just want to leave a message, okay?"

She didn't answer for a full ten seconds. "I'll get a pencil," she said quietly, and put down the phone before I could say another word. For Christ's sake, woman! I didn't say I was going to dictate a memo. I counted to fifty, then fifty more. Then—

"Okay. Go ahead."

I took a deep breath and held my temper and the timbre of my voice. "Tell him I think I'm on to something about Ayn. It has to do with Marlboro Man. We're going to have to go find him. Tell him—"

"—Is that Anne with an "E?""

"Jesus, Mother, I'm trying to give you a message! I don't care how you spell it!"

"You don't have to swear. It's not nice and I won't have it."

She's doing this on purpose. She's trying to aggravate me. Stay cool. Stay cool. Don't let her win. "Nevermind, Mother. Just tell him to get up and get dressed. I'll call back in a little bit."

"He really ought to sleep in today."

"I'll call later. Goodbye."

The sweat was standing out on my face. In the Middle Ages, they took people like that and boiled them alive for being scolds. Highly civilized times, the Middle Ages.

I took a deep breath and jogged around the room a few times and then held my face under the cold water faucet in the kitchen. I toweled off and dialed Kasi.

Little Eva answered. "Hi, Eva. Can I speak with your Mommy?"

"She's not answering any more phones," she informed me. I thought she was about to hang up on me.

"Wait, Eva, it's Eliza. Tell your Mommy it's Eliza calling."

"She said no more phones."

"Aw, please just tell her who I am," I pleaded.

"Is Mickey there?"

"No, Mickey's not here right now."

"I want to talk to Mickey," she announced.

Oh, great, I'm being screened out by a four-year-old with a crush on my brother. "Mickey and I will come see you soon, okay? But now I've got to talk to your Mommy. Please?"

"Okay." And she relented, just like that.

A moment later, Kasi came on the phone.

"I just barely got through. She's a tough cookie."

"Yeah, well, everybody's been bugging me. I'm sick of it. I told her not to answer, but she insists Daddy might call..." She sounded tired and depressed.

"I'm sorry. I can only imagine what you're going through. It's just that I was hoping if we reviewed a conversation together, maybe your impressions could help me figure something out."

"Why not? I've got nothing better to do. The dog shrink isn't due until 2:00."

"Dog shr—""

"—A joke. It's a joke."

"Ha-ha. I'm sorry. They're really giving you a hard time, huh?"

"Actually, Lt. Franken is bringing in an expert on dog tracking," Kasi said dryly. "They're brushing the neighborhood for pawprints to see where Marbles has been. Following her droppings would make about as much sense."

"It gives you paws, doesn't it? But you've really got to hand it to them—"

"I've heard them all, Eliza. They don't work any more."

"I'm sorry. Just trying to lighten things up."

"I know, and I appreciate it, but I've had enough." And her voice quivered.

Whoops! I switched gears quickly. "Well, this is serious. And I really hope you can help me."

"Go ahead," she said wearily.

"Remember when we went back out to the car on Raritan Circle after the cops came, and the black guys that were hanging around by the car said something to us as we were crossing the street?"

"Yeah. They thought Ayn was Mickey's sister."

"Yeah, well, that's because that's what Mickey told them earlier to get them to look after her instead of *at* her while we were inside, you know?"

"Oh, yeah, I see. I must have missed that part."

"You were a little preoccupied at the time — anxious to find J/J."

"Fools rush in..."

"Don't be hard on yourself. I'd have done the same. But what I've been flashing on was what the one dude said, and how he said it. He called Mick 'Mac,' and then he said he'd keep what he knew to himself. Do you remember that?"

"I don't remember the guy calling him 'Mac,'" Kasi sounded dubious.

"Don't you remember? He said, 'You shouldn't have brought your sister, Mac. This is a bad scene...'"

"No, that's not how I heard it," Kasi countered. "In fact, I re-member it because what he said confused me at the time. That and the 'sister' comment. But I just figured I'd missed something. I thought he said, 'You shouldn't have brought your sister back.' 'Back,' not 'Mac.' That's what confused me."

"Back? My god! Are you sure?"

"Yeah, that's what I thought he said. I was wondering why he said 'back' and why he said 'sister,' but then—"

106

"—You've got it! You've got it! 'You shouldn't have brought your sister back.' That means she was there before, don't you see? He must have seen Ayn there before!" I was doing a joyous little clogging step by the phone.

"You mean she'd been there already? You mean she already knew that—"

"I don't know how much she knew. But I'm going to check into it. Something's not adding up. Maybe there's another explanation. Maybe we're putting it together all wrong, but we've got somewhere to go with it now," I enthused. "You've been a great help, Kasi. Sometimes a different point of view makes all the difference!"

"Well, I guess." She didn't sound all together happy with her discovery, and I couldn't blame her, but it might take the wandering J/J off the hook. Who knows? We still didn't know if this Ayn was legitimate or not. Maybe she had more to offer us about the death of Ames than the mere identification of his remains. I said my parting thanks to Kasi and hung up.

Time to round up Mickey D. and go do some real sleuthing!

So five minutes later I'm tooling down Route 320 on my way to see Mickey, with Ayn and that strange roommate of hers on my mind, when I hear a siren, glance down, and see I'm doing 52, maybe 53 in a 35 zone. Shit! I pull over, take my license out of my pocketbook, and have it hanging out the window on the end of my hand when the officer steps up to the car. We all know the routine, right?

"You know why I stopped you, ma'am?"

"Yes sir."

"You were going 54 in a—"

"—Yeah, I know." So sue me.

He stands there for a minute, like I've really ruined his script. He's supposed to ask for my license, but there it is staring him in the face already. Drives them crazy. This guy looks a little old to be doing traffic stops. Usually they're on the desk or in investigations at his age. Finally, he takes it, affixes it to his clipboard, and peruses it. "Eliza Daniels." (It was good for five years when I got it, almost four years ago, and so still has my maiden name on it. Some day I'll get around to changing my name back, so why bother changing all the official stuff when I'll just have to change it back?)

"Ain't you Roderick's little girl?"

I looked a little closer. Well, what do you know? "That you, Snuffer? Snuffer Jefferson?"

"That's right."

"How you doing, Mr. Jefferson?" and we shook hands. Damn, I never would have recognized the man if he hadn't spoken up. He looked a lifetime older than I remembered him as a kid. Snuffer was in the Phily P.D. with Dad back in the day. Somehow he got caught up in whatever brought Dad down some fifteen years ago, and soon after Dad's death, they dropped the investigation, but Snuffer got demoted to traffic patrol and ended up quitting the P.P.D. when they leaned on him too hard. By gosh, here he is, still at it, trying to make pension, but now with the Springfield Township Police.

"Gonna retire next year, 'Liza," he said, pursing his lips into a pink double line and soberly shaking his head.

"Good for you, Snuffer, good for you. You deserve it."

"You doin' okay?" He looked at me real serious, like I better tell the truth, now.

"We're doin' fine, Snuffer."

"Your Mama?"

"She's fine, thank you."

"That's good. That's good." And he nodded his head as though he were remembering something sad, looking from me to the picture on my license. "You have a good day, 'Liza," he said finally, handing me back my card with hands as leathery and dark as his boots. And he ventured a smile, but the eyes behind it were full and sad.

"Thanks, Snuffer. You take care, now." And I started the engine.

Jefferson turned as if to go back to his patrol car, then swiveled around and looked me in the eyes. "He didn't do it, 'Liza. You remember that."

"Yes sir, I know," I said, real quiet. "Thank you."

And he turned and walked away.

I tried not to think of the blood visions in that basement from half a lifetime ago that welled up suddenly in front of my eyes. "Snuffer Jefferson," I said, over and over to myself. "Snuffer's made it to retirement. Snuffer's gonna retire. He said he didn't do it. Dad didn't do what they accused him of. He didn't do it. He didn't do it." The mantra got me to Mother D.'s.

108

I practically ran in the front door. Mom was dusting the knick-knack shelf in the foyer, and I almost plowed into her. "Oh, hi! Where's Mickey?"

"Ftt!" she blurted.

"Sorry, didn't mean to startle you. We had a break in the case. We've got to go see Ayn Curtis. Where is he?"

"He's resting," she said, and returned to her dusting. I swear there's not a speck of dust on those shelves. Never has been. Dust is on a perpetual circling and hovering pattern in this house. And it will never be cleared for landing.

"Well, he can't rest now," I declared, brushing by her. "He's not still in bed, is he?" and I started toward the stairs.

"You are *not* taking him out of here!" she exclaimed in a shrill voice, dropping her feather duster and rushing ahead of me.

"Mother, this is ridiculous, we have work to do!"

"*You* do it. Mickey needs to rest," she said, standing like a sentry at the bottom of the stairs, a hand on either banister.

"Mickey is my partner. I need him to help me with this case. Life does not stop because one gets a cold," I snapped. "Every time he coughs, every time he sneezes, you can't protect him," I hissed. "He's a grown man. He can make his own decisions. And he needs to work while he can," and I tried to extract her fingers, curled tightly around the balustrade.

"You! What do *you* know!" she shrieked, instantly passing the line into hysteria. "You've never been sick in your life! You've always had your way with everything. You don't like your courses, you change majors; you don't like jobs, you change careers; you don't like a husband, you dump him! Always changing, always having things your way, always running the show, running away from everything!" She was standing there, trembling, her hands tightly gripping the oak banisters, knuckles as white as Mickey's corpuscles, face red as blood.

I stood there watching her, and ceased to understand what she was saying. I knew only that she was livid with rage at me. Just like when Dad died. I'd found him in the basement, a bullet in his brain, a gun by his side. In horror and disbelief I finally climbed that long, dark, steeper-than-hell climb to the kitchen, and when I blurted out the news, she slapped me and screamed, "No! How could you! How *could* you!" As though *I* had killed him.

Funny, that's when *I* started blaming *her*.

Does she want to blame me now for Mickey, too? No, you're just the messenger, I kept telling myself. Like Rosencrantz and Guildenstern in Henry IV, she wants to kill the messenger to kill the message. You were the messenger when Dad died, and now you are your brother's mirror and his keeper.

We just stood there, glaring at each other, blue eyes sparking enough to set the room on fire; aristocratic features — chins and eyebrows and aquiline noses, jutting out all over the place like armor against the fray. Finally, down the stairs behind her, came Mickey D. She started at the touch of his hand on her shoulder, then seemed to almost physically melt before my eyes as he forcefully but gently unpried her fingers and walked her slowly up the stairs, cautioning me with a warning look and pursed, dry lips, not to come upstairs.

I went outside, out back to the old stone wellhouse, and sat down on the mossy patch made by its shade. I put my hands on the green softness and caressed it like a baby's velvety cheek. I swore. I cursed. I screamed inside. I argued with her and with myself. It's possible I may have cried.

It seemed like hours, but he finally came and sat down behind me, back-to-back, like we did when we were kids. His back is three inches taller now than my 5'10" frame. At some point in our adolescence, he grew when I wasn't watching. Taller. Stronger. Wiser. Kinder. Adversity makes some people grow. Others it makes ornery, like my mother. And yes, maybe, sometimes, like me.

If Mick and I had a pushing match now like we used to when we were kids, the moss beneath our shoes would not be torn, because he could easily bowl me over before I could dig in my heels. Still, thank god, still.

We said nothing for a long, long time, just touched, back-to-back, each stroking the moss beneath our hands silently.

"She needs a whipping boy, Eliza," he said finally.

I pretended to ignore him, rocking gently, patting the cold earth.

"When the crown princes were young, they sometimes needed to be disciplined, like any other child," he said in a story-teller's voice. "But you can't whip a prince or a king. He is the embodiment of god on earth, afterall. And besides, he's going to grow up to be king, and then where does that leave *you* if you've whipped him as a child? So they had a whipping boy — a peasant lad, a servant. And he would take the prince's beatings when the prince misbehaved. You are the whipping boy Mom has selected for me. She feels she can't confront me with my illness or my sexuality, but she must confront someone. So she picked you as the whipping boy. Because you're strong. Because you can take it," he said.

I did not answer.

"I told her that," he continued. "I told her she should stop punishing you. But she won't listen. She denied she was punishing anyone. She said she only wants to make sure I get well quickly."

"See no evil, hear no evil, smell no evil," I intoned.

"The ancient Jews had a whipping boy, too — a scapegoat," Mickey mused. "The high priest would confess the sins of the people over the head of the goat on the Day of Atonement."

"So I'm a sacrificial lamb, hey?"

"No, the scapegoat gets away," he said.

"What, no bloodletting?"

"The scapegoat is released. On the Day of Atonement, he escapes punishment. That's where the word comes from. He escapes. They let him go. He's only a symbol of suffering, like the whipping boy. He is innocent of other's sins. She's harsh with you because she knows you're going to get away. She needs a scapegoat in order to forgive me for being sick — for making her afraid."

And the echo of his words said, I'm not going to get away. I'm not going to get away.

It's only 11:30 a.m. and I've been on an emotional roller coaster all morning that's had more dips and curves than anything we road at Palisades Park when we were kids. "Look, can we please get out of here? We have to talk about the case," I said.

"Yes. Mom's in bed. I told her I was leaving for now. She'll just have to deal with it."

"Thank god!" And we pulled each other up off the ground.

When we were seated at Pedro's Mexican Restaurant, I filled Mick in on my conversation with Kasi.

"Huh!" he exclaimed when I was finished.

"Can't you do better than that?" I groused, stuffing in another mouthful of chimichanga.

"Not until I get some water. The jalapeño in my tostada has opened up my sinuses like a drill up my nose." He motioned to a waitress, who came and filled our water glasses. M.D. blew his nose.

"Ayn obviously lied about running out of gas," Mickey D. noted, stuffing his ever-present handkerchief back in his pocket. "And she was so different from the day before, when we first met her," he mused. "It was obviously more than the nervous anticipation of seeing her father after all this time."

111

"And she must have been at Raritan Circle before, from what The Marlboro Man inferred."

"Maybe. That would explain her reluctance to go in the building."

"And maybe why she was late?"

"Maybe." He was chewing on a toothpick.

"Do you think she could have known in advance that he was dead? Her reaction to seeing the body was almost — well, eerie," I offered.

"Hmm."

"She was genuinely upset," I allowed.

"No doubt about it," Mickey agreed. "She was admittedly dating the guy. It *is* rather upsetting to see your boyfriend and possibly lover lying there with a bullet through the brain," he said dryly.

Seeing the scene had upset *me*, I know. Gave me wicked flashbacks that crept into my dreams two night running. "We're not getting anywhere," I concluded. "I think we need to confront Ayn," I opined.

"Yeah," Mickey D. said glumly. Obviously, neither one of us was excited about the prospect.

"Maybe we should go find The Marlboro Man and Malcolm X Jr. and Sad Sack for more information," I suggested.

"You think so?" Mickey looked dubious. "Maybe we can get something out of her by just confronting her."

We sat in silence for several minutes, mulling the situation, as the waitress left the check, collected the business credit card, had Mickey D. sign the receipt, and then deposited two little foil-wrapped mints on a plate between us, and left. I was watching an Hispanic couple in the next table, as the man pinned a corsage on the woman's dress.

I turned to Mickey D. and said, "Let's take her some flowers."

"What?"

"Some flowers. Her boyfriend just got killed. Isn't that an official occasion for flowers?"

"You mean butter her up?"

"I mean be her friend. Console her in her time of need."

"What about Chakra?"

"Chakra can console herself."

"Eliza!" and he threw a napkin at me.

I rang the bell. Through the windowpane over the door, I could see Chakra approaching. "Shit," I muttered under my breath.

112

"Damn," Mickey D. agreed.

She peered at us, opened the door three inches and said, "Hello. This is very nice of you. But Ayn is resting. I will take them for her." And she reached out for the roses.

Mickey D. pulled back. The young woman was drawn out a step. The door opened wider. "We'd like to see Ayn, see how she's doing," I said in my sweet voice.

"I'm sorry, she is quite distraught. The police have been calling. The doctor gave her a sedative. She must rest. I will tell her that you called." And she reached again for the flowers. I wished now I had them. I would have given her the flowers right where it counts. But Mickey D. has more self control than I.

"We need to talk to her," Mickey D. explained. "We have some information I think she should know before the police start to question her about it."

I thought I detected movement in the foyer behind Chakra. "Ayn?" I called, taking a step forward and peering into the shadows.

Chakra tried to block my way. "She must sleep. The doctor says she's had too much—"

"—Ayn? We'd like to talk to you about Tadford."

Just a moment's hesitation, and she stepped into the light. "It's okay, Chakra," said Ayn, putting a hand on her roommate's shoulder. The girl immediately relinquished her guard post, though her eyes remained wary.

As Chakra stepped back, Ayn and Mickey D. stepped toward one another, and the bouquet of flowers more or less collided with her outstretched hand. "Ouch! Why thank you! Ouch!" She was simultaneously grimacing and smiling.

"Oh, I'm sorry! The thorns!" Mickey D. apologized, and reached into his back pocket for a clean handkerchief.

When I see blood and Mickey D. in the same space, my brain gives this bizarre intercept command. I saw him reaching for his handkerchief, and the drop of blood on the end of Ayn's thumb, and my body completed my brain's maneuver. I somehow managed to slip the handkerchief out of M.D.'s hand and press it into Ayn's, all in one movement. When I dared look, Mickey D. was standing there with his mouth open, a mixture of surprise and a fair dose of disappointed hurt on his face. I had to look away quickly. "Here, I'll take that," I said, as Ayn rather clumsily juggled the flowers and the soiled handkerchief. And I stuffed it quickly into the back pocket of my corduroy skirt to hide the incident from view, if not memory. "We should have gotten gladiolus or irises," I apologized.

"Oh, that's okay, these are lovely," Ayn said, putting thumb to teeth and sucking sharply. "You shouldn't have," she smiled warily.

"Ayn *is* tired," Chakra piped up from behind Ayn. "The doctor said—"

"—What was it you wanted to tell me?" Ayn asked, backing up just a little so we were able to squeeze into the foyer. "I've told the police everything. Twice."

"They've been here, then?" Mickey D. asked.

"This morning, yes."

"Did they tell you anything? Any clues they might have on the killer?" Mickey prodded gently.

"Killer? Why, he killed himself!" she said, valiantly attempting a look of disbelief.

"Ayn, you should—"

"—Not now, Chakra," Ayn cut her off. "Would you take these, please?" And she handed her the roses.

"Ow!" Chakra exclaimed as she received them.

Mickey D. almost laughed out loud, caught himself and turned it into a cough. I patted him on the back solicitously as he played it to the hilt. "Maybe a drink of water?" I suggested.

"Why don't you come sit down in the living room?" Ayn offered. "Chakra, could you bring Mr. Daniels—"

"—Mickey," said Mickey.

"Could you bring Mickey and Eliza—"

"Ms. Samuels," I said. Why not draw some good cop/bad cop lines right off the bat? Nevermind that we were all chummy yesterday. I want her to think we know more than we do, and we're upset at what we know. Besides, I'm better at the bad cop routine.

Ayn glanced quickly at me, then away. "Why not iced tea for our guests?" she asked weakly as Chakra disappeared rather brusquely into the kitchen and we followed Ayn into the living room. She moved a bit stiffly and awkwardly, as though parts of her needed oiling.

"Chakra said you weren't feeling well?" I prompted.

"Just a little sore," she said, seating herself in an overstuffed chair and motioning for us to take the opposing couch. "I must have pulled a muscle in my neck when I was hunched over the engine the other day, trying to figure out why the car had stopped. And all the time it's out of gas!" She laughed a patently fake chuckle. Very bad acting, I thought, exchanging glances with Mickey D.

Now's the time to zap her. "You didn't run out of gas, did you, Ayn?" I attacked, standing over her. Mickey had taken his designated seat.

She started, her hand leaping to her neck as though she wanted to protect it. Then she got ahold of herself, and the high, chiseled cheekbones seemed to acquire definition as her facial muscles tightened. "What do you mean? I told you that's why I was late."

"And yet you got gas that very morning, didn't you, Ayn? At least $10 worth. Mr. Daniels saw your car wash ticket."

"Oh, that!" she exclaimed, her hands suddenly expressive. "Chakra got gas in *her* car," she almost gushed. "She gave me the ticket because my car was so dirty, but I didn't get a chance to use it!"

I almost blurted, "You mean she doesn't wash it *for* you?" But I caught myself. Just then Chakra entered with a tray of glasses filled with iced tea.

Mickey D. smiled, took a glass, and drank. "Thanks, I needed that," he said. The woman actually smiled in return.

She came to where I was standing and offered me a glass. "No thank you," I said.

"Why don't you have a seat?" she suggested.

"I'd rather stand," I replied. She lowered her head like a geisha girl bowing slightly to a client, then offered a glass to Ayn, who accepted. Finally she placed the tray on the coffee table and went to stand at my back, by the window facing the street.

Now where were we? "Mr. Ames did not kill himself, Ayn," I said matter-of-factly. "And I'm sure you know that." I paced to the opposite side of the coffee table and turned so that my back was no longer to Chakra.

"I don't know what you're talking about. His gun was right there beside him," she said plaintively.

"How do you know it was his gun?" I prodded.

"The police said so. They told me it was registered in his name."

"In which name?"

"Why, Tadford Ames, of course!"

"Did you know Tadford Ames died over 35 years ago?"

"What?" She truly looked startled.

"The real Tadford Ames died when he was three," I said. "The man you knew as Ames took his identity."

"Why would he do that?" she asked, putting the glass down, untouched, hard on the coffee table. A few drops slopped over the edge and down the side of the tumbler.

"That's what we were wondering," I said, standing right over her.

"I don't understand," she said, quite obviously flustered.

I glanced at Mickey D. for help. He took the ball. "There's another problem, Ayn," he said gently.

She just stared at him, a wary, hunted look in her dark eyes.

"You were at Raritan Circle before we took you there."

She blinked, grimaced and recovered quickly. "No I wasn't. I'd never been there before in my life." She began to rub her neck under the high turtleneck and to stare at a spot just to the right of Mickey D.'s head.

"Do you see now why it's important you tell us the truth?" I prodded. "The police will come asking you soon."

"Asking her what?" Chakra said, moving from behind the chair. "She barely dated the guy. Twice. Right, Ayn?"

Ayn was still looking off into space.

"Right?" she repeated.

"Right," Ayn said, finally focusing. "I didn't see him Saturday," she affirmed. "I swear. In the morning I went grocery shopping. We had lunch, right?" she looked at her roommate for support.

"Rice and beans," Chakra added.

"Banana cake," Ayn added, really getting into it.

"Right."

"Then I studied my Intro to Crim and left for our meeting," she added. "And I ran out of gas," she insisted, looking straight at Mickey D. Her gaze did not waver.

"I know you're under a lot of stress, Ayn," Mickey offered sympathetically. "It's been hard to deal with your mother's death and your father's re-emergence and Tadford's—"

"—I don't know anything about his death!" she said sharply. "I told you, I know nothing!" And the hand went to the neck again.

"I think you'd better leave," Chakra suggested strongly, moving toward the door with her outstretched hand showing us the way we should go.

"I didn't mean to upset you, Ayn," Mickey D. tried again, but she only turned her head away from him. Her lower lip was trembling. I caught Mickey's eyes, and tipped my head in Chakra's direction.

"I hope you feel better, Ayn," I offered.

"Yes, I hope you feel better," M.D. echoed. And Chakra showed us to the door, shutting it behind us sharply, without a word.

We were halfway down the block, Mickey D. driving, when he finally said, "Well?"

"Guilty," I affirmed.

"Of what? Covering it up?"

"Or doing it," I offered.

"No..." he said, albeit doubtfully.

"Well, she was there. She knew he was dead. Maybe she knew because she killed him."

"She just doesn't seem—"

"—Like the type to kill? What's the type that kills? You of all people... I can't believe you! You saw that fear in her eyes!"

"Fear, yes; confusion, yes; guilt...I don't think so."

"Oh, come on, you're just a bleeding heart."

"I don't know, there was something about her. She knows something she's not telling us, there's no doubt about that, but to have killed him and then tried to set it up as a suicide? Why?"

"I don't know. That's what we have to find out."

"Aren't we getting off the beaten track here a little bit?" M.D. asked. "Aren't we supposed to be finding Kasi's husband, not Tadford's murderer?"

"Well, until this morning, I thought they were one and the same. Right now I'm not sure. The question is how to prove that."

We sat in the office. Mickey D. was making one more reluctant call to Darnell Pigeon.

"No, Darnell, I can't meet you for lunch," he said, eyes seeking the ceiling above the desk as I sat in my swivel chair sipping a Diet Coke. "I've got to get to the bottom of this thing with Tadford. I need to know who tipped him as to Jack Curtis's supposed whereabouts — the caller who sent him off to the sad side of town." He shuffled his feet under the desk, obviously listening to Darnell's reply.

"Yeah. You heard the tape, right? To get the address?" More toe tapping.

"Aw, damn! They took it?" A disgusted look; a sigh.

"Really? All right!" He put his hand over the receiver and whispered to me, "He wrote it down. He's got the name and phone number of the informant!"

Back to Darnell. "Give it to me, man." And he scribbled what Darnell told him on the pad he carries in his back pocket. "All right! Thanks, man! I owe you big." More toe tapping.

"Not *that* big, Darnell," he said, his all-American face flushing red. "How 'bout *basket*ball? You like the Sixers? I'll send you tickets." Eyes to the ceiling once more. "And Flyers. Yeah. Okay. You drive a hard bargain, man. Catch you later." And he hung up.

"The guy wanted blood," he groused as he popped a top on a Coke.

"Should have given it to him," I snickered.

"You're sick." And he curled his lower lip at me.

"I know," I smiled.

"But it's your turn," he smirked, handing me the pad.

"Marcquita Smith. 555-6030," I read. Great.

It took fifteen minutes of dialing, but the busy signal finally turned to a ring. "Mrs. Smith? My name is Eliza Samuels of Samuels & Daniels, Private Investigators."

"I done already told them cops everything."

"We're not police, Mrs. Smith. We're private investigators. We were hired by the wife of the missing man to find him."

"I thought the wife was dead. TV said she dead. Was the daughter what was looking for him."

"This is a different wife," I explained.

"What you mean, different wife?"

"The show on TV was with a daughter from a previous marriage. Mr. Curtis has left two families."

"My old man done the same thing."

"Then you know how she must feel, Mrs. Smith."

"It ain't 'Mrs.' Didn't marry the asshole."

"Well good for you! You were smarter than me and Mrs. Short — she's the second wife, you know — we both married *our* assholes."

Mickey D. snickered into a bag of cheese popcorn. I kicked the desk he was sitting at.

"Can I call you Marcquita?" Reminds me of a banana. And I began to unpeel Marcquita's defenses, one by one. Soon she was telling me how many times her old man left her and came back, how he never took care of her and their kids, how many girlfriends he had on the side, and what she intended to do to him next time he crossed her path.

"Did Mr. Curtis have girlfriends over to his place?" I interjected.

"Naw. Never saw him with nobody," she allowed. "Real quiet. Never heard a peep. Rented to him four weeks ago. I'm the super, you know."

"Oh, is that right?"

"Yep. He paid in cash, first month and last. Got a security deposit out of him, too. Least that's what I call it. Not exactly a security deposit. Owner doesn't require it. But it comes in handy, you know?" Then she paused. "That's between you and me, right?"

"Oh, absolutely. Who's to know?"

"Nobody now, I guess, huh?" and she cackled.

"What did Mr. Curtis look like? Was he like the guy on TV?"

"Well, that's the funny thing. We was watching that show on Wednesday, and Terrance — that's my oldest, he's ten — he says, 'That's the honk— er, white guy — in 1B.' I says, 'Hell, you say!' but he insists. Does sort of favor him a bit, I think, but he's a lot older than that." She chuckled. "Then I said to myself, 'Marcquita, you stupid, girl! Course he's older. That pictures gotta be ten year old!'" She laughed self-deprecatingly. I chuckled for support.

"Well, by then his rent was due again (we go by the actual day, you know), so I decide I'm gonna collect it in person and get another look at that there fella. He been so quiet, we almost never hear from him. Goes in and out and that's that."

"So you went to his apartment?"

"Damn right! Took me a few days to catch him, though. He's out a lot, and when he's in, he don't answer the door. Finally on Friday I yells through the door, 'This is Ms. Smith. I come for the rent,' and he opens the door. And Lordy, there he is standing there without a shirt on, ya know? And there's the scar on his arm they mentioned on TV!" she crowed triumphantly. "So I'm real cool, I just tell him I need his rent, and he gives me it, in cash, and that's it. I go and call the number they gave on the show about tips and you know the rest. Then that poor TV man got killed. They say could be suicide, but I ain't no fool. Don't sound like suicide to me! And to think I was living right down the hall from him all this time! You're not safe anymore in your own home. Used to be this neighborhood was something to be proud of."

"It's a shame," I agreed. "Did you see Mr. Curtis the day Mr. Ames was killed?"

"Naw, I was busy. My youngest's got the chicken pox and my knee went out on me again."

"You didn't see Mr. Ames before he died?"

"Naw, didn't see nothing."

119

"How about the young lady on the TV show — Mr. Curtis's daughter, Ayn?"

"Seen her on TV. Pretty thing, ain't she?"

"Yes, she is."

"What a shame to have a daddy like that."

"Yes, it is," I allowed. "Did you hear the gunshot?"

"No, I don't think so. The TV was on. There's loud noises all the time 'round here. Could kill somebody in the next room and I wouldn't notice." And she chuckled, sickly amused. "Guess that's what happened, huh?" The laugh changed suddenly into something more doubtful, nervous.

"Did Mr. Curtis have any company while he was living there? Any guests?"

"Nope. Kept to himself."

"How'd he get around? Did he take the bus?"

"Had a car when he first came, but it disappeared quick. First I thought it got ripped off, then I heard he sold it to Larry what runs the chop shop over on Sabin. Be long gone by now, in little bitty pieces, all over the place." And she laughed. Just about everything tickled this woman. Well, so much for Kasi's Toyota.

"Well, thank you very much for your help, Marcquita. Hope you feel better."

"Who did you say you was, now?"

"Eliza Samuels. I'm a friend of Mr. Curtis's daughter."

"Oh. Okay. Goodbye." And on that disjointed note, we hung up.

"It was our man," I told Mickey D. "She saw the scar. He paid the rent in cash and he sold Kasi's car to a chop shop."

"She didn't see Ayn or Ames?"

"Saw nothing, heard nothing."

"I bet we'd get the same story from all the other tenants."

"You better believe the cops have already tried. You know, we've got to go back there," I added.

"Yeah," Mickey agreed glumly. "Let's go!" And he snatched the car keys from the desk.

It was a lot easier finding Raritan Circle the second time around, especially without Kasi feeding erroneous directions in my ear. But

120

when Mickey pulled up in front of number 939, the street was deserted. We parked behind a stripped car. Even its fenders and taillights were gone. "What now?" I asked.

"Hey, it was your bright idea."

"That's not fair!"

"Well, how the hell are we supposed to find these dudes? Do we go knock on a door and ask for 'The Marlboro Man,' as you so quaintly call him? How about 'Malcolm X Jr.?' Like to see you asking after him!"

"Well, do you have a better idea?"

"Hey, got a light?"

Mickey D. practically hit his head on the car roof, and I instinctively grabbed for my gun. But there's Marlboro Man, bent over, one hand resting on Mickey's half-open window.

"Jeez, you scared me, man. Where'd you come from?" Mickey D. panted, his hand to his chest. I glanced around. The door to the "abandoned" car was open. I looked back at M.D. He'd changed the chest grab into a motion of patting at his shirt pocket. "No, sorry, I'm all out. You got any, Eliza?"

"No." Like he's not perfectly aware I wouldn't touch a cigarette if it puffed Channel Number 5 when you lit it.

Mickey D. moved to open the door and get out. I did the same. "Here," Mick said, reaching into his pocket and extracting a twenty. "Buy some. You helped us out yesterday."

Marlboroless Man stuffed it in his pocket and nodded. "Your sister okay?"

Mickey D. glanced at me. "Yeah," he said doubtfully.

"No, the other one, man."

"The other – oh, *Ayn!*" And his face lit up like the sun hadn't been out all along. "You know, I been wanting to talk to you about that. Saturday things were kind of hectic, you know?"

"Once you come out, I split, man. Ain't no pig askin' me none of *my* business," Marlboro scraped his sneaker around the outline of a large pothole. With his charcoal eyes downcast, he was innocent, almost baby-faced. It was when you saw his eyes that the wary threat inside them — a protective wall of deep distance — frightened you and caused you to disregard whatever else you had seen. At his sudden revelation of vulnerability, I felt an uncharacteristic urge to reach out and touch him. Then he looked up. "Gotta go, man," he said, suddenly hard once more, and I pulled back.

"Wait!" Mick said. "I'm worried about my sister."

"I ain't tellin' nothing," he promised as he turned away.

"Can you tell *me*? Tell me what you saw so I can protect her!" Mick pleaded. "She won't talk. She's afraid."

He paused, turned his body half-way, looked us up and down.

"Did you see the man that took the apartment — the white guy that used to drive the Toyota — come out or go in on Saturday?" Mickey said it fast like he was on a timer.

"I was copping Z's in my V."

"Your V?" I asked.

"Vehicle."

"So you didn't see the man that was living here — the one that was on TV as missing — you didn't see him that day?"

He shook his head no.

"What about my sister and the man who was killed?" Mickey asked.

"Saw both of them go in," Marlboro allowed. "Saw her come out." Question time over. He turned and walked away, slamming the door of the vandalized vehicle as he passed.

"Oh boy!" I said as Mickey drove us away. "Oh boy!"

"She's no cold-blooded killer," Mickey D. argued.

"Warm-blooded, cold-blooded, what's the difference?"

"A lot."

"A bullet through the temple is not warm."

"We've got to go see her again, you know," Mick declared.

"I think I'd rather go visit Mom," I mumbled.

"Oh, my Lord," Mickey D. exclaimed. "It can't be that bad!"

"Yep."

"I thought you liked playing bad cop," he sneered.

"Must be getting old," I mumbled. I mean, look how close I came to hugging that kid back there. Wouldn't that have been a hoot! Old Mrs. D. would have called for an exorcism if she'd seen that. And her Presbyterian persuasian doesn't allow for things like possession.

We were closing in on Ayn's neighborhood. "Just one thing I want to know," I said.

"What's that?"

"Is this getting us any closer to finding J/J?"

"Doesn't feel like it, does it?" Mickey agreed.

"Nope."

"You think Kasi's good for this?" Mick looked across at me. "I mean, if it doesn't lead to anything as far as her husband's concerned?"

"Hope so."

"I thought you were going to get a deposit," Mickey accused.

"I forgot."

"Forgot?"

"Well, why do I always have to do the paperwork?"

"That's not paperwork, it's negotiating," he scoffed. "It's good business."

"I didn't get a degree in business," I complained.

"Obviously not."

"Well, you do the negotiating, then. You do the paperwork. I'm fed up with it!" And I sulked the rest of the way to Ayn's.

So I was in a real foul mood by the time we pulled up about half a block shy of the apartment. Mickey wasn't exactly jolly, either. We both slammed the doors extra hard.

"My God!" Twice in one day, the people we want to see come directly to us. I pointed up the street. There was Ayn, walking down the sidewalk toward us, her hands bunched up inside the front pouch of her pullover sweatshirt. She glanced up and a wild, hunted look was in her eyes.

"Ayn! What a surprise! We were just coming to see you again," I said, giving her my most reassuring smile as I felt for the gun at my side. If she killed once.... I released the safety.

"I was just going for a walk. I had to think, you know?"

"Yeah?" Mickey D. and I waited. She was looking at the ground now, at the car, anywhere but at us. But she stood there, hands still working in the pouch, out of view.

I was ready to draw if necessary. My eyes never left that bulge where her hand disappeared into her sweatshirt pocket. Mickey D. had come around to the end of the car, between the two of us, but off to the side. I took another step forward. Well, it has to be said. "We know you did it, Ayn," I said softly, my hand grasping the grip of my revolver.

She blinked, her mouth slightly open. Her hands dropped to her side. A balled-up tissue fell from her right hand. I expelled the breath I'd been holding. "You were there, Ayn. We have a witness who saw both you and Tadford go in, and only you come out. Do you want to tell us about it?"

And the dam gave way. "I d-didn't m-mean to do it!" she gasped. "I didn't mean it. He was trying to kill me! I swear!" And she virtually collapsed onto the sidewalk, heaving deep, wracking sobs of pain.

Mickey D. rushed forward and propped her up in a seated position. I rather stupidly stood there looking down at them. "Eliza!" Mickey ordered.

"What? What?" I have no idea what to do in the face of such unbridled raw emotion.

Micki glanced back over his shoulder. We were next to a triangular wedge of green — one of the city's little mini parks. It had a few concrete benches and a goldfish pond shaded by two large willow trees. "Over there," Mickey directed. "Here, help me. Upsy-daisy, Ayn!" And he lifted her bodily from behind as I tried ineffectually to boost her from the front. He hissed in my ear, "I do *not* want to have to go back to that house!"

I nodded in agreement. If we could keep her away from Chakra, we would undoubtedly get more answers. We managed to cart the limp and moaning form 200 feet to a bench and prop her up on it with her back against a light standard. I sat next to her and inanely repeated, "Now, now," and Mickey D. crouched in front of her.

She seemed to have gone into some sort of shock, as though the verbal acknowledgment of the act had released a flood of overwhelming emotions. Soon she settled into a deep drone, rocking slowly and moaning, tears making tiny rivulets down her cheeks and onto her sweatpants.

Mickey D. handed her one of his handkerchiefs. "Tell us about it, Ayn," he coaxed.

She moaned some more, rocked some more, cried some more. And then she began to talk. "I killed him," she said, and looked at Mickey D. for a reaction.

He patted her knee. "Tell us about it," he prompted.

She bit her lip, gasped several times, as though struggling to catch her breath after rising from a great depth underwater, and then she began, pausing now and then to rock herself and swipe at the tears which coursed down her cheeks.

Ames had called her up Saturday about noon. He was so excited he practically screamed into the phone in his thick accent, "I've found him! I've found your father! I know where he is! I'm going to my suite for a camera. Pick me up there in twenty minutes!" And he hung up before she could even think, much less respond.

She didn't know what to do. She didn't really want to see her father — not like that, not by surprise. She'd waited ten years for this. She wanted to be ready for it, prepared. She needed more than twenty minutes to organize herself. But this was Tadford calling her. He'd been so nice, so solicitous. And now he was so excited — for her! Tadford would make sure everything was okay. So she quickly told Chakra where she was going, jumped in the car, and took off.

When she picked Ames up at the Embassy Suites, he was practically jumping up and down, his enthusiasm was so great.

"How do we do this? I'm nervous," she confided.

He was dismissive of her fears. "Don't worry, don't worry, I'll take care of everything. When he sees you it will all be resolved. Just wait!" And he told her to scoot over and he got in and raced through the streets of Southeast Phily, driving like he was in a Hollywood car chase scene. She pleaded with him to slow down but he ignored her. He hardly seemed to acknowledge that she was there, intent only on getting to the apartment and catching J/J.

"What if he runs? Shouldn't we call the police? Don't you take a film crew to cover stuff like this?"

But he waved away her protestations. "There will be plenty of time for that. Once he sees you he'll know he's been caught. Don't worry."

"Caught" wasn't quite the word that described what she wanted for her father. Identified, discovered, located, yes. But what do you do with him if you "catch" him? She hadn't thought this far in the process. "But I don't want to see him like this!" she wailed.

"Don't be silly! You've been waiting half your life for this," he looked at her as though she were crazy.

They finally pulled up near the building and he signaled her to follow behind him. "Where's your camera?" she asked.

"In here," he said, patting his windbreaker.

They entered the foyer. "Stay here," he hissed, holding her firmly with one hand against the entrance wall. With his other hand he withdrew a revolver from inside his windbreaker.

"What are you doing!" she blurted.

"Shh!" he clapped a trembling hand to her mouth and rasped in her ear, "We have to take him by surprise. He may be armed. I don't want either of us to get shot." He removed the hand slowly, cautiously from her mouth, put a finger to his lips and whispered, "I'm going to make sure he's not armed first, then you can come in. Stay here!"

She looked around her with panic, thinking, what should I do, what should I do? Tadford's gone crazy. But she stayed there. "I stayed there," she moaned softly to herself. "I don't know why, but I just couldn't make myself move." And she cried quietly.

"That's okay. That's okay," Mickey D. assured her, still patting a salty, wet knee.

Ames went from door to door, peering at the numbers, and came finally to the end apartment on the left side. He stood for a moment and listened, but there were noises from other apartments which served to drown out any ordinary sounds from inside this one. He stood with his back to the wall on the side opposite where the door would open, and he knocked. He listened, waited, and knocked again. Then once more. There was no sign of life from inside 1B. He bent down and looked in the keyhole. Then he took something out of his pocket, fiddled with the knob for just a few seconds, and, giving her an almost threatening warning motion to stay, opened the door slowly and slithered inside, his back hugging the doorframe. She could hear some thumping and pounding, and imagined him lunging, commando-style, from room to room. She held her breath. Finally he returned to the door, his face one raw sheet of disappointment, and beckoned her to come in. She breathed a sigh of relief. Her father was not there.

"What if he comes while we're here?" she whispered as she entered the almost vacant apartment. "Let's get out of here. I don't want to be here."

"Don't be silly. We'll lock the door. I want to look around for clues. If he comes back, we'll be ready. You'll see."

He was super hyper. She'd never seen him like that before. He had always been so courteous, so solicitous. Steady and reassuring, actually, not jumpy and almost manic like he was now.

"You loved him," Mickey D. commented.

"I thought so. But I was wrong," Ayn stated, blowing her nose on Mickey's handkerchief.

Ames locked the door behind her and rummaged around in the bedroom for a few minutes. She stayed just inside the door, refusing to go any further. Finally he came back and walked to the far window of the living room and leaned up against the sill. "Come here," he said.

"I want to go home," she said.

"Just for a minute," he cajoled. "I want to show you something."

"I want to leave," she said more plaintively.

"First come here," he said, half plea, half command.

"Okay, then we go?"

And he shook his head yes. She walked through the kitchenette and across the scuffed and dirty wooden floor of the living room. He reached out for her and pulled her to him. "Tadford, I don't want to. I want to go home." They had exchanged one long, lingering kiss on their second date just days before. But not here, not now—

"—Give me a kiss, Ayn," he said, putting his arm around her and pulling her face to his.

"Not now, Tadford."

"Just one." And he kissed her passionately. She half-heartedly returned his kiss. "Aw, come on. You love it, don't you? he teased, and kissed her again, more forcefully. She tried to worm away, feeling very uncomfortable. "Aw, Eva, come on!"

She started and pulled back. "What did you call me?"

He just smiled in a knowing way.

"You called me Eva. That's what my father called me."

"I know, you told me."

"No, I didn't."

"Yes, you've just forgotten."

She was becoming frightened. "I want to go now," she said. He still had ahold of her hand.

"In a little bit. There's something I want to tell you first."

"In the car," she urged. "Really, Tadford, I want to go. Let's go."

"I love you, Ayn," he said.

And now, in the telling of it, she broke down. "No man ever said that to me before," she gulped. "I didn't know what to do, what to feel."

"That's okay," Mickey D. assured her. "That's okay." The sun was going down behind the willow trees. Willows are the first trees to pop out new leaves in the spring and the first in the fall to change. They have always been able to hold me because of that. The willows shown like a gold maize through the waning sun behind Ayn's head.

Ayn took two big gulps, blew her nose, and bit her lip. "Okay," she said. "Okay," as if to pump herself up for the ordeal ahead.

"You're doing fine," Mick encouraged her.

When Tadford told her he loved her, her resistance melted. She felt somehow she needed to reciprocate. She was afraid to be there, in that apartment, any longer, but he wanted her there, for whatever reason. So she let him take her back in his arms. She let him stroke her face, run his hands through her hair, kiss her again and again. She tried to respond but something held her back. Something was not right. When he began to fondle her breasts, she said, "No, no, not now," and she squirmed away. "Tadford!" but he kept on. "Stop it!" she said sharply, trying with all her might to pull away.

And he slapped her!

Her resistance ceased immediately as she gazed at him in horror.

He was instantly contrite. "I'm sorry! I'm sorry!" he wailed. "I didn't mean to hurt you. But I need you to stay. You must stay until I tell you." And he held her all the tighter. His eyes, under those bushy dark brows, were sparking like flint. A minor tic in his face had become exaggerated, almost rhythmic. His accent, which she had once found romantic, was suddenly stronger, harsh. She trembled at his touch, not daring to pull away, unable to take her eyes from his twitching face, yet terrified of what she saw in it. Her heart was beating rapidly. His unwelcome advances had ripped the top buttons of her shirt open and exposed the top of her bra. She shivered.

He put his face inches from hers, his hot breath mingling with her shallow, panicked panting. And he hissed, "Your father is a monster."

She blinked, had trouble catching her breath. "What?" she asked incredulously.

He smirked. "A monster," he repeated. "Let me tell you about Jack Curtis," he panted. And his eyes seemed to gloss over. "I didn't start looking for your father just last month," he said almost in a monotone. "I've been waiting for the chance to track him down for years and years and years," he said. "Since he was a boy. You see, Eva, he was born bad and he's always been bad. And you don't know how lucky you are that he left you." The twitch was more controlled, the eyes almost hypnotic in their intensity. Ayn felt as if she were locked to them, like a powerful magnet. They drilled into her and held her captive. And all the while he held both her arms tightly, squeezing her breasts painfully between them, as he sat with his back against the wall beneath the window, with her half-sitting, half-kneeling, her legs trapped beneath her, in front of him.

Suddenly he screamed full into her face, "Your father raped a little girl when she was thirteen! Thirteen!" he shrieked inches from her face, spattering spittle in her eye. "He ruined her! Turned her into a carrot, a piece of potato, a rutabaga!" And he laughed a madman's cackle.

Then he said softly, as though from another room, "He did it and they blamed it on me!" And he gulped and reached to wipe his eyes, momentarily releasing her arm. She shifted her weight ever so slightly and he lunged at her, grabbing her tighter, squeezing her thin fore-arms until she cried out in pain. "He did it, and I paid. For twenty-nine years," he spat.

128

"So you know what I did when I got out?" he hissed in her face. "I tracked him down!" he crowed. "I dogged him. I chased him. I found you. And I found him," he said, shaking her. "I tracked you from that little one-diner town you come from." And his eyes bugged out like a frog's. A manic, mad urge to giggle welled up in her, but she suppressed it quickly, seized by the awful fear that she was turning into him.

"You know why I tracked you?" She said nothing, only trembled beneath his harsh touch.

He paused for effect and then whispered: "Because I knew he was watching you, too."

Ayn blinked. What did this madman mean? Nothing made any sense. When will he let me go? Why won't he let me go? What does he mean to do?

"You didn't know it, but he brought you here — his little girl, his little plaything. He saw to that when your mother died — manipulated you into a place where he could watch you more easily; arranged a college where you could study on scholarship — his phony 'scholarship.' Very subtle, very slick. I gotta hand it to him. Taking care of his little girl. So noble of him, wasn't it?" he smirked. "Noble for a man who molests little girls and abandons wives and children, don't you think?" he snarled.

Her mind was racing, but she couldn't think clearly. She wasn't thinking about what he claimed had happened, but what his next word, his next expression, his next move would be.

"The fact is," he said, "your father was afraid he was about to do the same thing to you that he did to that little girl long before you were born. That's why he left!"

Ayn reflexively shook her head no.

"Oh, yes!" he asserted. "If he hadn't already done it, he was afraid he was about to!"

This was so bizarre, so incredibly bizarre. She could only shake her head in denial.

"Don't you remember him coming to your bed at night?" he almost whispered.

She shook her head more slowly.

"Standing over your bed?"

She just stared at him.

"Just standing there."

And she saw a flash of her father's body above her, the silhouette of his form lit by the backdrop of a window on a night soon before he disappeared. "Yes," she whispered unthinking. "But—"

"—He wasn't looking after you, he was lusting after you," he breathed. "I came just in time. For you and for your little sister, Eva." And the name on his lips sounded like frigid water flowing deep in a hidden cavern.

"I saved you. Can't you see that? I saved you," and his voice was almost plaintive.

"He made me pay for his sins. Twenty-nine years in a stinking, rotting, fucking hole. That little girl a rutabaga in a rutabaga cellar. And as his reward for ruining our lives, they sent him away to school!" He was roaring now, shaking her violently.

"Stop it! Stop it!" she screamed at the top of her lungs, the fear drowning her words like an underwater solo. Why doesn't someone come? He slapped her again and she lost her balance, falling backwards, her feet trapped beneath her in the kneeling position. He lunged at her and tore the shirt off her and ripped her bra off over her head.

"I'll show you!" he roared. "I'll pay you for raping that little girl and throwing me to the dogs! The next best thing to killing you is to have my way with your daughter!" And his weight bore upon her thrashing form, his hands fumbling wildly at her jeans zipper.

She fought as if her life depended on it. She knew it did. When he couldn't fend off her blows and pull down her tight jeans as well, he put his hands around her neck and squeezed.

She thrashed. He squeezed harder. She lay still, eyes bugging, tongue hanging out. He released his grip and went for her pants again. She kicked and thrashed. He was at her throat again. He squeezed and squeezed. She clawed at him, her hands grabbing his wrists, and she tried with all her strength to pry his hands from her throat. He simply increased the pressure, his face just above hers, facial muscles twitching violently. "How's that feel, little Eva?" he hissed as her peripheral vision started to fade. "You're mine now, little Eva, little girl. How's it feel to be taken by the one that everybody picked on? The one they locked up. I'm just paying your father back. You're not Daddy's little girl any more, are you? He can't protect you now!"

She had no strength left to resist. The lights seemed to have gone out, and there was a ringing in her ears. Sounds came as from a long distance, through a thick barrier of memory and pain. She could not swallow. She could not breathe. Then suddenly he relaxed his hold and her hands flopped to her side, motionless, as she panted and panted to bring air into her lungs.

As if in another body, she sensed, rather than felt him tug on her pants until he had pulled them off. And she sensed the weight of his body as he lowered himself upon her.

Her right hand twitched involuntarily against the wooden floor, touched cold metal, and formed itself around it.

"The gun," she said simply, her face blank of emotion.

Mickey D. looked at me. I looked at him. Ayn sat silently, staring into a nightmare.

"You shot him," I concluded needlessly.

"You poor thing," Mickey D. said. "You poor thing."

"I must have passed out for a while," Ayn continued, an eerie, emotionless quality to her voice now. "When I came to and I realized what I'd done, I panicked. Who would ever believe this bizarre tale? I can't even fathom half of it myself. In the back of my mind, I still expected my father to walk in any minute and see us there. Then I said to myself, nobody saw us. Nobody knows I came here. They'll think my father did this. I felt like I'd been set up royally, why not set him up?" Then she paused. "No, actually I thought most of that later, when I was trying to justify it all to myself. At the time, I was only trying to figure out how to get out of there without anyone knowing I was there. I myself wanted to pretend it hadn't happened. He'd fallen back against the wall, almost as though I'd propped him there on purpose. I zipped up his pants. I wiped my fingerprints from the gun and pressed his hand to it, then laid it beside him."

"You were hurt?" I asked.

And she pulled up the sweatshirt and the sweater beneath it to show her belly. Long, red, raw scratches ran from her navel to as far as I could see, where her bra began to show. Mickey looked away. Then she lifted the sweatshirt over her head, wincing and biting her lip. She pulled the cowl of the turtleneck down to show red and blue blotched skin where his hands had almost choked the life out of her.

"That's okay," I said softly, almost embarrassed that she felt she had to show us. And yet I asked it: "Did he rape you?"

"No. He didn't make it." And the side of her lip curled slightly. "I thought no one could trace me there," she said. "Naive, huh? About as stupid as they come," she berated herself.

"Don't say that," M.D. said. "You were brave. Very brave."

And her bloodshot eyes seemed to brighten a little. "Half the things he said, I didn't know what to think. And for a while I thought maybe I imagined some of it as he was choking me. It was too crazy. Somehow the crazier it was, the easier to treat it like it didn't happen.

So I got in the car, drove home, took a shower, changed my clothes, and came to the hotel. I didn't feel the pain. I didn't feel the hurt. I didn't feel anything," she said, her lips pursed in a hard line. "Somehow I blocked it out, didn't think, couldn't think. After all, I reasoned, he was crazy. Certifiable. Deviant. Sick. Not my father — this guy who was after him." And she blew her nose again. "I told myself no one will ever know I was there earlier. The only way to forget this thing is to simply forget it. Disassemble. Deny. Then I went home from the police station," she said glumly.

"And talked to Chakra?" Mickey D. offered.

"No. I looked at the pictures."

"What pictures?" I asked, glancing at Mickey.

"The ones I found in his apartment."

"In your father's apartment?"

"Yes."

Oh boy!

"There were pictures on the wall of the bedroom in my father's apartment, affixed with thumbtacks. I almost died again, right there — this time of heart failure," she laughed shallowly.

She sniffled and continued. "I glanced at them — enough to see some of Kasi and the kids, and I really knew then that he had actually been there — that my father had been in that apartment recently and he might come back. I ripped down the photos and I searched quickly to see if there were other personal effects. I was in such a hurry to get out of that place that I grabbed a manila envelope and I ran, slamming the door on the way out. That's when the blood got on the door, I guess. Somehow I thought if I could take away all his personal things, I could erase him from the place, and that would erase Tadford and me and me and Tadford and on and on and on." She was looking from Mickey to me, begging us with her eyes to understand.

"But he followed me home," she sighed.

"Followed you home?" I said in alarm.

"Figuratively, Eliza, figuratively," M.D. chirped in for my edification.

"Duh!" I said, as though I'd only been kidding. I mean, honestly, stranger things have happened in this case, right? And they were getting weirder all the time.

"The pictures?" Mickey D. prompted.

From inside the large pouch of her sweatshirt, which now lay across her knees, Ayn extracted a 5" x 7" manila envelope. She carefully unloosed the string wrapped around the catch and opened it slowly. She extracted a photograph and handed it to Mickey. He got

132

up stiffly from his crouched position in front of her and sat down on the other side of me on the bench. We examined it together.

It was a pre-adolescent candid shot of Ayn, her face turned to some unseen individual, her hand pointing to someone or something off-camera.

"One of his old pictures of you?" I asked.

"No," she said simply. "I had long hair until I was 12. This was taken at least a year after he left. He took this picture with a telephoto or had it taken for him."

I shivered involuntarily and glanced glumly at M.D. "Here's another," Ayn said, handing it to me. A developing young woman romping with a dog. "And another." Ayn at about 16, helping an older woman — her mother, I supposed — unload groceries from the trunk of a car in front of a house.

"How about this?" she offered. A small group of people at a fresh gravesite, a hearse in the background.

"Your mother's funeral?" I asked in disbelief.

"Um-hmm," she said, lips pursed tightly.

"And this one." It was Ayn and another young woman hugging in front of Ayn's current vehicle, in front of the same house. There was a U-Haul attached to the car. "That's the day I left home for here," Ayn said, her lip trembling. "That's my best friend saying goodbye."

"Jesus!" Mickey D. exhaled and shook his head.

"Incredible!" I pronounced. And we just looked at her.

"For nine years my mother cried for my father," she paused, her eyes staring off into yesteryear, a bitter set to her mouth. "And all that time he was watching us."

"That means he cared about you, Ayn," Mickey said hopefully.

She snorted in irony. The snort turned into a chuckle and then a sort of chortle, and finally full-blown hysterics, as all the while tears simply streamed down her cheeks.

"Well, at least you haven't lost your sense of humor," I offered tentatively. Mickey grimaced.

But after a few minutes, she got control of herself and drew another photo from the envelope.

"Not more!" I grimaced.

"Oh, wait 'til you see this!" she smirked as she passed it to me and Mick peered at it over my shoulder. It was an old black and white snapshot, well worn, its edges dog-eared and thin. Three children stood in front of a stone stoop at an open door. They were dressed in basic school clothes, apparently clean but a bit frumpy. There were two boys on either side of a girl. The boys looked to be in their mid teens, and the girl just reaching puberty. The younger boy had a scowl on his face, his hands plunged into homemade wool pants too short for him. The older boy was holding the girl's hand and smiling almost shyly. It looked like a Depression-era family.

I took the photo from Mickey's hands and peered closely at it. "That guy on the right — the older one...." I paused and looked at Ayn.

"Yes, I think it's my father when he was a teenager. He always said he didn't have a family — that he was an only child and his parents died when he was young. That he didn't have any photographs and he didn't have any relatives. But everything he said was a lie." And she bit her lip and that far-away look came into her eyes again. Then she turned abruptly and her eyes focused straight at me. "And I want you to find him for me. I *need* to know now. I *have* to know. Will you do that?"

I know my mouth was in my lap. I was afraid to look at Mickey. I took a deep breath and just plunged in. "Let me just see if I have this right, okay?" I said, putting my hands on my knees and attempting a smile.

Ayn nodded. There wasn't a peep out of my partner.

"Stop me at any time if I go wrong or go too far, okay?"

And she nodded again.

"Okay. You have just put a bullet through the brain of your would-be lover as he was raping and strangling you to get back at your father, who presumably raped a thirteen-year-old decades ago in God-Knows-Where, and for which said rape said would-be-lover was allegedly framed and spent 29 years in prison. Am I right so far?"

Ayn nodded and looked at the ground. Mick sighed heavily, as though in disapproval, but said nothing.

"Your father, who left you when you were about the same age as the girl he allegedly molested, has, since his disappearance, apparently kept track of you via telephoto and some sort of telepathy to get you to move here for Who-Knows-What. And about the time you moved here, he left his second wife and family — a family that also consists of a daughter named Eva, the name for every-one in this sorry saga who actually has a name." I took a deep breath. "Where-upon, He Who Will Be Avenged, who has also been watching you in order to catch your father, concocts this elaborate scheme to get you on television so that he can flush out your father and do him in — after, of course, raping his daughter for good measure.... Have I left anything out?"

"Yeah," M.D. chimed in helpfully. "The hand."

"Oh, yes. Excuse me. The dog and the hand slipped my mind."

"Understandable," Mickey D. allowed.

"Do I have the rest about right?" I asked.

"Yes," Ayn said softly.

"Just checking."

The three of us sat there for the longest time, watching the leaves turn.

"Well?" Ayn finally ventured, almost in a whisper.

I looked at the young woman beside me. "You're serious — you really want to hire us to find your father?" It was a statement, actually, not a question. I already knew the answer, as did Mickey D.

"Would you?" Ayn pleaded.

"Could we?" I doubted.

"Should we?" Mickey countered.

Whereupon we took on our second client in regards to one missing person that no one should have given a damn about in the first place. "Double or nothing," I groused. And you know where *my* money was.

Chapter 9
Turn Around

As the three of us walked back to the house from the scene of the confession, Mickey D. whispered to me, "How do we find out if Chakra's involved in this?"

I turned to Ayn, "Mickey D. wants to know if Chakra has any part in this," I parroted.

"Eliza!" M.D. hissed under his breath and elbowed me in the side.

"What?" I asked guilelessly.

If Ayn noticed, she was too polite to let on. "No, Chakra's just my roommate," she said nonchalantly.

Still, Mickey D. and I exchanged "Yeah, sure" looks on our way up the front steps.

Naturally, Chakra insisted on coming with us to the police station. "Well, why don't you drive Ayn and we'll follow," I suggested. "That way, Chakra, you can come back here tonight, because Ayn will probably have to at least spend the night before bail can be set. Can you meet bail?" I asked Ayn.

"It depends. I have the proceeds of the sale of my mother's house..."

"Well, if they buy the self-defense, which they should, seeing the physical evidence of trauma, and take into account the fact that you've turned yourself in, bail shouldn't be too bad," Mickey D. commented. "Are you ready?"

"Well, yeah," Ayn said.

"You want to follow us, then?" I asked.

"Well, we could, but I'd have to leave my car there and ask you to give Chakra a ride back."

"Oh, no, I'll stay with you!" Chakra blurted.

"You can't stay in the cell with her!" Even Mickey's disgust was showing.

"But she'll be alone," the woman accused, as though we were proposing to feed Ayn to the wolves.

"She's been alone before," I noted, glancing at Ayn for confirmation. "It'll just be a holding cell, a temporary thing." Inside, I was screaming, "Get a life, girl!" But what I said out loud to Chakra was, "Why can't you drive?"

"Chakra doesn't drive," Ayn piped up sheepishly. "I lied about the car wash ticket. She doesn't have a car."

Chakra just looked at Ayn, her face washed free of emotion. How much did she really know about the case, and when did she know it? Whatever Ayn told her to say, to do, to feel, she would, it seemed. It made my stomach turn. Thoughtless compliance and blind loyalty are not in my book of desirable attributes. Whether it was just disgust at these overwhelming traits in Chakra or something much more insidious that made me distrust this woman so, I couldn't tell you. The only positive thing I could say about her was that she made me feel better about Mrs. D.

As I've always maintained, digression is the better part of valor. Or something like that.

·   -------

So we all trucked down to the main Philadelphia police station, from which Sergeant Staszewski was thankfully absent. There a very professionally-mannered detective by the name of Tranh Danh took Ayn's rather brief statement. We made sure it was as bare-boned as possible until Attorney Caroline Atkins, the lawyer Mickey D. had called from Ayn's house and asked to represent her, arrived. Caroline is an old friend of The Mick's who used to represent the FBI in racial discrimination and sexual harassment cases, then left to start her own practice. She does a variety of legal stuff, but has made representing abused women her specialty. She has been an advocate for several women who ended up killing their husbands and boyfriends after years of abuse. Caroline calls such cases her "por buenos," — not "for the good" of the public, like some charity Latin-based *pro bono publicos,* but the more down-to-earth Spanish "for good," because she feels the world is better off without such monsters and she's happy to help any woman who finds herself in such a position.

Caroline would expect Ayn to pay what she felt she could afford, without unduly strapping herself (and hopefully with something left to pay us to find her father). In Caroline's hands, Ayn was as secure as she could be, given the circumstances.

There was little more we could do for our new client once we'd explained everything we knew to Caroline and introduced her to Ayn. "We'll take you home now," I said to Chakra.

"I will stay, thank you."

"You can't — Oh, hell!" What's the use? She would get home however she damn well pleased, or she'd sleep like a dog outside her mistress's cell. Either way, it was her choice and her problem, not ours.

"Let's go, Eliza," Mickey D. prompted.

Fact was, we had another stop to make, in the opposite direction, before we could go home. And I wasn't at all looking forward to explaining to Kasi that her husband had been accused of being a child molester. Nor that her husband's oldest daughter was at this very moment confessing to putting a bullet through the brain of a TV programmer while the latter attempted to rape and choke her. Nor that J/J had been spying on his ex-wife and daughter for years and apparently actually orchestrated Ayn's removal to his second family's back door. And I certainly didn't think she'd be real thrilled to see some of the photos he'd taken of her, including the one I'd noted of she and George Diego in close embrace on the Short's back porch...

"She said she was sending a check yesterday," I told Mick as we approached the car in the police station visitor's lot. "Do you think she'd stop payment?"

Mickey shrugged. He's got this real flippant attitude about money. If it's there, fine; if not, somehow it'll show up. It bugs the hell out of me. "That's right, AZT must cost $2,000 a month now, which is $2,000 more than you have anyway, so what's a couple grand less to pay the bills with?" And I shrugged, too.

"That's what I like about you, Eliza," he snarled sourly. "You've got a real talent for finding the positives in life. Helps a man get through the day."

"You're welcome." And I tossed him the keys.

I was relieved to see the Ribbonos' '69 Mustang parked out front of Kasi's and to find Glory having coffee in the living room with Kasi. It might be easier to get through all this with Glory there. In my book, she was worth ten Chakras any day.

"We've got something to tell you," I announced after we were seated around the coffee table and Mickey D. and Glory had been introduced.

"Did you find him?" Kasi sat on the edge of the couch next to Glory, her face simultaneously hopeful and wary.

"Well, no, not exactly," M.D. admitted. "We found out who Ames was, though," he offered.

"We don't know his real name," I noted.

"I thought you said you knew who he was," Kasi's anxiousness bordered on annoyance.

"Well, actually he claimed to have been tracking Joe for years," I ventured, wincing a little.

"What! This guy's been watching us?" She jumped to her feet and started to pace.

"Well, that may be what scared Joe off, though we're not sure how he came here first, if in fact he did. But we do believe Ames was following Ayn, in order to find Joe. In fact, we think Joe may have manipulated Ayn into moving to this area. Then when Ayn moved down here, Ames found all of you."

"What?" It was downhill from there. Kasi went through a swearing jag, a crying jag, a panic period during which she ran to check on the kids three times in as many minutes, another yelling session, and a quiet spell. Through it all, Mickey D. and Glory tried to comfort and mollify her. I basically told the story and gave the picture show. Ayn had reluctantly entrusted the photos to us. Kasi agreed that the older boy in the well-worn picture was the spitting image of her husband. "The girl favors my daughter," she added, almost whimpering. It was hard watching her emotional upheaval, impossible not to. I felt like a voyeur at the scene of a hit-and-run.

At one point she started, whirled toward the front door, and blurted, "I *didn't* imagine it. He *was* here. Ames *was* Al. "He came here looking for Joe after Joe disappeared!" And an involuntary, collective shiver ran through us. "I need to go see Ayn," Kasi ultimately announced. "The child needs me."

"It's too late, Kasi," Glory said gently. "Almost midnight. She'll have bunked down by now. I'll go with you in the morning if she's still there."

"Glory's right," Mickey D. concurred.

"Um-hmm," I added.

"You're sure?"

"Yes," we chorused. And thankfully, that was that.

I was dead tired, and after M.D. dropped himself off at his apartment (the man's been playing musical bed tag recently for some inexplicable reason), I drove straight home, peeled off my clothes, threw on my nightshirt, and plopped thankfully into bed. I pulled the covers up to my ears and tried to fool my mind into taking me on a blissful, thoughtless sleep ride. But I slept fitfully, awakening again and again to capture pieces of dreams bobbing to the surface of my consciousness.

There was a deep hole in my mother's back yard, the size of an Olympic-sized swimming pool, only bottomless. Sometimes there was water in it; sometimes, mountains of industrial strength bubbles or firefighters' foam. And wallowing in it were Kasi and Ayn and Mickey D. and me. We were pushing through the damn bubbles, thick like cream that's been whipped and is just about to harden into crests of marshmallowness. The bubbles held us back, made us choke and struggle to keep our heads above the surface, so we could never gain footage on the slippery sides.

Standing on firm ground on the lip of the hole, and peering down at us were three children — the children in J/J's old worn photograph. They stood and watched us struggle. The oldest one — J/J — moved close, beckoned, and held out one hand, his other behind his back. Just as one of us was about to grasp it, he'd snatch it back. His face was a mask. The younger boy laughed and laughed and laughed, a mirthless, hollow laugh. His hands were stuffed into his pockets. The little girl simply watched it all and cried.

Then Mother D. came out and scolded us for making such a mess. The children ran away. I woke up, shook the webs of goo away, went back to sleep, and it started all over again.

At 7:30, I dragged myself out of bed and washed the taste of soap out of my mouth. The mirror over the bathroom sink said time is passing you by, girl. I stuck out my tongue at it.

I took a shower and held my head under the hot stream of water, relishing in the shortness of my recently-cut hair. I don't have the thick waves Mickey does, but at least it's got some body. Now all I have to do is wash it and let it dry. It's low maintenance now, like the rest of me. Six months to the day after I said good riddance to that man my mother thinks I "lost," I had my long hair chopped off. It's sort of a Samson story that worked in reverse for me. No hair. No make-up. No ties that bind.

The sun was flirting with the morning as I took my usual breakfast snack onto the sunporch and maneuvered the rocking chair into its sunniest corner. I sat and rocked, nibbling away on my cookie, eyes closed, absorbing the sun like a turtle basking on a rock.

Suddenly the hand popped into my head. Uninvited, unwelcome, unexpected. Not the severed one the dog had brought home, but

Ames's hand, with the writing on it. I inspected it in my mind. That damn thing was bugging the hell out of me. Even if Ames *did* make a habit of taking notes on his palm, that one, most-recent scrawl kept gnawing at me. "Dog." "Hdog." "Shdog." Something very awkward about this writing. I swallowed the last bite of oatmeal cookie, put down my empty glass and put the fingers of my right hand to the palm of my left, like a pen writing. "This way it reads 'dog,' or whatever. But what if someone else had written it, from the other side?"

I got up and went over to my desk in the corner and took the best print I'd made out of the file marked "Kasi Short." And I turned it upside down. "B-o-p. Bop," I read. "He got bopped, all right," I mused. "Bopric?" And I looked closer. Then the average-watt, 100 IQ lightbulb in my brain went on so bright it virtually overloaded and exploded in my head. "It's not our alphabet!" I whooped out loud in Eurekan glee. "It's Cyrillic!"

I ran all over the apartment, looking for my seven language dictionary, and finally found it in a box of books I hadn't unpacked since the move following my divorce. Then I spent fifteen minutes trying to figure out how one looks up a word one doesn't know in an alphabet one hasn't a clue about. Can not be done.

So I dialed Mickey D. It rang and rang and rang and then the answering machine went on. "Micker!" I screamed into the receiver. "Get up! The hand has spoken to me. Call Geli Korlov. Tell him we need a Russian translation. Get him immediately! Micker, you lazy oaf! Answer this phone!"

"What's this about a handsome Soviet?" he came on, trying to act like he'd been wide awake the whole time.

"It's Cyrillic. When you turn it upside down — which is right-side-up for anyone but Ames — it's something written in the Cyrillic alphabet."

"Russian?"

"No, I'm taking my time."

"Ahah! Darnell said Ames told everyone at the station that his parents had immigrated to Canada from Eastern Europe."

"We need someone who reads Russian to look at the photos," I said. "I thought maybe Geli would do it." Geli Korlov and his family were among the Jewish refuseniks who managed to emigrate from the Soviet Union in the mid 80's and settle in the United States. At first they had settled in the Brighton Beach, N.Y. area, where there were thousands of their fellow countrymen. But a few years later they followed Geli's brother Vadim to Philadelphia in search of opportunity. Here Geli and his wife Eleanor were at first unable to find more than minimum wage jobs — she in a supermarket, he in a convenience store, to support their two small children.

Seven years ago they had reached for the American dream — home ownership — through Habitat for Humanity, an ecumenical organization that builds houses in partnership with people like the Korlovs — folks who work hard but can never quite get ahead. The families help to build their own simple homes, and then they pay for them through no-profit, no-interest mortgages.

Mickey D. has been a long-time volunteer with the Southeast Philadelphia Chapter, and when the Korlovs applied, he helped them through their transition to home ownership as their "Nurturing Partner." (See — he's even got the official title!) Anyway, Geli and Mickey became friends and Mickey D. helped him get a management position in a restaurant where he's more than doubled his income. He even brought his younger brother Vadim into the business with him as assistant manager.

"Geli will do it. He owes you," I said.

"He doesn't owe me anything," Mickey D. replied. "But I'm sure he'll do it. "We'll probably have to see him at the restaurant. I'll call and see if he's got time. Pick me up in half an hour."

"Will you be decent by then?"

"I'll be ready."

"Okay, I'll settle for that this time."

Forty-five minutes later, we were seated in a booth in the otherwise-empty overflow back dining room at The Fireside Family Restaurant, across from Geli Korlov. I was wolfing down pancakes and syrup and a mound of greasy, limp bacon. But I let the half-cooked hashbrowns sit on my plate. They'd obviously come straight out of the freezer and been stirred around on a grill for 30 seconds. "You don't like?" Geli gestured to my plate. "I will have made for you eggs? Sausage? Ham?"

"No, no, Geli," I spat, a piece of bacon flying out of the side of my mouth and landing on the plastic checkered tablecloth. I swiped at it with a napkin and then wiped my face as if to stifle the offending orifice. "It's good. Very good. I'm just full, thank you."

"You, Mickey, my friend, you must fatten up. Like Hansel and Gretel you are!" And he called to a waitress as she emerged from the kitchen. "More French toast for Mickey!"

142

"No, no, Geli," Mickey pleaded, pushing his half-finished plate away. "Really. I can't eat any more. I told you, I ate just before I called you. This was more than enough. Thank you."

Geli sat back in the booth, pulled out a cigar, and offered it to Mickey D. Mick shook his head. Geli nodded at me, more on the lines of, "you don't mind, do you." Not a question, just a passing courtesy. I smiled slightly. Actually, I hate smoking, and cigars in particular, but I'd rather smoke one myself than have someone else smoke one in front of me. But hey, he hadn't offered. Silly me, and I thought the women wore the pants in Russia!

Geli stuck the cigar in his mouth, lit it, and exhaled across the table. "So you want a translator, Roderickovich." Ooh, I love the sound of that. Maybe I'll start calling Mickey Roderickovich. That would make me Roderickovna, Daughter of Roderick. Pretty nifty.

"I am not Russian, you know," Geli said between puffs. "I am from Kazakh. It is Autonomous Soviet Republic," he puffed, with emphasis on the "Autonomous." "Is joke," he added. "Or at least it was when I live there. Nothing autonomous in Soviet Union! Now is called Kazakhstan."

"But you *speak* Russian," I emphasized.

"Oh yes, in Kazakh we have our own language, but we also speak Russian."

"And read Cyrillic."

"Cyrillic?"

"The Russian alphabet. In English it's called Cyrillic," Mickey D. explained.

"Oh yes. The alphabet. A-B-C."

"Here, this — this is a picture of the writing," I said, drawing the photographs from the file between Mickey and myself. "It looks to me like it's in the Russian alphabet." And I handed him one of the crime scene photographs.

He put it on the checkered tablecloth in front of him and placed the cigar in an ashtray by the window. He studied the photograph closely, and his nostrils began to flare. "What is *this*?" he spat, his mouth screwed into an ugly scowl.

"That's what we were hoping you could tell us."

"No, no," he brushed at the air as if to remove cobwebs. "What it's written on?" His voice had raised about two octaves. Mickey D. and I looked anxiously at one another.

"A hand," Mickey said.

"A what?"

"A hand."

143

"Is dead hand or live hand?"

"Dead."

And he threw the photo down on the table and jumped up from his seat. "Why are you doing this? You bring death to my livelihood, to my doorstep, to my family! I thought you were my friend!"

"I am, Geli!" Mickey cried and rose, too, snatching up the discarded photograph. "We just need someone to translate. It's the only clue we have about who this guy was!"

"I thought I left them behind!" he bellowed. "They follow me everywhere! Now you, my friend!" And he stomped off across the empty dining room, toward the kitchen. Vadim, coming from the main dining room, saw his brother's obvious agitation and Mickey D. with his puzzled look, trailing after.

"Vadim!" Mickey D. hailed him. "Vadim! I don't understand. Geli thinks I have insulted him. All I wanted was a translation. Please talk with him!"

I stayed put. Mickey D. stood twenty feet away, showing Vadim the photograph and trying to explain the situation to him as the younger man peered at the photograph, shook his head, and clucked like an old babushka over a scandalous situation. "I see. I see," he said. "The man belonging to this photograph is dead. Here. In America."

"Yes. We need to know—"

"—He is Russian."

"Well, apparently whoever wrote this knew Russian. We don't really know. We need to find out—"

"—He was murdered."

"Yes."

"Organizatsiya," he said, shaking his head and pursing his lips.

"I'm sorry, what did you say?" Mickey D. asked.

"Organizatsiya," he repeated.

"I thought that's what you said," I answered, still completely baffled.

"Just a moment, I get Geli," he said, patting Mickey D. on the arm. "You are good friend to us. Geli is upset. Is not your fault. We will explain." And he strode into the kitchen, the swinging doors slapping shut behind him.

Mickey Roderickovich looked at me and I looked at Mickey Roderickovich. I shrugged and helped myself to the rest of M.R.'s nice, fatty bacon. There was loud arguing coming from the kitchen, in what I presumed to be Kazakhstani. Three waitresses emerged, looking alarmed. Then a woman in a chef's hat and apron came out,

144

wiping her hands on a towel and looking back over her shoulder as if someone might come after her. I eyed The Mick's toast, but thought better of it, and was considering another stab at my hashbrowns when the noise from the kitchen finally subsided.

Within twenty seconds, the kitchen door swung out and Geli emerged, big hands at his side, his wide face florid. He walked directly to Mickey D., held out his arms and embraced him. "Forgive me, Mikhail Roderickovich," he said, his head bowed. "I behaved — how you say it — foolishly?"

"Oh no, whatever you—"

"—Vadim, my little brother, is wiser than I," Geli said, a sad smile touching his lips. "He showed me I am wrong."

"Siblings do that sometimes," Mickey D. smiled.

"Sometimes?" I mumbled. But they were ignoring me.

"It is that this thing — this man — it looks like Organizatsiya." And he whispered the last word.

"What *is* that?" Mickey steered Geli back to our booth. Vadim, coming out of the kitchen, beckoned to a waitress and she removed our dirty dishes as Vadim sat down next to his brother, across from Mickey. Coffee appeared.

"Is a terrible thing," Geli exhaled deeply, reached for his cigar and relit it.

"I've never heard of it. What is it?" I prompted.

"Russian Mafia." Vadim pronounced the words like an epithet. "It is the number one reason we move to Philadelphia."

"To escape the Mafia, you came to Phily?" I snorted, incredulous. Mickey D. gave me a dirty look. Vadim ignored me. Geli seemed lost in memories, puffing on his stogie.

"The Russian Mafia, they are hoodlums — crooks, murderers, thieves. Felons who came here many years ago with the blessing of the Soviet government and the KGB," Vadim stated. "To disrupt America. Common crooks posing as political enemies of the state or as refuseniks. But even more, they come to harass the Russian immigrant community here — the legitimate, honest people."

"How?"

"Extortion, protection, drugs, scams. They send millions of American dollars back to Russia. In Brighton Beach, they are boss," Vadim stated flatly.

"We tried — Eleanor and I — to start business when we first came to New York," Geli spoke softly. "Computer repair shop. You know, in Kazakh, I was computer engineer?" And his eyes met mine for the first time.

145

"No, I didn't know that. Did you, Mickey?"

"No, I didn't."

"We put little ad in the paper. Vadim paid for first," Geli said, nodding at his brother. "We got some work. But we also got call from Organizatsiya."

"Who was it?"

"First time, just one man. Russian. He said we must pay work permit fee. He wanted $800 cash. We did not have. He gave me week. I went to Vadim, who came to U.S. one year earlier than we. He said there is no such thing. Then two men come back for money. I said no such thing as work permit fee. He said yes there is, and showed his knee to my balls — excuse me, Mickey's sister," he glanced in my direction. "He hurt me bad. Eleanor, she chased other man with broom. First man takes out gun and points it at my head. I give them all the money I have and he shoots out customer's computer and leaves." He puffed heavily and sat back in the booth. "There is more, but was enough for us."

"Why didn't you go to the police?" I asked, knowing as soon as I said it how naive it must sound.

"You have heard of code of silence?" Vadim asked, but didn't wait for a reply. "Russians are used to police state. Also used to neighbor telling on neighbor to save own ass. And before you know it, you are counting trees."

"Counting trees?" Mickey asked.

"Banished to Siberia," Geli explained.

"Nice expression," I opined.

"So people are used not to trusting authority. Here they are new. They have opportunities, hope. Things they do not want to risk. They are afraid they will be deported. But more, they are simply afraid. These people are brutal," Vadim pronounced, curling his lip with the last word. He motioned for more coffee. A waitress refilled the cups. There was only the sound of spoons stirring cream and sugar.

Geli blew smoke toward the window and continued. "A man we came to know from Kuybyshev fell in with them. They owned many, many gas stations — how you say, a chain with many links. Instead of paying the government for tax which people pay when they buy gas, they were making bean bags with the books, juggling them. Millions and millions of dollars they were keeping that way," he said, wiping his forehead with a napkin. "This man we knew, he took too much for himself, didn't give enough to Organizatsiya." He paused and wiped his forehead again. "The Organizatsiya killed his wife and

146

took out her eyes," he sighed. "Is Russian peasant belief that the reflection of the murderer is in the victim's eyes."

"Not nice people," I commented.

"Because they are so not nice, this is why they were dumped here," Geli explained. "Is on purpose. KGB gets them out of Russia, where they harm society, and gives them to America for same reason. Castro copied the Soviets same way with his boat people. Just open the prison doors and show them to the nearest rubber raft. Is happening now with Communist Chinese. Americans sometimes are very gullible," he said, looking at us almost apologetically.

"When you show me the picture of the hand, I feel they will come here to where I work and do the same as in New York. They will demand money. I can not run again." And Geli looked down at his own hands.

"What was it about the photograph that made you think of the Organizatsiya?" Mickey D. asked.

"Writing on someone's hand, like warning or message. In this case, like signature. A Russian dies violently in this way, and it can be only one thing," Geli said.

"But this man's murder was justifiable — it was in self defense," I protested. "A young woman — a client of ours — was attacked by him and defended herself."

Geli looked dubious. "What do you know of this man?"

"He apparently did time in jail, though we don't know where. He had an Eastern European accent. His Social Security number traces to a child who died in Canada at the age of three. He had ready access and sufficient resources to obtain illegal drugs, was violent and possibly psychotic." Mickey D. pretty much had Tadford's known history covered.

"I had friend in the Brighton Beach Police Department," Vadim said softly, almost secretively. "They had no power against these people. What he told me so much frightened me that I talked Geli and Eleanor into moving here with me and starting over. My friend said that the Organizatsiya brings in assassins from the Ukraine and Siberia. Cold War is over, but Mafia has its own war. To get temporary visa, you need only Letter of Invitation from citizen of U.S. Can buy such letter in Brighton Beach for $100. Get visa, come to States, do murder for contract here, hop back on plane and return to Russia."

"This body could be one of them," Geli said, jabbing his cigar at the photo.

"Was he the target or the assassin?" I wondered out loud.

"Dead either way," Mickey D. said blandly.

"I have heard that the enforcers who live in the states change their names to fool the police," Vadim explained. "They move from one Russian-American émigré community to another. They fence stolen goods, launder money, and exchange enforcers. This way, is like a serial murderer, police can not keep track of them."

"How far would they go to get back at someone?" I asked. "Would the Organizatsiya follow a man for years, from state to state, even country to country, to get revenge?

"There are many reasons to kill," Geli sighed, stubbing out his cigar. "If it is personal, price is cheap, effort has no boundaries."

"Can you tell us what the writing says?" I asked gently.

"Of course. Forgive me." Geli smiled sadly, sighed and picked up the photograph. He looked at it.

Борис

He smiled faintly, flipped it over, and read.

Борис

Almost immediately, he pronounced, "Boris." Then handed it to Vadim.

"Da, Boris," Vadim concurred.

"The name Boris?" I asked.

"Yes."

"That's all?"

"That's all."

"What does that mean?" I asked Mickey D.

"Maybe Ames's real name was Boris or his killer was Boris," Mickey said with a sigh. "Thank you, Geli, Vadim," he said, rising and shaking both men's hands. "I'm sorry if we stirred up bad memories."

"No, no, it is my memories, my problem," Geli brushed the apology aside. "It was foolish of me. We are safe here, now. We don't live and work in Russian-American community. We live in Habitat Village," he said with the warm smile I was more used to. "Our friends are American. We are American!"

And the brothers walked us to the door of their genuine American greasy spoon and told us to come back again real soon.

"Should we check on Ayn?" I asked, as we got into Cabri.

"In a little bit. But first let's hash this out," Mickey D. suggested. "How 'bout Friebert Park?"

"Really?" I was surprised because it's been a while since The Mick has wanted to walk. He must be feeling better. Walking and talking out a case together is the method we often use to sort through a puzzling situation.

Mickey D. drove to one of our favorite walking parks. Friebert has a two-mile, mostly-paved trail that circles a 30-acre lake. There are areas of open field, portions with tall, thick woods, and sections where the trail becomes a boardwalk skirting the edge of the water. Willows line the banks and ducks swim in and out, bobbing for food and calling to one another. In the fall, the geese land en masse and rest for long periods in the course of their southern trek. The trail is wide, and Mick and I can walk side-by-side and talk without having to move aside for others. Mick sometimes jogs here when he's feeling well, but I'm not particularly fond of pain, so I don't jog.

It takes us about 45 minutes to circle the lake going counter-clockwise, and when we reach our starting point, there's a deck and a docking area where you can rent paddleboats or rowboats. We usually sit there for a few minutes afterwards as a sort of reward, letting ourselves cool down and amusing ourselves watching people trying to figure out how to steer those ornery paddle things. "Let's rent a boat," Mickey D. surprised me as we approached the dock that should have been the beginning of our walk. "Makes my leg muscles work," he explained. He's been getting leg cramps at night, a side effect of the medication he takes regularly for the HIV. In the morning he often hobbles around, his muscles all knotted up.

"It might cramp 'em up more," I cautioned, honestly dubious. Paddling sounds too much like unnecessary exertion to me.

"No, if I work them, it should strengthen them," he insisted. "Then they won't cramp so easily. We can see parts of the lake we've never seen before," he cajoled.

Mickey doesn't know it, but I've already seen those parts, with The Ex. And the memories are painful. But so are Mick's leg cramps, I imagine. "Well, if we get way out there and I get tired, what then?"

"You can just hang out. I'll get us back."

"Doesn't it take two?"

"It'll just take longer if only one of us paddles."

So I skipped Paddleboating 101 and went right into Petting 102. So sue me! "Okay, okay."

It was a lovely early fall day. The leaves had begun to change ever so subtlely, and there was a warm breeze from the west. The sun was in-again, out-again, and it felt like there was a storm off on the horizon somewhere, up over the next chain of mountains, but not anytime soon. It was about 70 when the sun was out, 65 when it ducked behind a cumulus cloud.

So we rented the paddleboat. I insisted on steering, because I'd never gotten to do that before. "I don't know, if you drive in the water like you drive on land..." But he gave in, and I found I liked it. You just have to move the stick – or the rudder – to the left and then to the right and to the left, and the right, and so on, to keep it going straight. If you hold it continually to one side, you go in a neat little circle, which I tried for a while, until Mickey said he was dizzy and he refused to paddle any longer, so I resumed the back and forth.

"Okay," Mickey D. said after a few minutes. "What's the story?"

"Well, I can buy that Tadford/Al was in this Organizatsiya thing," I opened.

"He could very well have come out of a Russian prison after doing time for rape, and then been shipped over here to get rid of a violent and obviously unstable individual," Mickey said.

"Do you think they'd do that nowadays?"

"Who knows how long he's been here. He said he'd been looking for J/J since he was a kid. Twenty-nine years in jail can be meta-phoric; it can be a lie. Who knows?"

"Okay. So let's say he was loosed on the immigrant community with the dual purpose of getting rid of a bad seed and to destabilize the American people and the government. He obviously came in under a different name and then just took on whatever identity he wanted. There are hundreds of would-be immigrants who come to the States every year and ask for political asylum. If they ask, the law says the INS has to give them a hearing date and let 'em go. A lot of them never show up for the hearing. They're just floating out there somewhere."

"Yeah, doing who knows what!" We paddled on silently for a while. It was a little chilly out on the water. I was glad we'd both worn long sleeves.

"And I can see him doing criminal things here – using an illegal network of crooks to make money and live well," I said after a while. "He was obviously a real con man, getting into that studio with abso-lutely no credentials. And I wondered how a TV producer for a small station could live in a hotel suite like that for months at a time. Must be at least $90 a day, even long-term. He had to have outside income," I noted.

"The drugs," Mickey D. said.

"Yeah. He was giving them away at the studio to get what he wanted accomplished without too many questions being asked. He had to be selling them somewhere else."

"So he was using the Organizatsiya to do whatever dirty work he did — drugs and whatnot..."

"...And he was also using it to find J/J and get his revenge. I bet the Russian and Italian mafias do some information swapping," I mused. "J/J worked at those clubs with the band..."

"...And he did some money running for Old Man Ribbono's Joker Poker business..."

"...And somewhere along the line Ames might have asked enough questions of enough people to find J/J."

"But this was personal. He may have used their tactics and resources, but this was a personal vendetta, not a sanctioned Organizatsiya thing, right?" I said, pausing in my leg pumping. "I mean, it *feels* so personal – everything he said and did to Ayn, the way he struck out at her when her father didn't materialize. Don't you think?"

"I guess. I guess," Mickey pursed his lips. "But I feel there's something more." He hadn't slowed in his pumping. My feet were pushed up and down by the jointly-connected pedals even though I put no muscle behind them. Might as well pump if you're going to *be* pumped, so I resumed my pedaling.

"What else could it be?" I asked, steering us under the hanging boughs of a shedding willow tree. The skinny, yellowed leaves littered the placid water.

"I don't know," Mick allowed. "But where does J/J fit in? How did he get over here? Why's he been running?"

"You had to bring that up, didn't you?" It felt warmer here, sheltered, under the willow. The wind seemed to have picked up in the last few minutes. I steered us in and out of the little inlets, hugging close to the bank. We were on the opposite side of the lake from the boat dock now. "He's obviously been here a lot longer than Ames."

"But J/J knew he was being pursued."

"That's why he ran. But from one man?"

"Why not tell the cops and get protection? This other guy was found guilty, not him. Even if he *had* framed him."

"He's obviously not here legally, either. He couldn't go to the cops. At the very least, he'd get deported."

"You know what bothers me the most about J/J?" I said, letting my hand dangle in the chilly water.

"What?"

"His accent. He apparently didn't have any. Kasi always thought he was from the Midwest. Ayn said her mother told her his folks were from some part of Canada. He never let on he knew a thing about the Soviet Union."

"Maybe it was too painful to dwell on. He was obviously very private, very secretive," Mickey D. mused. "He started completely from scratch. He reinvented himself, including the background, the accent, the whole bit. He's been here at least 21 years. Some people are just better at languages than others."

"I guess." I steered back toward the dock. "Let's go back. I bet the FBI's involved by now. If they haven't figured out this guy's background yet, we'll have to give them a boost. They've got the resources to track down Tadford's origins, and that might lead us to J/J."

"Oh God, I forgot, we've got to check on Ayn!" Mickey reminded me, and we started paddling harder.

We called Ayn's apartment from a pay phone inside the park entrance. She was home already. They had booked her and arraigned her on a general charge of manslaughter, but given the circumstances, released her on her own recognizance and $10,000 cash bond. Caroline sounded quite positive that the district attorney would go easy with this one. They were on their way to a physician to have Ayn checked out and to document her injuries for evidentiary purposes. Chakra was still planning to tag along, having kept guard duty in the police lobby with the whores and the druggies all night.

"She's giving loyalty a bad name," I grumbled, as I hung up.

"Why do you dislike her so?" Mickey asked.

"Oh, come on, you do, too."

"Well then, why do *we* dislike her?"

"If she were a dog, I would like her. In a human, it's distasteful."

"Speaking of pets, I've got to go home and feed Churchill. And myself, come to think of it."

When we got back to Mickey D.'s apartment there were several messages on the answering machine. The first was from Ira Fahnstock, saying he had some information for us and to call him back whenever we wanted. The second and third were from Mom, reminding Mickey she had made him a doctor's appointment Friday and to be sure to take his antibiotics. And the fourth was from Jake Janus. "They think they've got an ID on your body," Jake said, traffic noises in the background. "But don't call me at work. I'm calling from a pay phone now. Meet me at 3:30 at King of Prussia Mall, the older part, at the Food Court."

"Bingo!" Mickey D. whooped and we high-fived.

We decided to catch a late lunch at the mall before the meeting with Jake, but we still had some time to kill, so I gave Ira a ring.

"How's the sleuthing business?" I asked him after the usual opening pleasantries.

"Well, I think I'll stick to the camp business, Eliza, but it's been interesting, I must say."

"Find out anything?" I flicked the phone on speaker and sat back in Mickey's recliner.

"Well yes, yes, I did."

There was a pause during which neither of us spoke. "Ira?"

"It's most curious," he said.

"Curious?" Both Mick and I prompted in unison.

"—Miss Ayn Curtis appears to be legitimate," Ira said.

"What?" This time just me.

"Yes, apparently a very nice young lady. Graduated seventh in her class from Wallenpaupack Area High School. Played the saxophone in the band." Mickey D. and I exchanged knowing looks. "She worked throughout much of high school and a year afterwards as a waitress at Paradise Regained. That's a—"

"—honeymoon resort," I mumbled.

"What's that?"

"I know about Paradise Regained."

"That's right, they advertise all over, don't they? Big champagne glasses that you and your spouse can take bubble baths in, heart-shaped pools—"

"Typical Jewish Renaissance decor," I said before my mind caught up with my mouth.

Mickey started to snicker.

"Yeah, that's about right, come to think of it," Ira said, laughing easily. "You've always said it like it is, haven't you, Eliza?"

Well, actually, I thought that was something I'd developed over the years. Certainly not back in junior high... "I didn't mean anything derogatory by that," I declared defensively. "Some of my favorite decora— well, you know what I mean." And I changed the subject. "What else did you find out?"

"Well, about her mother..." He paused and another moment of silence fell upon us.

"Ira?"

"Yes, I'm here."

"What about her mother?"

"Well, I want to look into that a little more," he said.

"Into what?"

"The things I've heard. I want to check into them a little closer."

"Such as?"

"It's all just rumor, innuendo, nothing solid. I'd like to verify it somehow. Gossip is a major pastime up here. Ranks up there with beer gardens and cruising Main Street."

"What's a beer garden?" Mickey D. asked.

"Excuse me?" Ira asked.

"Nevermind," I said, snarling at M.D. and motioning him to shut up. "When can you tell us more about Mrs. Curtis?"

"I'm not sure. I'm going to sleuth some more this afternoon. I'll let you know when I have something solid."

"Well, okay. Hey, thanks, Ira, for your help."

"Glad to. It's been an interesting change."

"That's good."

"Give my love to your mother and my regards to Mickey."

"Sure, you too — to your family, I mean."

"Goodbye."

"Goodbye."

I hung up and looked at Mickey D. He was watering his plants. "Who knows?" I shrugged.

"Who knows," he agreed. "Everything but us has been fed. Let's go," he urged, putting down the watering can and grabbing a sweater.

I had finished my Arthur Treacher's chicken and chips and was started on a McDonald's hot fudge sundae, and Mickey D. was just polishing off a cheesesteak and fries when Jake Janus slid into the seat in the foodcourt next to me. He shook hands with Mick and offered his hand to me when Micker said, "You remember my sister, Eliza. We're in the business together."

"Sure, sure. How you doing?"

154

"Fine," I said, managing to finish the sundae without missing a stroke. "Would you like one? It was good."

"No thanks, trying to lose weight. Eating kind of early, aren't you?"

"Late, actually," Mickey D. said. "Had breakfast twice, but missed lunch."

"Irregular hours," Jake commented.

"Not a Fib anymore," Mick responded with a smile. "My time's my own."

"I hear ya," Jake shook his head appreciatively.

"Can I get you some coffee? A soda?" Mickey offered, placing the tray with the remains of his meal on the table behind him.

"No, I'm fine, thanks."

"So what have you got for us, Jake?"

Jake leaned forward, his hands stretched out in front of him. "This can't go any farther than the three of us. If they knew I told you this stuff, they'd have my neck."

"Understood. Don't worry," and Mickey D. patted Jake's hand reassuringly, automatically. Jake didn't seem to notice. He was excited about what he had to tell us. He glanced around as if to make sure no one could hear, then he began.

"Your Tadford Ames is one Demetri Fyodorovitch Dagronsky," he announced dramatically. I felt the pit of my stomach fall. Not Boris? Then who's Boris? But Jake went on. "He was a Russian national of mixed Polish-Russian descent, born in Odessa in 1951. We don't know much else about him, except his visa says he was trained as a jeweler. He seems to have led a pretty quiet life, publicly, at least until now. If indeed that's his real name. It's still hard to get any concrete information from the Russians. They continue to tell us what they want us to know and nothing more. The old paranoia and fear of openness is still quite alive, while at the same time, they've got their hands full just trying to get by day-to-day. We do know Dagronsky came into the country less than six weeks ago on a tourist visa."

"He's only been here six weeks!" Mickey interjected.

"Yep. Under *this* name, at least."

"Well, he hasn't been touring a whole lot," I scoffed.

"Well, we're pretty certain he's got organized crime connections. He's been giving away drugs like candy, and it takes some heavy connections for a jeweler to get a job as a program coordinator for a television series."

"The Organizatsiya," I said knowingly.

"You've heard of them?" Jake looked impressed. Mickey D. filled him in on our morning conversation with Geli and Vadim.

"Well, your friend hit the clown right on the nose," Jake stated when Mickey had finished. "These guys are getting big and out of control. They're even working in conjunction with the Sicilian Mafia now. The greatest fear internationally is that Dagronsky and his ilk may be presiding over the sale of the former U.S.S.R.'s nuclear arsenal to the highest bidder."

"Well, *he's* obviously not doing that now," M.D. commented.

"No, your friend Miss Curtis should get a medal for putting this guy out of commission. When the D.A. hears the whole story, I'm sure he won't seek an indictment." If word spread half as fast to the D.A. as it had to the FBI, the indictment could well get quashed before it got signed.

"What about his family?"

"No family here in the states that we know of."

"And back in Russia?"

"I don't know, really. We'll have to do more checking for that. By the way, Ayn Curtis's father's prints were all over the room that Dagronsky died in. They matched latents the police picked off of things from his house. But we couldn't find an ID for them, so apparently he's not had any previous run-ins with the law in the states."

There was more small talk, shop talk, let's get together and go out for a beer sometime talk. Eventually, Mickey thanked Jake, we shook hands, and parted.

"Damn!" I swore on the way back to the office. "Ames isn't Boris afterall. Either that or it's *another* alias."

"Maybe J/J is Boris," Mick suggested.

"Maybe."

"We shouldn't be disappointed. We at least know who Ames was and that he didn't belong here in the first place. Ayn deserves a citizenship award."

"Yeah," I said absent-mindedly.

"Hey, come on home to supper with me."

"What are you making?"

"Mom's cooking her pot roast."

"Very clever, Mickey," I said sourly. "After what happened yesterday? I think not. Let me know when it's Mother's Day."

I dropped Mickey off at his apartment so he could get his car, and then headed for the office to check on something. Those photographs were calling to me.

156

I took the manila envelope we'd gotten from Ayn out of the filing cabinet and sat back in my swivel chair, feet propped up on the desk. I looked at them one by one. Ayn in her yard at 12 or 13. Ayn playing tennis at 14 or 15. Ayn and her mother unloading groceries from a car. Ayn and a young man kissing goodnight in front of her house. The funeral. The U-haul. And Kasi in the back yard with the kids. Kasi and George. And the old photo of the three children in front of the stoop. I kept coming back to that old photo. We still don't know who J/J was and why he left. Even if he was scared off by Dagronsky, why not come back into his family's life now that Dagronsky was out of the way? If he kept track of everything that went on in their lives before, why not assume he still was, even at this moment? Granted that he was still alive, of course. And whose hand had Marbles brought home and what, if anything, did it have to do with J/J?

I kept staring at that old photograph. There must be something there — some clue — that would help. I rummaged in the desk drawer for a magnifying glass. I held the picture up to the light and examined it, centimeter-by-centimeter, with the magnifying glass. Nothing. I turned it over. On the lower center of the back there seemed to be indentations. I could vaguely detect what looked like handwriting. But the ink was long faded and the writing illegible. I peered and peered through the magnifying glass, but could make out nothing. Suddenly I remembered Darnell's phone number on Dagronsky's hand — an earlier writing, brought out by ultraviolet light. I grabbed the photo and ran into the bathroom.

The human eye is a marvelous thing, but sometimes wear and tear, the passage of time, or obliteration by outside agents hides objects from the naked eye. This does not mean that they no longer exist. It just means we have to look at them in a different light, both literally and figuratively.

In the energy spectrum between X-ray and visible light bands is a band of rays called ultraviolet. Many objects, such as handwriting and fingerprints, emit a visible glow when irradiated by ultraviolet (UV) light. By allowing UV to shine on an object and then photographing its reflected glow, we can often produce a magical phenomenon that I call "wigginwus" (WYGINWYS) — What You Get Is Not What You See.

I took my trusty Minolta, focused the camera, screwed on my old Wratten 18A UV filter, and popped in some highspeed black and white Kodak film. Using a basic 200-watt lamp, I set the F-stop at 16, screwed the camera base on the copystand, placed the old snapshot face down on top of the copystand, and fired away. I took a couple of shots, came down two more stops, and then two more. Then I took out the film, developed it and enlarged it. And when I was done, I had words, written clearly in Cyrillic, on the back of the photograph. Eureka!

Three hours later, Mickey D. and I were sitting at Geli Korlov's kitchen table. We had been through half an hour of pleasantries with Eleanor and the kids, drank a little vodka and sampled Eleanor's delicious apple pie, and were finally getting down to the business of our visit. Mickey D. expounded on what we had found out about Dagronsky, thanked Geli for steering us in the right direction, and explained why we were seeking his help once again.

"Okay," Geli said almost reluctantly, and held out his hand toward the manila folder. "I will look."

I quickly withdrew the clearest print I had made and placed it in his hand. "There," I said, pointing to the writing. "What do you think?"

"Eleanor!" he said, waving his hand behind him. Eleanor got up, walked across the room, and brought him his glasses. He put them on. She returned to her seat at the opposite end of the table.

Mickey D. and I, sitting between them, on opposite sides of the table, leaned forward expectantly across the small rectangular table.

"It says Balta."

"What is that?" Mickey asked.

"It is a town."

"In Russia?"

Eleanor and Geli exchanged a few words in Russian or Kazakhstani. We looked back and forth between them. Eleanor got up again and went to a bookcase, extracting a large book. "An Atlas," she explained. She thumbed through it for a moment, spoke to her husband again.

"It is near Kotovsk, in the Ukraine," Geli explained. "Eleanor knows a woman here in Philadelphia from Kotovsk."

"They are seeking Habitat house," Eleanor explained.

"What else does it say? There's more," I urged hopefully.

"There are names."

"Tell us."

"Three names."

"Of course, Geli, tell them." Eleanor teased her husband. "Geli is so — how you say, dramatic?" she smiled at us.

158

"Oleg, Ida and Elias," he said quickly.

"What, no Boris?" I was severely disappointed. After all this...

"No Boris," he acknowledged.

Mickey D. sighed and looked at me. His eyes said, "What now?"

"May I see?" Eleanor asked. Her husband passed the print to Mickey, who handed it to Eleanor.

"You thought this was clue to man you are looking for?" Geli asked.

"We were somehow hoping that Boris was the name of one of the men in this picture. The original photo was found at the scene of the murder, and apparently belonged to the man we all were searching for," I explained.

"It is not 'Ida,'" Eleanor interrupted.

"Excuse me?"

The couple had another foreign-language discussion. Eleanor got up and walked around to Geli's end of the table and the husband and wife apparently discussed interpretation of the writing. Finally Geli said, "Okay, maybe so."

"What's that?" M.D. asked.

"The letters," Eleanor said, "they are faded and badly formed, like a child would write, but it looks to me like what you say here, 'Eva,' not 'Ida.'"

"Hallelujah!" I leapt up, Mickey jumped up, and we high-fived across the table. Mickey D. grabbed Eleanor and enveloped her in a bear hug.

"What, what? What did I say?" Her broad, open face showed raw bafflement.

"You put together another piece in the puzzle," Mickey assured her, finally releasing her. "I'm not quite sure what it means, but it means something."

Eleanor, obviously pleased at the prospect of being able to help us, promised to call the woman from Kotovsk and get back to us.

I took Mickey home to his apartment, and then called Ayn from mine. "Aunt Eva," she said quietly when I told her about the photograph. "He named us after his sister Eva, not his grandmother," she said.

"Are you okay, Ayn?"

"Yes, I'm okay. I'm fine, just fine."

"Well, goodnight, then."

"Eliza?"

"Yes?"

"Do you think — I mean, do you think it's possible — to find Aunt Eva or Uncle Oleg?"

"I don't know, Ayn. We'll try if you want. But it's a big world out there. Let's just hope they want to be found more than your father does."

Chapter 10
Tradition

When I got off the phone it was 10:30. I heated some leftover spaghetti in the microwave and ate in front of the TV, falling asleep in the middle of the 11 o'clock news. Next thing I knew, I was swimming in that damn pool again.

But this time Elias's mask was gone. In its place was a cavernous blank hole. He continued to tempt and taunt us, while his brother, Oleg, his hands still in his pockets, smirked. And now little Eva sat disinterestedly, dangling her feet in the pool. Behind her, with her hand on Eva's shoulder, was my mother. And it was I who cried into the whipped cream/bubble water as I exhaustively tread.

Awakening in a cold sweat in the middle of the night, I turned off the TV and dragged myself off to bed. But I couldn't get back to sleep.

Finally, at 6:00, I got up, took a shower, and got dressed. I slipped into Cabri and started to drive. I drove aimlessly through Delaware County up to Montgomery County, touching a corner of Philadelphia, and back into Delaware again. I drove up and down the tree-lined streets of Lochmore, past the houses of friends, up and down the streets of old elementary and high school classmates, past the offices of Samuels and Daniels, Private Investigators, past Mickey's place, past my own apartment, and eventually onto the street where I grew up. I pulled up in front of the stately Georgian that Great Grandfather Longacre had built in the 1880s. I turned off the ignition, got out, and walked down the driveway and opened the little white picket gate that leads to the back yard. And there was Mrs. D. in her gardening smock and slacks, by the rose trellises.

"Morning, Mom."

She started and glanced up at me, a brief look of surprise followed immediately by a blankening shield. "What are you doing here? It's early. Mickey's not here."

"I know." She had large, long-handled red shears in one hand. There were clippings at her feet. "What are you doing?"

"Cutting out the dead rose bushes."

"But Dad planted those!" And I stepped forward. I don't know if I meant to keep her from cutting more, or what, but her eyes met mine, and the warning, shaded look in them stopped my advance.

"They were his pride and joy," I ventured weakly. The house was always Mom's domain; the yard, Dad's. You didn't mess with Dad's roses any more than you messed with Mom's Wedgwood.

"They're dead, Eliza."

"But he planted them when we were little." I heard my own voice. It sounded whiney and plaintive.

"They're dead. Everything dies." And she took the shears and snapped off a thick, dry stalk at its base.

"Yeah, Mom. You're right." Everything dies.

"Mickey's not here."

"I know. You already said that. I know." And she whacked off another. I just stood there, watching her. Finally, I simply blurted, "Mom, why did you name me Eliza?"

"That was my sister's name." She didn't even glance up.

"I know that, but why'd you name me after her?"

"She died young. It's traditional to name people after dead relatives." She glanced at me with what looked like mild puzzlement bordering on annoyance.

"Hell of a tradition!"

She gave me a sharp glance and dumped an armload of rose remains in a little red wheelbarrow, but said nothing.

"How old was she, Mom?"

"Why are you asking me this now?"

"I just want to know."

"She was sixteen." And she dropped another handful of stalks into the cart.

"Tell me again what happened."

"You know what happened. Her scarf caught in the wheel when she was out driving with her boyfriend in his new convertible. You know all that."

"And you were a few years younger than her?"

"Younger than she." She corrected, paused, clipped, continued. "I was fourteen. What difference does that make?" she asked gruffly. And she stood up straight, in perfect coming-out posture. "Are you having your period, Eliza?"

"Am I what? Shit, Ma! Why'd you ask me—"

"—Don't swear at me, young lady!"

"I'm not swearing. I just want to know why you named me Eliza. Does that make me hormonally challenged?"

She went back to clipping, her face in profile. "Don't you like the name Eliza?"

"Eliza's fine. That's not the issue. Why did you name me after Aunt Eliza?"

"She never got to be an aunt."

"Neither did you."

"You probably won't either."

Wow!

She clipped in silence for a while. I moved the wheelbarrow so that she could drop the dregs in it without moving. "Did you love her, Mom?"

She went on clipping. A bee swarmed around her head. Two squirrels in the willow chattered loudly. I knew she'd heard me, but she kept on clipping, her face in rocky silhouette. "I could never be as good as she was," she finally said softly. "My father always said he lost the light in his heart when she died." And I thought I heard a sigh, though she'd turned her back to me again.

"Did you love her, though, Mom?"

"I named my only daughter after her, didn't I? Now stop this foolishness!" And she cut off a perfectly good rose.

Then she invited me in for breakfast.

"No eggs?"

"No eggs."

I'd forgotten how the sun shines in the window of the breakfast nook on a fall morning, and the taste of pancakes with real maple syrup. I wonder when Mom stopped coloring her hair.

After breakfast, I went driving again.

I met Trisha Petersen for lunch, as prearranged, at a little restaurant called The Easel, near The Gallery, Philadelphia's downtown mall.

Trisha got there first. I stood there for a moment at the hostess's podium, watching her from across the room. She was sitting in a corner booth, looking out the window, her cute pug nose and fresh face framed by russet hair. I felt a warmth engulf me as she turned and flashed her familiar, open smile at me. I crossed the room quickly and we embraced tight and long. I'd forgotten how much her friendship really means to me. She was my anchor throughout college; the steady rudder to my confused, often irrational, sometimes self-destructive seeking.

"How the heck are you?" she asked. "You look tired." And we were off on a catch-up of each other's lives.

I kept shooing away the waitress when she came for our orders. Finally Trisha said, "Hey, I'm hungry! They make great omelets here."

"Yuck!"

"Oh yeah, I forgot. Well, they've got other stuff, too. Good salads and sandwiches.

We finally ordered and a few minutes later we were served — Trisha with a huge mushroom omelet; me, a grilled chicken salad. When she was finished, Trisha put down her fork, wiped her mouth and said, without preamble, "Very unusual patterns. It took me a long time to figure it out."

"What do you mean?"

"The blood samples. First I typed them. Both 0 negative, RH positive. No great surprise there. That's the most common blood out there," she mused, pushing back her long, gorgeous hair.

"Um, I kind of, uh, forgot to tell you I don't need the blood analyzed any more." I gave her a 'don't hit me' look and a fake cringe.

"What do you mean?"

"Well, we already know who killed the guy. It's just that when I got up this morning and remembered I hadn't told you, I didn't want you to cancel our date on account of you being real busy and all, so I didn't tell you you'd done all that work for nothing."

"Oh! Then you know the relationship."

"Huh?"

"Between the two samples."

"Like I said, we know who killed the guy – the young woman who ID'd him. Turns out she went there with him to find her father and he went wacko, tried to rape and strangle her, and she shot him. It's self defense."

"She went there with her father?"

"No, no, she went there with the guy who was trying to find her father for her."

"He's not her father?"

"No, no, her father's been missing for years. It's a long story."

"This is screwy."

"I'm sorry, let me start over again," I apologized, and drew a deep breath.

Trisha put her hand on my arm. "Wait a minute," she said. "Obviously I'm missing part of the puzzle, but I think there's something here you're missing as well."

"How so?"

"Do you know what auto radiography is?"

"Auto what?"

"Nevermind. How about a DNA fingerprint?"

"No, not really. I've heard the expression…"

"It's an analysis of sequences or genomes found in DNA. You know what that is?"

"Well, I know what DNA is. I remember Biology 101 and those spirally things with the little chromosomes on 'em."

"Right," she said, smiling at me gently like I was some pathetic, simple-minded thing. "DNA stands for deoxyribonucleic acid. It's what provides the genetic coding that makes an individual who he or she is. It's based in the nuclei of cells. All of your hereditary traits are in your DNA."

"Right." I knew that.

"When we do auto radiography, or genetic fingerprinting, as it's popularly called, we subject samples of a person's DNA — from blood or saliva or semen, and increasingly, even hair or skin or bone tissue — to analysis by breaking down the repetitive patterns within a person's genetic code into bands in order to compare their characteristics with another, or known sample." She paused to see if I was with her. I nodded. "We take special restriction enzymes and cut the chromosomes into pieces, use a starch, and then apply an electrical charge which causes the DNA pieces to migrate across a field according to size. This causes them to arrange themselves in a distinctive pattern. We then take a probe, which is labeled radioactively, and it binds to the mate we are seeking, which allows us to capture the image of bands on X-ray film. These bands consist of a genome, or two units of markers — one inherited from your mother, and one from your father."

By now I'm just nodding automatically, hoping soon she'll get to a part I can identify with, and perhaps even understand.

"Okay. Now when you've got two samples and you're not sure if they come from the same person, you want to compare them, right?"

"Obviously."

"So I did that, but once I had, I immediately knew that wasn't enough."

"Why?"

"Well, before you knew who your killer was, the police had said the blood samples were 'possibly related,' but you'd claimed they were definitely different — that it was the killer's blood which some-how got spattered on the door, not the victim's."

"Right."

"But when I did the first band comparison on the radiograph between the victim's blood and the blood from the door, I thought I'd made a mistake."

"What do you mean?"

"They matched."

"They were from the same source?"

"Well, at first I thought they must be. The chances of one band matching — that is, both markers of a genome in any given segment — is 1 in 100 amongst the general public. But you had been so adamant that they were unrelated, I initially thought I might have made a mistake and tested the same sample twice. So I tested a different band on a different chromosome to give me a broader genetic picture."

"Yeah?" Just what is the point here? "I don't get it."

"Let me give you an example," Trisha said, bouncing the eraser of her pencil on the tablecloth. "Remember the last Russian Czar and his family — the Romanovs — who were executed in 1918 and supposedly buried in the woods by the Bolsheviks?"

"Uh, yeah. So what?"

"Well, remember that woman who claimed for years that she was one of the daughters — the Grand Duchess Anastasia? That she had somehow survived the massacre?"

"Yeah, I remember reading about her."

"Well, in the late 1970s, in Yekaterinburg, they dug up the bones of what were supposed to have been the remains of Czar Nicholas and his family. There wasn't much left of them after all that time — some of the bones had literally turned to dust, and the skulls were so fragmented they couldn't compare them with computer simulations of photographs to conclude if they were the Romanovs or not."

"Uh-huh." She kept bouncing that eraser on the tablecloth. "Trisha, this is fascinating, but what does it have to do with Ayn Curtis and Tadford Ames?"

"I'm trying to explain how you can trace relationships. Just shut up and listen, will you?"

"Huh!"

"Anyway, like I was saying, they had these fragments of bones, but that's all they had. Except for mitochondrial DNA. That's DNA inside of the bones. The bones carry less DNA than living tissue or blood or semen, but it's there, nonetheless. Anyway, a few years ago they were able to extract a tiny amount of it, amplify it through a polymerase chain reaction, which I won't get into now—"

"Gee, thanks."

"—and then they had to have something to compare it to."

166

"Are we getting to the relationship part?"

"Yes. What they did was they had to find relatives descended from the same maternal line for comparison. Czarina Alexandra's grandmother and the grandmother of Prince Philip, Queen Elizabeth II's husband, were sisters. So they asked Prince Philip to give a blood sample. And when they matched several bands of chromosomes, they found enough similarities to prove that they were related. They matched! They matched Philip's DNA with the remains of who they now know was the Czarina, and three others — the bodies of three of her daughters. Interestingly enough, the body of the czar's son, Alexei, and the fourth daughter were missing."

"The mysterious Anastasia?"

"Well, for a while they thought so, but just recently they determined it was Maria's body that was missing."

"Couldn't they have dug up the woman who always said she was Anastasia and proved she wasn't related in the same way?"

"Well, I suppose so, yes," and she gave me an exasperated look. "But what I'm trying to explain to you is that when I tested more than one band of chromosomes from your samples, and found them similar but not exact, I realized that the samples were not from the same source. The blood samples from your murder scene were related, but not like the cops initially meant it. They're not from the same person, they're from a related person!" and she smiled a self-satisfied smile.

"Related as in related, related, like from the same family?" I queried. Little warning signals were going off in my brain, like artillery bombardments or flares on the next hill. Not here yet, but approaching, coming close.

"Either related by family, or so alike genetically that they should have been," Trisha declared. "The chances of two unrelated people having such a close genetic match-up would be about the same as me winning the Pennsylvania Lottery without buying a ticket."

"But two different people?" I pressed.

"Yes, I've checked and rechecked. Two different people," she affirmed, shaking her head.

"You get this often?"

"Only when it's a family matter, and the bodies have been so damaged or are so decomposed that they can't identify them by sight. A man goes crazy and wipes out his family and then kills himself. Usually some domestic deal where the wife threatens to leave him and he decides if he can't have her, nobody can. And for good measure he takes the kids with him, then sets the house on fire and it consumes them all," she said matter-of-factly. "Of course, we're expecting to match blood, then. The children will get half of their genes, including half their antigens, from each parent. Siblings will more closely match one another than they will their parents for that reason. Of course, husband and wife won't match any more closely than any other two strangers who meet on the street."

"Even I can follow that!" I remarked. By now the bombs were dropping right outside the door. "So the killer — or at least, the person who left their blood on the door — is almost certainly related to our body."

"Closely related."

"How closely?"

"That's impossible to say. All I can tell is that they're reasonably recent descendants of a common ancestor."

We sat there for several minutes, Trisha sipping her coffee, me looking out the window, watching my own private revelatory artillery show.

"How does this affect your case?" she finally asked.

"I think it's blown it all to hell! I'm completely baffled," I admitted. "Just yesterday we thought we'd finally found out who killed this bastard, what his true identity was, and why Ayn killed him. Now I'm not even sure who either one of them is, except that they're apparently related."

Trisha put her cup down and pushed it away, a look of tired distaste covering her face. "It's a crazy, bloody world."

"Job getting to you?"

"To put it mildly," she sighed. "It's hard to go home to Tom and the kids after you've spent all day analyzing the same bastard's semen that's been scraped out of twenty different rape victims!" she scoffed. "Ronnie's only eight. He asked me the other day what I do for a living. 'I'm a serologist,' I told him. 'What's that?' 'I analyze body fluids.' 'What fluids?' he asks. 'Blood and other bodily fluids.' Next thing I know, we're discussing rape and AIDS and fathers who don't want to acknowledge their children. My third-grader and I!"

"Wild world, huh?" was all I had to offer. But my mind was on so many things. We sat silently for a few more minutes. Finally I blurted it out. "HIV leads to AIDS, which is an immune deficiency, right?"

"Yes..." It was a question more than an answer. I could feel her eyes on me and I didn't want to meet them just now.

"You said that related people can have some of the same blood patterns. Does that mean they have the same antigens?"

"You develop antigens both through heredity and through experiencing illness," she said softly. "Your DNA pattern and Mickey's would be very, very similar, but that doesn't mean anything when it comes to one of you contracting a disease. HIV is a virus that attacks the body's ability to protect itself — its natural shield against disease."

"My antigens couldn't be, like, transfused into his body to help him fight disease?" I whispered.

"HIV is much, much stronger than that," she said, putting her hand gently on mine. "No, Eliza. You can't help him that way."

I got up quickly before either one of us said or did more, thanked her, hugged her quickly, paid the check and left. I won't see her for another three or four months, but everything will be the same when I do. That's how close relationships should be. The same. Never changing. Sound, secure, stable. Undying.

Once again I rode around in Cabri for a bit, trying to figure everything out. But I couldn't focus. Everything kept running together — blood and DNA and fathers and brothers and aunts and mothers and daughters. I just got more and more confused. I finally ended up at the lake where Mick and I often walk. But I didn't feel like walking. Instead, I sat on a bench by the boat dock and looked out over the water. With school in session, the place was practically deserted on a mid week morning.

There was a little spaniel mix dog sitting by the edge of the lake, looking out at is as though she were also lost in thought. I called to her, and she looked back at me with patented disinterest, flicked her bushy tail in brief, polite acknowledgment, then turned her attention once again toward the lake.

Did you know that in only ten years' time, the offspring of one female dog can total 4,000? For a cat, the numbers are even higher. But cats and dogs simply seem to couple, give birth, suckle their young, and then, as soon as they can walk and eat on their own, they are completely cut off from "family," instead becoming attached to humans. That dog sitting there might have thousands of living descendants, but she probably wouldn't recognize or remember any of them at this point, and she doesn't seem to care.

But we humans, even when we've been emotionally maimed by members of our own family, can't seem to manage to separate ourselves from them. We cling to one another at the same time we are pushing each other away. It sometimes drives me crazy.

I walked down to the edge of the water, several feet from the dog, and began to pitch stones into the lake, trying to make them skip across the surface like Mick and I used to do when we were kids. But they just plunked, making small, ineffective ripplings on the lake, then sank.

"You're holding it wrong. Here, like this." I controlled the jump my heart had made so that my body showed no outward trace of what my inner organs were doing. I didn't even turn. Mick skimmed a beaut across the surface, jumping one-two-three. He stood beside me, his long, thin body casting a slanted shadow. "I wondered where the heck you'd been all day. Finally I called Mom." He paused and I let myself turn slightly. He was looking at me real quizzically, as though he were examining my face for a rash or something equally eruptive. "She reminded me you were going to meet Trisha. So I called her. She told me about the blood tests. When you didn't call, and I couldn't find you at your apartment or the office, I came here."

"I hate you something terrible, Mickey."

"I know, but you'll get over it."

We walked along the path circling the lake. Just walked, saying nothing. A noisy gaggle of ducks kept up a cackling along the shoreline. A muskrat skittered in front of us and plunged with a slap into the water's edge, disappearing among the cattails. Frogs made their deep-throated garumphs and birds sang warnings to one another. We watched an army of ants dragging a large peanut across the paved walkway. A few joggers passed and nodded hello. Walkers overtook us. And the little dog followed us at a twenty-foot distance.

Finally Mickey spoke. "Are you okay?"

"I'm fine."

He looked at me, looked away again at the water, then began. "Okay, so Ayn Curtis is related to this Ames guy."

"Apparently, yeah."

"Okay. How is she related to him?"

"Obviously through her father."

"Right. But how?"

"By blood."

"You're a big help. Come on, Eliza! We're supposed to be detectives." We passed a woman wheeling a baby carriage with twins. Mickey D. smiled at her.

When she had passed, I said to Mickey, "Did you know a woman can have two wombs and be pregnant by two men at the same time?"

"Eliza!"

"Just making conversation."

"Detect, don't converse," he said gruffly, "I swear, as soon as I think you might possibly turn into a normal human being, you say something so typically bizarre." A young man on roller skates whooshed by and we walked on. A minute later, Mick's face lit up suddenly like a birthday cake. "Maybe Ames or Demetri Dagronsky or whatever his name was -- was actually a son from a third marriage or relationship!" he enthused. "Another family he left behind -- but this one back in Russia. Only Demetri somehow found out about his father's later relationships, and tracked down Ayn. Then he produced the TV show to flush out his father, but somehow the reunion went terribly sour," he concluded triumphantly. "He may have even set it all up for revenge, meaning to kill his old man for all the heartaches he'd caused, only instead, when J/J wasn't there, he turned all of his anger at J/J's daughter."

"Brilliant!" I applauded.

"Thank you," Mickey D. grinned.

"Only one problem," I said smugly.

"What?"

"What's the shortest age spread between generations?"

"Oh..." he said, turning up his nose. "Well, it sounded good for a minute there."

"It sounded like a week's worth of plots for a soap opera. What other brilliant ideas do you have?"

"I'd be willing to throw in Chakra as a prime suspect," he snickered and gave me a wide smile. And we laughed. It felt so good to laugh with my brother, I could have died right then and been happy.

We were driving back to the office, with me following Mickey D., when we passed the entrance to Vortex Institute. I laid on the horn and pulled over to the side of the highway, and Mickey pulled over 50 yards down the road. I jumped out and ran up to Mick's window. "Let's go see Kasi. Afterall, we're right here. Maybe she'll have an idea about Ayn and Ames."

"How do you get in there? It looks more secure than the state pen."

"We just go to the gate and have them call her."

Mickey looked dubious, but he swung his van around and a minute later we pulled up to the Vortex guardhouse. There was an ornate-appearing but obviously electric fence stretching on either side of a bullet-proof glass booth. Beyond, a winding road turned past well-manicured shrubbery so that the buildings themselves were obscured from the highway. From inside the glass cage, five feet from my car window, a male uniformed guard spoke into a microphone as a female guard looked on blandly.

"May I help you?" the voice said through a speaker pointed directly at my car.

"We're here to see Kasi Short," I spoke loudly.

The guard paused for a moment, looking down at a ledger of some sort. "Do you have an appointment?" he asked.

"No, we don't. But we'd like to see her."

"Is she expecting you?"

"No, but I'm sure she'll see us."

"And who might you be, ma'am?"

Jeez, what is this, The White House? "My name's Eliza Samuels. And the guy in the van behind me is my partner, Michael Daniels," I said crossly. My Social Security number is—

"—Your partner?"

"Yes, partner." And I fished in my glove compartment for a business card. "Here, see?" I held it up so he could see it. Suddenly a drawer popped out of the wall and came toward me on a hinge, like at a bank drive-through.

"Please place the card in there, ma'am," the guard said.

"Jeez," I said under my breath, and stretched to drop the card in the drawer. It was drawn back into the wall of the building. The woman got up and retrieved it, glanced at it, and handed it to the man.

"Do you have Ms. Short's security number?"

"Her what?"

"Her security number."

"I just want to talk with her. Can't you call her on the phone and tell her we're here? We don't want to steal your software, we just want to speak with our client."

"We have highly sensitive equipment and software at Vortex, Ms. Daniels," he said humorlessly, still looking at the card.

"Samuels."

"Excuse me, Ms. Samuels. Security is important to us."

"No, really?" I was getting touchy.

"If you go to the phone over there, I will contact Ms. Short for you," he said finally, pointing to an ordinary-appearing Bell telephone kiosk recessed in the stone wall to the right of the guard house.

"I don't have a number," I complained.

"I will call her for you," he said. "That phone will ring if she can speak with you. Just pick up when it does."

"Why didn't we do this five minutes ago?" I mumbled, pulling Cabri over to the side in a marked parking space next to the wall. Mickey pulled in beside me. The phone rang as soon as I got out of the car. "Jeez, Kasi," I said when she said hello. "This security is ridiculous."

"Yeah, they're very careful in some ways, but incredibly sloppy in others," she allowed. "Are you really outside?"

"Yeah. We were driving by and we thought we'd stop in. Mickey and I discovered something very interesting."

"Great! I've got something to tell you. But not over the phone."

"Well, can we come in?"

"Yes, but I'll have to come get you."

"Is it a bad time?"

"No, no. It's okay. Hang loose, I'll be right there."

Five minutes later, Kasi came to the gate. She inserted a card into a slot on the far end of the guard building and the gate swung open. "You'll have to leave your cars here, but it's not far," she said. "We'll go to the cafeteria."

We passed through a metal arch.

"What's that?"

"It's magnetic. So you can't bring computer disks in or out."

"Oh." Like I'd know what to do with them anyway.

We walked on a wide sidewalk adjacent to the curving drive. When we rounded the bend seen from the public road, half a dozen dormitory-like three- and four-story brick buildings could be viewed in a campus-like setting, surrounded by beautifully landscaped and planted lawns. There were walkways going from building to building. "I work over there," Kasi said, pointing to the second building from the left. "The cafeteria is over there, adjoining the gym."

"Gym?"

"Yes, we have our own gymnasium. You can work out in the morning, after work, or on your lunch hour. But we can go to the cafeteria now and have a snack. They make the best desserts here. Death by Chocolate is my favorite."

Mickey looked at me and smirked. I adore chocolate. We walked into the cafeteria. It was three stories high, with tables on the first floor and around the perimeter of the balconied second and third floors, so you could look down on your fellow diners. "Great for food fights," I noted to Mick.

"Come on, you've got to try D By C," Kasi urged, taking Mickey's arm and drawing him toward the cafeteria line. It was mid afternoon, and there were only fifty or so people in the place. "They come here on their breaks, or even just to think. It's encouraged," Kasi said.

I raised an eyebrow as Kasi reached into a case full of delectable-looking desserts and plunked a six-inch-high many-layered concoction down in front of me. "Ten layers of different chocolate," she said.

"Really?"

"Yeah. You'll love it." And she set one down in front of Mickey, too.

"Oh, no. I'll have some of this," he said, replacing the cake and selecting a bowl of tapioca pudding with a little dab of whipped cream on it.

Kasi took a Death by Chocolate too, and we moved to the cash register. "Six-four-oh-nine," she said to the cashier as Mickey D. reached for his wallet. "Don't bother, I've got it. They'll just take it out of my pay, pre-tax."

"But you don't have to—"

"Oh, it's only $2.50, total," she said, waving her hand dismissively at Mickey.

"But the ingredients in mine alone are worth..."

"I know, I know, but it's subsidized. You should see the prime rib dinners we have sometimes for $3.50."

"I think I went into the wrong business," I groused.

"You'd be an elephant if you worked here," Mickey D. said.

"You're right. But what's your news, Kasi?" I changed the subject as we approached a table in the corner.

"I found out about the hand," she said, a look of triumph flashing across her face.

"You mean Ames? Didn't we tell you his real name is supposed to be Demetri Dagronsky?"

"No, no, the hand that Marbles brought home," she said.

"Oh, that hand." I'd almost forgotten about that hand, what with confessions to murder and nasty little Russians interrupting my sleep and DNA fingerprints and fatal diseases and disappearing ink and naming your kids after dead relatives and assorted sordid stuff like that.

"I called the police station last night to see what had happened with the investigation into the hand, because they stopped nosing around all of a sudden," Kasi said.

"Oh, really?" Then I took a bite of Death by Chocolate and almost forgot to pay attention.

174

"Yeah. And I just want this thing behind me, you know?" she sighed.

"I can appreciate that," Mickey offered.

"Um-hm." I added, around a mouthful of the most wonderful calories I've indulged in since puberty.

"Well, Lt. Franken tells me the case is closed."

"What!" I almost spit out a morsel of real, rich, dark stuff. I rescued it from my lips with the tip of my tongue.

"Yeah, that's what I said, along with a few other choice comments," Kasi toyed at her cake with a fork. "I asked him whose bright idea was that? And he said it was 'confidential official police business.' I said, 'Oh yeah? Well, I'm officially, and not at all confidentially, telling you I have a right to know what this has to do with my husband!'" Her voice was strident now.

"And he said, 'Don't worry, Mrs. Short, it's not your husband's.' 'Then whose is it?' I asked him. 'That's not your affair,' he said. 'Oh it isn't, huh?' I screamed, and I hung up on him!" And she emphasized this point by slamming down her fork on the table.

I looked at Mickey D. and Mickey D. looked at me. The arrogance of officialdom!

"How do they know it's not him?" I snorted. "All we've got is one building super who liked the looks of J/J without a shirt on. She might have been so busy looking at his bare chest and his birthmark to match him with the description on TV that she failed to notice a small thing like an extremity." And I ran my fork across my plate to pick up the last moist crumbs.

"Well, that's what I wondered," Kasi said, picking up her fork again and taking a little bite out of her cake. "I was so peeved about their attitude, that I steamed all night. I couldn't sleep, thinking about what a bunch of morons they were and that if they're not going to prove it to me that it wasn't Joe and that it didn't have anything to do with him, then I've got to find out for myself."

"Well, we've done all we can, given the—"

"No, not you, *me*!" she interrupted Mick, again forcefully setting her fork down.

"Oh?" Mick and I said simultaneously, though mine was a question and Mick's sounded more like an exclamation.

"So this morning I set to work." Kasi leaned forward. "And I broke in!" she whispered.

"You what?" I hissed.

"I broke in and found the records."

"You broke into the police station?" My mouth was on my plate.

"I don't think she means physically, Eliza. Electronically?" Mick asked.

I raised an eyebrow and looked sideways at Mickey D.

"That's right," Kasi acknowledged, her eyes on her dessert again.

"How did you do that?" Mickey asked.

"It's what I do," she said, taking the tiniest of bites.

"It is?" I couldn't help staring at her plate. I felt like tapping into it.

"Mm-hm," she said, cutting off the most minuscule of itsy-bitsy, tiny pieces, putting it coyly into her mouth, then laying her fork tines down, European style, as if signaling she was done so the plate could be cleared from the table. There was still three-fourths of a piece left on her plate. My index finger twitched involuntarily and I tried to ignore the tinny taste of saliva in my mouth.

"You do that for a living?" Mickey D. brought me back.

"The government has paid this company big money to write programs that can do that automatically," she whispered, glancing around us to make sure no one was listening in. "But I can't talk about that," she said in the next breath.

"Well, how did you do it?" I asked.

"It doesn't matter," Kasi waved the question away like a pesky fly. "But the Lochmore police have handed it all over to the FBI — Franken just didn't want to admit it. Wounds his pride, I guess."

"It's possible he was told not to," Mick surmised.

"If it's been turned over to the FBI, how did you find anything out?" I asked.

"It was right there."

"In the Lochmore records?"

"No, the FBI records."

"You mean you tapped into the FBI's computers?" Now even Mickey's mouth was jawing the tablecloth.

"Lower investigation levels," she shrugged. "I haven't cracked the more secret stuff. And this whole thing is now marked with some code that must mean 'secret' or 'confidential' or something like that."

Mick and I just sat there and looked at each other.

"But I did find out where the hand came from, and that it's definitely not Joe's," Kasi continued blithely.

"How do you know that?"

"They think it happened the night of the 4th. Joe didn't disappear until the morning of the 5th. He had all of his limbs at the breakfast table that morning."

"What happened the night of the 4th? Where did the hand come from?" I pressed.

"Well, from all I could find that wasn't sufficiently protected, there was a report that night by a freight engineer that his train may have possibly struck what they initially thought was a dog. They think now that it was probably a man who was struck."

"This was the night before Joe disappeared?" I asked. "The night he went out for a walk with Marbles and came home kind of damp and disheveled?"

"Now wait," Mickey D. jumped in. "The train runs near your house, right?"

"It's four blocks away."

"Did Joe ever walk the dog near there?"

"I guess so. The two of them walked all over the place."

"Is the grass high over there?" I lept back in.

"I imagine, down by the tracks, if you go that close."

"Did the police search down there after Marbles brought the hand home?"

"They must have. They searched a good half-mile radius, they said."

"And the FBI obviously has a theory about who this hand belongs to. But for some reason, they're not telling us," I mused.

We were quiet for a minute, each lost in our own thoughts. Finally Kasi spoke up. "I know now that the hand wasn't Joe's," she said, her lips pursed in a straight line and her hands playing with a balled-up napkin. "But this morning I really got scared. The police say the hand's got nothing to do with Joe, but I know the FBI thinks it does," she said firmly. "The police can deny it until their noses grow so long they can touch their toes without bending over, but that's not going to change anything. The man that belongs to that hand was here to find Joe the night before he disappeared, and somebody — Joe or someone else — found him first. I don't know who he was or why he came or what really happened to him. And I don't know why that Ames/Dagronsky guy was after Joe or why he attacked Ayn or why Joe kept leaving his families but still hanging around and spying on them. All I know is it's starting to scare the shit out of me!" Her usually low voice was a couple of octaves higher and there were tears now in the corners of her eyes. She began to dab at them with her napkin. I offered her mine. Mickey D. patted her on the hand.

"I can't take much more of this," Kasi squeaked. "I'm thinking about quitting my job, selling the house and moving somewhere far away. The only thing that's stopping me is the feeling that no matter where we go, he'll be following us, and we'll never know when or why!"

I got up to get Kasi a glass of water. Coming back, I glanced up at the second floor tier, and there, directly above where Mickey and Kasi were seated, was Chakra. She sat at a table near the balcony, her dark hair framing her face, which was lowered as though she were intently studying something in front of her on the table.

"Pasternak like mistletoe," I bent over and hissed in Mickey's ear. "Huh?" he says.

Now in the good old days, Mick would have caught it right away. He would have remembered our childhood dog, Pasternak, who was purchased to be a guard dog, but never quite got the message; and of course the fact that said guard dog was directly overhead, as in mistletoe hung to be kissed under.

Instead I get a, "Huh?"

So I wrote on a napkin, "Chakra's upstairs listening. Let's get the hell out of here!" and discretely applied it to his face as though I were chasing stray pudding stains on his chin.

"Oh!" he said, glancing at it, then handed the napkin to Kasi, who blew her nose on it.

I rolled my eyes at both of them. "Show us where you work," I prodded Kasi.

She wiped her reddened eyes. "Well, I really can't—"

"—Just show us the building. I'd like to stretch a little." Finally Mickey D. stood up and Kasi rose, leaving her lovely D By C huddled on her plate, half-finished and forlorn. I reverently buried it in the trash can.

As we walked to the front of the building, I hissed at Mickey to turn around and look. "Can you see her?" He played gentleman and opened the door for us, and in the process, turned his body sideways and glanced up as discretely as possible. "Well?" I prodded as we went out the door.

"No, she's gone." And sure enough, when I turned and looked, she had vanished.

"You really think Chakra was watching us?" Kasi asked.

"Have you ever seen her here before?"

"No, but there are a thousand and a half employees on campus. We're spread out between all these buildings, and she apparently just started here. I hadn't even met her until last week. And why would she be watching us?"

"Believe me, I wish I could answer that," I mumbled. "But we've got an even weirder one for you." And we told her about Ayn being physically related somehow to Ames/Dagronsky.

Kasi, who'd been setting the pace along the walkway, pulled up short and whipped her head around, her shoulder-length hair slapping her flushed cheeks. "But Ayn? She — how could she be....?" and the sensitive hands fluttered in the air as if to rearrange its very molecules into logical, programmable, understandable sequence.

"We don't know how. We only know their DNA profile is very close. If they're not related by blood, they should be. Chances of their not being, with the profiles they show, are apparently astronomical," I explained.

"But then Ames—"

"He's most likely related to Joe," Mickey D. concluded. "There's no reason to believe Sally Curtis's family would have any interest in finding J/J. And according to Ayn, there is no family to give a damn."

"Joe said he didn't have family, either," Kasi said, beginning to walk again, this time with a frenetic energy. We hustled to keep up with her. Those little biker's legs were pumping.

"No, but we've found out Joe did have a family, and they may still be out there somewhere," I reminded her.

"Is the whole goddamn family watching us?" Kasi spat. We were jogging now, headed, thankfully, for the gate.

"At this pace," I panted in Mickey's direction, "I doubt it."

Chapter 11
Balta

I got to the office a good five minutes before Mick, only to find Geli Korlov parked on our front stoop. "I have spoken with the woman who is from Kotovsk," he announced proudly with a broad grin. "She has to me given a family from Balta. They are professors at Lochmore College. We go now and see them."

"That's wonderful!"

He started to lead me down the sidewalk.

"Hold it, Geli, just a minute. Mickey's on his way. Let's wait for Mickey."

"Oh," he said, and his broad shoulders sagged ever so slightly. The sight of him standing there in his manager's white shirt and tie, a spot of dried sauce on the collar, obviously so anxious to help, was endearing.

"Eleanor's friend from Kotovsk didn't know the Dagronskys?"

"No, the towns are many kilometers distant. But she gave us the names of Tanya and Mikhail Vakarov, from the same town as your Dagronskys. I phoned them. They are ready to see us now." He stood there tapping his black shoe on the sidewalk. The 4:05 commuter train pulled into the station across the way with a slowing chug and the squeal of air brakes. "They are important people," he said more loudly as the train started up again with a clatter. And he turned impatiently as though he were going to go off to meet them by himself.

"Here comes Mickey now!" I called as his Plymouth Voyager pulled into a parking space across the street.

"Come on, then," Geli said and headed off down the sidewalk.

"But shouldn't we drive? Where do they live?" And I motioned to Mickey D. as he sauntered across the street. "Come on! Geli's here. He's found some folks from Balta and we're going to see them!" We both stepped lively after Geli, who was halfway down the block, headed out of the business district.

"Geli!" Mickey D. caught up and patted him on the back. The two shook hands, but the Kazahki kept on walking. "Where are we going?" Mick asked.

"The Vakarovs are very important people," Geli responded. "We must not keep them waiting."

"Where do they live?"

"They are professors," Geli repeated. "He is political science professor. She is psychology professor."

"Is it far?" I was breaking out in a sweat. Too much exercise for one day. Mickey D. was panting, too.

"—Mikhail Vakarov testified against the KGB when Yeltsin banned the Communist Party," Geli threw over his shoulder. Mickey D. had fallen back a step and I was right behind him, when Geli stopped abruptly, and we two practically ran into him like a rear-end pile-up.

"Whoops!" I yelped involuntarily.

"Here," Geli pronounced simply and almost triumphantly.

We were standing in front of one of the grand old stone homes that skirt the periphery of Lochmore College. Considering they were relatively new immigrants, it looked like the Vakarovs were doing okay.

"I guess these aren't the folks who wanted the Habitat house, huh?" I said.

We walked up to the front door and Geli rang the doorbell. "You have the picture?" he turned and hissed at me suddenly.

"The picture?" I answered blankly. The picture! "Oh, yes, it's in my briefcase." And I patted the briefcase I had been about to take into my office when he accosted me. Just then the door opened and a striking, statuesque woman in her early fifties smiled at us politely.

"Mrs. Vakarov? I am Geli Korlov. These are Eliza Samuels and Mickey Daniels, who I told you about."

"Thank you so much for seeing us on such short notice," Mickey piped up, shaking Tanya Vakarov's hand. She shook hands all around, motioning us into the foyer, and after closing the door behind us, ushered us past a curving staircase into an old fashioned drawing room. The furnishings were turn-of-the-century sturdy Victorian pieces. At a harpsichord in the corner a bearded man was deeply engrossed in performing a Bach fugue. "Mikhail!" his wife said, but he did not hear.

I motioned to her to wait until the piece was done, but again she said, "Mikhail!" And he raised his head. He stopped mid-chord. "Excuse me!" he said, pushing back the bench and rising immediately. "I hear nothing when I am playing. Or trying to play." And a wide smile spread across his face and wrinkled the skin under the eyes of the Santa Claus-like face.

"Oh, but it sounded beautiful," Mickey offered his hand. Introductions were made all around.

"Come, come, sit down," Mr. Vakarov gestured expansively to the many pieces of period furniture in the overstuffed room.

"We've gone overboard with the fact we have room," Mrs. Vakarov apologized. "Always in Russia there was no room. Now we have room and we still try to fill it up like a formerly hungry child, now with plenty, who hoards for the lean times. We are funny creatures, yes?"

"Yes, we are," I agreed as we all sat down. Some of us more than others.

"You are here about a compatriot of ours?" Mr. Vakarov noted, lighting a pipe.

"Mikhail!" his wife warned.

"Oh, I'm sorry. Does my smoking bother anyone?" he said around the stem of the pipe.

"We are still behind on American health habits," Mrs. Vakarov apologized for her husband. Social commentary number two.

As long as Geli doesn't take this as the opportunity to light up his cigar, I'll survive, I thought. But he made no move, and no one objected, so Vakarov started to puff away.

"Actually, it is Tanya who is from Balta," the political scientist noted. "I call her my country girl, because she is from little Balta, which is only 25,000 people. I am from the nearby "big" city, Ananyev, of 50,000."

"Balta is very small," Mrs. Vakarov agreed. "It was quite a surprise to hear you were seeking information about someone else from my little town. We have been here ten years, however, and before that, we lived twenty years in Odessa, so I doubt if I will remember one family from thirty years ago."

"I have a picture," I said, unsnapping my briefcase and withdrawing the envelope with J/J's photographs. "This was obviously many, many years ago," I added as I handed the photo of the three children across a lion-footed coffee table to Mrs. Vakarov.

"Just a moment," she said, turning on a tassle-shaded lamp next to the sofa, picking up a pair of reading glasses from the table beside her and positioning them on the bridge of the long, thin nose. She then took the photograph gingerly, held it up to the light and examined it with interest. "Why, these are children. They look like country children. Not even town children. They are dressed very rural, what I think in America you call 'hayseed,' yes?" And she peered at it as if it would talk to her. "They are of low status," she declared. "Not a Party Member family."

"I thought everyone was of equal status in the Soviet Union," I smirked.

She glanced up at me over the half-rim of her glasses to confirm the facetiousness of the remark. Having done so, she asked, "How do you know they are from Balta?"

"Eliza found writing on the back," Mickey commented, as she turned the photo over. "You can't see it. It was photographed under ultraviolet, and the writing then became legible."

"Hm. Very interesting," commented Mr. Vakarov, looking over his wife's shoulder. "What did it say?"

"Geli and his wife Eleanor translated it for us. It had the names of the town and of the children," I said. "Oleg, Elias and Eva."

"Their last name?" Mrs. Vakarov asked, removing her glasses.

"Well, that wasn't on the photo," Mickey D. replied. "But now we feel that they may be Dagronskys or related to the Dagronsky family."

"Dagronsky," she repeated. "Dagronsky." She tasted its sound with her tongue and her eyes looked far away into the past. "I don't know...I'm not sure...It may be that—" and she stopped and looked searchingly from me to Mickey D. "Why is it that you are seeking this family?" she asked pointedly.

"We represent the family of those children there," Mickey D. said. "There are two families trying to find their missing father and husband, and seeking to discover why he left. We believe the boy there on the right is that father and husband, and that if we find someone who knows his past, we may be able to determine his present whereabouts, and if not, at least provide enough answers so that they can resign themselves to his disappearance and get on with their lives."

"You are seeking closure," Mrs. Vakarov commented.

"To put it simply, yes," M.D. agreed.

"And what if what they find out is not pleasant?"

"The present situation is not pleasant," Mickey pointed out. "There are three children without a father; a wife without a husband."

Mrs. Vakarov sat and, holding the photo carefully between both hands as though she were weighing a heavy object, looked thoughtfully at Mickey D. "Okay," she said finally. I felt pressure being physically released from Mickey's direction, as though he had been holding his breath. "I do remember the name Dagronsky," she said, after an interminable gap. "I do not remember much about it, and this is why I hesitate to say anything, but I will." And again she paused. Finally she sighed and said, "There was a murder."

183

"Oy!" Geli exclaimed next to me.

"Murder of a Dagronsky? By a Dagronsky? What?" I prodded.

"Eliza, let her—"

"—Now that is why I did not want to say. It was a long time ago. I can not remember the exact circumstances. It feels to me as though it was a sordid mess, somewhere out in the country. I don't know exactly. But that is what I think when I hear the name Dagronsky." And she shrugged and raised her pencil-thin eyebrows in an apologetic manner.

"There must be some way we can find out," Mr. Vakarov chimed in, and then started to speak Russian with his wife. They talked back and forth for a few minutes. I glanced at Geli to see if he was eavesdropping. He was looking at his lap, pretending to pick at a spot on his trousers.

Finally, Mrs. Vakarov handed the photograph back to me and put her hands together like the church and the steeple. "This is what I shall do," she said. "I have, er — contacts still in Balta."

Mr. Vakarov coughed loudly behind his pipe and turned his head aside, but not before I noticed a smirk.

His wife patently ignored him. "I will call them and ask what they can find out about the family," she promised.

"That would be wonderful," I said, handing her my card. "If we could find one of them, it would answer many of our questions, I'm sure," I enthused. "Thank you very much."

"Yes, thank you," Mickey D. rose.

"Sbasibo," added Geli, shaking hands.

"Sbasibo," I attempted, and Mr. Vakarov showed us to the door.

"Murder!" I nudged Mickey D. excitedly as we walked down the sidewalk to the road, turned and waved to Mr. Vakarov, still in the doorway.

"I thought she was never going to tell us," Mick said more loudly as we were out of earshot.

"She was not," Geli concurred, nodding his head knowingly.

"Why not?" I asked.

"It is a family matter," he said cryptically but knowingly.

"What do you mean?" I prodded.

"A matter of pride," he said.

"Not to tell about a murder? Why? We know murders happen in Russia the same as here," I scoffed.

"No, that is not it," he said, picking up his pace again.

"Hold on, Geli," Mickey D. urged.

"Don't hold back on us, Geli," I begged.

And he stopped still in the sidewalk. "Well, which one do you want?" he asked, looking flustered.

"What do you mean?" Mick said.

"Hold on or don't hold back?" Geli raised his eyebrows at us as though we were trying his patience.

Mick and I looked at one another and smiled. "I meant slow down," Mickey said.

"And I meant please tell us what you know," I added.

"Well, why did you not say so?" And he mumbled to himself and started off again, this time more slowly. We reached the corner of Cornell, turned onto Oxford, and he began to talk again. "She did not want to tell you because she did not know herself, and to find out, she must ask a favor. To ask a favor, she will owe a favor."

"We could pay her something," Mickey D. offered.

"Oh, no, she would not take it," Geli waved a large hand in dismissal. "What she owes she owes already, but she apparently does not want to pay, and to ask favor of someone you already owe a debt draws attention to the debt."

"Is this a riddle?" I asked, and Mick shot me a warning look.

Geli glanced at me. "Her mother is still in Balta," he said.

"Oh," I said, suddenly understanding completely. "The old woman wants to move here, but her daughter doesn't want her to."

Geli raised an eyebrow as though surprised at my easy but apparently correct analysis. He shook his head in acknowledgment. "It is cause of friction between Mr. and Mrs. Vakarov," he added.

We walked the rest of the way in silence. When we got to the office, Mickey D. offered to drive Geli home.

"No, no, I ride the train. It is fun, brings back memories," he said with a grin. Mickey shook his hand. He held out his hand to me, but instead I put my arms around him and gave him a hug — an un-WASPish and wonderful feeling. He chuckled and embraced me.

"Thank you, Geli," I said. "You've been a tremendous help."

Chapter 12
The Day It All Fell Apart

Mick and I spent all day Thursday giving depositions in a messy divorce case we'd been working on for what seems like years. It's days like those that make me wonder how sane I was the day I said "I do" in regards to Mr. Samuels. I surely wasn't.

Friday turned out to be a day of rest. Ayn's preliminary hearing was postponed for some vague reason she wasn't able to logically relate to us. I slept in late and did my laundry, and Mickey D. had a doctor's appointment in the morning.

I was hoping for more of the same on Saturday, but no such luck. Instead, I was brutally yanked from a deep, wonderful slumber at about 10 a.m., had clothes shoved at me, which I apparently put on in my sleep, not realizing until later that they were Friday's leftovers, and then I was hustled outside. The next thing I remember was opening my eyes and seeing an Interstate 95 highway sign fly by.

"Where the hell are we?"

"Wilmington," Mickey D. said.

"Delaware?"

"No, North Carolina."

I hoped he was kidding. "There's a law against kidnapping, you know."

"You wanna get out?" We were in the Voyager. He slowed down and started to pull over to the side of the highway. The traffic whizzed by at 70 m.p.h.

"No, no, just tell me where you're taking me."

And he sped up again. "Baltimore."

"Maryland?"

"No, Ohio."

"My, aren't we getting snippy!"

"I've been taking lessons from a pro."

"Well, the repartée is good, but you really need to polish up a bit on the sarcasm. It sounds unnatural, almost contrived. Repeat after me, 'No-o-o, O-hi-i-i-o.'"

"No, Ohio."

"No, draw it out, 'O-hi-i-i-o.'"

"O-hi-i-o."

"Not bad! Mickey, why are we going to Baltimore? Are the Orioles playing the Phillies?"

"I've found Aunt Eva."

"You what?"

And he grinned triumphantly, like he'd beaten me to the prize in the Wheaties box.

It seems Mrs. Vakarov had reluctantly contacted her mother in Russia on Thursday evening, as she had promised. Her mother had then spoken to several friends, and one of them had heard that the entire Dagronsky family was gone from Balta — dead or moved away. The last, the daughter, had gone to the states just a year before with her own grown daughter. The woman had heard they were living in a port city on the East Coast.

This was all passed on to Mickey D. by Geli Korlov on Friday when he got back from the doctor's. In the afternoon, Mickey went down to the public library, copied the appropriate pages in every Bell Telephone directory in the East that had a Dagronsky in it, and came home with a folder full of DAGs from Portland to Miami. There weren't any Olegs, and we'd already figured J/J for Elias, so he started by calling the three E. Dagronskys, and when that didn't bear fruit, he went back to the northern cities and moved south. In Baltimore, he struck the motherlode.

"The listing was under the name Sophie," he said. "When a woman answered, I asked if Eva was there. She said yes she was, but what did I want? I practically peed in my pants!"

"I can't believe you found her, M.D. I can't believe it!"

"I told her I had some family news for Eva. The woman said Eva was her mother, but she didn't speak English, and that I could tell her the news and she would pass it on."

"What did you tell her?"

"Well, at first I just stuttered along. I couldn't believe I'd found her. I mean, really, what are the chances? Of course, I wasn't even sure it was the right Eva Dagronsky, and I hadn't worked out in advance what I was going to say, because I never figured I'd actually find her."

"Well, what did you tell her, already?"

"Well, finally I asked her if she came from the town of Balta. She said yes, kind of hesitantly. And then I asked her if her mother had two older brothers. There was a pause and then she finally said, 'Who are you?' as if suddenly she thought I might be an obscene caller or something. So I just blurted it all out — that I represented two women who were trying to find Eva Dagronsky, because one of them had been married to a man we believed was Eva's brother, Elias. And the other was Elias's daughter from a previous marriage."

"And what did she say?"

"Nothing. She didn't say anything for the longest time. I kept asking her if she was still there, and if she was all right. Finally she said yes, it was just such a shock. They all thought Elias was long dead. They had no idea. It would be quite a shock to her mother. She kept using the word 'shock.' Not 'surprise' or 'thrill' or anything like that normally associated with finding a long lost relative. 'Shock.'"

"You were expecting them maybe to kill the fatted calf?"

"Eliza!"

"But she did agree to meet with us?"

"Well, first she said she would have to talk to her mother and get back to me. I was afraid she would never call back. I really laid it on — how important it was to Kasi and Ayn to know about Elias and his background, and that he had just disappeared without warning a few months ago. That last bit seemed to shake her. 'Disappeared?' she said. And then she took my number and promised to call back. She didn't call and she didn't call. I ordered pizza delivered because I was afraid to leave the apartment. I watched a lot of boring TV. Mom called about 9:00 and I hustled her off the phone. I waited and waited. I'd almost given up on Sophie, when the phone rang again about 10:15. She said her mother had agreed to see us. 'My mother is very strong,' she allowed, as though the thought exasperated her. It definitely sounds like the meeting will be against Sophie's better judgment, but luckily for us, her mother has prevailed."

"So we're going to see them today?"

"At 1:30. I have the directions."

"I have to pee."

We stopped at Harborplace, Baltimore's showcase harbor revival area, used the bathroom, and had sandwiches in the international food court.

Then we got back into the van and, following Sophie's excellent directions, pulled up fifteen minutes later in front of a '50s brick apartment house in an area of working-class duplexes and apartment buildings.

Mickey D. grabbed the folder with photos, news clippings and other information, and I took the camera.

"Shouldn't we have brought Kasi and Ayn?" I said as we approached the sidewalk leading to the building.

"Don't you remember what happened last time we did that?" Mick snorted.

"Oh, yeah."

We rode the elevator to the third floor and found 314. Mickey D. took a deep breath, exhaled slowly, and knocked. I halfway expected we'd get no answer — only an open door and another body. But almost immediately there were voices, footsteps, and the sound of a deadbolt pushing back. The door opened. A young woman stood in the doorway. She had the same cheekbones as Ayn, the same wavy hair as J/J, and the intense eyes of a long-term pediatric cancer ward nurse. She shook hands and in a quiet voice, said, "I am Sophie. Please come in."

I followed her measured, almost mechanical steps and Mickey D. brought up the rear. A quick glance about revealed an eat-in kitchen to the right. Everywhere we looked were paintings — oils, watercolors, pastels, pencil sketches. Streaks of light, brilliant colors, haunting shadows, dark landscapes. They filled the rooms.

We followed Sophie into the living room, and there were even more paintings, covering all the wall space to within inches of the ceiling, breathing of an emptiness trying desperately to fill itself. The sparse furnishings on the floor — a second-hand couch, two folding chairs, two draped easels on either end of the small room — barely relieved the heaviness upon the walls.

A short, thin, balding man with wire-rimmed glasses rose from the couch. "This is Mr. Marcinkovitch," said Sophie.

"Pleased," he said softly, with a slight nod of his head. "I must go now." I turned around to measure Mickey D.'s reaction to our surroundings, and when I turned back from the calm, deep absorption behind those familiar, wide, penetrating eyes, Mr. Marcinkovitch was gone.

"Please be seated," Sophie said. "I will get Mama." And she left the room.

But neither of us sat down. Mickey placed the folder on a chair and stood expectantly by it at parade rest, breathing shallowly, as if testing the air. I found myself drawn to the paintings. One drawing especially pulled me to it. It was a realistic oil of a man standing at a street corner. But there was a hole where the man's face should have been. It was the man of my dreams — the boy at the edge of the bubble pool, grown up. Joe. Jack. Elias. A shudder streaked through me. The signature, in the bottom right corner, was in Cyrillic, but I recognized the characters as the simple "Eva" on the back of the photograph.

Just then Sophie entered the room, followed by an older carbon copy of herself. She had dark hair with streaks of gray, sharp, piercing eyes, and a bearing of intense composure, as though she were holding herself distant, shielded. I felt an instant familiarity I could not name.

"This is my mother, Eva Dagronsky," Sophie said. And then she introduced us, in Russian, to her mother, and stepped aside.

"Hello," Eva said simply, but she did not offer to shake hands. Instead we nodded, smiling politely at one another. She motioned toward the couch, and Mickey D. and I sat as directed, he clutching his folder as I lay the camera on the seat beside me.

"Mama speaks no English," Sophie explained, placing a folding chair in front of us. "I will translate," she said, as her mother took the chair her daughter had arranged there, and watched silently as Sophie put the other chair beside hers.

Eva spoke softly to Sophie. "Oh yes," Sophie said, rising instantly. "Would you like coffee or tea? We have doughnuts, too."

"Oh no, no, not now, thank you," Mickey replied, shaking his head. "We've just eaten. Thank you." And he made eating motions, then patted his stomach to show he was full. Eva smiled politely to show she understood. Sophie sat down again.

"The paintings — they are — remarkable," I said, pointing to the walls and trying to convey an impressed expression. I got a nod of affirmation from Eva.

"Most of them are Mama's," Sophie said. "I, too, am learning. But it is Mama whose art has brought us here," she said. "She is doing very well. Mr. Marcinkovitch — the man who was here when you arrived — is her agent. He arranged for us to come to the States. He is scheduling shows for her. She has one coming up in November in the State Capitol building. She is beginning to sell."

"Has either of you had formal training? From what little I know of art, these are very good — unique. Very emotional," Mickey commented.

Sophie translated.

"Thank you," Eva said in a deep, heavily-accented voice.

"She is self-taught," Sophie added. "It comes from inside."

"Yes, I see that," Mickey D. nodded, looking straight at Eva.

The older woman lowered her eyes and looked down at her hands.

"Your English is superb," I changed the subject, turning to Sophie.

"Thank you. I have studied many years. It has finally come in handy," and she smiled her most open smile yet. "But you did not come to discuss painting and English," she added, raising an eyebrow slightly. "My mother is — she is ready to hear about her brother."

Mickey D. opened the file and withdrew the old photograph of the three children, rose, and, holding it gingerly with a finger on either side of the white border, passed it with both hands, like a precious relic, to the older woman. She held it just a few inches from her face, the only sign of an emotional reaction the blinking of her steel-gray eyes. "Da," she said. "Da."

Sophie, looking over her mother's shoulder, seemed the more shaken of the two. "I can't believe it!" she shook her head. "We have a print of the same photograph. She has painted it many times, many ways." And I could see a shudder run through her.

It was then that I became consciously aware of my fear of what was to come. Up until then it had been only a gnawing itch in my gut — a feeling I'd attributed to the rare roast beef sandwich and sour pickle I'd consumed for lunch. But this was not a food-related distress, it was family related — much more insidious than heartburn.

Suddenly Eva began to speak, and Sophie to translate. Mickey D. came back and sat down next to me on the couch, and we simply listened.

"The picture is of Mama and her brothers," Sophie began. "It was taken in the nineteen-sixties, outside of their home in Balta. Soon after that photo was taken, it all broke apart."

"Her father was a cruel and angry man," Sophie continued. "He fought in the war. He saw and did horrible things. He survived Leningrad. But perhaps it would have been better if he had perished there. He was a man who needed violence in his life to make him know he was alive." Sophie paused, sighed. "It is easier if I translate exactly, as my mother speaks," she interjected. "I will use her point of view," she said. And her words began to sound like Eva's tongue, Eva's memories.

"My father was a laborer when he worked, and a drunkard when he could find drink. We were very poor. Don't believe them when they say that in communism everyone is taken care of. We were often hungry. We were often cold. We were always frightened.

"This photo was taken at one of the good times. My mother — may she rest in peace — did her best to clothe and feed us. She just didn't have the strength for much more. If you wonder why she didn't

191

leave him, I can't answer that. I believe now that it simply never occurred to her that she could. So she stayed. We stayed."

Eva sat, her head lowered, one worn, artistic hand fingering the photo. "Oleg," she said, and her hand shook, her voice quivered.

"Mama—" Sophie's voice was anxious, her hand on her mother's shoulder.

But the older woman sighed and continued. Sophie translated a phrase, a sentence behind.

"Oleg was just a year older than me. When we were little, we played together. Scraps of wood from the carpenters' jobs were our toy soldiers. The clothes on the line were the walls of our playhouse." A faint smile touched Eva's lips. "Elias — he was three years older than I. He was more serious, more studious and intelligent. But very sensitive. He wanted what was right.

"Our father was a tyrant. There was no time to play when he was at home. If he caught us having fun, he would make us work. And if we did not work hard enough, he would beat us. He beat Oleg most, because Oleg pretended it did not matter. Oleg would not cry. Oleg would not yield. Oleg held it all in and became a — a masochist inside out. He tore out his own fingernails. In his sleep, he ripped out great locks of hair. He sometimes sat and hit his head repeatedly against the wall. Father began to beat him for his self-mutilations, and little by little, Oleg turned his violence outward, until he became a sadist. He tortured the cat. He killed the neighbor's rooster. He picked fights with Elias. He became a bully, like our father. Only in this did he gain Father's respect. Only this way did Papa back off and leave him alone. He would egg him on against Elias, against me, and the neighborhood children. When father did beat him, Oleg sometimes would come to me and twist my arm or pull my hair, as though by doing so he could transfer his own hurt or have control over it.

"Once Oleg picked a fight with Elias over who would make the tea. Elias finally boiled the water just to shut him up, even though it was Oleg's turn. Oleg, furious that Elias would not fight, grabbed the pan and threw the boiling water into the air. Elias was badly burned, here—" and Eva pointed to her upper left arm, the spot where Elias's supposed "birthmark" was.

"Florida," Mickey said softly, in understanding.

"Excuse me?" Sophie looked at him questioningly.

"The scar — it was in the shape of the state of Florida," I explained.

Sophie repeated this to her mother. A look somewhere between bemusement and incredulity crossed the artist's face. "Florida," she repeated to herself. And suddenly I imagined her painting it — the state of Florida in a scar across the gap in her brother's face. I shook off the image as she continued.

"One day," Sophie translated in her mother's voice, "when I was thirteen, Father came home in a particularly foul mood. Elias was not there. Father started knocking our mother around. Oleg and I tried to stay out of his way, because to interfere only made things worse. But it was a tiny house — just two rooms — and suddenly Father turned on Oleg. He got him up against the kitchen wall and he started banging his head against it.

"And for the first time, Oleg did something none of us had ever done — he fought back against him. There was a great rage inside of him — a great force like a tornado whirling in a vortex. He took our father by surprise, with his defenses down. He stormed at him like a bull, knocking him over, crashing through the kitchen chairs, smashing over the glasses on the table and strewing the pots and pans about the room. He went at our father like a mad dog unleashed after years of being kicked by its owner. He grabbed Father by the throat and he throttled him with his bare hands until he lay dead on the floor, a harmless sack of bones. When Mama saw what he had done, she began to scream. Oleg chased her around the room screaming at her to shut up, but she only became more and more hysterical. He grabbed her in the other room and began to choke her, too. Finally, I reacted. I jumped on him, but he just shrugged me off, threw me against the wall like a rag doll. He had the strength of a thousand unanswered beatings still trapped in him; the anger of a thousand tortured creatures.

"And he killed her, too."

There was silence. I could feel the wild staccato beat of my heart and the sweating of my palms. I heard a clock ticking in the kitchen and the sound of traffic on the street outside. The salty smell of sweat filled my nostrils and my mouth was filled with an acidic bile. I smelled fear as though it were breathing from the very pores of the pictures on the walls.

Eva sat, staring out past us — past today and into a scarred world of anguished memory. She was reliving The Day It All Fell Apart. But her eyes were dry, her voice steady. Her paintings apparently served as the vehicles for her emotions. She herself seemed sad, resigned, calm. So when she spoke again, I almost jumped.

"Then his eyes landed on me," Sophie repeated after her.

And I felt my heart skip.

"When I saw him — when I saw his eyes, I must have screamed. They were the eyes of hell," she pronounced. "I ran. I ran toward the door, but he caught me. He scooped me up like a hawk snatches a rabbit. He headed me off and he lunged and grabbed, slamming me to the floor. And he raped me."

I gasped. Mickey gasped. How in the world could we tell her history had repeated itself? That there was another victim of the horror of The Day It All Fell Apart. Mick and I glanced at one another and shook our heads. Sophie was breathing heavily, her lips tight together. But Eva began to talk again, and Sophie dutifully translated.

"When he was done, he took his hands — the hands without fingernails — and he put them around my neck. I struggled. I kicked. I thrashed. But I was beginning to lose consciousness. Then suddenly, from nowhere, Elias was there. He pulled Oleg off of me. He knocked him across the room and they began to go at one another. Then all of a sudden the neighbors rushed in and the room was full of shouting people, flashes of movement. They pulled the two apart. They wrapped me in blankets. They covered the bodies of our parents. And the police came and led both of my brothers away."

Eva paused, looked down at her hands. "That was the last I saw of either of them. Oleg went to prison — a labor prison. Elias, they told me, went to some sort of government boarding school. I was sent to live with cousins."

Eva looked up at us again. "And now you are here, telling me my brother Elias is alive, here, in the States. I thought they were both dead. And if not dead, then far, far, away, in my past."

"We believe he is alive, though we don't know now where he is," I said softly. "And we have news, as well, of Oleg."

Sophie flashed a look of shocked surprise, then translated for her mother. "Oleg?" Eva breathed, obviously stunned. A look of raw shock passed between mother and daughter.

"We wanted to tell you in person," Mickey D. said. "And until now, we weren't sure of Oleg's identity, though we knew he was related to Ayn in some way. Now, knowing what went before, I'm glad that we came to see you, though this won't be easy." And he paused and took a deep breath.

"Please, continue," Sophie directed. They were her own words, not a translation.

"Speak it," Eva confirmed in heavily-accented English.

So Mick spoke it. He started at the beginning — the beginning as we knew it, that is — about Kasi and the children and their life with Joe Short and how he disappeared one August morning. And then he told them about the TV show, and how Ayn, daughter of Jack Curtis, came into the picture. And about how a man called Tadford Ames cleverly manipulated Ayn into telling her story on TV; how she trusted him and went with him to find her father. And how he took her to her father's empty apartment, turned on her, and, telling a story of alleged betrayal and revenge, abused her, strangled her — and was ultimately killed by her in self defense with his own gun.

The telling was slow and tortuous, with Sophie struggling to hold back her emotions enough to translate for her mother, while ever cautious of the older woman's feelings. But Eva listened with nary a question nor interruption. Her eyes seemed filled with a heavy knowing, a weighted acceptance, as though evil were a palpable, constant presence she dealt with on a daily basis. Only when Mickey related the assault and attempted rape on Ayn did she briefly shut her eyes. And at the self-defense murder of her brother, she opened her eyes and actually raised a heavy eyebrow.

Mickey told her of the eventual identification of Oleg's body and his probable connections with the Russian Organizatsiya. "Until now, we weren't absolutely sure that Oleg was your brother," Mickey D. explained. "We were told his real name was 'Demetri Dagronsky.'"

"Yes," Eva nodded. "Oleg was what we called him. I don't know why. I really don't know why."

"Then who was Boris?" I asked.

"Boris? I don't know Boris," she said almost distantly. It was as if we had overloaded her and she was fading away, shrinking.

"I am sorry," Sophie apologized for her mother. "Mama is getting one of her migraine headaches. She needs to rest."

"I'm so sorry. But I wonder if she could answer just a few questions — there are so many missing pieces. Does she have any idea why Elias would flee? Why he would leave? And suggestions as to where we could find him?"

"I am sorry," Sophie translated as Eva slowly rose, clutching the back of her chair. "My brother who was dead in me is finally truly dead. He was the brother I truly knew. I knew the core of his evil, because I watched its birth and its growth, and now you have told me of its death. And my brother Elias, who was my savior and yet was gone from me, is still gone. I can not help you. I do not know him. I never knew him. Nobody knew him. He is the man of the empty face."

I shot a pleading look for help at Mickey D.

"Oleg is dead, and Elias is still missing to you," Mickey said. "But Elias left family behind — a wife, your nieces and nephew," he begged, rising with her. "They would love to meet you. They would love to share their lives with you, if you will let them. They need to know what they can about their roots."

"Tell them their roots should be pulled up and burned, and the land that they grew out of salted so that it will bear no more fruit," Eva intoned.

"Elias burned many of his roots," I said. "But not all. Something held him to you," and I held out the worn photograph.

She glanced down at it and away, running a hand across her face.

"And he named his daughters Eva, after you," I added. "A parent doesn't name his child after someone he wants to forget."

She raised her dark, pain-filled eyes to mine and held them without blinking. The sounds of the outside world faded as her eyes locked to mine. There was so much in those black orbs I could have lost myself there. I could have melted into them and come out of the tips of her fingers as one of her paintings, the way she looked at me. "Okay," she said finally, simply, and, shaking her head in dignified leave-taking, walked with a controlled, deliberate and measured bearing from the room.

"Give us a few days," Sophie asked. "I will call you." And she followed us to the door.

We mumbled niceties, thanked her for her hospitality. "It must be difficult for you and your mother to come alone to a foreign country," I said as we stood in the doorway. "Your father — did he stay in Russia?"

"No," Sophie said, a wan smile on her lips. "As a matter of fact, I never met the man. And, from what you've told us, I have apparently been spared that eventuality. My cousin obviously took care of that for me. If she hadn't shot him, I would have. Goodbye. Drive carefully."

And with that the door shut softly and I struggled to pick my jaw up off the ground.

"You know what's really been bugging me?" I said to Mickey D. as we neared Wilmington. We had ridden in silence since Baltimore, each absorbed in his or her thoughts.

"The name Boris?"

"No."

"The pictures?"

"Un-unh."

"The cycle of violence?"

"Uh-huh. But do you realize that Sophie is her own cousin?"

"What?"

"The daughter of your uncle is your cousin. Also, her mother is her aunt because she's her father's sister. That makes her her own cousin!"

"Jeez, Eliza!" Mick groaned, shaking his head.

"Well, things like that can drive you nuts, you know?"

"Jeez!" he repeated, sighing.

Chapter 13
The Eye of the Hurricane

Saturday evening we called Kasi and Ayn and asked them to come to the office. I didn't tell Ayn in so many words not to bring Chakra, but thankfully the message got through.

Mickey D. mixed up his patented Hurricane Horror, made of everything alcoholic we could find and just enough fruit juice to disguise the stuff as harmless, and we sat the women down, plied them with a couple drinks each (any more, and you don't know which way the wind is blowing), and then we told them as gently as possible everything we'd learned from Aunt Eva and Cousin Sophie.

Kasi paced, bit her lip, cracked her knuckles, then sat and stared. Ayn cried, swore, cried, and pounded her fist against the filing cabinet. Finally the two women met in the middle of the room, embraced, and locked together.

Mick and I slipped out and walked around the block, then another block, and another. When we stopped, we were standing in front of the old homestead. There was a full moon. The night was comfortable with an unseasonably warm wind, but Mother D. had a fire going in the fireplace. You could smell the sweet, tangy flavor of burning applewood rising above the slate roof, its smoke mixing with the russet and golden maples and oaks.

"She cut his roses down."

"They were dead, Eliza."

"That's what she said."

The wind blew softly through the trees.

"She named me after her sister."

"I know."

"I'm afraid, Mickey. I'm afraid. Aren't you?"

"Sometimes, yeah. Sometimes." And he squeezed my hand.

We stood for a while at the edge of the sidewalk, just looking at the big old house, its bittersweet memories and broken promises, in the dark. And finally we walked back the way we'd come. Kasi and Ayn had gone home.

Sunday, Mick and I worked a Workmen's Compensation case. A pressman who claimed to have hurt his back lifting newspapers had been collecting compensation, but was suspected by the insurance company of faking it. We'd been following this guy off and on for some time now, and hadn't seen anything suspicious. The man didn't do much. He walked slowly, now and then, to the corner of his block and back again. He stood outside his house and watched his wife do the yard work. And he spent a fair amount of time in the local tavern. We'd sat outside that bar on more than one occasion, hoping for him to come out and dance a jig or something.

But this day, after following his car two miles to his favorite watering hole, we were intrigued when he entered a door adjacent to the one everyone uses during the week. This was especially interesting because this particular establishment didn't have a license to sell liquor on Sunday, and wasn't even officially open.

We parked and wandered across the street and kind of hung out, nonchalant like, picking our noses and whatnot, until another dude came up and went to the alternative door and knocked three times. Then he said, "Travis in two," and the door opened and he went in.

I looked at Mickey. Mickey said, "I'll bet three."

"Try four," I said.

"How do you know there can be four?"

"How do you know there can be three?"

We went up to the door and Mickey knocked three times and said, "Travis in five." And the door opened up.

"Ten buckth each," the doorman, a toothless African-American septagenarian with shocking wisps of white hair, lisped.

I gazed about vapidly, as if money were no concern of mine, batted my eyelashes at Mick like I was his date and he was my sugar daddy, and he was forced to fish in his wallet. He found a twenty and handed it to the doorman.

The room was one big wall of smoke — a back room of the same bar, no doubt. There were about forty people — all male — sitting in a circle of small tables, drinking and smoking and yelling and swearing at two guys on a slightly raised platform in the middle of the room. The guys at the tables were slugging down beer and whisky, and the guys on the stage were slugging one another.

And lo and behold, back in the corner, behind the stage, was our fearless paper pusher in the process of peeling off his shirt and then his Sunday slacks to reveal bright red boxing trunks. Senor Pressman, it turned out, was next up on the ticket! We hung around long enough to get some wonderful color action shots of our man, through an ingeniously contrived hole in my lovely faux handbag-come-camera case. Pressman was pretty roughed up by the end of the match, but not half as sore as he's going to be when the Workmen's Comp people pull the plug on his free ride.

As a result of our sleuthing, we now even had a tip to feed to the cops — something that earns us well-needed points with the local constabulary so that they might return the favor sometime when we need help or information. Every once in a while this job can be rather satisfying.

Sunday evening Mickey convinced me to go to Mom's for dinner. Okay, it was palatable.

Monday morning I went to see Trisha Petersen.

Monday afternoon I ran into Mikhail Vakarov coming out of the Lochmore Public Library and filled him in on our search for Elias Dagronsky. He invited Mick and me over that evening and treated us to Tanya's pot roast and a fascinating lecture on post Cold War political strategy in Russia.

Tuesday we shot photos for an accident lawsuit and then spent most of the afternoon chasing all over Chestnut Hill, following the poor unsuspecting mistress of a two-timing attorney who suspects her of having an affair with some other guy who most likely doesn't even exist. Every once in a while this job sucks.

We got a call from Ira Fahnstock, and had a meeting with the accountant. A check came in from Kasi.

Finally, on Wednesday evening, Sophie called. After much discussion, the women had agreed that it might be best to stay close to home rather than go to Philadelphia to meet with Elias's families. Eva's migraines had intensified and the stress of travel and new surroundings aggravated them. Mother and daughter did, however, agree to meet their long-lost family — but perhaps not at the apartment, with "things the way they are." The "things," I imagined, were the paintings staring down from the walls — those which could stare and those which had no eyes and yet still stared. Perhaps meeting at a neutral site was a good idea, we agreed, especially given little Eva's impressionable age and already overloaded emotional state.

So we arranged to meet at a city park Sunday at noon and to bring a picnic luncheon.

Micker got the results of his latest series of blood tests on Thursday. "Thumbs up," he grinned.

I had a hard time stifling the urge to jump up and down on the furniture, but I played it cool, nonchalant, Celtic.

Mick was sleeping regularly at his own apartment again.

On Friday, I took the photo album from my wedding and burned it in a barrel in the back yard. Mrs. Doyle's dog chased the blowing wisps of burning paper around the yard and barked and snapped and barked and snapped.

Saturday I got a delivery from the Paperback Book Club. I stayed in all day, curled up with my books on the sunporch and occasionally looked up and watched the rain fall lightly against the windowpanes. In the evening I made pasta salad and stored it in the refrigerator.

Chapter 14
Boris

We pulled up in front of Ayn's apartment at 9:00 a.m. on Sunday. Ayn was sitting on her front porch steps, a wicker picnic basket beside her. Chakra was nowhere in sight. Mick got out of the driver's seat of the van and met her halfway up the walk. "You all right?" he asked with a smile.

"Yeah," she replied unconvincingly. She looked tired and excited, like she'd been up all night thinking about today's trip to meet Aunt Eva.

"I brought my photo album. Do you think that's okay? It's in here."

"Sure, that's great. Let's put that in the back. We have to pick up Kasi and the kids yet." Mick took the basket, slid open the back door and placed it on the far side of the third row seat. Ayn started to climb in as Mick stood at the door.

"Yes!" he exclaimed with a wide grin, pulling back Ayn's windbreaker and motioning to me to look at what she had on underneath. From the front passenger seat I could glimpse the Groucho Marx T-shirt we had seen flapping in the wind on her front porch the first day we met her. I smiled approvingly.

"I remembered what you said about my father — how it's too dark inside him to see what's real and what's not," she smiled sadly and settled into the window seat behind Mickey D. Black and blue marks were still visible above the T-shirt's rounded collar. She looked vulnerable, yet determined.

"Then you're ready for this?" I asked.

"I guess. It's not like I'm going to see him again, I'm going to see part of his past. Kasi says it's like having an operation so that you can get better — a healing process you've got to experience. I guess she's right." And with that she turned her face to the window and looked out it as if to signal her readiness to get on with the process.

General havoc predominated at Kasi's. Brando had had her up every hour on the hour all night with teething pains. Eva had wet the bed for the fourteenth night in so many days, and the washing machine was broken down. The little girl was running around the house naked, screaming, "No, No, No!" and Kasi was standing there with her arms hanging at her sides, a look of exhausted defeat on her no-longer-pert face.

"Eva Ayn Short!" Mickey bellowed sternly as he stepped inside the door, putting his hands on his hips. "Where are your clothes?"

She stopped dead and gaped. "Brando peed in 'em," she said tentatively, eyeing us questioningly.

"Wha-a-t?" Ayn drew it out doubtfully, stooping to the four-year-old's level.

"He peed in 'em?" This time it was a hopeful question.

"I don't think so. But whoever did pee in them better go get some clean clothes and let me help her put them on, because we're going to go see Aunt Eva."

"I don't have an Aunt Eva."

"Well, I do, and if I do, you do, 'cause you're my sister."

The little girl scowled at Ayn. "I don't have a sister, I have a brother."

"And a sister," Ayn insisted.

"Un-unh."

"Who makes a sister and a brother?" With Eva's full attention on Ayn, Kasi knelt down beside her and began to dress her. Eva automatically and unconsciously cooperated by lifting her legs to step into the panties, and raising her arms to allow her mother to slip on an undershirt and a frilly yellow smocked dress, all the time devoting her attention to Ayn, who crouched just in front of her.

"A mommy and a daddy," she pronounced after a moment.

"That's right!" Ayn smiled.

"And who's your mommy?"

"Mommy," Eva said, with a "you dummy" look.

"And who's your daddy?"

"Daddy."

"Well, my daddy is the same as your daddy," Ayn said. "I just have a different mommy."

The little girl eyed her suspiciously. "Where's your mommy?"

"She died."

"What about *them*?" Eva said, changing the subject and pointing at Mick and me.

"Well, Eliza and Mickey are not related to you or to me," Ayn said, "But they are related to one another. They're sister and brother, just like you and me and Brando. They have the same parents, but you and I and Brando and I have only one parent who's the same — our daddy. Some people would say I'm your half-sister, but I just say you're my sister, because a half is as good as a whole when it comes to family."

Eva was getting little yellow ribbons tied to her hair now as her mother worked quickly to finish the job before the little girl's attention was distracted.

"And the people we're going to see today in Baltimore," Ayn said, taking a washcloth from Kasi and reaching out to wipe more artistic attempts at make-up application from the little girl's face, "are family, too. Do you know how?"

"No."

"Aunt Eva is our daddy's sister. They had the same mommy and daddy, like you and Brando have the same mommy and daddy and Eliza and Mickey have the same mommy and daddy."

Thankfully she didn't get into cousin Sophie's family history, because it could confuse a lot more than a smart four-year-old. I was still lying awake at night trying to sort that one out.

At any rate, by now Eva was dressed. Brando had thankfully fallen asleep and Kasi was busy bundling him up, collecting baby paraphernalia, food, wraps, and other odds and ends.

"Don't forget photos," Ayn reminded Kasi.

"Yes, they're in the refrigerator."

"The refrigerator?" I asked.

"I figured if I put them in there, I'd remember them when I took out the potato salad and the kielbasa."

"You already took out the potato salad and the kielbasa."

"Oh, yeah. Well, can you get the photos, please?" She was putting a knitted turquoise jacket on the baby. "And Mickey, could you please get the baby seat out of the back of my car? You'll have to unbuckle it from the seatbelt. The keys to the car are by the phone there."

We finally got everything and everybody situated and were on the road to Baltimore by 9:45, one nerve bundle of humanity on the way to a family reunion. "Hey, wouldn't Unresolved Histories love a clip of this one?" I mumbled to Mickey D.

———————

Sophie's directions and my navigating skills again proving themselves to be excellent. We found Randall Park, three miles north of the Dagronsky residence, with some time to spare. We had initially agreed to meet at another city park — Woodruff. But just as we were going out the door, Sophie had called and said they'd found out there was a big wedding being held there, and so she suggested Randall instead.

When we arrived, the Dagronsky women were not yet there, so we selected a table by the little pond Sophie had described, and began to lay out our picnic. Brando was deposited on a blanket beside the table and little Eva helped Mickey place the charcoal in a park grille and watched him light the fire. Ayn unfolded a plastic tablecloth and we anchored it with our baskets. I passed around sodas from a cooler and we sat down on the benches and tried not to be too obvious in our studying of one another.

It was a tranquil, bucolic setting. The sounds of city traffic were faint and removed. A large grassy area between the picnic tables and the parking lot and a bank of rhododendrons leading down to the water's edge, which was lined with tall sycamores and maples, made it feel as though we were truly outside of the city. The air was a snappy 65 degrees. The leaves were turning shades of amber and gold and russet. The air smelled of fall — damp from yesterday's rain, musty with a hint of decay. An arrow-head line of geese honked overhead, pointed south.

No one spoke. Ayn sat at the table in a sort of daze. Kasi paced nervously along the bank of the pond, coming back periodically to sit down for a minute and stare out across the grass in the direction of the parking lot. Mickey D. was keeping an eye on little Eva, who was quietly drawing with a stick in a pile of sand. The baby was asleep on the blanket.

I sat thinking about all of our still unanswered questions. In the past week, Mick and I had uncovered partial and possible solutions to Elias Dagronsky's disappearance, most of which we had yet to share with our clients. But much remained little more than speculation and innuendo — half answers which would raise even more doubts in the already tangled and tortured lives of these people we had grown more than a little attached to. Yet it appeared we had gone about as far as we could go with this.

So we'll have this little reunion, I thought to myself. What little closure we can offer will be accomplished. Everyone will get everything off their minds. We'll have reunited the parts of the family that can be reunited, fit the puzzle pieces together that are there to be fit, and we can collect our little fee and get back to the simple cases, like trip and fall documentation, errant husbands and insurance fraud.

I was in the process of mentally patting us on the back for a job well done when M.D. tapped me on the arm with the barbecue tongs and motioned toward the parking lot. He waved at two distant figures carrying a basket between them. "There's your Aunt Eva and your Cousin Sophie," he said softly to Ayn. She bit her lip and rose. Kasi called to her daughter and the three of them walked together slowly toward the approaching women.

"Should we—?"

"No, let them go," Mickey waved me away as I rose to follow. And we watched as the women slowly converged and awkwardly made contact in the middle of the dewy grass.

A moment later we were all gathered around the picnic table, setting out food, arranging tableware, using the meal as a means of common ground and communication. Mickey's burgers and hotdogs began to sizzle and the conversation hugged the safe arena of everyday normalcy in food preparation and consumption.

Little Brando woke up and began to fuss. Sophie and Aunt Eva cooed over him and he became the safe center of maternal attention. "Mama says I fussed just like this when I was teething," Sophie translated as she held her little cousin.

"Who's your mommy and your daddy?" interjected Little Eva, standing at Sophie's knee and eyeing her suspiciously, her little brows knit and her mouth set in a tight line. The look signaled a determination to get this relative business sorted out.

"I've been trying to explain that she and I are sisters," Ayn related to Sophie and her aunt. "She hasn't quite grasped it, I'm afraid."

And that opened up the flood.

Mick and I sort of sat in the background, listening, as they went around and around, exploring family history, characteristics, skeletons, and filling in each other's gaps as best they could. But the more gaps they filled, the more obvious the chasms that remained: What happened to Elias and Oleg between the time they were "sent away" and when they showed up in the states? Why had Elias run, not once, but at least twice? Most of all, where was he now, and why?

I finished off a cheeseburger, a kielbasa sandwich, a handful of taco chips, a helping of potato salad, one of pasta salad, a slice of watermelon, two Diet Cokes, and a leftover bite of hotdog that Little Eva had abandoned. I was just starting on a piece of carrot cake when Aunt Eva grabbed her daughter's arm and motioned wild-eyed at her namesake.

Everybody shut up except little Eva. She was sitting on the picnic bench between her mother and her aunt, singing a little song and swinging her leg back and forth, kicking playfully at a clump of grass grown up around the table leg. As soon as she realized everyone was listening, she grinned broadly and sang louder, oblivious to the look of shocked surprise on the faces of her aunt and cousin. Suddenly Ayn, seated across from the little girl, joined in.

With a jolt, it came to me — they were singing in Russian.

Aunt Eva rattled something off to her daughter and Sophie, a deep pool of wonder darkening her sharp eyes, questioned pointedly, "Where did you learn that?"

"I learned it long ago," Ayn responded in a dazed, almost atonal fashion. "My father used to sing it to me when he put me to bed."

"Yep!" piped up Little Eva.

Ayn continued. "I'd almost forgotten it until I heard Eva singing it just now. He said once it was an old folk song his grandmother taught him. I believe he claimed it was Finnish," Ayn recalled.

"No, it's a Russian folk song," Sophie corrected. "A lullaby." And she translated a string of excited verbiage from her mother. "She says her mother would sing it to her, but with different words — the *real* words. Mama sang it to me, too," she recalled. "But the words you are using are not the original words, they are made-up words. Please sing it again, slowly."

And the two sisters sang their father's lullaby, phrase by phrase. After each phrase, Aunt Eva would gasp and shake her head, and Sophie would translate.

"Little girl of mine..."

"You are my sunshine."

"Boris is my name."

"I am not quite what I seem."

"Maybe someday when you are grown..."

"Some day when I am gone..."

"You will understand."

"Little girl of mine..."

There was silence except for the unaffected humming of Little Eva, providing a background to the adults' emotions.

"So his name *was* Boris," I finally interjected softly.

"They called him that when he was little. I'd almost forgotten it until now," Sophie translated for her mother. "It was a nickname, I guess. I don't know where it came from. I think they used it when he was very young, but by the time we were split apart, everyone was calling him Elias. It was a childhood thing. A childhood name."

"And from childhood, he sang you this song! He gave you the clues from the start that he was someone else and that he would be leaving some day!" I shook my head in amazement.

Ayn held her head in her hands. "But the song says we will understand. It was a lie, like everything else he stood for. I understand less now than ever," she moaned.

Kasi put her arm around Ayn's shoulder and squeezed her tight. "Somehow I believe he brought us all together, though," Kasi said tentatively. "I don't know why, either, but if he hadn't left, we never would have found one another."

"He's not here, though, so what good is it?" Ayn cried in anguish. "My mother's not here. He killed her by abandoning her. And he made me kill Oleg!"

"No!" I said, rising from the table. "That's wrong."

"I never would have been there if I hadn't been looking for my father. Oleg wouldn't have hated me, he wouldn't have betrayed me. He wouldn't have attacked me like he attacked Aunt Eva. I wouldn't have had to kill him!" Great sobs were coming out of her.

"You didn't kill him!" I said forcefully.

Ayn continued to cry. Kasi, though, looked up. "What are you saying?"

"Yes, what do you mean? He's dead, isn't he?" Sophie's penetrating eyes blazed.

"Oh, he's dead, all right," Mickey D. assured her. "But Eliza's right, Ayn did not kill him."

"What are you talking about? I told you, I shot him with his own gun. I killed him!" Ayn jumped up now, her face a red sheet of anguish and confusion.

"Your father killed him," I said evenly, my face a foot from hers. "Your father, Boris, came home and found his brother attempting to rape his daughter just as he had raped his sister thirty years before, and he shot him. When you came to, you found the gun next to your hand and assumed, because you were all alone and Oleg was dead, that you had done it. You hadn't seen the writing on his hand before the murder, but it was on his palm, and as he was strangling you, you could not have seen his palms. Then when you pressed his hand to the gun to impress his fingerprints, you used his right hand, not his left, which was the one with the writing. So you assumed, as we all did, that the writing had been there all along, especially when we heard about his known habit of writing things on his hand, and the fact that there was no pen in the vicinity of the body.

"But Boris left his calling card with the man who had known him by that name in childhood — the name among many names that he owned — the one he kept as his own and sang to his children. He killed Oleg before Oleg could kill you, and then he propped his body up against the wall. You could not have moved his dead weight there by yourself! And before he could do more cleaning up, no doubt with an idea to setting it up to look like a suicide, just as you later attempted yourself, you started to come to, and he chose to leave before you saw him."

"But how do you know it was him?"

"—Because of this..." And I pulled what was left of Mickey D.'s handkerchief out of my jeans pocket — the handkerchief I had used to dab Ayn's hand from the rose-prick the day we used flowers as an entree to find out what she was hiding about Ames's death.

"Remember what I told you about genetic blood patterns — how we found out that the blood on the door was related to, but not the same as Oleg's, and so we assumed it was yours since you had confessed to his murder? And the relationship of the two bloods is what led us to the relationship between you and Oleg?"

Kasi and Ayn just looked at me with their mouths open. Sophie was excitedly translating for her mother.

"Well," I continued, "after we heard your Aunt Eva's story, and how Elias saved her from Oleg under such similar circumstances, I was convinced that your father had a hand in this, as well. And I remembered I hadn't yet laundered Mickey's handkerchief from the day you got pricked with the roses. And so I took it to my friend Trisha Petersen and she analyzed it. Sure enough, the blood on this handkerchief — your blood — is not the same as the blood sample from the door in your father's apartment. And the blood on the door was not the same as Oleg's blood. Because the blood on the door was your father's. He was there. He saved you. He killed Oleg."

A gaggle of geese flew overhead. The baby whimpered on his blanket. No one else spoke.

"We've talked to the police and the FBI," Mickey D. said. "And they had begun to come to the same conclusion. That is why they postponed your preliminary hearing. They'd found out the blood didn't match the sample you gave at the police station, and a handwriting analysis of the 'Boris' scribble didn't look anything like Ames's writing. And with the hand that Marbles brought in ruled out as belonging to your father, they weren't about to write off any possible involvement in anything by your dad."

I was standing behind Ayn now, who had sat back down and was staring at the plate in front of her in a kind of stupor. Mickey, at the other end of the table, said, "Does anyone want another burger or should I dampen the coals?" He raised the tongs and the sun, just beginning to come out in full force for the first time that day, glistened off the stainless steel. When no one responded, he lowered them. A flash of light still glittered behind him. I refocused on the thick rhododendron bushes twenty yards away, behind the grille. There was the flash of light again, like a reflection off a shiny metal object.

"What's that?" I said quietly.

Mickey D. turned around. "What?"

"There, something shiny."

The angle of the light switched instantaneously and there was a rustling and the unmistakable sound of diminishing footfalls. "Mickey!" I hollered and we both took off running toward the bushes. Mickey crashed through as I scooted around, just in time to see a thin male figure racing toward the parking lot, a camera or a set of binoculars with a strap dangling from one hand.

"Get him!" I screamed as Mickey quickly took the lead, his long legs pumping after the fleeing figure.

"Damn it, stop!" M.D. bellowed as Boris/Elias/Jack/Joe Dagronsky/Curtis/Short dove into a beat-up green pickup truck, revved the engine into life, and threw it into reverse.

"Quick! The van!" I shouted, plunging my hand into my jeans pocket for the keys Mick had entrusted to me earlier, and running catycorner to him, scrambled into the driver's seat. "Hurry up!" As I squealed out, M.D. grabbed the passenger door and hauled himself in a split second before I gunned the engine into first. We peeled out of the parking lot, slamming down the other side of a speed bump 500 yards behind the rapidly accelerating pickup. In the rearview mirror, I saw Ayn's figure running behind us, arms flailing, legs pumping, getting smaller and smaller. Never take a client on a high-speed chase of a man she loves and hates in equal measure. No telling what she might see.

"That yellow-bellied bastard's got a hell of a nerve spying on us!" I spat as I shifted down in preparation for the quick left Boris had just pulled. "Shit, I wish I had Cabri!"

"You think a Volkswagen could outrun a pickup? This is crazy! We'll never catch him in this thing, either! And if we do, how are we going to stop him?" Mickey's weight, bent over me as we took the curve, pressed hard against me.

"Jeez, man, sit down!"

"I was trying to save your life when we crash," he chided, as we took an immediate sharp right and he was thrown to the other side of the van. "Damn it, I was trying to put your seat belt on!" he barked, righting himself and moving over again to reach for my belt. The pickup swerved around a car. We followed. Mickey D. plunked down in his seat with a thud, bracing his hands against the dashboard. "Put your own belt on," he pronounced sourly.

"All right, here, hold the wheel a second," I directed, and he reached over and steered as I snapped on my harness. "Now you do yours." And as soon as he had, a car came out of nowhere across our path. I slammed on the brakes. We both jerked forward, but the van skidded safely to a stop.

"Shit!" I slammed the palm of my left hand against the steering wheel, threw the van in gear and put the pedal to the metal. The truck was just pulling out of sight half a mile up the road. "Come on, come on, come on!" I screamed at the van. "Follow that damn bastard!"

By the time we rounded the corner, he was out of sight. "We've lost him," I moaned.

"No, wait," Mickey said. "This road is straight. We should still be able to see him. He turned off somewhere."

"Well, great, where? There's like a road every 200 yards." All the time I was racing through the gears, getting up my speed.

"There!" Mickey barked.

I slammed on the brakes and a car that had just pulled in behind us screeched to within inches of rear-ending us.

"Back there!" Mick pointed frantically to the street we had just passed. "He was sitting in a driveway about five houses down."

And I pulled a U-turn directly in front of a Cadillac full of Sunday spit and polished people. The Caddy jolted up onto the sidewalk to avoid us. I zipped past them and around the car that had been behind us, and which was still stopped dead in the road, waiting to see what crazy bumper car move I'd make next, and we scooted down the side street. Just as we neared the driveway in question, the pickup came barreling out, straight for us, the driver's face a concentrated intensity of determination — a man with nothing to lose. I instinctively swerved and the truck squealed by, back out onto the street we had just left. "Shit!" I swore. "I should have hit him. I had my chance. I should have blown him away!" And we went racing after the s.o.b., past the two cars we'd run off the road, and, a mile down the highway, up a ramp, trailing the green pick-up onto Interstate 83.

"And they say my *private* lifestyle is dangerous," Mickey growled as we merged into the midst of a line of cars going 60 miles an hour and rapidly accelerated to 85.

We flew up Route 83, zigging and zagging between cars, along shoulders, past honking semis. I could see the drivers jabbering on their CBs, glaring down at us from their cabs. But we managed to keep Boris in sight. Luckily, the pick-up was in less than mint condition, and Mickey's van was perkier than I would have imagined possible. But the unhurried Sunday afternoon traffic was slowing Boris down. At one point we were right on his ass, behind two semis stubbornly riding tandem, no doubt on purpose.

"Now we've caught up with him, what do we do?" Mick said.

"I don't know. Should I ram him?"

"Yeah, right. Cause a forty-car pile-up and a few deaths, most likely ours included. It's bad enough that we've endangered this many people already."

"Damn, Mick, what am I supposed to do?"

"I don't know, Eliza."

"We can't let him go. He's the guy we've been after all this time!"

The second the words were out of my mouth, our man swerved violently to the left and exited. I squealed after him just in time, sideswiping a guardrail and shooting gravel across two lanes.

"Thanks," Mickey groused. "I have this van two years in the city of Philadelphia and I never get so much as a shopping cart bing!"

"I'm sorry already. Where the hell are we?" I hollered.

"I don't know. With those trucks obliterating the signs, I couldn't even see which exit we took."

We barreled down a ramp and onto a two-lane road, running a stop light and bouncing off a curb to avoid a collision with a guy on a motorcycle.

"Jeez, I'd never forgive myself," I gasped.

"Then slow down!" Mick yelled.

"I can't! He's getting away!"

Suddenly there was the sound of a siren converging from the east. "Oh, shit!"

"No, that's good!" Mickey enthused.

"I'm not so sure. We're the last in line. They'll get us first. While we're explaining ourselves, he'll get away."

We hung another right, almost parallel to Route 25, and headed south, back toward the city. The sirens got louder. "I can see them," M.D. said, looking back over his shoulder. "Maybe we should stop. We're gonna be in deep shit."

"And we're not now? In for a penny, in for a pound."

"Now you sound like Mom!"

"I wish you'd stop saying that!" And I executed a perfect swerve left directly after Boris, into the entrance of a wooded state park, just over the crest of a hill.

"I bet they didn't see us pull in here," Mick said as we crashed over a speed bump. "Ooph!" he grunted, his head hitting the ceiling.

"Sorry. You're too tall."

We chased Boris around winding curves and over speed bumps, beeping at recreationists, hikers and bikers to clear out of the way. "Oh, shit!" I moaned, as the pick-up pulled suddenly down a rough dirt road a third of a mile ahead of us. The van jolted along the rutted road, bordered by thick woods and bushes that scraped at either side of the vehicle, but we began to lose ground almost immediately to the sturdier pick-up. The terrain was just too rough for its suspension. We were getting further and further behind. "Damn it! We're done for now. Maybe I should shoot his tires out."

"No!" Mick said, grabbing my arm as I reached inside my blazer. "This might be a dead end."

"For who?"

"I doubt he knows this park. He may run out of options soon. We could catch up."

I glanced at Mick. "You think?" Suddenly the thought frightened me. I patted my shoulder holster for comfort. With the next turn, the pick-up was out of sight. We kept bouncing along the rocky terrain as fast as conditions would allow without ripping out the bottom of the low-lying vehicle. The undercarriage scraped against rocks in the road. We rounded another turn and came upon a small stream which had overrun the trail. We forded that without much trouble, then bounced up over a crest. As we came down a long hill, I heard a crashing thud up ahead. "What's that?" I yelped.

We rounded a turn and Mick screamed, "Stop!" as I slammed on the brakes to avoid rear-ending the pickup, which had run head-on into a huge fallen pine, canted sideways across the trail.

Both doors were ajar. Nothing in sight was moving. I cut the engine, pulled my gun from its holster, released the safety and cocked it, and we slid out of the van. Glancing cautiously about, we approached the truck from the rear, peeking first in the empty bed, then sneaking along either side of her. I leaped to the open door, revolver outstretched, finger on the trigger. A shot whizzed in Mick's direction, slamming into the underbrush beyond. As I positioned myself to return fire, hesitating only to confirm Mick was out of my line, Dagronsky, his body splayed awkwardly across the seat, swiveled his shoulder toward me, the gun in his right hand rotating almost in slow motion, his dark, raven-like eyes peering out between rivulets of blood, locking onto mine. "Go ahead," he said, in a deep, bottomless voice so cold and empty that I knew the physical damage he would sustain were I to pull the trigger on the bead I had drawn on his forehead, at the very spot where his head had smashed into the windshield, couldn't touch whatever was damaging him from inside. "Go ahead," he repeated, the gun in his hand aimed not at me, but at his own temple. The words were Hollywood, but the man who spoke them was not acting.

"Drop it!" I hollered.

He only looked through me, his eyes searing holes through my skull, beyond to another world.

"Drop it!" I repeated. I could feel a drop of sweat trickle into the corner of my eye, and I blinked involuntarily. Instantaneously, I heard a click and blinked again to see Dagronsky's trigger finger repeat the motion with the same result. Click! He turned his face toward the nonresponsive weapon and squeezed once more, point-blank, into his own bottomless eyes. Click!

At that moment, Mick leapt from behind him, his long, muscled arm reaching and grabbing the wrist, pushing the muzzle toward the ceiling, struggling to loosen Dagronsky's steel-like grip of the recalcitrant suicide tool. Suddenly the trigger clicked again. Boom! A live bullet shot through the roof of the truck. In the split instant of frozen disappointment I saw in Dagronsky's eyes, I smashed the butt of my revolver down on his exposed knee, his grip on the gun recoiled in reflexive pain and Mick wrested it from his grasp and threw it into the woods behind him.

Dagronsky, now half-seated with his feet out the driver's door, his left hand cupping his bashed knee, his right gripping the steering wheel for support, taunted me once again to finish him off. "Go ahead," he almost whispered it this time. "They're not going to catch me. I have nothing to lose. Go ahead," he urged.

I shook my head. "You're going to face your family," I snarled, waving the gun at him. I saw my hand shaking. I lowered the gun, took a deep breath. "They need answers. You owe them answers."

Behind him, Mickey D. shook his head slowly in agreement.

"I can't," Dagronsky said, almost plaintively. The black of his eyes had somehow grayed, clouded over, as though the spark of life which colored them was gone.

"You must," Mick said matter-of-factly. He had come around the back of the truck and was standing at my right shoulder.

"They'll hate me." The words were deep, cavernous, spoken with a fathomless sadness that made me tremble again.

"Maybe," Mick acknowledged. "But now they don't even know you. They will never know you. They will never understand why."

214

"What they will know," I said, finding my voice, "is that their father ran out on them without a word; that their mothers were abandoned; that their husband didn't so much as leave a note, didn't even have the guts to face them."

"Hit and run, that's what you've committed. Hit and run on their lives. Own up. Take responsibility," Mickey urged.

"They'll never understand. I can't come back. It's too late. It's too much. It's gone too far. It's dangerous for them now, too. I must run forever or die." Blood dripped from his jaw onto the knee of his jeans. Mickey extracted a handkerchief, handed it to him. Dagronsky took the handkerchief without understanding, letting his hand fall immediately to his lap. Mickey bent over, took the handkerchief out of the man's slack hand and administered to his face, dabbing at the nasty gash on his forehead with almost maternal care. Dagronsky looked up at Mick as though it had been a long time since an alien creature of unfathomable motives had administered to him in such a fashion. The look on his face was not unlike that on the faces of the devout witnessing stigmata coming from marble statues of Christ. But he said nothing, allowing Mick to examine the cut, watching with vapid silence as he removed a pocket knife from the front pocket of his jeans, knelt on the ground in front of him and slit a hole in Dagronsky's left jeans leg at the ankle, ripping a tear to the thigh which exposed the bruising gash on his knee.

"She packs a wallop, hey?" Mick smiled ironically at his patient, who could only look back at him, incredulous but silent. "I don't think anything's broken, though, do you?" he said rhetorically. Then he ripped the pants leg off at the thigh, stripped a tear down the middle of it to make two pieces of cloth, and took one and bound it around Dagronsky's knee wound, and the other and tied it around the gash on Dagronsky's forehead, like a headband to stop the flow of blood. "There!" he pronounced and reached to grab Dagronsky's left arm to assist him from the truck. "Help me, Eliza," he directed, and I lowered my gun and took his other arm as we eased him out of the cab.

"What are you doing?" he finally grunted as we walked him, unsteady and limping, to the van.

"We're taking you to meet your family," The Mick said.

"But They're after me," he mumbled half-heartedly, the fight in him gone, the fear replaced by a sad submission.

"We know that," Mick said, his own blue eyes peering into Dagronsky's grayish orbs. "We want you to tell your family that, and why. All of it. The whole story. The real story. Then we'll see what to do. We won't promise you anything. But you must do this."

"But I—"

"This is your one chance to come clean, Mister — to explain your side and redeem what you can," I urged. "The authorities will be here soon. It's only a matter of time. We need to get away before they show up. What happens afterward, I really don't care," I said coldly, still holding the grip of my gun as we eased Dagronsky into the back seat and I scooted in beside him. Mick might want to nurse and nurture this man back into the bosom of his family, but I had come to believe they would be better off in the long run without him. If he was intent upon killing himself, well — I looked at Mick's flushed face as he put the van in reverse and turned his shoulder to back down the dirt path. His eyes flickered across my face, and I saw the fear beneath the surface calm — the fear of death seen in others; the fear of life left unfinished. I knew then that Mickey couldn't stand to see this man die — that somehow he had made Dagronsky's life a kind of tangled metaphor for his own — our fathers' unanswered suicide, Mick's own impending mortality. As for me, I wanted only to know what had brought this man this far — all the whys, all the why nots. Mick, being Mick, wanted to see him rise above it, to redeem himself in whatever way he could.

But we all knew there wasn't much time. It wouldn't be long before *they* — the cops or the Feds or the CIA or whomever was on our trail by now — caught up with us and wrested all decision from us. That thought brought a sudden bolt of fear and immediacy. "Stop!" I screamed, and Mick slammed on the brakes.

"What is it?"

"The gun!" I shrieked as I pulled the sliding door open, jumped down and ran into the woods. I fumbled about in the brush for about forty seconds before I sighted it. "I got it! I got it!" And I ran with it back to the van. "Okay, let's go. Quick!" Mick's prints were all over that gun. Of course, it was bad enough both of ours were in the truck, but who knows what *they* could pin on us for the gun... I checked the chamber, making sure all the bullets were spent, and then tucked Dagronsky's gun inside my jeans.

As we approached the paved road, a park ranger stood at the intersection, suspiciously eyeing our vehicle. "Get down!" I hissed, and Dagronsky grimaced and slid painfully to the floorboards, holding his knee with one hand and his chest, where the steering wheel must have bashed him good, with the other. I draped his own little daughter's pink blanket, left there from this morning, over him as the officer came to Mickey's opened window.

"What's going on? That road is not authorized for non-employees," the ranger warned. "I could have you arr—."

"There's been an accident," Mickey cut him off. "Someone's been hurt. Call an ambulance."

"An accident? You weren't shooting illegally at game back there? I thought I heard gunshots!"

"I'd call the cops if I were you," Mick acknowledged, then slipped the van in gear and started to drive away.

"Wait!" the ranger called, waving a ball-point pen in the air. "You can't leave! Come back!"

But we drove away as quickly as the abused vehicle would allow. "That will distract them for a while," Mick offered as Dagronsky came out from underneath his blanket, clutching it like a talisman, his now-grey eyes almost hazy, fogged under. This one symbol of his child's vulnerability and closeness had softened him into a kitttenlike shell of the former tiger we had witnessed just fifteen minutes earlier.

Chapter 15
Confrontation

When we got back to the park where the picnic had been held, Mickey parked the van and left us to check. He came back with a note written on a napkin that had been tacked to the picnic table, penned with Kasi's blood-red lipstick. It said, "Come to Aunt Eva's place."

Seven minutes later, we arrived at Eva's apartment building. By then, Dagronsky's body had begun to curl toward a fetal position. He huddled, unresponsive, as Mickey tried to coax him out. Finally, I pushed Mick aside. "Eliza!" Mick warned as I released the safety on my revolver once more and crowded in on the broken pink form. I shrugged off his restraining hand upon my shoulder. "It's okay," I said softly only inches from Dagronsky's face. "It's okay. I won't hurt him. Not if he gets his sorry ass out of this van and goes up there and faces his family. But there's one thing I've never understood, and that is cowardice. I'm amazed that after all you've been through, you're afraid of your own family more than *them*." And with that, I crowded in so close that I could see the clouds over his pupils start to clear and a flicker of black flare like an ember in the dark. He stirred and stretched out his legs. A corner of the blanket dropped from one hand and he eyed me with hatred. "Good," I continued in the same even, quiet tone. "Because you are one catch I am not letting go. Even if I have to shoot little pieces of you off one by one, beat you senseless and then revive you in there on the kitchen table. You are going to face the music!"

I backed off a foot. Mickey D. curled his lip at me and mimicked with false incredulity, "Little pieces?"

I poked him with an elbow to shut him up. Something was working. It was undoubtedly the threat to his pride rather than his bodily parts which had sparked something in Dagronsky, but expressing the latter had felt extremely satisfying.

Finally, Dagronsky uncurled his form and Mick and I backed out of the van as our captive painfully emerged, still wrapped in his daughter's baby blanket. He stood upright, wobbling a little, like a buoy in a rough sea. Mick stood on one side of him, and I on the other, and we ushered him as quickly and unobtrusively as possible into the building and onto the elevator. When we stepped off onto the third floor, Mickey turned to the now subdued Dagronsky. "Are you ready?"

Dagronsky glanced up and down the hallway and then at me. My hand now resting as unobtrusively as possible on the shouldered weapon concealed under my blazer. "They deserve this," I said quietly. He nodded his head and bowed it, a sinner prepared to do penance. Mickey reached to knock at Eva's door. Suddenly Dagronsky stepped forward and waved him away.

So when Sophie opened the door, niece and uncle stood face-to-face for the first time in their lives. She expelled a guttural exclamation in Russian and just stood there in the doorway, her normal wall of composure cracked, floundering and awash. Boris stood on the doorstep, facing her, swathed in bandages, wrapped in his daughter's blanket, as vulnerable as a baby. Finally, Sophie reached out to him. One strong hand grasped his, the other took his elbow in a supporting gesture. "I am your niece, Sophie," she said softly. "Thank you for saving my mother's life, and mine." And she drew him into the foyer. He followed without a word.

Mick and I exchanged looks as we entered behind them. I could see into the kitchen beyond, where Ayn and Kasi, their backs to us, were absorbed in examining one of Eva's impressionistic paintings upon the wall. Eva was making motions as if explaining the laying of the paint upon the canvas. Suddenly she stopped, mid-gesture, and looked up, her eyes meeting her brother's across the room. A faint smile crossed Boris's face — a lightening of skin tone, a loosened degree of tightness in his stance and around his eyes. Eva stepped wordlessly from the side of her niece and sister-in-law, crossed the kitchen, and, taking Boris's outstretched hands in hers, raised them to her lips and kissed the backs of his hands like a pilgrim seeking the blessing of a pontiff. He took her care-worn face between his musician's hands and drew her to him, kissing her with feeling on the left cheek, the right cheek, and gently on the forehead.

The crash of a porcelain cup against the metal edge of a table, and a startled squeal brought us quickly back to reality, as Kasi hurtled her small frame across the room and bowled into Boris at waist level. Eva was jostled off to the side as Boris staggered backwards, struggling to maintain his balance while trying to fend off the pummeling force of an emotional tornado released from captivity. He lost. Down he went, Kasi tumbling with him. She thrashed about on top of him, screaming invectives and landing glancing blows as he squirmed about beneath her, like a beetle trapped upside down on its back, being tormented by a small boy with a stick.

"That's my father!" Ayn suddenly screamed. "Get off of him! Get off!" And she tugged at Kasi with all her might, her brown hair whipping the air, her eyes gleaming with a religious-like fervor.

Unsure if her intent was to get a piece of Boris for herself, or to keep Kasi from pounding him to a pulp, I glanced quickly from Eva to Sophie, seeking some sort of consensus on whether to join in on the toffee pull, or to let them work out the damages between them. Personally, I had the urge to sneak in a good quick kick myself. Anyone who takes a shot at my brother — even if only to keep him away — deserves what he gets. And I certainly couldn't fault Kasi for trying to beat the shit out of the man who had abandoned her and her kids without so much as a fair-thee-well. Ayn — well, Ayn's desire to both embrace and kill the man she felt equally responsible for her mother's agonizing decline and death and her own rescue from his psychotic brother carried enough emotional baggage to leave in doubt anything she might do to the man. He was her father, but at the same time his abandonment of her and her mother was tantamount to emotional gang rape.

I didn't have long to cogitate on the quandary, because Eva and Sophie soon jumped in and Mick lent a hand. Ayn was pulled off of Kasi and Kasi was pealed off of Boris. The sudden absence of physical contact had the effect of a breaker tripping from voltage overload — the emotional energy was suddenly zapped into submission; all impetus seemed to go out of the encounter. People stood about or lay or sat there, spent, panting, sobbing, moaning.

Finally Boris broke the silence. He said something in a whisper, a kissing breath of air, a sigh. I glanced at Mickey, confirming that he, too, had failed to catch it. But no one said a word. We all just stared at him, sitting there on the checkered linoleum on top of his pink blanket. His makeshift bandages had been dislodged. The one tied around his forehead was knocked askew, partially covering his right eye, and the blood had begun once again to trickle down his long nose. "I'm sorry," he said more loudly when some time had passed. "I'm so very, very sorry. Please, please forgive me."

"I can't," said Kasi, rising slowly to her feet from a kneeling position. "That time is past. Had you come to me of your own free will and explained things weeks ago, months ago, I would have tried to understand. I would have tried... Your daughter cries for you at night. She wakes with nightmares. She sings your song — your God damned 'Boris's song!' She turned her back on him and her shoulders slumped. "I was going to fix you lobster, for Christ's sake. I don't even like lobster! The police said you'd found another woman. The dog brought me a hand, but it wasn't yours. You gave me your hand in marriage. Why did you take it back? Why?" They sounded like nonsequiters, but they weren't. To Kasi they made perfect sense.

"I didn't mean to hurt you — I thought the less you knew the less They could—"

"Didn't mean to hurt?" It was Ayn now, standing by the kitchen table, her arms at her side, her hands in tight fists, tears streaming down her face. "Didn't mean to hurt? When you just up and leave your family — your families? When you disappear forever without a word? You killed my mother. It took her nine years to die, but you killed her. And then your crazy brother almost killed me when you weren't available. Why did you kill my mother, then save me? Why?"

Boris's face showed shame, concern, and embarrassment, but mostly, confusion.

Mickey stepped in to save us from ourselves, but also to try to salvage what little honor Boris still held in his daughter's eyes. We knew Dagronsky hadn't been the one to save Ayn, but it had seemed expedient and kind to give her that scenario to help her deal with the situation. That, of course, was back when we thought Boris was going to remain some wispy, surreal entity out there in the mist. "Ayn knows you saved her by killing Oleg before he could kill her," Mickey prompted, a stern, warning look in his demeanor.

Boris, glancing up at Mick, quickly realized this spin on things was to his advantage, and grasped at it like absolution on his death bed. He was anxious for redemption, even if it was rightly someone else's. His face lit up. "But you're okay?" he asked Ayn tentatively. "He didn't—"

"Thanks to you, he obviously didn't kill me," Ayn spat sarcastically. She would give him no more than that. Unconsciously, her hand went to her still-bruised neck, but her eyes could not meet his.

"He didn't—?"

"What difference would it make?" Ayn bit the words off and spit them in his face.

He cringed, his hands rising before his face, almost in supplication. "I'm sorry, Ayn, Kasi... I never wanted it to get like this. I never — my life.." And he struggled awkwardly to his feet, wincing from the pain. He stepped toward his older daughter, reaching out his arm.

Ayn shuddered and backed up, shaking her head. The tears continued to flow unabated, her eyes resisting his.

"Kasi—" And he turned to his wife where she stood by the sink, his eyes imploring. "I didn't mean for this to happen, Kasi," he begged. "It was beyond my control. I thought that if They knew that you knew, They might come after you, too. If you didn't know, it wouldn't hurt so much. You could get on with your life, forget about me."

"Like your first wife forgot about you?" Kasi snarled and curled her lip in disgust. "If I didn't know what, Joe? That your name wasn't Joe? That it wasn't Jack and it wasn't Elias? Maybe your name's not really Boris, either? Huh, Dagronsky? Is that it? Is that what you were shielding us from? That you don't have a name? Is that what made you run and hide? Why, Joe, why? Who the fuck are you to tell me what I shouldn't know? What happened to you to make you play God with our lives? Just who the fuck do you think you are?" She screamed the last and stood there trembling, her knuckles white from grasping the corner of the sink as though it were a life raft, her lips drawn in a tight, bloodless line, and her bright eyes wide with anger and hurt.

The line of Boris's shoulders sloped in dejection, his face pale with anguished pain amid the rivulets of blood — a road map to a hellish place of fear and dread. "I'll tell you. I'll tell you all I know. I'll tell you now and then I'll leave you alone." And he all but collapsed into a kitchen chair, beneath a painting of Oleg with dead daisies coming out of assorted facial cavities.

Sophie came to him with a warm, wet washcloth and bathed his forehead, wiping the blood from his face. He seemed in a trance, his eyes clouded again as they had been in the woods when we'd disarmed him.

Aunt Eva silently pulled out chairs at the table and motioned the rest of us to sit down. Kasi refused, choosing to lean instead against the stove. Ayn took the chair furthest away from her father, opposite and catycorner to him. Mick sat next to him and I positioned myself straight across from Boris, next to Ayn. Sophie produced coffee and placed it in front of us, then sat beside her mother at the head of the table, next to her uncle. I noticed Little Eva's absence.

"Mr. Marcinkovitch and his wife came to take Eva for a few hours," Sophie explained. "They're going to the zoo." Gee, and they could have attended one here for free! But all Little Eva needed was to witness this little family reunion, and she'd be wetting her bed forever.

"Brando is asleep in the other room," Kasi added.

In the empty space after the mention of his son's name, Boris's smooth baritone growled reluctantly to life, his hands lay flat on the table before him, his eyes staring through me into oblivion. "They're after me," he said simply. "When they take me, they will take my body, but not my soul. My soul they ripped from me years ago, when I was a boy. It is in a hut in Balta; in an apartment in Gaczyna. As much as I wanted it to follow me here, when I came to Pennsylvania, it would not; it could not. I hope only that you can try to understand and try to forgive."

He said the words, but his affect was flat, distant, as though he had turned on a recorder inside himself and was only releasing words he had rehearsed throughout a lifetime. He seemed only peripherally aware of his audience and our reactions to his words, speaking almost in a monotone, yet pausing to allow time for Sophie to quietly translate to her mother. The words had a strange, poetic distance to them, like an actor's narrative.

"What I am going to tell you will sound crazy, I know. That's because it is. But it is true. As much a lie as my life has been, what I tell you now is the truth. You must know this and believe this.

"By now, my sister Eva has told you of our beginnings — of the poverty, the despair, the violence of our upbringing. I myself believe we were born afraid, and that fear made us creatures of the darkness — separate from normality, unable to function in the mainstream. The day I came home to find my brother Oleg had killed our parents and had raped Eva and all but killed her was a day that the fates had prescribed. It was not so much a surprise as a destiny. Since that time, I came to realize that something else — some hand of fate — controlled my life and it seemed I could do nothing about it.

"And until two months ago, I let it control me. I thought I had broken free, but the freedom was only smoke and mirrors. It chased me, this freedom. It hunted me down. Now fate has captured my shadow. I thought I could get away, but I was only a greyhound running after an artificial rabbit, on a senseless treadmill life prescribed for me the day I was born. It is time now to tell you, because my time is up. Ayn has waited nine years for my explanations. Eva and Sophie waited longer, without even knowing it."

Boris reached into his shirt pocket and extracted a package of Kents, removed one, tamped it on the table, lit it, inhaled, and tilting his head back slightly, expelled smoke toward the ceiling. The whooshing exhalation of his breath was the only sound in the room until Kasi unexpectedly placed a bread plate in front of him as an ashtray. Their eyes did not meet. He continued, unbidden.

"On the day of Oleg's bloody rampage, after they peeled me off of him before I could snuff out the devil bastard's soul, the police took me to an orphanage in nearby Ananyev. I was frightened, lonely and confused. I was just 16. My family had been wrested from me in the most horrible way in a day's time. I asked them why I could not go with my sister. They would not give me a reason. I asked them where she was. They would not tell me. They left me there for eight weeks. No one visited. No one called. I was the most alone I have ever been. I wished fervently that Oleg had killed me, too.

"Finally one day I was called into the superintendent's office. There were two men in full military uniform of some sort. I was afraid I was to be arrested. The superintendent left the room and closed the door. They asked me to sit down. I did. They asked me questions about myself — how I felt about my family; how I felt about myself; how I felt about my brother; what I would have liked to have done to him; was I glad I had been stopped before I killed him? What did I think would happen to me? They also asked me political questions, of which I was quite ignorant. We were country folk. Father fought in the war, was injured protecting the Motherland, but I didn't have any political feelings. I don't remember how I answered most of the questions, I only remember that they asked how I felt. No one had ever asked me that before.

"After three hours of this, they left.

"Two weeks later I was again called to the superintendent's office. One of the same military men was there. This time he gave me a long questionnaire to fill out. After that, I filled out a general knowledge test. He left, taking the papers with him.

"Several weeks later, I was summoned once more. The same officer told me I was to come with him. 'Where?' I asked.

"'You'll see,' he answered.

"And I went with him. I had nothing but the clothes on my back and the picture of the three of us — Oleg, Eva, and me, tucked in a pocket I had sown inside my shirt, next to my heart.

"When we left the orphanage, much to my surprise, I was ushered into a big limousine. I sat in the back, across from the man with the uniform, and we drove a long, long way without speaking. I was afraid to ask him questions. He did not offer anything. Finally he fell asleep and I sat, looking out the window. We drove many miles, finally arriving in Kishinev, the capital city of the Republic of Moldavia. It was the largest place I had ever seen — then about 350,000 people, now probably even larger. The chauffeur took us to the Kishinev airport. My escort said we were going to fly. To fly! We had never had a refrigerator or even a radio, but I, the son of a drunkard wife-beater and the brother of a murderous, incestuous shadow of a human being, was going to fly on an airplane!

"We flew all the way to Gorki. The city was even larger — over a million people! At the airport we were met by another big car, and driven into the city. The car pulled through gates set in high brick walls and I saw as we got inside the walls that there were armed guards all along the periphery of the wall. Whether they were to keep us in or to keep others out, I had no idea. Just as we pulled in front of one of several large stone buildings set well back from the streets, my escort said, 'You are to go to school here, son.' And that's the first I knew it was school and not prison and not another orphanage or who knows what that I was headed for. I suddenly felt an overwhelming warmth for the man who had said only a few dozen words to me over thousands and thousands of miles of travel. I had to strongly resist the urge to hug him. And then he was gone.

"Young men in uniform immediately marched out of the building and ushered me in almost goose-step fashion, inside. They promptly sat me down and produced another questionnaire. It was exactly the same as the one I had completed back in Ananyev. 'I did this already,' I protested.

"'Do it again," they ordered. And so I did.

"When I was finished, they brought out a folder with my name on it and extracted the earlier questionnaire. They then compared the two documents, question for question. 'Good,' said one, presumably satisfied that my answers matched.

"Another document was produced. This one they made me read out loud. It said that I promised never to communicate to others anything about the school, and to work to the best of my ability to become an outstanding specialist in any field to which I might be transferred. As I hadn't any idea what field or specialty they were referring to, nor did I know anyone to whom I could confide anything, nor did I have the courage to ask questions, I readily agreed.

"And thus began my life and education at the Marx-Engels School. We were told that we were being educated for future careers in the Communist Party — a prerequisite for advancement in Soviet society at any rate, and one which a poor peasant like me from a socially disadvantageous background, as the Americans would have put it — could never have dreamed of under normal circumstances. At first I wondered why they had plucked me out of an orphanage in the Ukraine when there were plenty of Party members' sons who would have given their left hands for the opportunity I was being given. But little by little, I forgot about my background and buried my past. I convinced myself, bit by bit, that my past had all been a bad dream, that I was the social equal of my fellow students, that my

225

presence there was my right and to my country's honor. And I settled in to submerge myself completely in the life of the Marx-Engels School.

"For the first four months, we learned nothing but the history of the workers' movement throughout the world and the history of the Communist Party of the Soviet Union. We rose in the dormitories, on the upper floors of the school buildings, at 7 a.m., dressed, did calisthenics, ate breakfast, and then attended lectures and did classwork until 6:30 in the evening, with the exception of a short lunch break. Then there were more physical exercises, supper, homework, and lights out at 10:30. Every day was exactly the same. I welcomed the discipline, the routine, the surety of it all. I felt protected and secure, as though I were in a womb — the womb of the Party. Others missed their families. I had no family to miss. Even Eva, I am afraid to admit, was buried in the back of my mind, beneath the pain and fear of childhood. I felt I had left all that behind. I was a grown man now. I had a new family — the Communist Party.

"There were young women there as well, in the classrooms and at the cafeteria, but I did not become involved with them. My mind was on excelling — at garnering approval from my teachers and the administrators.

"Eventually, I graduated with honors. Officer Vasily Somonov — the man who had taken me from the orphanage — was there. He shook my hand and called me son. I was so proud! He took me alone into a room and told me he would be keeping an eye on me and watching my career. Then he told me you were dead, Eva. That you had committed suicide when you found out you were pregnant with Oleg's seed.

"....I was deeply disturbed. I had comforted myself with the thought that I had at least saved you. You were the only family I had, and now you were gone, another fatal victim of our brother's madness. Officer Somonov put his hand on my shoulder and comforted me. I felt he was the only one who truly cared about me now. I asked permission to write to him in the future. Permission was granted."

A chill went up my spine at his words. "Oleg's seed" quietly finished her translation and glanced, expressionless, from her mother to her uncle. Sophie's taut, focused demeanor remained unchanged. Boris crushed out his second cigarette, his eyes cloudy and distant behind the trailing smoke. It felt as though the man's soul were in that smoke, drifting away in the atmosphere, dissipating in the molecules about us. This was less than a shadow before us; this was an apparition, a vestige of life, a whisper of a man. I got up and started another pot of coffee as the voice resumed. Boris's "explanation" of his life and experience hung thickly in the air about us, but the underlying answers to *why* it was his life — as to why his soul, his loyalties, and his honor were so shallow they could be purchased by the promise of a penpal — could never truly be explained by anyone but God, I told myself. Would I have done the same? I knew that haunting question would follow me indefinitely. But Boris continued.

"Directly following graduation, my comrades and I were transported in large automobiles to the Lenin Technical School in Verkovnoye, ninety miles north of Kazan, and some 200 miles east of Gorki. It was in a very isolated spot, near the border of the Autonomous Tatar Soviet Republic, and could be reached only by private road, after approved access through closely-guarded sentry stations along the perimeter of a vast brick wall. I doubt the people of the area even know that it exists in their midst.

"And it was here that they told us the important job we had been chosen for. Sitting on a cold bench in a gymnasium with 120 other young men and women, I learned that, if I was good enough and smart enough and quick enough and brave enough, I could become a future Secret Service agent for the United Soviet Socialist Republics."

A startled yelp from Kasi broke the narrative. She stood next to me at the sink, her face flushed and her eyes wide, staring in horror at her husband. Suspecting the substance of Boris's revelations in advance had not been sufficiently concrete to prompt us to warn our clients of his probable role. Kasi, apparently, had thought of everything but this — infidelity, gambling debts, a secret life as a bigamist or trigamist, even — but spying?

Ayn, too, looked as though she were in shock. Even Sophie faltered in her translation and touched her mother's arm.

Boris hesitated briefly, his only acknowledgment of our presence and reaction. Then he continued.

"Unlike the Marx-Engels School, the buildings were modern and the grounds extensive. But the pattern of teaching and the discipline were much the same. It was still highly regimented. But now, on top of academic classes, we learned about firearms, explosives, how to set up and operate portable radios, how to use photography equipment and to develop prints, to tap phones and determine when they were tapped, to doctor tape recordings for possible blackmail, and to prepare poisoned food.

"I excelled at all my lessons. And with my mastery of English, I was ready, before my 18th birthday, for the next step: Gaczyna.

"What I am telling you now could get me killed in the old Soviet Union, and in the new Russia, where you can no longer tell where loyalties lie, who knows? Whichever, it does not matter, because I am like a dead man anyway. So, because I told you so little for so very long, I will tell you what few know and even fewer would admit to." At this, Boris lit another Kent, sat forward a little further in his chair, and released a long, slow breath.

"There is a place," he said, " — or there *was* a place in the '60s and '70s, when I was coming of age, and well before and after that — called Gaczyna."

Mickey D. and I exchanged glances. What Mikhail Vakarov had surmised from our information on Dagronsky had been right. Dead right.

"You could not find Gaczyna on a map, you could not reach it by car, and you could not fly over it by airplane without being shot down," he continued. "It lay approximately 100 miles southeast of Kuibyshev, and stretched along what was the southern border of the Tatar Autonomous Soviet Republic with the Bashkir Autonomous Republic. It covered over 400 square miles, and from an outer ring thirty miles away, was guarded by crack state security troops who admitted no one without a Secret Service permit.

"Even more than the Marx-Engels School, even more than the Lenin Technical School, the public never dreamed what was behind the walls of Gaczyna. When I arrived, I did not know what I was coming to. They flew us in on special aircraft, and when it flew away, the last of the world outside flew away with it, as far as I was concerned. I wasn't to step back into it for almost ten more years. And when I emerged, I was a different person, with a different identity, a different country, a different mission.

"I was an American.

"From the moment I stepped off the plane in Gaczyna, I was allowed to speak only English — no matter how primitive at first. And as I shed my mother tongue, I shed my Russian identity and took on a new one — that of Jack Curtis, Canadian immigrant to the United States. I lived, breathed, slept, and ate Jack Curtis's life and the life of an American, for I was, for all practical purposes, in a miniature America.

"You see, Gaczyna was a perfect duplicate of foreign countries. It was a miniaturized world, sectionalized into completely independent zones and countries, so that the cadets could live immersed in the atmosphere of the country in which they were to be drilled. For the entire purpose of Gaczyna was for its graduates to eventually be able

228

to penetrate the countries themselves — to live as natives among the people; to think, to act, to speak and appear like a Toronto native or a New Yorker or someone from Sydney or Paris or Tokyo.

"I was, of course, in the English-speaking zone, because of my fair command of English and my physical appearance. Within the English zone, there were sections broken down into the United States and Canada, United Kingdom, Australia, and New Zealand. In other parts of the compound that we did not visit, there were divisions for each of the language groups and geographical regions of the world where our comrades were assigned, depending upon which country was to be their 'native' one.

"Every division of Gaczyna was a true replica — a town or village of the country it represented. There were streets, buildings, businesses, parks and even cemeteries that mirrored the real thing in the real country. 'My' town had corner drugstores with soda fountains, theaters with American movies, laundromats, restaurants, houses and apartments — even churches, just like a town in North America would have. The area was large, with a city area as well as a rural section, so that it actually felt as if we were in the United States.

"The people in the town lived like they would live in America. We took apartments or lived in homes. We ate at the local restaurants, shopped at the grocery stores for American products with American money, chatted with the workers, in English, of course, about everyday life. When I had a toothache and needed to see a dentist, it was an American dentist, and an American dental office. The scar I had from my scalding water escapade with Oleg was operated on by an American doctor in a small American hospital to make it look more like a birthmark than a scar.

"No matter what we did, we pretended we were in America. We immersed ourselves in Americana. And little by little, year after year, we became more and more American and less and less Russian.

"For the first five years, we had continuous tutoring in English. We learned it inside and out, concentrating on idioms, pronunciation, and intonation until we sounded like natives. We listened to tape-recorded American news broadcasts and watched film after film, movie after movie. I became an expert on American actors and actresses and on current affairs. We had actual Americans as teachers — not just in the classrooms, but everyone — down to the bus drivers, the waitresses and the store clerks. They were ex-patriots from the countries we were going to. And they were there for life.

"The cemeteries in Gaczyna were more than authentic, they were real. Because you don't leave Gaczyna unless the KGB tells you to.

And the only way you leave Gaczyna alive is to go on a mission to the country you were picked to spy on."

"I don't believe this! It's preposterous. It's a lie, a fairytale!" Kasi's explosion broke the spell. She came at Boris, her face livid with incredulity and disgust. "How can you expect us, after all that you've done, to believe this?" she screamed, her hand flailing the air inches in front of his face, taunting him with her anger.

Boris moved not an inch, did not even blink. Like a recorder with its button pushed to "Pause," he sat silently.

Mick rose from his seat next to Boris, stepped smoothly to his right and put a hand gently on Kasi's trembling shoulder. "Believe him now, Kasi," he said softly. "The past has been a lie. This is not."

She looked at him, her lower lip trembling, glanced down at the man she had raised two children with, and a tremor of pain, palpable and raw, coursed down her tiny frame. She turned her face away, and stepped to the other side of the room, leaning against the far wall, her arms hugging her chest. Ayn, a bewildered wildness in her eyes, pushed back her chair and looked furtively from her father to Kasi, but remained seated. Eva sat now, a hand shading her closed eyes, Sophie's hand in hers. Mickey sat down. I poured coffee all around and resumed my seat. Only then did Boris continue, picking up the story as though it had never been interrupted.

"We learned history and general knowledge, read classics and modern writers — many of them banned in Russia — and we listened to American music. This is where I began my love affair with music. My music teacher was a jazz musician from America. I won't tell you his name, because he seems to me now more a metaphor than a man, but I assure you, all Americans from that era with any knowledge of music knew him, for he was famous once in the U.S. I'll call him Zeke. Zeke experienced discrimination in America because he was black, and he became disillusioned with the fact that America pretended to treat all its citizens fairly, while its government publicly decried the 'lack of personal freedoms' in the Soviet Union. So in the mid '50s, at the height of his career, he defected. And he ended up in Gaczyna, teaching American music to Russian spies.

"Zeke taught me the saxophone. I picked it up very quickly, because it was something I could feel, and for years I had needed to feel something. And so music became a way for me to express myself. I realize that eventually it became practically the only way I could express myself... I am sorry for that.

"After a short time, my affinity for music, especially jazz, became obvious and encouraged. We each needed to have a 'cover' occupation in the country we were assigned to. After a while it was decided that mine should be music, possibly combined with photography, as a hobby or a vocation. Both occupations would give me the access I would need — a reason to travel, to view the countryside, to meet new people, to interact and socialize without suspicion.

"During all these years my only correspondence outside of Gaczyna has been with Officer Somonov. He would write me, too, sending small presents at times. When I became involved in music, I took to writing him on musical scores, telling him that in English it was, afterall, 'notepaper.'"

Boris's lip curled at his own pun. No one else so much as cracked a smile.

"We learned other practical things which would also transfer to additional skills, from skeet shooting, which I was to one day take up with you, Kasi, but which was also a means to keep my shooting skills intact; to the game of baseball, in case we ever had to play in a pick-up game at a company picnic. Everything was covered. I even took driver's education, learned to shift a '68 American Rambler, drive on the right side of the road, and to stop on red and go on green.

"The last five years at Gaczyna, we underwent more extensive training in coding, decoding, and call-sign techniques. The codes change sequence in an irregular fashion, so you must learn several codes and use them randomly, changing them from transmission to transmission. Periodically, all of the codes are changed, so they must be learned again and again.

"While radio communication is effective, it is dangerous and must be done infrequently lest it be detected. So microdot communication was also taught. We learned how to record long bodies of information on microfilm, reduce them to the size of a pinhead and to affix them and transmit them — often under stamps; sometimes by 'dropping' them where they would be retrieved by other agents — all of the things you see in James Bond movies.

"We were taught how to take apart everyday household objects — clocks, books, toothpaste tubes, etcetera, and make them carriers for film, microdots, even cameras. We learned how to rebind books, how to repair clocks, and to drill holes in bottle corks and reclose them without detection.

"And eventually we learned how to recruit informers and sub-agents; how to trail and to avoid a tail; how to find weak points in people who could provide information, how to approach them without arousing suspicion, how to assess the vulnerable and — and — how to use them."

Boris coughed and took a deep breath. When he resumed, his voice was less assured. Ayn appeared to lean closer over the table, into his words.

"Finally, after ten years of preparation, there is a test. The test is the test of your life. It lasts three weeks. Specialists in every field grill and examine you to see if you are ready to be an American. If they decide no, you go to school for another year, and perhaps another and another.

"I passed the first time. I was 28 years old and ready to leave Gaczyna."

"He lied even about his age," Kasi piped up. "You weren't forty. More like fifty."

Boris didn't even glance up. He just continued. "I was ready to become a mole. Officer Somonov came and wished me luck. We embraced. I knew I would miss him. He was the closest thing to family I had left."

Boris coughed again and rattled his coffee cup. The listening faces looked glum.

"The manner of my entry into American society was discussed. I was given the materials I would need, and some cash to get me started. I was flown from Gaczyna. We went by a circuitous route which doesn't matter, but they actually flew me eventually into a remote area of Michigan, landed the plane in a farmer's field, and set me and my belongings off. There was a motorcycle waiting for me half a mile away with a map marked for my route. I hopped on it, strapped my suitcase, my American-made saxophone and my Kodak camera on behind, and set off for Northeastern Pennsylvania.

"I stopped that night at a motel outside Toledo, Ohio, and radioed that I had arrived safely. I was pulled over the next morning by a state trooper on the Ohio Turnpike. I had never been so afraid. I knew from training that I hadn't been speeding because we had been taught the speed limits. I also knew the uniform of a state trooper. I could even tell you that I was supposed to produce my driver's license. What I had gotten screwed up on was that I hadn't taken my ticket at the toll booth. I hadn't been paying attention, and when the car in front of me went through the turnstile, I did, too, without taking a ticket. A trooper, ahead on the highway, had been alerted. He issued me a citation for failure to stop at the tollbooth, looked at my fake driver's license (I would obtain a new, genuine one as soon as I became established in Pennsylvania), and waved me on.

"I arrived in Scranton, Pennsylvania at 6 p.m. on August 31, 1972 and checked into a small, family-run motel on Route 6 outside of the city.

"My handlers had picked Northeastern Pennsylvania, from Scranton up into the Poconos, for many reasons. There was a large ammunition manufactory in Scranton, and other defense-related contractors which might provide opportunity for sabotage and information retrieval; there was a high-tech Army depot at Tobyhanna which dealt in military and defense communications and had an obvious value; and there was an American Telegraph and Telephone satellite station in Kimbles, near Hawley, which might provide easier egress to state-of-the-art satellite techniques the U.S.S.R. was very interested in, as well as the obvious possibility of large-scale sabotage."

This time Ayn gasped and blanched. I bit my lip and looked at Mick. This was not going to be pretty.

"...And there was an unsophisticated, trusting population, secure in the impression that they were safe from anything as insidious as spies among their midst. The last thing they would think at the Hawley Diner on a Friday night was that the man sitting next to them asking them about their simple job wiring circuits at the Tobyhanna Depot was a Soviet spy.

"And so I settled in. I rented an apartment, looked around for a band that I could join, and found a position taking photos at a honeymoon resort. All the time I was getting to know people. The resort management turned out to be 'connected,' as they say, and by simply talking to people who knew people who knew people, I found some folks who were a little less than patriotic, or just simply naïve — folks who would tell me things; folks who would get me things and do things for me — first at the Depot, then at the ammo manufacturer. I even got into the private files of a former governor from the area and a prominent congressman who represented the region, was on the Defense and Appropriations committees, and who stupidly and illegally kept confidential files in a safe in his home. In neither case did the families know I had been in their homes, among their private belongings. I took nothing, only photographed material. I was doing pretty well. My handlers were pleased.

"Then I met Sally."

He lit a another cigarette. Ayn was shaking her head back and forth very slowly and biting her lip. She got up and started to pace.

"Sit down," I urged, patting the chair beside me.

Ayn shook her head.

Boris cleared his throat. "I want you to know, Ayn, that I didn't know I would have a family. I didn't think of it that way. I'd never known real family. Or if we had one, I'd buried it way back in that little shack in Balta. I didn't go into the relationship with your mother thinking about family. I never understood the word, the concept. And so I didn't know how it would feel and what it would do to me, to you, to all of us."

He paused again, breathed heavily, and actually looked up at her for the first time. She turned her back to him.

"I met Sally in the spring of 1973. She was an innocent. She was a respected secretary at AT&T. She seemed perfect for — for infiltrating the AT&T station at Kimbles."

He drew on his cigarette. Kasi crossed from the other side of the room and put her hand on Ayn's shoulder. Ayn shrugged her off. Kasi bit her lip and stood by warily.

"She knew nothing about it, Ayn, I swear. Nothing. I wooed her. She responded, but would not commit. She was unsure. I poked a hole in my condom and she conceived. We were married."

Ayn's shoulders were heaving and little gulping sounds rose from the bottom of her chest.

Boris kept on. His voice held shades of real emotion. He was saying his lines with almost convincing sincerity. If you didn't look at his face...

"You were born the following spring. Sally picked your name. I was a bit chagrined that it was the same name as that capitalist writer, Ayn Rand. But Sally said she thought it was just an interesting spelling for 'Anne,' and I was ashamed at what I was doing to her, and so I gave in. I picked your middle name, Eva, telling her it was my grandmother's name.

"I was confused — so confused! I didn't expect to feel what I found myself feeling. At first I was afraid of what having you meant — of what we had done. But I loved you. I do love you!"

At this, the tears flowed freely down Ayn's face, but still she kept her back to him, her hands balled in fists. Boris continued to look at her back, but did not reach out to her.

"Your mother — I'm sorry, but I never loved your mother. And she knew it. She tried everything to get me to love her, but I couldn't. I just couldn't. The more she tried, the more she fawned over me, the more I turned away from her. I felt sometimes like my father. I wanted to strike out at her. I wanted to punish her for my fears, my doubts, my guilt. Oh yes, I had guilt. I had doubts. But I was in it up to my neck and beyond. Don't you see? I couldn't get out — no more than the people in Gaczyna. They would kill me, don't you see? One side or the other. They had me and they knew it. And I — I was digging my own grave. I was in a sewer with shit up to my eyeballs. And the harder I pumped, the more shit that came at me.

"So I did the best that I felt I could under the circumstances — I pretended and I tread water, and finally, I left her. And in leaving her, I left you. But I didn't see any other way, don't you see? I'd gotten all I could from her. These investigators you and Kasi hired discovered that, I'm sure. They've told you what they found out about your mother—"

Mickey and I shot looks between one another and Ayn, who had turned toward us with questioning, tear-packed eyes. We had almost as much explaining to do as Boris here, once this was over.

"...But I want you to know that she didn't know what it was all about; she thought she was helping me advance my career, which she believed was something altogether different than it was. She was very vulnerable, very naive — characteristics I picked her for. And I took advantage of those characteristics. She was an innocent, and I used her innocence. It haunts me still. I swear, it does."

"You bastard!" Ayn spat between clenched teeth, striking her hand against the kitchen sink. "You fucking bastard!"

"...I know you hate me, and you have a right to. I just want you to finally understand why I did what I did, as much as you can understand — as anyone can understand. Not only had Sally outlasted her usefulness to me as an information gatherer, but I was destroying her by being there.

"And things were getting hot there, and at the same time, the area had run dry for me. So I asked to go to another place. It seemed logical to go to a larger city where I could blend in a little easier. My handler wanted me to go to Philadelphia where some high-tech companies were doing advanced computer work the Russians were only dreaming of. By then industrial espionage was coming to the forefront, with the hint of a thaw in relations between the two superpowers. It was 1985.

"I took several trips to the Philadelphia area. I found a company to target — Vortex Institute, which was dealing in highly sensitive government contract software for everything from the defense industry to a spy system it had developed for the CIA. My handler arranged for an operative to do preliminary scouting and identify several individuals — all women — he felt would be in sensitive, and possibly vulnerable positions at the Institute.

"I was hungry for romance at that stage of my life. I had had forty loveless years. Forty years of stifled emotion I would let out only in my music, sometimes in my photography. I was aching over the thought of leaving my daughter. They showed me photographs of three women.

"You picked me out of a line-up?" Kasi gasped, her mouth wide open.

"...I saw your picture. I watched you in the grocery store, at the coffee house with your friends..." He looked in her direction, but not directly at her face.

"You tracked me? You had me in your sights like a clay pigeon with your little skeet shooter?" she roared.

"...And I fell in love with you."

"Yeah, right. You bastard. You cowardly, cheating—"

"..I know you won't believe it, Kasi, but I did. I fell in love for the first time in my life. I fell in love with you. You must believe me."

Kasi was steaming, but she said no more, biting her raw lower lip and pacing on the far end of the room, as if there was a barrier between them she would not cross for fear of losing all dignity. I couldn't believe this man's arrogance. But it was a blind arrogance — a naive, childish thing — claiming to fall in love with a woman before he'd even met her. It was pathetic!

"...I had found you, so then I needed to find a job and then a way to meet you. I planted myself in a bar where a band needing a new horn player was performing, but I hadn't set everything up yet, so I didn't officially approach the band.

"I found out you were going to Atlantic City with a friend. I arranged to 'run into' you there, claiming to be there with the band. It was beautiful! We hit it off right away. I couldn't believe it. I was so happy! In fact, I was so ready to show you off, I almost jumped the gun. I stupidly brought you to the club before I'd approached the band about a job, and I think I might have mentioned to Billy Randolph before that that I was going up to Atlantic City. Anyway, if he picked up on it, he never said anything.

"At any rate, you and I, Kasi, had fallen in love. I really mean that, Kasi. I did love you."

"You said 'did,'" she hissed. "Well, I never did, you blood-sucking bastard! I was faking it the entire friggin' time!" she screamed, her expressive hands flying again, knocking sideways on the wall a self-portrait of Eva standing on the top of a cliff with blood red wings coming out of her back. I had a hard time swallowing a nervous laugh welling in my chest. This scene was more bizarre than the oils of Eva's imagination. I realized now that to her, the paintings were realistic, not surreal as they seemed to the casual viewer. But before I could analyze this whole scene more thoroughly, Boris started in again.

"...I had received new identification prior to arranging my meeting with you, and I took a crash course in computers — enough to understand what it was you did so that I could figure out a way to use your extraordinary skills and access the information you had available to you without your knowing I was doing it."

Kasi snarled. "You bastard! You acted as if you didn't even know how to turn a computer on!" Then, "My God!" she gasped as the realization hit that Boris had somehow been accessing her highly sensitive work. You encouraged me to do a lot of my work at home. You said it would give me a leg up on my career if I did. Convinced me no one would ever know!" Her mouth and eyes were wide with incredulity as her husband's voice droned on, confirming, almost echoing, her very words, sticking to the script, performing the role.

"...I helped you buy the computer you used at home, and talked you into doing work there, pretending I didn't know the least thing about your work. 'What harm can it do?' I said, noting no one would know your passwords, and that if anyone tried to break into your machine, you had it protected to self-destruct any information. You weren't allowed to carry disks to or from Vortex — everything was searched; employees walked through powerful magnets that would destroy any information carried in or out. But ideas — logarithms and code — ran through your mind like musical notes run through mine. When the muse hit, you could get it down at home, then study what you'd done, memorize it, and copy it down the next day at work.

"The only thing I really had to know about computers was how to attach the keyboard jack to the computer. That's because I took the regular keyboard that came with your computer, and replaced it one day while you were out with an exact duplicate. Inside the new keyboard was a minuscule device which transmitted the ASCII signals made by each stroke of the key to a remote receiver hooked up to a recorder kept camouflaged in a developing canister inside my dark room. Every so often I would take the cassette tape and 'drop' it for pick-up by an operative who eventually passed it on to someone who could make sense out of it all."

Kasi shook her head and closed her eyes. There was sweat standing out on her forehead and her fists clenched and unclenched.

"...I'll sign something now to this effect, if you want me to. When they investigate, they will know you were innocent — a dupe and nothing more."

"A dupe," she said softly, almost purring. "Gee, thanks, sweetheart. Thank you so much. I'm sure the CIA and the FBI will take the word of a Russian mole in regards to my career. That's awfully kind of you!" she snarled. "Not only have your ruined our family, you've most likely ruined my career, just like you did with poor Ayn's mother!"

He chose to ignore her response, continuing with his narrative. "Everything seemed to be going well. I was getting enough information from Vortex to keep my handlers happy, and odds and ends from people I talked up during my gigs with the band. There was an old guy who was ostracized from his community back in World War II for claiming conscientious objector status. He gave me all kinds of goodies that a pal in a high position at the Naval Ordinance Laboratory in Maryland fed to him for a price. We would meet at the bars after the band played and he would pass me stuff.

"And there was a woman from Connecticut who liked to gamble big at the Jersey casinos. She had a sensitive job with a submarine manufacturer, and I fed her gambling habit as long as she fed my info habit.

"Then Gorbachev came to power and things began to loosen up. Perestroika was the catchword. The Soviets and the Americans played games with one another's diplomatic corps, which were, as they both knew, nothing but spying mechanisms. It was an argument over who had the most spies. I found it rather amusing."

Boris's lip curled in a sort of smile-come-grimace. I saw Mickey shudder.

"...When they got over the spy wars saga, they started on talks about nuclear arms — a different spy wars. In the meantime, the Soviet Union was going bankrupt. I didn't notice it at first, because I didn't want to. If I noticed it, it would mean I was in an even more tenuous position than I already felt, and there didn't seem to be any more dangerous a position than the one I held. What it boiled down to was the fact that the center was falling apart. They couldn't afford to control everything everywhere anymore — Eastern Europe, the Baltics, the interior dissension. Somewhere along the line, it had occurred to some of the people in the government that in the global scheme of things, they were faking it. They had come to realize they were a Third World country putting on the airs of a World Power. That the bread lines and the toilet paper lines and the special treatment for the elite few just wasn't making it. And they lost the faith. They lost the effects of smoke and mirrors. They lost control.

"By then I was disillusioned, too. But I was comfortable. The wall was coming down in Eastern Europe. The Soviets were thrown out of Afghanistan in disgrace, like the Americans had been thrown out of Vietnam before them. The natives were restless. But I was the most comfortable I had ever been. Eva was born. I had lost Ayn — Oh, I saw you from afar, through the lens of a telephoto camera when I just couldn't make myself stay away any longer — but I couldn't touch you or hold you. So we made another little Eva, my Eva Ann.

"And the walls kept falling down. I kept sending information to my handlers, but I was beginning to question why. When I mentioned quitting for a while, they talked of calling me in. I resisted. I didn't know just how much it was falling apart. I hadn't been in the U.S.S.R. for two decades. I buried myself in my music.

"Then came August of 1991. The faction run by the KGB tried to wrest control from Mikhail Gorbachev. The government collapsed. The KGB was castrated. I was indeed out in the cold. I panicked. Would they abandon me? Would they disavow me if I tried to return? I had always thought I would return, afterall. Should I go home? Did I have a home? Where was home? Where did I stand? And then real fear overtook me. They would all want me dead now, I thought. All the files would be released, as in some new Russian equivalent of an American Public Information Act orgy. Some misguided pompous ass in Yeltsin's new holier-than-thou government who mistook himself for a patriot might get up in front of the Politburo and read off the names of KGB operatives across the world. The names would be published in Pravda. And I and my once patriotic comrades from Gaczyna — now spread across the world — would end up in body bags that even our countrymen would no longer accept for burial.

"I was frantic. I was overcome with doubt and indecision. Should I flee to the Motherland, or from it? For the first time in my life, I was truly attached to something — my family. I didn't want to leave. And I didn't want to die.

"Finally I dropped a note to my contact that I wanted to speak to the man who had recruited me, Officer Somonov. It had been many years since I had had any contact with him — since my days with Sally and Ayn. I needed some advice from the man I thought of most as a father — the man who knew my past and had made my present, and who I felt I could trust. The note was not answered.

"I slowed down the frequency of my information drops. I stopped trying to recruit agents and solicit information. I sent another request to speak to Somonov. Again nothing. I thought, fine, they have all forgotten about me. Maybe it doesn't matter any more. And I became creative in a way I felt only in my youth. I began to write music. Brando was conceived. I allowed myself to feel almost free.

"I sent messages two times more to Somonov, this time on the back of musical scores, as I had from Gaczyna 25 years previous. They did not contain his name, but I knew all my messages were supposed to go back to headquarters to be decoded and acted upon. If he was there, he would see them and respond, I was sure. Still nothing.

"Until one night on the way to our weekly gig in Ardmore, I saw the message. It was disguised as graffiti written on a concrete highway underpass I drive beneath every Friday. A prearranged signal to make contact at a preordained location — Longwood Gardens, southwest of Philadelphia. I almost ran off the road when I saw it. It had appeared within the previous week.

"I agonized. I considered approaching the Americans about defecting — the Spy Who Came in *After* the Cold? I decided against it. I was too ashamed, afraid. I didn't know what to do. I convinced myself I could talk my way out of whatever it was my handlers wanted me to do. I had decided I wasn't going to be a spy any more, and I wasn't going back to Russia, and that I would tell them to just forget about me. It was quite mad, actually. There was no way they would allow that to happen. Too many had too much at stake. They can claim the KGB is dead, but trust me, it has only changed its colors.

"But I suspended reality and the next day I drove to Longwood Gardens. I bought my ticket and entered the grounds and stood off in the shadows behind the topiary, watching. There he was by the colored fountains — a middle-aged man carrying a brown-handled umbrella, a copy of Sports Illustrated peeking conspicuously out of his right rear pocket. At the time I knew him only as Alexei, my contact, even though he had 'handled' me for over 15 years. We had met face-to-face perhaps only half a dozen times. The routine was simple. I was supposed to take off my hat, scratch my head and be the first to comment on the marvelously-timed water display.

"I walked slowly to the fountain. I removed my baseball cap. He glanced at me, started to smile pleasantly. My frustration caused me foolishly to attempt to play games with him. I put the cap back on. He glanced away, then back again. 'Remarkable, don't you think?' he prompted anxiously, jumping the gun, appropriating my line.

"He was nervous, I realized. I thought I would press my case. There was no one within hearing distance of us. 'I think I've watched too much falling water,' I replied, still looking at the fountain.

"'Oh, there's never too much,' he said hastily.

"'Too much for me,' I responded.

"'Oh no, oh no. Water is needed more than ever. There's a scarcity of water where I come from. It's very valuable. Very necessary. Those who supply it are revered.'

"'Let's cut the bullshit,' I said, leaning over with my Philadelphia Inquirer and pointing at a picture of Martina Navratilovna under a story about her possible retirement, as though we were discussing the article. 'Why have you been ignoring my requests?'

"'Great serve and volley, hey?' he smiled through his teeth and shook his head. Then soberly, quietly, he said, 'Your friend Somonov is dead. I'm sorry. He died six months ago. We didn't want to upset you.' And his voice rose as a couple passed by. 'I think it's about time the lezzy retired, don't you?' Then he said under his breath, 'I could have you sent back. They'll put you in Gaczyna for the rest of your life. Is that what you want?'

"I was still trying to digest the news of Somonov's death. I felt empty, bereft, abandoned. 'No,' I said simply. I was in a daze. I promised more code and more recruits. He promised extra money I intended to use for Ayn's education. We parted.

"When I left, I covered my tracks, making sure no one was tailing me, then I kept on driving. I ended up going all the way to Hawley. I stood in a grove of trees in an oversized mackinaw and watched in the pouring rain as my daughter buried my first wife.

"I decided then that it was finally time to bring my family together. Ironically, the decision was to be my downfall. I put the bug in your ear to move to Philadelphia, Ayn. I wanted you close by, and now that your mother was gone, nothing tied you there. I paid for your 'scholarship' at college and maneuvered you to Philadelphia. I was feeling strangely confident that some day soon I might be able to get my entire family back together. Little did I know you would be together, but without me."

Boris tamped and lit another cigarette. I looked around at the drained and shell-shocked faces — the angry betrayal and loathing on Kasi's flushed face; the colorless confusion and fear on Ayn's; the haunted sadness of Eva and Sophie. All of these women had loved this man in some way, at some time. Some of them loved him still. But I saw no respect, no empathy for his position. The eyes still questioned, the faces still sought understanding. Even Mickey had a guarded look of dread in his demeanor as he glanced up at the clock above the stove. His eyes met mine. "When will the authorities catch up with us?" they said. "What should we do when they do?" I pursed my lips and sighed. I wasn't sure we had control over that anymore. But Boris had flipped to the other side of the tape in his mind's recorder, and I returned with the others to the act of absorption.

"Kasi, it happened the night before I left. I was restless. When you were out of the room, I switched the TV from your movie. And there, on CNN, was a meeting in Moscow between America's Secretary of Defense and military officials of Russia, to discuss further controls on the nuclear weapons in the former Soviet Union. The camera panned a group of officials as they stood in a hallway sipping cocktails before dinner. And there was Somonov — General Vasily Somonov — the man my contact had told me was dead. My heart felt like ice. I had to get out, so I took Marbles and went for a walk."

Suddenly Boris rose from his chair, the pain in his knee apparently forgotten, the look in his eyes distant. He paced, cigarette in hand, in front of the door, four steps this way, four that. Kasi watched him warily from the other side of the room. Mickey turned in his chair to watch. I sensed his readiness to tackle him, should Boris decide to bolt. But the man seemed lost in his own memories, reliving that night a few short months ago. One hand was at his side, the other held the cigarette, almost unconsciously, as he paced.

"It was only a matter of months since the talk at Longwood Gardens," he continued. "Since then I had left two drops with some rather useless information, and tried half-heartedly to talk up an older man at the bar who was a longtime employee of a Trenton, New Jersey defense contractor. But now I knew that my contact was lying to me. He had not passed on my messages. And Somonov was alive!" He was animated now, agitated and restless. The pacing quickened. "I was not sure if Gaczyna even existed any more. I was not sure if I, Boris, still existed. Who was I? This crazy life I'd led confused even me. Who should I be afraid of? I trusted no one. I needed to think.

"Marbles and I walked quite a ways and before I knew it, we were on an isolated spot of Beechwood, by the railroad tracks. Marbles slowed, sniffed, and squatted by a bush, next to a street lamp. From behind me came the crack of a dry twig." And with that, his head turned quickly to the left, as though he had just heard the noise, there, in the kitchen. "I pivoted," he almost whispered, crouching in a defensive stance and waving the cigarette at an apparition in the room. "Out of the shadows came the silhouette of a man. I reached into my shirt as if to withdraw a weapon." And his left hand reached inside his shirt in demonstration.

"'Hold it, man,' he said, his hands held, palms out, in supplication. 'I'm not going to hurt you.' It was the thick accent of my handler, Alexei. He had never accosted me like this before. Always, when we met, it was by prearrangement. I was petrified. My immediate reaction was to flee — to run and never look back. But they knew where I lived. They knew how to find me and my family! I stood still, every fiber on end. The man stepped to my left, and with the light of the streetlamp no longer in my eyes, I could see his ruddy features, florid even in the lamplight. He was wearing a jacket too bulky for a warm summer night. He seemed nervous, yet somehow cocky all at once. He stepped closer and bent as if to pet Marbles. Marbles growled at him! 'I guess he doesn't like strangers, huh?' And he backed up a step and sort of hugged himself around the middle with both arms.

At this, Mickey stood up.

"What are you doing?" Boris asked, warily.

"I'm just stretch—"

"No, no, that's what I said to him," Boris dismissed him, waving Mickey off like a heckler distracting a performer on stage, and snuffed out his cigarette in the plate in front of me. "I said, 'What are you doing?'" Boris repeated.

"'Actually, I was hoping we could talk man-to-man,' Alexei said.

"'What do you mean? We talked just recently,' I said. And then I added, 'Actually, I talked and you lied.' Saying that to him felt something like stepping on the toe of one's executioner as you walk to the scaffold," Boris almost chuckled. He seemed to be playing off of Mickey, now, talking to him as if he were a member of the audience called up on stage to act the part of Alexei, while relating asides to us as though we were the studio audience watching a demonstration of how to use a Ginsu knife.

"What more could it hurt me at that point?" Boris asked rhetorically. "Because I knew he was there to either kill me or send me back to Russia. The way I was feeling then, it didn't make much difference which to me. They are both death sentences. I fear I know too much for the 'new' Russia. They won't even have a Gaczyna any longer to warehouse me in. They would not want me, a potential loose cannon, out there. You do not change the stripes of tigers just because you put them under different handlers. They would undoubtedly make me disappear."

And with that, Boris snapped his fingers. I started in my chair at the hollow, popping sound. Mickey stood, eyes alert yet body working hard at appearing casual. He stood now next to Boris's chair. Boris hovered by the sink. Everyone else seemed transfixed, caught up in the story.

"The only thing that made me a little cocky," Boris continued, "was the man's manner. He didn't seem capable of killing me. I suspected he'd been a diplomat for so long he'd forgotten everything else they taught him. I had been so stunned at the timing and the manner of the rebirth of my nightmare that I had left my own pistol at home, concealed in a hidden pocket under the lining of my saxophone case. He hadn't answered my insult. He seemed to be sizing me up. 'Are you alone?' I pressed, glancing about.

"'Your dog doesn't hear anyone else, does he?'

"Marbles was just sitting there, looking at him curiously. He hadn't moved since the first growl. I had time to regret buying a pet instead of an attack dog. We were truly isolated out there. The only sounds around us were night sounds — crickets, katydids, the high-pitched whistle of a freight train a few miles distant.

"'You're not doing your job,' Alexei said more loudly.

"'What are you talking about? You wanted code. I'm giving you code.' And with that I moved quickly to go by him, feinting disinterest in the conversation."

Boris demonstrated this by walking to the right of the table. Mickey swiveled almost naturally in response.

"Suddenly he put out his left hand, like this, to stop me, and his right hand swept inside his jacket. 'You can't go yet,' he hissed, extracting a .358 Magnum from underneath his coat.

"'What are you going to do?' The train was getting louder, about half a mile away. I moved slowly to my right and he circled around to the left, where I had been before."

The actions of the two men mirrored that of the narrative. Boris stood now next to me, his back to Kasi. Mickey faced him.

"'Nothing if you cooperate,' he said. 'But you stopped doing your job — stopped making dead drops, supplying us with computer information. You're not even trying to get information anymore. We still need information. We still need to compete in the world market. We're not a threat militarily any longer, but we can become an economic threat. Everybody's doing it these days.'

"'What's this 'we'?' I scoffed. 'Were you sharing my information with the old comrades back home? Did you pass all my valuable information to Mother Russia?'

244

"'Are you accusing me of treason?' And his eyes began to bug out in his red face. Behind him the slow freight train was in view, 500 yards distant, down the tracks which passed just 30 feet away, over a bank and down a slight incline covered with high grass.

"YOU — TOLD — ME — HE — WAS — DEAD!" Boris screamed the words.

We all jumped. My heart pounded wildly. Boris was crouched now, in a fighting stance.

"And like a flash it came to me — 'It's me who is dead, isn't it? It is me who has been reported as nonexistent. They think I'm dead back there! You wrote my obituary so that you could collect my insurance by selling me and my information to the highest bidder!' And I spat in his face!

"Phht!" Boris spat on the floor. "He flinched and shifted his weight to wipe the spittle away. As the first car clacked by noisily, I lunged toward him with all my might."

At this point, Boris's actions and words seemed to meld. He became part of the fight he was relating. Mickey stepped in and seemed to follow, even anticipate, his direction, taking the part of Alexei. The punches were pulled, as though they were shadowboxing; the action was purely for demonstration. It was choreography in action. No longer did I see a man relating an event, but the event itself, in slow motion.

"Alexei reflexively pulled the trigger, and the bullet whizzed off to his left, in the direction his body was moving, three feet to the right of my head. My body weight slammed into his arm a millisecond later, the force knocking the revolver through the air and over the bank. We tumbled together after one another and the weapon, down the bank, with Marbles scrambling after. We rolled in the thigh-high grass within feet of the tracks, the cars chugging in our ears. It felt as though they would run us over. I could not reach the gun, could not see it.

"He grabbed me by the hair. I pulled at his jacket, punched him in the face. He swiped at my coat, grabbing the sash that held it on. With one pull he managed to rip all but one arm of the coat off of my body. I struggled with him, trying to roll toward the train when he was on top; trying to push away when he had my back to the rails. At one point we were so close, my shirt was nicked by a passing car, ripping off the sleeve. I managed to push back with all my might, reversing the advantage and pinning one of his shoulders to the ground. I leaned my knee against his chest, applying pressure to his throat. But he pulled a leg free and shot a knee to my groin. I released my grip and with a burst of strength, he heaved me off of him and started to scramble on hands and knees in the direction the gun had gone. I recovered quickly, jumped to my feet and raced after him. He started to reach for a metallic object on the ground. I lunged, flying through the air from behind and flattened him as his left hand came down on the grip of the gun, just inches from the track. The gun was in his hand. My body was across his, both my hands squeezing his arm. He struggled to push the barrel of the gun toward me. I pushed back, easing his hand closer and closer to the rails. 'You can't do this!' he screamed. 'I have diplomatic immunity! You are a ghost!'

"'No, you're a ghost, Al!' And with that I heaved with every ounce of my strength. The gun went off, the bullet ricocheting past my ear, the metal of the muzzle sparking as the iron rail scraped against it a split second before the hand followed underneath the train, the sound of rumbling rails muzzling a blood-curdling scream that rivaled a pig at the moment he is pierced through the heart.

"He went limp under me. I moved away from the still form on my hands and knees, searching for the gun. It had been knocked clear somewhere. I had lost it again in the darkness and thick undergrowth. I crawled inch by inch down the track, eyeing the ground. I finally found it in some brush I had crawled over three times before. I picked it up, checked the chamber. One more bullet!

"I turned in time to realize the last car was rumbling away into the darkness and that Alexei was nowhere in sight. He must have had just enough energy to get up and to struggle onto the back car and pull himself up with one arm, taking my future with him.

"The faint hope of a moment before — the dream that they had all forgotten about me now — was dashed. If Alexei got away, I was doomed. He was the only one who apparently knew I still existed — the only one who could destroy me. And he would because it was him or me. All that I had known was finished and gone — my family, my job, my security. I must find him and kill him to save myself!

"I ran after the train. It was slow but it had a good start on me. I stumbled on side railings in the darkness. I cursed and jumped up and ran with all I had only to stumble again. The slow train was almost out of sight. 'Damn you!' I screamed into the darkness, my fist raised against the night. And I tripped again. Over a body. It was Alexei, cowering, panting, his bloodied stump clutched to his chest." (At this, Mickey sank to the kitchen floor and Boris stood over him, his arm outstretched.)

"'Didn't make it, huh?' I said to him. He kind of shook his head no. His eyes were bulging and bloodshot. I could smell his fear, and behind it, his defeat. I could smell his death. I finished the job."

And with that, Boris's finger pulled the trigger on the imaginary pistol held to the head of my brother as he lay on the Dagronsky's kitchen floor. My hand reflexively jerked to the pistol under my own arm and I jumped to my feet. "Okay! That's enough," I panted, hearing the panic in my own voice, my heart thumping in my eardrums. "Get off him!" I ordered, feeling a fear racing through my body I had never felt before. "Get off him!" I repeated, more frantic, tugging at Boris's sleeve.

"I'm okay, Eliza. It's all right," Mickey said, struggling to his feet with a look in his eyes that mirrored my fear. Something inside of me felt wounded and helpless, like a mother deer watching her fawn caught frozen in the headlights of a car. I did not want to see Mickey like that. I would rather be out there in the road facing down a car by myself. I held my right hand on the gun under my blazer, motioned with my head for Mickey to go back to his seat, and with the other hand, pushed Dagronsky toward his.

"It's okay," Mick said softly, soothingly, but he sat back down and Dagronsky followed suit. The air crackled with tension. No one said a word.

"Go ahead," I ordered. "We don't have much time." And I leaned against the sink, my hand touching metal inside my blazer.

"I hid his body in the grass," Boris resumed, an almost smug look on his face. "...and trailed by Marbles, went home to get the Toyota. I brought it back and loaded the body in the trunk and took it where I figured it belonged — to our 'dead drop.'" And Boris sneared and chuckled.

I shook my head in disbelief.

"I imagine the Russians have found the body, but if they haven't, it's at the McCarthy farm family cemetery, West Chester Pike, in between a 'Broward McCarthy' and a 'Sarah McBride.' I used to leave Kasi's computer code in a hollowed out tree next to the grave of Cyrus McCarthy III." He sneared again, pleased at his own sick joke.

"Once I'd disposed of Alexei, I wandered through the night, thinking of my options. I knew that even if Alexei were the only one in the KGB who had known I was still alive — if indeed he had reported me as dead to Moscow, and then kept me as his personal agent in order to use the information I provided to make money for himself — he was undoubtedly still in a highly visible position. His disappearance would cause waves — probably international waves. Perhaps he had left evidence behind of my existence. They would come after me. If not the successors to the KGB, then perhaps the CIA and the FBI.

"The kindest thing to do for my family would be, once again and forever, to leave them. In Gaczyna I had a teacher of literature who quoted Shakespeare's Hamlet, 'I must be cruel only to be kind.' Maybe some day if things cooled down, I could come back. Or so I tried to convince myself... And so I spent the night preparing to leave. I destroyed all of my old spy paraphernalia. Then I sat in the dark and watched Kasi and the children while they slept, just as I had the night before I left Ayn and Sally. And the next morning, after I dropped the kids off at the day care center, I left. I didn't know any other way." Boris looked from Ayn to Kasi and back again. Their faces seemed almost bland, drained of emotion.

"But I didn't know then what the death of Alexei would unleash," Boris continued. "With the money I took from our account, I got an apartment, as you know, in South Phily. I thought I was relatively safe there. But the superintendent suddenly showed an undue curiosity. It felt as though it might be time to move on.

"The day you came, Ayn, I was on the street, watching the apartment at a distance. I recognized your car pull up. But then a man got out. I knew immediately it was Oleg. Every nerve, every tendon, every cell in my body cried out, but I did not move. Everything came at me like a wall of angry, raging debris down a flooded river. They had sicced the wild wolf upon me!" And with this, he pounded the table in anger. The empty coffee cups rattled and Eva blinked and sat back a little in her chair. "After all I had done for my country, they had loosed the one man who would find me at all costs — the one man who would go to any limits for his crazy revenge. It was betrayal of the worst kind. A Judas, a Brutus with a mad touch!

"I had had no inkling Oleg was out there. Somonov — the man I had trusted," (his voice rose plaintively) "—the man I had looked upon as a father, had told me, long ago, that Oleg was no longer a factor. I took that to mean I would never see him again — that he had most likely been executed. For the KGB knew well that he could never be let out of prison while I was alive. They would never do that and risk his compromising everything I had accomplished for the Motherland.

"But that was obviously exactly what someone wanted now. When he was let loose, Oleg would know precisely how to find me. He knew me better than I would have believed. He knew somehow

248

that I had been watching you and that I couldn't totally abandon you any more than he could abandon his vengeance. He had a terrible, mad vengeance which had been building up inside of him since the day of the attack in Balta, and long before. He hadn't been able to finish the job because of me. He hadn't been able to kill all of his demons, and in his mind, I was the worst of them. If he could only get back at me, he would be free. I knew Oleg felt a crazy sort of untouchableness. I was the only one who had ever stopped him. If he could get me, he thought, he would be invincible, indestructible, eternal.

"I had become convinced that Alexei had taken the opportunity of my move from the Poconos to 'disappear me' in the eyes of the KGB so that he could use me as his own private spy. So the last contact the official organization had for me would have been through my family there. Through subtle maneuvering, I had gotten you, Ayn, to move to Philadelphia, and he followed you there. I had paid for your scholarship at college. Oleg surmised that I was nearby, but he didn't know for sure. I imagine they set him up with underworld connections — the Russian Mafia. They would help him with money, drugs, whatever he needed to get what he wanted. Somehow those connections gave him a tip on where I was hiding.

"When I saw him outside of my apartment, I was immediately shocked and furious. But when I saw you, Ayn, get out of the car as well, I almost grabbed you. I was confused. You were obviously with him willingly. I didn't know what was going on. So I decided to hold back, wait and watch. But finally I could wait no longer. I went inside the building and listened outside the doorway. I realized immediately that I had almost waited too long. When I got to you you were unconscious, lying there exposed and battered, that monster on top of you."

At this point, Boris glanced quickly at Mick and then at me. This was a portion of his story he was not about to act out, because he had surmised by now that we knew parts of it that he did not. Things that would put him in an even worse light in his family's eyes. But he also knew by now that we had told Ayn a white lie about Oleg's death in order to spare her feelings. So he rushed into it awkwardly to get through it and salvage what he could of honor in his daughter's estimation of him. "Oleg lived long enough to see me and recognize me before the bullet met his brain," he lied. "It felt as though a job long delayed had been finally accomplished." By the blinking of his eyes and the almost imperceptible shift of his shoulders I could see we were now past the lie. He went on more confidently. "As I was moving him against the wall, I scraped the back of my hand on something from his pocket, opening a cut that began to bleed. It was the bent metal pocket clip on a fountain pen. I took it out and wrote my name on the palm of his hand — the name that only he and my sister Eva and one other person — General Somonov — had known. The message was for Somonov — to show him I knew of his betrayal, and had risen above it. Then I stuffed the pen in my pocket. Just then I heard you stir and I slipped out of the apartment.

"You saved my life, but you couldn't stay around long enough to answer the most basic question of my life — Why? Why did you do all of this? Why did you live a lie?" Ayn said softly, gazing pointedly across the table at her father. There was a deep sadness in her voice, the heavy emptiness of loss.

"But don't you understand? I had no choice! I had no choice!" And Boris rose with his voice, reaching across the table to touch her, to make contact, to pull her toward him.

Simultaneously I heard the sound of car doors slamming outside. I turned quickly and peered out the window to the street below. Several men in dark suits and ties, congregating in a huddle between four dark cars of the same make. It was Them.

"They're here," I said.

Boris's reach for Ayn stopped in midair. He turned toward the window. "I can't," he said, his hand dropping to his side. "I can't let them catch me."

"What do you have to lose now?" Mickey, rising also, countered. "We know your story. They will soon, too. You might as well face them." He placed himself between Boris and the door to the foyer.

"No," Boris shook his head. The cloudiness in his eyes was gone. They were charcoal black again, with a touch of flint. He turned around in a little circle as if searching for a way out. "My gun," he said, looking straight at me. "For God's sake, woman, give me my gun!"

All I could do was shake my head. What had we gotten ourselves into? If he thought I was going to arm him he was more unhinged than even I had imagined. We were already in deep shit from having brought him here. All we could do at this point was plead complete ignorance and stupidity — bumbling private eyes who got in over their heads trying to help two women find their father and husband. We would explain the spent shell at the park as a suicide attempt that we staved off, subduing the man, then, out of the kindness of our hearts, bringing him here to meet with his distraught family. Ever since then, he'd been babbling nonsense. Gee, Mr. G-Man, can you please take him off our hands? I was mentally preparing my "Officer

Krumpke" speech in my head, hoping Mick had some good lines of his own. But Boris was having none of that. He headed for the door, trying to shove Mickey aside. Mick pushed back.

"Oh no you don't!" I said, drawing my revolver, releasing the safety and cocking it. "Get away from him!" I warned. Ayn had rushed up behind Boris. Sophie and Eva were standing now, watching. "Stand back!" I shouted at Boris.

"They're coming up," said Kasi, peering now out the window.

Boris pivoted away from Mickey, turning now to face me. "You know that won't stop me," he said coldly, his gaze staring down the gun. "It worked once today because you convinced me I could make them understand. I've told them now. They don't understand. They can't understand. No one can understand."

"I want to understand," Ayn said weakly, only a foot away from him. She reached out to touch him, perhaps to prove to herself he was not just a figment.

"I'm sorry I kept following you — all of you," he said to her, but made no move this time to touch her. "I'm sorry I didn't just let you go. It would have been easier on everyone. It's just that if I quit following, there would be nothing left. I can't start over. I don't know how. There is nowhere to go. There's no one to teach me how to live any more. I can't pretend any more. My whole life has been pretending." And he looked past me at Kasi. "I'm sorry I used you. I'm sorry I had to leave. But I didn't know what else to do. I can't go back. Not to Russia, not to prison, not to a life I'll never fully live." And he turned once more toward me. "You must let me go. Because you'll have to shoot me to keep me here, and you won't — not with them." And he gestured to his family. "Give me your gun. Both guns. If I leave with the guns, you can say I wrested it from you after the crash and you were forced at gunpoint to drive me here. If I leave and you still have the guns, you are an accomplice to my crimes. You become a traitor. Shoot me or give me the guns. It's as simple as that." And he held out his hand.

"Are you crazy? I'm not giv—"

"Traitors don't get P.I. licenses."

"You think I'm going to give up my gun to a spy?" I hissed.

"I'm through hurting other people, lady. I'm trying to save your ass because you brought us together," he sneered.

"Eliza, give him the guns." It was Mickey, his hand on my shoulder. He reached out and took the gun out of my hand, flipped it open and removed the bullets from the chamber, clicked it shut and put it in Boris's outstretched hand. He turned me around deftly by the shoulder, pulled up my blazer and extracted Dagronsky's pistol from under my waistband and handed it to Boris, too. And I just stood there, allowing myself to be disarmed, manhandled and manipulated.

Boris turned toward Eva and said something in Russian. She nodded and responded in Russian, pointing toward the back of the apartment.

"Spasibo," he said softly, glancing briefly at his daughter, his wife, his sister, his niece, then pivoted and walked out of the kitchen.

"But we can't—"

Mick grabbed my arm as I ran after Boris. "Let him go. *They* are." And he gestured back toward the women following slowly, faces bereft, desolate, angry and confused. "The authorities will probably catch him. He's no threat any longer to anyone but himself."

We stopped inside the living room and watched as Boris leaned over his son sleeping peacefully on a blanket on the living room carpet. A tear fell from his eye and landed on the child's face. Little Brando swiped unconsciously at the drop. Father and son did not touch. Boris rose from the baptismal and, looking back over his shoulder, said softly, "I didn't mean to hurt anyone. I didn't mean it." And with that he passed out of sight, into the hallway which held the bedrooms. A second later we heard the sound of a window being boosted and the soft thud of sneakers dropping onto the metal stairway of a fire escape.

Forty-five seconds later we were seated "nonchalantly" around the kitchen table when They pounded on the door.

"Let Them in," I said to Mick with false bravado, and exhaling deeply, prepared to face the music.

Chapter 16
See No Evil

"Thank God you're here, officers," Mick played his part with gusto. "You wouldn't believe the shit that just went down," he gestured as they pushed past him into the apartment. There were Maryland State Police, City of Baltimore Police, FBI, unidentified officials I assume were CIA, and even a lone officer of the Park Service.

From overheard radio conversations, it was apparent They had known there was to be a family reunion, but had staked out the wrong park. Chakra, I assume, had known of our original planned rendezvous point — the location we had mentioned to Ayn — but not our ultimate meeting place, which we intentionally switched at the last minute just in case such a tip-off occurred. It wasn't until the car chase, and ultimately the crash in the state park, that the Powers That Be had had any idea that Boris had shown up for the picnic. From that point on, it had been just a matter of time before they reconnoitered and made their way to Aunt Eva's.

But they were too late. Boris had disappeared.

They cordoned off a 20-block area, searched from house-to-house, and practically dismantled the apartment, even down to removing pictures from the wall and threatening to take them away as evidence.

"Evidence of what? That the woman came from a dysfunctional family?" I hissed at M.D.

Then they were going to charge us with harboring a fugitive.

"Fugitive from what?" Mick asked. They hadn't yet bothered to inform us what crime he was accused of. Seems they didn't want to acknowledge Boris was a spy, nor that he had murdered one. As for his brother's murder — well, that was one we knew he hadn't committed, even though he would have liked to. Abandonment is a crime, I guess. It certainly should be. But harboring was obviously the opposite of what we had been doing for the past several weeks. We sheepishly proffered Boris's suggestion of having been brought by him to the apartment at gunpoint, but they remained skeptical.

When the threat of charging us with abetting a fugitive to escape didn't appear to move us, they accused me of speeding, various other traffic offenses, and ultimately, leaving the scene of an accident.

They wanted to know all we knew, and questioned us all repeatedly, separately and together, on that account, yet feigned incredulity at the recitation of Boris's story. It was bizarre, really. It was as if they wanted to deny all signs of his existence while chasing willy-nilly after a ghost they denied existed. I had the creepy feeling that if they could have easily wiped us out too, they would have.

It almost felt as though Boris were an alien landed from a different galaxy — a not-so-harmless ET who had lived among us, captured people's trust, been found out, and then chased off by the government. They now wanted only to learn what we knew of him, then exume his memory because the idea of there being others like him out there was too frightening to face.

It was well after midnight when they finally departed, leaving us drained and empty, and insinuating that if they were us, they wouldn't talk to anyone about this, because we would look quite foolish, now, wouldn't we? But still, the questioning, the explanations, were not over.

"Tell me about my mother," Ayn demanded. She was seated again, her long-fingered hands pressed, palms down, on the table. The knuckles were white, like her face. The harsh overhead lights had been mercifully extinguished. One sixty-watt bulb over the stove shone dimly behind her head.

I glanced at Mick. He was fiddling unconsciously with the cover of the sugar bowl, lost in another place. His face looked as though it had aged since yesterday — or was it this morning?

"Please," Ayn said. "I have to know. No more secrets."

"You're right," I acquiesced. "You know everything else. No matter what They say happened. You deserve to know the truth."

And I took a deep breath and plunged in wearily. It was time to reveal what we had learned from our sources but had not yet told her. "You knew your mother was let go from her job before your father left. Do you remember when all the phones went down in the early '70s, all over the northeast corridor of the nation?" She looked at me blankly. "No, of course — you were a child, a little girl. Well, there was a communication outage then that affected the entire East Coast, the Middle Atlantic States, and into the Midwest. The phones went haywire. Some calls were rerouted to totally wrong connections; others dead-ended; many people couldn't even get a dial tone. It lasted for about half an hour. AT&T blamed a computer glitch. There's a computer program that balances out the calls and routes them all over the country. But they have back-up systems in case something goes wrong. The programs run in parallel: if one goes out, the next is supposed to take over; if it goes out, the third one steps in and over-rides it. But for some reason, they all failed. A call that was dialed to go to New York should have traveled via one satellite, and bounced off of that to another down station. Instead it would get rerouted somewhere else where there was no receiving number, thereby dead-ending it. People were getting crossed lines, hearing other conversations at random, or a constantly ringing line. The phones simply didn't work. Not a single call in the East got through to its intended destination."

Ayn was looking at her hands. They were clinched now. I could feel Eva and Sophie's eyes on us. Kasi stood with her back to the room, looking out the window, lost in another time, another life. "It was after your mom had met and married your dad," I said softly. "At the satellite station in Kimbles, it was obvious that someone, some-where, with total overall access to the programs, had overrun the system. The place was completely overhauled and the programmers quietly reassigned or let go. Your mother was just a secretary, and apparently never suspected. AT&T kept the whole thing as quiet as possible. They didn't want it to be known how vulnerable to sabotage the U.S. communication system was.

"Everything apparently went smoothly from then on at the station until just before your father left your mother. Then it happened again — a seven-minute massive phone short-circuit across the Eastern seaboard. But this time Sally Curtis was the only one still working at the station who had been there during the earlier scramble. They let her go."

"Did she do it?" Ayn whispered.

"She couldn't have done it without his help and guidance," I offered.

"But did she?"

"What do you think?"

"I don't know."

"Does it matter?"

She sat and looked at her hands. "Not any more," she whispered.

Not any more.

The Marcinkovitchs, kept away until then by the authorities, finally arrived with little Eva, Brando woke up and demanded to be changed, and we all bumbled about, awkwardly mumbling comforting platitudes to one another.

Phone numbers, babies, and kisses were exchanged. Aunt Eva asked her daughter to translate Ayn's shirt. After digesting Groucho

Marx's comment on life, Eva related something to Sophie. "My mother says it may be too dark inside a dog to read," Sophie told Ayn, "but not to draw."

"I think maybe it lost something in the translation," Mickey D. whispered in my ear.

"Well, maybe not," I replied, glancing doubtfully at some wild sketches propped haphazardly against the wall in the entranceway, in the wake of the FBI's search.

"Come again," Aunt Eva said in heavily accented English. The juxtaposition of polite niceties and unreal realities threatened a nervous giggle welling in my chest. We said our goodbyes and departed.

On the ride home, the children babbled and the adults sat in virtual silence, looking out at the impending dawn. Mickey dropped everyone off at their homes. I immediately went to bed.

There were chases in my dreams — shadows and fear and blood and anger, betrayal and denial, families and whole nations in screaming turmoil. I awoke to the stark realization that my dreams were real. I cried for the first time since Daddy died. No, since before Daddy died.

But as if to spite all evidence to the contrary, the sun rose on a beautiful morning — a different, parallel reality in the same space and time.

Chapter 17
Loose Ends

In the weeks and months that followed, agencies — from the CIA on down to the Lochmore Police — did all kinds of investigations, while simultaneously pretending a concentrated disinterest. Each government arm, in its own fashion, basically publicly denied most of what Boris had said and what we had uncovered independently. They pooh-poohed and downplayed the entire affair, as though minimizing and denial would make it all go away. "That'll do about as much good as me claiming I'm not HIV positive," Mickey D. declared.

Chakra was gone when Ayn got home that night. She had left a note saying she had been called away to see a dying grandmother in Bangladesh, and probably wouldn't be back any time soon. We discovered a tap on Ayn's phone. Curiosity on Mick's part led us to "find our way into" the unit on the other side of the house — the apartment Chakra had supposedly been "burned out" of before she convinced Ayn to let her move in with her. There was no fire damage and no sign of life — just a notebook with notations, in Chakra's handwriting, of some of Ayn's conversations, next to a tape recorder with weeks' worth of Ayn's phone calls on it. The next day, when we went back, even that had disappeared.

When we found out there was a tap on our office phone as well, I was all set to march over to old Miss Marsh's adjoining piano parlor to shake down her upright and anything else that might harbor listening devices, but Mickey stopped me. "It's a different kind of tap," he said. "There's no recording device around the corner. And just how could you suspect sweet old Miss Marsh?"

"She's always known more than anyone should possibly know about this town. That certainly would explain it, wouldn't it?" I was ready to suspect anyone at that point.

But we simply removed the taps and called the CIA and the FBI. They, of course, denied any involvement in anything, including any knowledge of an agent fitting Chakra's description.

We couldn't get much more out of Vortex. Chakra Patel had come highly recommended and with all the proper credentials. She had suffered a family emergency and quit to go back to Bangladesh. End of code. Kasi did seem to be holding onto her job at Vortex, but the company itself very suddenly and quietly lost several of its highly sensitive contracts.

What we finally concluded came from a mixture of good old fashioned investigating on our part, a considerable amount of help from good contacts in the right places, downright frightening stupidity on the part of more than one official government agency, a fair amount of conjecture or educated deduction, and some simple common sense and good luck. And it goes something like this:

Kasi had been right, there really *was* an Al — Alexei Bogati — an undersecretary with the Russian consulate in Washington D.C. And he most likely had been killed by Boris in the struggle by the train. It was Bogati's skeletal hand that old Marbles brought home weeks later as a souvenir of that night's bloody encounter. So if "Al" came knocking on Kasi's door two nights after he was killed — well, I'll let you interpret that one for yourself.

What we do know now for a fact is that the FBI had missed Bogati almost as soon as he failed to show for work the Friday of Boris's disappearance, according to information ferreted out for us by M.D.'s Fibbie friend Jake. The driveway of Bogati's Georgetown apartment was filled that morning, mostly with diplomatic-plated vehicles. Even Alexei's son's BMW was there, in spite of the fact the kid had finals scheduled that day at Bucknell University. Russian officials were closeted in Bogati's office for hours. Inquiries as to his whereabouts brought conflicting responses: first he had gone back to Russia; then, when no travel records to that effect could be found, the official word put out in response to inquiries was that he was traveling in the U.S. Two days later, his wife and son flew home to Moscow, with Mrs. Bogati weeping out the window of Aeroflot Flight 402.

The Vakarovs also confirmed much of what Boris had related. Mikhail, a highly respected political science professor at Lochmore College, and an expert on the KGB, had shared with us, just prior to our picnic reunion, his insights on the profile of a Russian mole, and the amazing lengths to which the Soviet government had gone to train its spies, including the secrets of Gaczyna. Now Mick and I revisited the Vakarovs and asked for more specifics given the information Boris had supplied. Mikhail's resources were vast, as were his inside experience and contacts, and he attacked the issue as though it were a treasure hunt with pots of informational gold at each station.

"The KGB did not just vanish," he warned, his face exploding with conspiratorial glee into a mass of crinkled lines fading into his white beard. Tanya looked on in reserved amusement, as though she were studying us prior to writing a social treatise. "Where do you think all those people went?" Mikhail said rhetorically. "They are selling themselves to the highest bidder, tapping into government computer banks or fomenting rebellion in places like Boznia-Herzegovina and Chechnya. Competition between the U.S. and Russia is not military any more, it is economic. But it is still political. Always political."

We gave Mikhail the information we had, and within a few days he came back to us with the following:

General Vasily Somonov, Boris's so-called father figure and recruiter, had been an original player in the August 1991 coup against Mikhail Gorbachev. In the 11th hour, however, he astutely threw his allegiance to Boris Yeltsin, providing the Yeltsin camp with valuable information to assess the hardliners' strength and support, and ultimately assisting in the peaceful quelling of the uprising, thereby earning himself Yeltsin's gratitude and indebtedness.

Immediately following the arrest of dozens of his compatriots and the downfall of Gorbachev, the General was assigned by President Yeltsin to an advisory position on intelligence affairs. American political analysts believe Yeltsin had recently been prepared to elevate him even higher — perhaps to a Cabinet position.

Vakarov surmised that, from his former position, Somonov had undoubtedly been the officer in control of Alexei Bogati and the agents under him as part of the old Second Division of the First Chief Directorate (Directorate S). The ostensible dissolution of the KGB in the time following the coup was actually a reworking of the old Cold War spy mentality into a new, modern '90s spy mentality. The outdated deep mole concept was an anachronism. Today's spies sit next to you on the boardrooms of corporations, Mikhail noted. Their loyalty is to the ruble, not the hammer and sickle.

Bogati had seen the writing on the wall and seized advantage of the changing climate before the slow political machine itself switched gears. He had apparently taken the initiative to get a piece of the action himself, and used Boris without his knowledge, and perhaps other agents as well, for his own personal gain. Reporting Boris's demise when he switched locations was a cinch. His superiors would no longer expect output from Boris, so Bogati could therefore sell the information he obtained from Dagronsky and other "disappeared" agents on the underground market, to his own financial gain.

When the political picture changed, Gen. Somonov had undoubtedly cleaned house — or thought he had. He had apparently felt secure enough to allow Bogati to retain his position, which indicated

Somonov was under the impression any former deep agents had been neutralized or recalled. Bogati's disappearance opened up a Pandora's box for Somonov, who could not afford at this politically sensitive time to have his dirty past rehashed. It could be highly embarrassing and potentially damaging to his political aspirations, which were apparently considerable.

Somonov, as a high level intelligence adviser, would have access to whatever notes or files the Russians removed from Bogati's residence following his disappearance. One look at Boris's musical "notes" to his former recruiter, if Bogati had been stupid enough to keep them (and, as Mickey commented, all indications pointed in that direction), and Somonov would have put two and two together and realized Boris was still very much out in the cold. Only Somonov knew who had sent the musical notes and what they meant. Only Somonov knew enough about the Dagronskys and their tragic familial soul to formulate a plan to leave Boris permanently out in the cold. And that plan involved releasing Oleg from his Lubyanka cage and siccing him on his family one more time.

So what happened when Oleg was let loose? Well, for that, Mick and I went to the source — Ira Fahnstock. That's right, we got in trusty Cabri and headed north three hours to the Poconos. We had asked Ayn if she wanted to accompany us, but she said she wasn't ready to go home just yet. "Maybe next year," she said. "I've got midterms." It was too soon, too raw. She had to digest her parents' past and come to grips with that first before she could go home again.

It was mid October by then. Northeastern Pennsylvania was gorgeously crisp and blazing of golden, russet and crimson hues. The clear air was full of honking geese and the mountain lakes in their cobalt depth rippled with the promise of deep winter dreams to come.

An ebullient Ira greeted us at the door of his spacious, modern log cabin, wearing an old-fashioned black hat instead of a little yarmulke over his undoubtedly bald pate. He and his wife were warm and gracious and his four home-schooled children anxious to show us around the 500-acre property with its now empty rustic bunkhouses, meeting halls, and worship center surrounding a lovely, spring-fed lake. After a delicious luncheon of lamb stew, Ira helped us find the right sources to trace Oleg's tracks to Ayn's childhood roots.

With a photograph of Oleg in hand, we located a taxi driver in Honesdale who remembered picking up a fare at a Hawley bed and breakfast in mid August. He had been offered $200 to ferry the man with the thick accent around the Lake Wallenpaupack area for a day. Oleg had told the cabby he wanted to find out what had happened to the Curtis family. He told the Curtis's neighbors that he was an attorney seeking Ayn as the recipient of a sizable inheritance from a distant relative who had recently passed away. Her next-door neighbor was pleased to give him Ayn's address.

"She was such a sweet girl and she had such a rough time, don't you think?" Mrs. Eck told Mickey, Ira, and me over coffee in her parlor. "The attorney was very charming, wasn't he? I gave him Ayn's address. That was okay, wasn't it? She really deserves whatever she's got coming to her and more, I think, don't you? Her father was such a ne'er-do-well, you know. And her mother, poor soul, well, she was a sorry thing, don't you think? Oh, I probably shouldn't have said that, should I? Ayn's all right, isn't she?"

"Mm-hm, Mm-hm, Mm-hm," we chorused as we backed out the door.

The reassurance the cabby required had not been lip service, but monetary reinforcement. In fact, he left his meter running. Mick had just handed over three twenties, and Ira and I were disembarking at the taxi stand, when the guy pulled Mick back into the cab and hissed conspiratorially in the direction of Ira's black-clad back. "Is he one of them spooks, too? Dresses kind of conspicuous for that, don't he?"

"Who, Ira? Ira lives here. He runs a camp up in Northern Wayne. He dresses that way because he's orthodox Jewish. What spooks are you talking about?"

And the guy allowed as how Dagronsky had given him an extra $100 as a tip and asked him if he wanted to buy some coke. "I didn't tell them other guys about it, 'cause I figured if they really wanted to know, they could find out themselves if they're such good spies, you know? But if you're local, that's different."

"Well, I don't live here myself, but my friend does. I wouldn't mind having a little cottage up here on a lake," Mick allowed. And he took out another ten and laid it on the dashboard. What did you tell the other guys? Where were they from?"

"Washington. They had cards and badges and all." And he licked his lips, his eyes got big and a self-satisfied smirk crossed his face. "Said Central Intelligence Agency. They came up here nosing around like they owned the place a couple days after the guy with the accent left. That guy wasn't no attorney, was he?"

Mickey chuckled and slapped him on the back in a congratulatory gesture. "You're damn straight he wasn't. You didn't miss a thing, did you? How was the coke?"

And he only hesitated a split second, having already formulated his judgment on old Mickey D. "Not bad. Purest stuff I've ever had. He said he could get me more but then he never got back to me," he said, lips turned down in a pout. "He's dead in that picture, ain't he?"

This guy was about as astute as they come. "Afraid so," Mick responded, shaking his hand.

"You don't know where I could—"

"Afraid not. Sorry. Thank you for your help." And Mickey backed out smiling.

As for Oleg's employment at the studio, that was obviously another case of drugs and money buying power and position, orchestrated, most likely, by Organizatsaya funds and connections.

For information on Grace Johnston, the temporary worker who had set up Ayn to be approached by Ames about Pennsylvania's Unsolved Mysteries, I looked up Dad's old associate Snooker Jefferson, who was more than happy to help. He in turn went to some old buddies still active in the P.P.D. who were able to search arrest records and come up with a prior on Johnston for shoplifting and prostitution. She turned out to be the live-in girlfriend of one Sergei Zazulin, a peripheral figure in the 1984 bootleg gasoline operation Geli and Vadim Korlov had told us about. In fact, in the process of checking up on her, the P.P.D. discovered an outstanding warrant on Zazulin for armed robbery and sales of narcotics and picked him up at his apartment. But by then Johnston was long gone, dead of a drug overdose.

We were left now with the question, what really happened at 939 Raritan Circle, Apartment 1-B on October 1? Mick and I recognized that the blood on the door, while undoubtedly Boris's, did not get there from a cut to the finger from a broken fountain pen. It was a splatter pattern more akin to blood flying from a trauma blow of some sort. We had set Boris up to be the hero in Ayn's horrid encounter with Oleg in order to make her feel better about her father and dispel unnecessary guilt feelings, but the pieces didn't quite fit his scenario.

So if not Boris, who had stopped Oleg? Who actually put that bullet through his sorry brain? And who beaned Boris outside the apartment door? My money was on Chakra and her associates. It was obvious that she was a CIA plant, and that there was more government involvement in this mess than anybody would ever let onto. What the CIA and/or the FBI truly knew, and at what point, I have no idea, and probably never will. But there is enough we know from what Ayn told us and from the physical evidence on the scene, to determine the following:

Ayn had told Chakra prior to picking up Ames the day that he was murdered that Ames had a tip on her father's whereabouts. Chakra could have followed them there.

Nobody had answered the phone the first time we called Ayn's apartment from the Embassy Suites, but the second time, some time later, Chakra answered, obviously out of breath.

The blood on the door was low, as though Boris had been bent over, looking in the keyhole or listening at the door to the commotion inside, when he was hit from behind, most likely on the head. That was where the blood spatter most likely came from.

According to the P.P.D. police report obtained by Snooker's buddy, ballistics showed that while Oleg was killed by a 9 mm — the same size as the Browning found at the scene — the bullet did not come from that gun. Many agents use 9 mm Walthars.

So my theory is that Chakra, or someone in cahoots with her, sneaked up on Boris and whacked him good with the butt of a 9 mm before he could go through the door. She/they then rushed in just in time to save Ayn's honor and most likely her life, dispensing Oleg as Ayn lay unconscious. They may have been on their way back out to secure Boris (the fact that they only knocked him out to begin with indicates they wanted him alive — which means they were probably agents of the U.S. government) when someone else appeared on the scene. This is the only thing that explains how Boris managed to get away. Not only did he get away with only a bump on the head, he had time to go into the apartment, determine that Oleg was dead and Ayn was alive, and to write his very own encrypted "Kilroy Was Here" message on his little brother's palm — probably because he felt frustrated that he hadn't been able to do much of anything else to help his daughter or to avenge his family.

I got to this point in my hypothesis, and I began to wonder again about that ugly, dark apartment at 939 Raritan — so much so that I talked Mickey D. into going down there with me one day to check it out. When we pulled up in front, Marlboro Man's "V" was gone, and he was nowhere in sight. The neighborhood itself felt like one never-ending, unsolvable crime occurred there on a daily basis. The crime was the neighborhood and the neighborhood was the crime. That day the neighborhood was eerily quiet.

We cautiously approached the front door of the dilapidated building. My heart beat like machine gun rat-a-tats beneath my .32.

The corridor was empty but lighter this time — due, no doubt, to the fact that the door to 1-B had been removed and the light from the curtainless apartment windows shown faintly into the hallway. We stood outside the door and looked in at the empty apartment, as though there were still a barrier to our entry. But I didn't want to go in there. All I needed was one glance through to the living room to envision Ayn's body trapped beneath Oleg's angry hatred, his fingernailess hands groping at her flesh.

"No, it happened out here," I said softly, standing at the threshold. It was quieter now than last time. Only one baby cried, softly, colicky, from behind a door across the hall.

Mickey turned to me, his eyes clear and searching. "Okay, Chakra or an agent in cahoots with her has plugged Oleg," he said, quickly setting the stage. "Now she's checked to see that Oleg's dead and Ayn's not. She hears a noise. She comes back through the living room. What does she see?"

"Boris."

"Right. Still lying on the ground?"

"Yes. Because he never saw her. So he has to still be out cold as long as she's still there."

"So he's unconscious. What makes her leave him there? Why wouldn't she neutralize him — tie him up, arrest him, even finish him off if that's to their advantage?"

"There's someone else in the hallway," I said.

"Who?"

"A resident?"

"But nobody saw nothin'."

"Someone else who's after Boris, then."

"Or even someone sent to knock off Oleg after he's done Boris."

"Possibly. Somonov may have sent a second assassin to clean out the Dagronskys for good. But the other guy isn't sure who's been 'done.'"

"So there's confusion."

"Definitely."

"She sees him, he sees her. Nobody's sure who's who."

"Wait a minute," I said, taking the flashlight Mickey had brought in from the car out of his hand. I snapped on the torch and trained it on the cobwebs along the stairwell in the middle of the hallway. The beam played along the opposite wall: the usual foul adolescent graffiti interspersed with so-and-so loves so-and-so; a yellow smear which could have been anything from dried vomit to spilled paint; a long gouge in the plaster which looked like somebody had run a knife blade along it.

"Okay," I continued. "You've risen from making sure Oleg is dead and Ayn's not. You're turning toward the doorway. Go ahead, Mick," I urged. Better he than I. Mick shrugged his shoulders and, taking the flashlight from me, sauntered, feigning nonchalance, into The Apartment. He walked toward the spot where Oleg's body had been found, propped against the wall by the window. But before he could turn around, I crouched outside the door, an imaginary body crumpled at my feet, and as he turned, shining the light upon me, I uncoiled and sprang to my feet, racing out of the beam of light, toward the exit on the other side of the stairwell. Mick's running steps followed behind and the light beam reached me just as my hand touched the cold metal of the fire door.

"See!" I cried enthusiastically to Mickey as he arrived at the door, virtually panting.

"See what? That doesn't prove anything."

"Oh yes it does!"

"How?"

"See this!" and I pointed to a bullet-sized indentation, chest high, in the metal doorframe.

"Oh, hell, that could be anything. Look at all the marks on there!"

It was true, there were dents and scratches all over the thing. But I wasn't ready to give up that easily. "Give me that," I demanded, and he handed over the flashlight again. I played the light along the wall, beside the frame, and even across the door of the closest apartment. Nothing. I even shone it on the ceiling. In the middle of a two-foot discoloration above the doorway from a probable upstairs water leak, was a darker mark. "What's that?" I asked. I couldn't see well enough. The ceilings were about 9' tall.

"I don't know," Mick replied.

"Well, boost me up there."

"Oh, come on!"

"No, bend over!" And I pushed down on his shoulders.

He moaned and mumbled, but he bent down and let me climb onto his shoulders. Then, with much grunting and staggering, he rose to his feet with all 130 pounds of me precariously perched up there.

"That Bobby Russell song's a bunch of crap," he groused. "Just because she's my sister doesn't me she ain't heavy."

"Hey, but it's worth it," I said, almost in a whisper as the flashlight gleamed off of something shiny. "Give me your pocketknife."

"Yeah, right! Why don't I whip up dinner with my spare hand while I'm at it!"

"The knife!" I stressed as though repeating it would make it leap from his pocket. But somehow he managed to juggle me and extract the knife without dropping either.

"Hurry up," he hissed. "I don't think I've felt this much weight on my shoulders since Dad died and left me the Man of the House."

Somehow I managed to carve one 9 mm slug out of the ceiling of the first floor hallway at 939 Raritan — a bullet which I bet the ballistics people — if they ever got their hands on it — would be able to match perfectly with the one found in Oleg's cretinous brain.

And better yet, we got out of there without being shot at, falling from a great height, or in Mickey's case, developing a hernia.

So anyway, I figure whoever bashed Boris and shot Oleg, had then caught someone in the hallway hovering over Boris's slack form, and come out shooting. The hoverer made it outside, with at least one bullet ricocheting off the doorframe into the ceiling. He or she was probably chased some distance, because by the time the shooter got back, Boris had come to, found Ayn alive and Oleg dead, propped the latter up against the wall, and written his signature in the palm of his brother's hand before vanishing once again.

And that ties it up about as neatly as I imagine it'll ever get tied. The circle of intrigue goes on and on, like the waves caused by a pebble tossed in a lake.

I fully believe Boris won't be taken alive. If he were, with our government's apparent grasp of the concept of "perestroika," we might never hear about it, anyway. Can you imagine the public panic and outcry at the revelation that there have been and may still be moles among us? I'm sure that's the last thing the FBI and the CIA want us having Congressional hearings on!

Well, things gradually settled back into their normal dull pattern. Ayn got involved in her studies and started dating a professor. Kasi actually got promoted at Vortex! Aunt Eva and Sophie had a successful showing at Harborplace. And little Eva eventually stopped wetting the bed. Scooter Jefferson retired with a full pension. Mickey D. sleeps in his own bed most nights now — alone, as do I.

One day soon after Kasi and Ayn made their last payment on the case, I went for a walk and ended up at Mom's. She met me at the door. "I know, Mickey's not here," I said, figuring I'd beat her to the punch.

"I have something for you," she drew me inside.

"You what?"

"He's in the back yard."

"Mom, what are you talking about? I can find my own—"

"—It's not a man, it's a dog."

"A what?"

"'Bow-wow. Arf-arf,' whatever they do. I found him at the pound. They were going to euthanize him this afternoon."

"A dog?"

I followed her, jaw unhinged. We went through the entranceway, past the living room, and onto the back porch. A medium-sized young mutt with long blond hair and soulful eyes looked up at me. It was tied to the railing of the porch stairs. It stood and licked me when I bent over. "Mom, it's a she, not a he."

"Well, whatever."

"But why did you get me a dog? Don't you want her for companionship? You're all alone now."

"I hate dogs. And I don't need anyone else to take care of. I've done that already."

I looked up at her. She was standing there, ramrod straight, her stubborn, aristocratic chin jutting out for all the world, hiding the vulnerability, shielding the fear of rejection.

"Yes, you have," I acknowledged.

"But you need a dog," she insisted.

"Why?"

"To teach you nurturing skills," she said.

I took the dog.

###

Following graduation from the creative writing program at the University of Arizona, Kristen Ammerman began her professional writing career as a newspaper reporter and eventually became managing editor of a community daily in her hometown of Honesdale, Pennsylvania. She has edited journals on forensic photography and roof consulting and is a member of the Carolina Crime Writers. Kris and her daughter Rachel currently reside in Raleigh, North Carolina, where Kris is a publications director. This is her first published novel.